PENGUIN CANADA

WHEN WE WERE YOUNG

STUART McLEAN writes and hosts the popular
CBC Radio show *The Vinyl Cafe*. He is the
author of many bestselling and award-
winning books, including five collections of
Vinyl Cafe stories.

Also by Stuart McLean

The Morningside World of Stuart McLean

Welcome Home:
Travels in Smalltown Canada

Stories from the Vinyl Cafe

Home from the Vinyl Cafe: A Year of Stories

Vinyl Cafe Unplugged

Vinyl Cafe Diaries

Dave Cooks the Turkey

Secrets from the Vinyl Cafe

Selected and Introduced by

Stuart McLean

When We Were Young

an Anthology
of Canadian Stories

PENGUIN
CANADA

PENGUIN CANADA

Published by the Penguin Group

Penguin Group (Canada), 90 Eglinton Avenue East, Suite 700, Toronto, Ontario, Canada M4P 2Y3
(a division of Pearson Canada Inc.)

Penguin Group (USA) Inc., 375 Hudson Street, New York, New York 10014, U.S.A.
Penguin Books Ltd, 80 Strand, London WC2R 0RL, England
Penguin Ireland, 25 St Stephen's Green, Dublin 2, Ireland (a division of Penguin Books Ltd)
Penguin Group (Australia), 250 Camberwell Road, Camberwell, Victoria 3124, Australia
(a division of Pearson Australia Group Pty Ltd)
Penguin Books India Pvt Ltd, 11 Community Centre, Panchsheel Park,
New Delhi – 110 017, India
Penguin Group (NZ), 67 Apollo Drive, Rosedale, North Shore 0632, New Zealand
(a division of Pearson New Zealand Ltd)
Penguin Books (South Africa) (Pty) Ltd, 24 Sturdee Avenue, Rosebank,
Johannesburg 2196, South Africa

Penguin Books Ltd, Registered Offices: 80 Strand, London WC2R 0RL, England

First published in a Viking Canada hardcover by Penguin Group (Canada),
a division of Pearson Canada Inc., 1996
Published in Penguin Canada paperback by Penguin Group (Canada),
a division of Pearson Canada Inc., 1997
Published in this edition, 2008

1 2 3 4 5 6 7 8 9 10 (WEB)

Introduction, Notes and Selection copyright © Stuart McLean, 1996

Pages 444–46 constitute an extension of this copyright page

*Publisher's note: This book is a work of fiction. Names, characters, places and incidents either are the product
of the author's imagination or are used fictitiously, and any resemblance to actual persons living or dead,
events, or locales is entirely coincidental.*

Manufactured in Canada.

LIBRARY AND ARCHIVES CANADA CATALOGUING IN PUBLICATION

When we were young : a collection of Canadian stories / selected and
introduced by Stuart McLean.

ISBN 978-0-14-316906-2

1. Short stories, Canadian (English).   2. Canadian fiction (English)—20th
century.   3. Children—Fiction.   I. McLean, Stuart, 1948–

PS8321.W48 2008   C813'.0108354   C2008-902722-1

Visit the Penguin Group (Canada) website at **www.penguin.ca**

Special and corporate bulk purchase rates available; please see
www.penguin.ca/corporatesales or call 1-800-810-3104, ext. 477 or 474

To W.O. Mitchell
writer, teacher

"And what a tricky teacher *he* was!
With what cunning sleight-of-hand
he palmed truths and insights and
hid them in his students without
their knowing it,
to appear magically years later."

—*from* SINCE DAISY CREEK *by W.O. Mitchell*

CONTENTS

Before We Begin

At one time, just like A.A. Milne, I thought I might write a lengthy note at the beginning of each of these stories. A note written in the manner of the poets who like to tell you where they were staying, and which of their friends they were walking with, and what they were thinking about when the idea of writing their poems came to them. The problem, of course, is that I didn't write the pieces in this book. But I was thinking, if I could not tell you where I was when I did not write them, perhaps I could tell you why I like them, and why I chose to include them in this collection. You will find a story later on (if you get as far as that) about a young girl who has an eye operation, and I would have explained, in my note, that when I was a boy, I, too, had an eye operation. In those days a four-year-old boy living in Montreal (me) had to go to the hospital alone (without me mum or dad)—or so the nuns instructed my mother. And in those days you did not argue with nuns. Or my mother didn't. Or, if she did, she lost. Because on the appointed day she dropped me off at St. Mary's Hospital and left me there.

I was taken to a long, lonely ward, the kind you see in black and white films where the doctors walk between the rows of beds and there are clipboards and someone dies or gets better and the men who come to visit wear fedoras. And though my father did wear a fedora he didn't come to visit. No one did—it was against the rules. I was miserable.

I remember the operating theatre and the moment they dropped ether over my mouth through a sort of strainer, like the kind you use when you make tea. When I woke up there were patches on my eyes. The nuns had to feed me.

Perhaps you will understand that I didn't like the nuns. First, they would not let my parents come and see me. Secondly, they lied to me, about my parents and about other things. Like food for instance.

—Porridge or Pablum? I asked one morning.

—Pablum, said the nun, pressing a spoon against my mouth.

—I don't like Pablum, I said.

—Then it's porridge, she said. Eat your porridge or your mother won't come to see you.

My mother says when she was finally allowed to visit they wheeled me out of my ward to a room where she had been told to wait. I was, she remembers, a pathetic little thing, head hanging down, eyes patched, crying and with a cold I did not have when she last saw me.

After I was discharged I had nightmares for over a year—I would sit up in my bed, my eyes open but unseeing, screaming for my mother, who was on the bed beside me, trying to tell me everything was all right.

After all that, only one of my two eyes has ever worked satisfactorily. And it is only as an adult that I have realized my athletic inadequacy, once the source of so much pain, has had as much to do with my inability to see in three dimensions as my (albeit woeful) co-ordination.

Like all doomed passions my relationship with sports was a source of initial pleasure. About Roch Carrier's contribution (the Canadian childhood classic, "The Hockey Sweater"), I would certainly have told you, had I been writing a note, that like Carrier, I too once lived for hockey. I played on snowy driveways, frozen lakes, and in school yards. Mostly, like the boy in Carrier's story, I played in my mind. I was cut from the school team when I was in grade seven—replaced by a boy in grade six.

In 1978, when I was making documentaries for the CBC Radio program "Sunday Morning," my friend Suanne Kelman sent me to Montreal to interview Carrier. We met in my room at the Château Versailles hotel and drank cognac, and talked for a few hours. At what seemed to be the end of the interview I asked him if he would mind reading something. He suggested a story he then called "The Sweater." He said that although it had not yet been published, it was a favourite of his. He was concerned whether his English would be up to the job, but was willing to give it a try.

He did a fine job—until we came to the last paragraph. When we got there the word moths came out as "motts." If you are familiar with this story you will appreciate that moths fly into the narrative out of nowhere and understanding that they are moths and not "motts" is … well it is not the point of the story, but it helps if you want to get it. We must have done twenty or thirty takes of that one word—maw-thhhh-ssss. But no matter how many takes we did, or how long we practised, or how clumsily I tried to demonstrate where Carrier should place his tongue, the moths were "motts." After some time we mastered a singular "MOTH," and we both realized that was as good as we were going to do. The recording made it into the CBC archives and is played from time to time on the radio. Every time I hear it, I listen for the edit, and the exaggerated "thhhh" and I remember, with affection, the hour I spent in that hotel trying to teach English phonetics to Roch Carrier.

Pronunciation aside, it seems to me that Carrier's memory of childhood is just right. For me his story's charm is not the narrative (as charming as it is) but the way Carrier captures childhood insecurity, when identity is so meshed with the things we identify with. I have marshalled the stories that follow with an eye to the chronological age of the protagonists. If you choose to march through this book in the order I have chosen, it should be a little like a walk through childhood—from the beginning of self-awareness as Robertson Davies tells it, to those familiar feelings of, there it is again, inadequacy, that flutter like moths around dating, and first love, as remembered for us here by Margaret Laurence.

How odd it is, this business of childhood memory. It is clear that a two-year-old can remember things—yet so few of us can remember being two. W.O. Mitchell is fond of saying that all the details in his stories are God's truth. All those details, says Mitchell, come together to form a more magic and meaningful lie. Alice Munro, I am told, bristles when she is asked which parts of her stories are autobiographical.

I wonder if anyone can really remember what it was like to be a child. That, it seems to me, is what the stories in this book give us. If not the details of our childhood, a lie about them that helps us find a more meaningful (and if we are lucky, magical) truth.

As I read these stories, memories emerged out of the wispy fog of my early life, sometimes with abrupt and surprising clarity. One evening, for no apparent reason, I found myself thinking of the time my mother took me for a ride on one of the trains that stopped at the station at the bottom of our street. We went to the village of Como, maybe an hour away, bought ice cream cones and then came home. There was no purpose to the trip except the pleasure I took in trains. The only time I ran away my mother found me at the Montreal West station—watching the huge steam-powered engines, the man who held out the hooped message-stick, the traffic on the worn wooden platform that smelled of oil.

As I continued to read more stories I began to scribble down the things I was remembering. My two pages of notes are a cryptogram of my childhood. *Breaking my leg. Hamsters. Red-winged blackbirds. Cold hands on Bedbrook Avenue. The smell of my parents when they had been out to dinner. Walking to school.*

Walking to school. I walked to school alone. Up Brock Avenue and along Parkside. I walked home for lunch. I liked the mornings when it was raining. It made me feel special to be allowed out, alone, in bad weather. I enjoyed the solitude of a grey sky. I believed that my black rubber raincoat and billy boots bound me to the landscape. There were puddles, leaves to kick.

Of school I don't remember much. I was not a scholar. But I do remember the readers, and the day we got ink pens, and the sense of rebirth every time we were given a new workbook. There was a box at the bottom of our report card called General Standing, and I understood it was the most important one, so in the weeks before reports were due I was careful to stand tall and straight though never, it seemed, tall or straight enough. Mostly I remember the constant battle to pay attention. Mostly I remember the seductive slide into my daydreams.

More than any lessons I recall with affection the commerce of the boy's playground. This is where we traded and flipped cards, knocked chestnuts and pulled stems from the restless poplars that lined the park. I remember the wars we fought in winter. Battling for possession of the rolling snow hills in the playground where the city dumped snow.

I have not forgotten how cruel we could be. How we ran in gangs. How we teased and were teased. How often I had trouble sleeping at night. How I would toss and turn, terrified if I didn't sleep *now* I would never sleep again. I would try to calm myself by getting up and washing my face, brushing my teeth again, trying to start over, but fifteen minutes later I would look at the clock and … panic.

I believe I had a happy childhood yet I know I was beset by insecurities and fear. I prayed that my parents

would not die. Sometimes I doubted even my own
survival. Seemingly harmless events could at any
moment turn sour. Mealtime for instance. With each
meal loomed the horrifying possibility that I might be
forced to eat something I hated. I knew with certainty I
would die if I ever put egg in my mouth. Often I was
left at the table long after everyone had been excused,
sullenly pushing a mound of cooked beans around my
plate. Or shovelling them under the table to the dog, or
stuffing them out of sight behind a radiator or under a
couch. There were so many things my parents wanted
me to do that didn't make sense. Like clean my room. It
was possible to commit an unforgivable sin and not be
aware of it. There were things that you couldn't ask
about.

Yet I would try to be the first up on Saturday
morning. I had a wagon, a blue tricycle, I got a red and
white bike for my sixth birthday. In the summer we
went to the ocean. In a good summer we would stop at
one of the amusement parks in upstate New York:
Storytown, Santa Claus's Village, or best of all, Frontier
Town. I knew all the words to the "Ballad of Davy
Crockett."

Once, I am told, I went missing at a restaurant in
Saratoga Springs called The Wishing Well. It was 1953
and no one was worried when I wandered away from
the table and did not return. When my mother finally
did go looking for me she found me in the piano bar
across the hall. She says I was standing at attention on
top of the grand piano while the large-bosomed pianist
played the song I had requested. I was singing it at the
top of my little lungs, and everyone in the bar was

singing along—to the old Arthur Sullivan hymn, "Onward Christian Soldiers."

When I was in grade six I broke my leg and, mysteriously, two girls from the neighbourhood, Judy Love and Diane Perodeau, came and visited. I didn't go to school with either of them any more, and I didn't understand why they would want to visit until they had been there for fifteen minutes and one of them suddenly reached out and, before I could stop her, removed the sheet that was covering me. The cast, which rose from my toes to above my knee, made it impossible to wear pajamas, or any sort of pants, and usually I wore nothing, and that, I suppose, is what Judy and Diane were hoping to find. But I have led a blessed life. That afternoon I had on a pair of underwear. I was still horrified. Only as I write this do I realize I should have been pleased—that they might have cared.

These moments, among so many others, are what is left of my childhood. Memories that have become the connective tissue of my life, the path I can follow backwards to my younger self. Although even as I remember I cannot say with any certainty what it is I am remembering—the moments or the memories of them; the person I was, or a construction of the person I wanted to be.

I am writing this at a desk I used when I was a child. It is a large, wooden desk with eleven fine thin drawers. It once belonged to my great-grandfather—a man who went to Australia from Scotland when he was twenty-five years old and began a publishing business. My father brought the desk with him when he came to Canada after the war. It was moved into my bedroom when I still had red cowboy curtains and a bedspread to match. At night when I was supposed to be doing my homework I would prop open the middle drawer and lay a book there and read it rather than study. I would spread my homework on the desk in front of me in case my mother or father walked into my room. If they did, I would lean on the drawer with my book in it and make it disappear. Mostly the books that disappeared were things like James Bond and volumes from the series by Leslie Charteris featuring the Saint. Great stories for a young boy.

There is a stain on the desk. Though you can't see it any longer because years ago my brother painted the desk. The stain was burned into the veneer when someone spilled a bottle of ink remover—a chemical sold in those days when children used fountain pens. You dripped the liquid onto the word you wanted removed and it would fade away, like a photograph developing in reverse. Somehow the bottle spilled (I wasn't in the room when it happened); maybe my brother did it, or maybe I left the bottle open and the wind, or the cat, which had tormented my father for so many years, knocked it over. Except I think by then the cat was dead. Like those nightmares and the sleepless nights and many other of my childhood memories I am not exactly sure how the stain came to be and whether it was my fault or not, just that it is still there—out of sight maybe—but there nevertheless.

Stuart McLean
Toronto

EXTRACT FROM

What's Bred in the Bone

by Robertson Davies

*Robertson Davies was born in 1913 in Thamesville,
Ontario. He was a student in Canada and in England,
returning to Canada in 1940. He had careers as an actor,
journalist, and Master of Massey College but was best
known as one of Canada's most distinguished men of letters
who gained worldwide fame for his three trilogies. He died
in 1995.*

THE EXTRACT THAT FOLLOWS is from *What's Bred in the
Bone*, the second novel in the Cornish Trilogy.

It was in a garden that Francis Cornish first became truly aware of himself as a creature observing a world apart from himself. He was almost three years old, and he was looking deep into a splendid red peony. He was greatly alive to himself (though he had not yet learned to think of himself as Francis) and the peony, in its fashion, was also greatly alive to itself, and the two looked at each other from their very different egotisms with solemn self-confidence. The little boy nodded at the peony and the peony seemed to nod back. The little boy was neat, clean, and pretty. The peony was unchaste, dishevelled as peonies must be, and at the height of its beauty. It was a significant moment, for it was Francis's first conscious encounter with beauty—beauty that was to be the delight, the torment, and the bitterness of his life—but except for Francis himself, and perhaps the peony, nobody knew of it, or would have heeded if they had known. Every hour is filled with such moments, big with significance for someone.

It was his mother's garden, but it would be foolish to pretend that it was Mary-Jim's creation. She cared little for gardens, and had one only because it was the sort of thing a young matron in her position was expected to possess. Her husband would have protested if she had not had a garden, for he had determined ideas about what women liked. Women liked flowers; on certain occasions one gave them flowers; on certain occasions one told them they were like flowers—though it would not have done to tell a woman she looked like a peony, a beautiful but whorish flower. The garden was the work of Mr. Maidment, and it reflected the dull, geometrical character of Mr. Maidment's mind.

It was uncommon for Francis to be in the garden unattended. Mr. Maidment did not like boys, whom he knew to be plant-tramplers and bloom-snatchers, but at this magical moment Bella-Mae had left him to himself because she had to go indoors for a moment. Francis knew she had gone to pee, which she did frequently, having inherited the weak bladder of her family, the Elphinstones. Bella-Mae did not know that Francis knew, because one of her jobs was to protect Francis from bruising contacts with reality, and in her confused and grubby mind, little boys ought not to know that adults had such creatural needs. But Francis did know, even though he was not fully aware who Francis was, and he felt a minute guilt at his knowledge. He was not yet such a close reasoner as to suspect that if Bella-Mae were thus burdened with the common needs of life, his

parents might also share them. The life of his parents was
god-like and remote. Their clothes did not come off,
obviously, though they changed several times a day; but
he had seen Bella-Mae take off her clothes, or at least
shrug and struggle them off under her nightdress,
because she slept in the nursery with him. She also
brushed her coarse rusty hair a hundred times every
night, for he had heard her counting, and was usually
fast asleep before she had reached the century stroke.

Bella-Mae was called Nanny, because that was what
the Major insisted she be called. But Bella-Mae, who
was Blairlogie to the core of her being, thought it a silly
thing to call her by a name that was not hers. She
thought Major and Mrs. Cornish stuck-up and she took
no pride in being a child's nurse. It was a job, and she
did it as well as she could, but she had her own ideas,
and sometimes smacked Francis when he had not been
very bad, as a personal protest against the whole Cornish
manner of life, so out of tune with Blairlogie ideas.

Within the time between his meeting and recognition
of the peony and his fourth year, Francis came to know
that Bella-Mae was Awful. She was plain, if not
downright ugly, and grown women ought to be
beautiful, like his mother, and smell of expensive scent,
not starch. Bella-Mae frequently made him clean his
teeth with brown soap, as she did herself, and declared it
to be wholesome; she took no stock in the tooth-powder
with which the nursery was supplied. This was Awful.
More Awful still was her lack of respect for the holy
ikons which hung on the nursery wall. These were two
vividly coloured pictures of King Edward VII and Queen
Alexandra, and once a month she scrubbed their glass

with Bon Ami, saying under her breath: "Come on, you two, and get your faces washed." If the Major had known that, he would have given Bella-Mae what-for. But of course he did not know, because Francis was not a squealer, a kind of person Bella-Mae held in abhorrence. But if he was not a squealer, Francis was a noticer, and he kept a mental dossier on Bella-Mae which would certainly have led to her dismissal if his parents had known what it contained.

There was, for instance, her contumelious attitude, expressed physically but not verbally, toward the other picture in the nursery, which was of A Certain Person. Bella-Mae did not hold with images or idols; she belonged to the small assembly of the Salvation Army in Blairlogie, and she knew what was right, and a picture of A Certain Person, in a room like the nursery, was not right.

To remove the picture, or alter its position, was out of the question. It had been hung beside Francis's bed by Aunt, Miss Mary-Benedetta McRory, who ought by rights to be called Great-Aunt. Bella-Mae was not the only one to have reservations about pictures of A Certain Person; the Major was not happy about it, but rather than have a row with Aunt he tolerated it, on the ground that women and children had soft heads about religion, and when the boy grew older he would put an end to all that nonsense. So there it hung, a brightly coloured picture of Jesus, smiling sadly as though a little pained by what his large brown eyes beheld, and with his lovely long white hands extended from his blue robe in the familiar Come-unto-me gesture. Behind him were a good many stars, and he seemed to be floating.

From time to time Aunt Mary-Ben had a secret little whisper with Francis. "When you say your prayers, dear, look first at the picture of Jesus, then close your eyes but keep the picture in your mind. Because that's Who you're praying to, isn't it? And He knows all about little boys and loves them dearly."

Bella-Mae was sure that Jesus didn't like to see little boys naked, and she hustled Francis out of his clothes and into them with great speed and certain modest precautions. "You don't think he wants to look at your bare B.T.M. with his big eyes, do you?" she said, managing to include both Francis and the picture in her displeasure. For her displeasure was immense. The faith of the Salvation Army expressed itself in her through a repertoire of disapprovals; she lived strongly in the faith of the Army, and from time to time she murmured the Army war-cry, "Blood and Fire," with the vigour usually reserved for an oath.

She saw that the Army figured in Francis's life as much as possible, though she would not have dared to take him to the Temple; the Major would not have stood for that. But at least twice a week he beheld her in the splendour of her uniform, and he was the first to see her in the glory of the Chapeau.

The Army uniform cost a good deal of money, and Bella-Mae bought hers garment by garment, as she could afford it. The sensible shoes, the black stockings, the skirt, and the tunic with its wonderful buttons, were achieved one by one, and then the great decision had to be made. Should she buy the bonnet, which was the familiar headgear of the Salvation Lassies, or should she opt for the Chapeau, a flat-crowned, broad-brimmed hat of blue fur felt, glorious with its red-and-gold ribbon, and strongly resembling (though Bella-Mae did not know this) the hats worn by Catholic priests in nearby Quebec. After deep inward searching, and prayer for guidance, she chose the Chapeau.

In full Salvation fig at last, she marched around the nursery, for Francis, singing in a style of her own, which included noises indicative of the band's contribution:

> *At the Cross, at the Cross*
> *Where I first saw the light*
>   *And my heart's great burden roll'd away (pom, pom)*
> *It was there through Blessed Jesus*
> *That I turned to the Right*
>   *And now I am happy all the day!* (Pish! scolded the cymbal)

>   *At the Cro—s—s—s!*
>   *At the Cro—o—o—s!*
> *At the Cross where I first saw the light (boomty-boom)*
>   *It was there through His mercy*
>   *That I turned toward the Right*
> *And now I am happy all the day!* (Boom, boom!)

It was irresistible. Francis hopped off his bed and paraded behind Bella-Mae, and under her guidance was able to shout, "Thine the glory!" and "Blest Redeemer!" ecstatically at the right intervals. He was elevated. He was free of the repressive influence of A Certain Person, whose sad eyes he ignored. He did not know what he was singing about, but he sang from a happy heart.

The nursery door opened. It was Aunt Mary-Ben, tiny and smiling, her little soft cap nodding pleasantly, for she was not a bit disapproving. Oh, not she! She motioned Francis back to his bed, and drew Bella-Mae toward the window, where she spoke very softly for a few minutes, after which Bella-Mae ran out of the room, crying.

Then Aunt said, "Shall we say our prayers, Frankie? Or I'll tell you what—you shall hear me say mine." And Aunt knelt by the bed with the little boy, and brought out of her pocket a sort of necklace he had never seen before, made of black beads of different sizes, strung together with silver chain, and as Aunt passed the beads through her fingers she murmured what sounded like poetry. When she had finished she reverently kissed the cross that hung on the necklace and, with a sweet smile, held it out to Francis, who kissed it, too. Liked kissing it, liked the reverential quietness, liked the effect of poetry. This was every bit as good as Bella-Mae's march, in an entirely different way. He held the cross in his hand, reluctant to let it go.

"Would you like it for your very own, Frankie?" said Aunt. "I'm afraid you can't have it right now, dear, but perhaps after a little while I shall be able to give you one of these. It's called a rosary, dear, because it's a rose-garden of prayer. It's the garden of Jesus' dear Mother, and when we say our prayers with it, we are very near Her, and we may even see Her sweet face. But this is our secret, dear. Don't say anything to Daddy."

No fear of that. Conversation between Francis and the Major was in a very different mode. "Come here and I'll show you my gun, Frank. Look down the barrel. See? Clean as a whistle. Always keep your gun clean and oiled. It deserves it. A fine gun deserves decent care.

When you're older I'll get you one, and show you how
to use it. Must learn to shoot like a sportsman, not like a
killer." Or it might be, "Come with me, Frank, and I'll
show you how to tie a trout-fly." Or, "Look at my boots,
Frank. Bright, what? I never let the girls do my boots.
You'd never think these were eleven years old, would
you? That's what proper care does. You can always judge
a man by his boots. Always get 'em from the best maker.
Only cads wear dirty boots." Or, in passing, "Stand
straight, Frank. Never slump, however tired you are.
Arch your back a bit, too—looks smart on parade.
Come tomorrow after breakfast and I'll show you my
sword."

A good father, determined that his son should be a
good man. Not entirely what might have been expected
of the Wooden Soldier. There were depths of affection
in the Major. Affection, and pride. No poetry.

Mother was entirely different. Affectionate, but
perhaps she turned it on at will. She did not see a great
deal of Francis except by accident, for she had so much
to do. Amusing Father, and taking care that there were
no unfortunate encounters when the Cornishes set
out for St. Alban's church on Sunday morning, and
the McRorys' carriage might be making toward
St. Bonaventura; reading a succession of novels with
pretty pictures on the covers; and playing the phonograph, which gave out with *Gems from the Wizard of the
Nile,* and a piece Francis loved, the words of which were:

> *Everybody's doing it*
> *Doing it, doing it*
> *Everybody's doing it*

> *Doing what? The turkey-trot;*
> *See that rag-time couple over there,*
> *See them throw their feet in the air—*
> *It's a bear, it's a bear, it's a BEAR!*

It was wonderful—better than anything. Just as good as Father's sword, or Aunt's mysterious beads, and far better than Bella-Mae in her uniform, which he never saw now, anyway. Mother took his hands and they danced the turkey-trot round and round her pretty drawing-room. All wonderful!

As wonderful, in their own way, as the ecstatic first moment with the peony, but perhaps not quite, because that was all his own, and he could repeat it in summer and remember it in winter without anybody else being involved.

All wonderful, until the shattering September morning in 1914 when he was led away by Bella-Mae to school.

This would have figured more prominently in the life of Chegwidden Lodge if the household had not been in disorder because of the many absences, which extended from days to weeks and then to months, of the Major and his wife in Ottawa, where they were increasingly favourites at Government House. In addition there were mysterious colloquies with military authorities; the Major acted as a go-between for the Governor-General, the Duke of Connaught, who was a field marshal and knew rather more about military affairs than most of the Canadian regulars. As the representative of the Crown, the Duke could not make himself too prominent, or cause the Canadians to lose face, and it was somebody's job to carry information to and advice from Rideau Hall without being tactless. That somebody was Major Cornish, who was tact personified. And when, at last, war was officially declared against Germany and what were called the Central Powers, the Major became something which was slow to be named, but was, in fact, Chief of Military Intelligence, in so far as Canada had such an organization, and he moved himself and Mary-Jim to Ottawa. They would not be in Blairlogie, he told the Senator, for the duration, which was not expected to be long.

The business of arranging for Francis's education had not been much considered. Ottawa and the pleasures and intrigues of the Vice-regal world were foremost in Mary-Jacobine's mind, and she was the sort of mother who is certain that if she is happy, all must certainly be well with her child. Francis was too small to be sent to board-school, and, besides, he tended to have heavy colds and bronchial troubles. "Local schools for a while," said the Major, but not to Francis. Indeed, nobody said anything to Francis until the evening before school opened, when Bella-Mae said, "Up in good time tomorrow; you're starting school." Francis, who knew every tone of her voice, caught the ring of malice in what she said.

The next morning Francis threw up his breakfast, and was assured by Bella-Mae that there was to be none of that, because they had no time to spare. With her hand holding his firmly—more firmly than usual—he was marched off to Blairlogie's Central School, to be entered in the kindergarten.

It was by no means a bad school, but it was not a school to which children were escorted by nursemaids, or where boys were dressed in white sailor suits and crowned with a sailor cap with H.M.S. *Renown* on the ribbon. The kindergarten was housed in an old-fashioned schoolhouse, to which a large, much newer school had been joined. It stank, in a perfectly reasonable way, of floor oil, chalk powder, and many generations of imperfectly continent Blairlogie children. The teacher, Miss Wade, was a smiling, friendly woman, but a stranger, and there was not a child in the thirty or more present whom Francis had ever seen before.

"His name's Francis Cornish," said Bella-Mae, and went home.

Some of the children were crying, and Francis was of a mind to join this group, but he knew his father would disapprove, so he bit his lip and held in. Obedient to Miss Wade, and a student teacher who acted as her assistant, the children sat in small chairs, arranged in a circle marked out on the floor in red paint.

To put things on a friendly footing at once, Miss Wade said that everybody would stand up, as his turn came, and say his name and tell where he lived, so that she could prepare something mysteriously called the Nominal Roll. The children complied, some shouting out their names boldly, some sure of their names but in the dark as to their addresses; the third child in order, a little girl, lost her composure and wet the floor. Most of the other children laughed, held their noses, and enjoyed the fun, as the student teacher rushed forward with a damp rag for the floor and a hanky for the eyes. When Francis's turn came, he announced, in a low voice: Francis Chegwidden Cornish, Chegwidden Lodge.

"What's your second name, Francis?" said Miss Wade.

"Chegwidden," said Francis, using the pronunciation he had been taught.

Miss Wade, kindly but puzzled, said, "Did you say Chicken, Francis?"

"Cheggin," said Francis, much too low to be heard above the roar of the thirty others, who began to shout, "Chicken, Chicken!" in delight. This was something they could understand and get their teeth into. The kid in the funny suit was called Chicken! Oh, this was rich! Far better than the kid who had peed.

Miss Wade restored order, but at recess it was Chicken, Chicken! for the full fifteen minutes, and a very happy playtime it made. Kindergarten assembled only during the mornings, and as soon as school was dismissed, Francis ran home as fast as he could, followed by derisive shouts.

Francis announced next morning that he was not going to school. Oh yes you are, said Bella-Mae. I won't, said Francis. Do you want me to march you right over to Miss McRory? said Bella-Mae, for in the absence of his parents, Aunt Mary-Ben had been given full authority to bind and loose if anything went beyond the nursemaid's power. So off to school he went, in Bella-Mae's jailer's grip, and the second day was worse than the first.

Children from the upper school had got wind of something extraordinary and at recess Francis was surrounded by older boys, anxious to look into the matter.

"It's not Chicken, it's Cheggin," said Francis, trying hard not to cry.

"See—he says his name's Chicken," shouted one boy, already a leader of men, and later to do well in politics.

"Aw, come on," said a philosophical boy, anxious to probe deeper. "Nobody's called Chicken. Say it again, kid."

"Cheggin," said Francis.

"Sounds like Chicken, all right," said the philosophical boy. "Kind of mumbled, but Chicken. Gosh!"

If the boys were derisive, the girls were worse. The girls had a playground of their own, on which no boy was allowed to set foot, but there were places where the boundary, like the equator, was an imaginary line. The boys decided that it was great fun to harry Francis across this line, because anybody called Chicken was probably a girl anyway. When this happened, girls surrounded him and talked not to but at him.

"His name's Chicken," some would say, whooping with joy. These girls belonged to what psychologists would later define as the Hetaera, or Harlot, classification of womanhood.

"Aw, let him alone. His parents must be crazy. Look, he's nearly bawling. It's mean to holler on him if his parents are crazy. Is your name really Chicken, kid?" These were what the psychologists would classify as the Maternal, fostering order of womankind. Their pity was almost more hateful than outright jeering.

Teachers patrolled both playgrounds, carrying a bell by its clapper, and usually intent on studying the sky. Ostensibly guardians of order, they were like policemen in their avoidance of anything short of arson or murder. Questioned, they would probably have said that the Cornish child seemed to be popular; he was always in the centre of some game or another.

Life must be lived, and sometimes living means enduring. Francis endured, and the torment let up a little, though it broke out anew every two or three weeks. He no longer had to go to school in the care of Bella-Mae. Kindergarten was hateful. There was stupid, babyish paper-cutting, which was far beneath his notice, and which he did easily. There was sewing crudely punched cards, so that they formed a picture, usually of an animal. There was learning to tell the time, which he knew anyway. There was getting the Twenty-third Psalm by heart, and singing a tedious hymn that began

> *Can a little child like me*
> *Thank the Father fittingly?*

and dragged on to a droning refrain (for Miss Wade had no skill as a choral director) of

> *Father, we thank Thee: (twice repeated)*
> *Father in Heaven, we thank Thee!*

Francis, who had a precocious theological bent, wondered why he was thanking the Father, whoever He might be, for this misery and this tedium.

It was in kindergarten that the foundations for Francis Cornish's lifelong misanthropy were firmly established. The sampling of mankind into which he had been cast badgered and mocked him, excluded him from secrets and all but the most inclusive games, sneered at his clothes, and in one instance wrote prick in indelible pencil on the collar of his sailor middy (for which Bella-Mae gave him a furious scolding).

He could say nothing of this at home. When, infrequently, his parents came back to Blairlogie for a weekend, he was told by his mother that he must be a particularly good boy, because Daddy was busy with some very important things in Ottawa, and was not to be worried. Now: how was school going?

"All right, I guess."

"Don't say 'I guess' unless you really do guess, Frankie. It's stupid."

> *Love the Lord and do your part:*
> *Learn to say with all your heart,*
> *Father, we thank Thee!*

WHO HAS SEEN THE WIND

by W.O. Mitchell

W.O. Mitchell was born in Weyburn, Saskatchewan, in 1914. He has lived in Saskatchewan, Ontario, and Alberta. His novel Who Has Seen the Wind *(1947) is one of the most popular and critically acclaimed novels ever published in Canada. He is also the author of many other novels, five plays, and two collections of short stories that inspired the classic CBC Radio series* Jake and the Kid. *W.O. Mitchell died in 1998.*

THE FOLLOWING is the first chapter of *Who Has Seen the Wind.*

Here was the least common denominator of nature, the skeleton requirements simply, of land and sky—Saskatchewan prairie. It lay wide around the town, stretching tan to the far line of the sky, shimmering under the June sun and waiting for the unfailing visitation of wind, gentle at first, barely stroking the long grasses and giving them life; later, a long hot gusting that would lift the black topsoil and pile it in barrow pits along the roads, or in deep banks against the fences.

Over the prairie, cattle stood listless beside the dried-up slough beds which held no water for them. Where the snow-white of alkali edged the course of the river, a thin trickle of water made its way toward the town low upon the horizon. Silver willow, heavy with dust, grew along the riverbanks, perfuming the air with its honey smell.

Just before the town the river took a wide loop and entered at the eastern edge. Inhabited now by some eighteen hundred souls, it had grown up on either side of the river from the seed of one homesteader's sod hut built in the spring of eighteen seventy-five. It was made up largely of frame buildings with high, peaked roofs, each with an expanse of lawn in front and a garden in the back; they lined avenues with prairie names: Bison, Riel, Qu'Appelle, Blackfoot, Fort. Cement sidewalks extended from First Street to Sixth Street at MacTaggart's Corner; from that point to the prairie a boardwalk ran.

Lawn sprinklers sparkled in the sun; Russian poplars stood along either side of Sixth Street. Five houses up from MacTaggart's Corner stood the O'Connal home, a three-storied house lifting high above the white cottage to the left of it. Virginia creepers had almost smothered the veranda; honeysuckle and spirea grew on either side of the steps. A tricycle with its front wheel sharply turned stood in the middle of the walk.

The tricycle belonged to Brian Sean MacMurray O'Connal, the four-year-old son of Gerald O'Connal, druggist, and Maggie O'Connal, formerly Maggie MacMurray of Trossachs, Ontario. Brian at the moment was in the breakfast room. He sat under the table at the window, imagining himself an ant deep in a dark cave. Ants, he had decided, saw things tiny and grass-coloured, and his father and mother would never know about it. He hated his mother and his father and his grandmother for spending so much time with the baby, for making it a blanket tent and none for him. Not that he cared; he needed no one to play with him now that he was an ant. He was a smart ant.

He hadn't asked Dr. Svarich, with his bitter smell, to play with him. He would never again ask anyone to play with him. He would make them wish they had never been mean to him.

"Brian!"

His grandmother stood high above him. Looking up to her he could see her face turned down, could see the dark velvet band circling high around her throat, hooping in the twin folds of skin that hung from under her chin. Light stabbed out from her silver-rimmed glasses.

"I told ye to go outside!"

He crawled from under the table and stood by her hand with large liver spots spattering its back, and blue veins writhing under the thin skin. Her hand had great knotted knuckles. When her stomach sang after dinner, Brian promised himself, he would not listen.

"I will not speak to ye again!" The loose folds of her cheeks shook slightly as she spoke. The winy bouquet of tonic was about her, reminding him of apples. Behind the spectacles her eyes looked forbidding to him. "If ye stay inside ye'll disturb the baby. Ye must go out!"

"Can I have a tent like the baby has?"

"Ye cannot. 'Tis bad enough having the baby ill without—"

"Is he ill bad?"

"Aye," said his grandmother. "Now, be a good boy and do as ye're told."

He would get Jake Harris, the town policeman, after her. He hoped Jake would bring his policeman's knife and chop her into little pieces and cut her head off, for making him go outside to play.

He stood on the step of the back porch a moment, feeling the warmth of the sun against his cheek, the wind,

which was beginning to rise now that it was late afternoon, delicately active about his ears and at his nostrils.

Slowly he walked to the sand pile by the high
Caragana hedge that separated the O'Connal back yard
from that of Sherry next door. He hated his grandmother. She made him go out to a sand pile where there
was nobody but an old shovel to play with. Reflectively
he stared down at the sand hump in one corner of the
box. It was like an ant pile, he thought; perhaps if he
waited an ant might come out. He watched impatiently,
and then as no ant emerged, he took up the shovel that
lay at his feet. He hit the bump, and wished that it were
his grandmother. He hit the bump again, being careful
that it was with the sharp edge and not the flat bottom
of the shovel. He was hitting his grandmother so awful
she was bawling her head off.

He stopped.

Directly opposite him, and low in the hedge, was a
round and freckled face—a new face to Brian. He began
again to punish the sand pile.

The boy came to the edge of the sand pile. Hedge
leaves hung to his sweater and to his hat, a blue sailor
hat bearing the legend H.M.S. THUNDERBOLT. It had
got twisted so that the ribbon hung down his snub nose.

"I'm coming into the sand pile." As he stepped over,
Brian saw that his knees were scratched, that his hands
were fat with deep crease-lines at the wrists, like the
baby's. "Let me hit some," the boy said.

"No," Brian said.

"I'm Benny Banana."

"Benny Banana—Benny Banana," chanted Brian;
"Banana-Benny-Banana."

The boy sat down; he picked up a thin pebble from the sand. "What's your name?"

Brian plumped himself down by the boy. "Brian Sean MacMurray O'Connal," he said.

"I'm Forbsie Hoffman." The boy touched the tip of his tongue with the pebble he had picked up. The pebble hung. To Brian it was magic.

"I'm going to do that. I'm going to hang to my tongue." He tried it. "Mine won't hang at all."

"Naw 'hinny enouch," said Forbsie, with the pebble still clinging to the tip of his protruding tongue.

Brian found that a skinnier pebble hung.

Forbsie said, "*Thpt.*"

Brian said, "*Thpt.*"

"Do you know anything more?" asked Brian.

"I'm hungry. Maybe if you was to ask, your maw'd give us a piece."

"The baby's going to heaven," explained Brian.

"My dad's a conductor," Forbsie said, "on the C.P.R. He has got silver buttons."

"It's where God stays," said Brian, "heaven."

"No it ain't," said Forbsie. He lifted his arm and pointed. "God lives right in town. Over there. I seen Him lots of times."

"Where?"

"At His house."

"You have not!"

"Oh, yes! He's all grapes and bloody. He carries around a lamb."

Brian got up. "Let's us go over to His place."

Forbsie got up. "I guess I'll go home. I don't feel so much like going."

"I've got something to say to Him. I'm going to get Him after my gramma. You show me where He lives."

"All right," said Forbsie.

The wind had strengthened; it had begun to snap the clothes on Sherry's line, where Mrs. Sherry, a tall, spare woman, was in the act of hanging up her washing. She took a clothespin from her mouth. "How is the baby today, Brian?"

"He's very sick," Brian told her. "This is Forbsie. We're going to see Someone."

Mrs. Sherry, with limp underwear in her hands, stared after the boys as they walked toward the front of the house.

At MacTaggart's Corner a tall man in shirt sleeves greeted them: Mr. Digby, Principal of the school. He walked a block west with them from the corner. Digby could not be called a handsome man, largely because of the angularity of his face. His skin had the weathered look of split rock that has lain long under sun and wind. His sandy eyebrows were unruly over eyes of startling blueness; his hair lay in one fair shock over his forehead.

"We're going to see Somebody," Brian told him.

"Are you," said Digby.

"Yes," said Brian: "God."

The schoolmaster showed no surprise. "I'd like to come with you, but I have a previous engagement."

"What's that?" asked Brian.

"It means that I can't go," said Digby.

When the boys had turned off Bison Avenue and left the Principal, they walked in silence over the cement sidewalk. Once they bent down to watch a bee crawl over a Canadian thistle, his licorice all-sorts stripes showing through the cellophane of folded wings. Down the road, from time to time, a dust-devil spun— snatching up papers, dust, and debris, lifting them up, carrying them high into the air, and leaving them finally to sink slowly down again.

"Step on a crack," Forbsie sang, "break your mother's back!"

Brian sang, "Step on a crack, break my gramma's back!" He did not miss stepping upon a single crack in the three blocks that took them to the great, grey, sandstone church: KNOX PRESBYTERIAN—1902.

"Is this it?" asked Brian.

Forbsie said that it was.

"Let's go see Him, then."

"I'm going home, I think. It's suppertime, and I better get home."

"Not yet." Brian started up the stone steps; when he turned at the top, he saw that Forbsie was halfway down the block, his head turned back over his shoulder. Brian knocked on the church door. As he did, he felt the wind ruffling his hair. Forbsie was down by the corner now.

A woman came out of the little brown house next to the church. She shook a mop, then turned to re-enter the house. She stopped as she saw Brian; stood watching him. A fervent whirlwind passed the brown house with the woman standing on the porch; at the trees before the church, it rose suddenly, setting every leaf in violent motion, as though an invisible hand had gripped the trunks and shaken them.

Brian wondered why Forbsie had not wanted to come. He knocked again. It was simply that God was in the bathroom and couldn't come right away.

As he turned away from the door, he saw the woman staring at him. She ought to know if God was in. He went down the steps and to the opening in the hedge.

"I guess God isn't anywhere around."

"Why—what do you mean?"

"That's His house, isn't it?"

"Yes."

"I'm going to see Him."

The woman stared at him silently a moment; under the slightly grey hair pulled severely back, her face wore an intense look. "God isn't—He isn't the same as other people, you know. He's a spirit."

"What's that?"

"It's someone—something you can't hear—or see, or touch." Her grey eyes were steady upon his face; he noted that her teeth had pushed back her upper lip slightly, giving her a permanent smile.

"Does He smell?"

"No, he doesn't. I think you better talk with my husband. He's the minister and he could tell you much more about this than I could," she said, with relief loosening the words.

"Does he know God pretty well?"

"Pretty well. He—he tells people about Him."

"Better than you do? Does he know better than you do?"

"It's—it's his job to know God."

"My dad is a druggist. He works for God, I guess."

"He works for God," the woman agreed.

"My Uncle Sean isn't a sheepherder—neither is Ab. Ab's got a thing on his foot, and one foot is shorter, so he goes up and down when he walks."

"And who is Ab?" the woman asked him.

"Uncle Sean's hired man that feeds the pigs and helps grow the wheat whenever there isn't any goddam-drought."

The woman looked startled.

"Has your husband got calfs?" Brian asked her.

"No—he hasn't any calfs—calves." She looked quickly back over her shoulder.

"He looks after the sheep and the sheep pups."

"Looks after the …!"

"I'm going to get God after my gramma," Brian confided. "She has a thing on her leg too. It's not the same as Ab's. You only see it on the heel. She's got room-a-ticks in a leg."

The woman cast another anxious look over her shoulder.

"She belshes," said Brian, "a lot."

"Perhaps your grandmother has stomach trouble."

"If your husband works for God, then he could take me in His house for a while, couldn't he?"

"Perhaps he could. Tomorrow."

"Not now?"

"Tomorrow—in the morning—after breakfast." She turned to the doorway.

"Does God like to be all grapes and bloody?"

"All what?"

"That's what I want to see."

"But what do you mean …?"

"Something's burning," said Brian. "I'll come back."

She hurried in to her burning dinner.

Brian walked back towards his home. He did not turn down Bison Avenue where it crossed the street upon which the church was, but continued on, a dark wishbone of a child wrapped in reflection.

The wind was persistent now, a steady urgency upon his straight back, smoking up the dust from the road along the walk, lifting it and carrying it out to the prairie beyond. Several times Brian stopped: once to look up into the sun's unbearable radiance and then away with the lingering glow stubborn in his eyes; another time when he came upon a fox-red caterpillar making a procession of itself over a crack that snaked along the walk. He squashed it with his foot. Further on he paused at a spider that carried its bead of a body between hurrying thread-legs. Death came for the spider too.

He looked up to find that the street had stopped. Ahead lay the sudden emptiness of the prairie. For the first time in his four years of life he was alone on the prairie.

He had seen it often, from the veranda of his uncle's farmhouse, or at the end of a long street, but till now he had never heard it. The hum of telephone wires along the road, the ring of hidden crickets, the stitching sound of grasshoppers, the sudden relief of a meadow lark's song, were deliciously strange to him. Without hesitation he crossed the road and walked out through the hip-deep grass stirring in the steady wind; the grass clung at his legs; haloed fox-tails bowed before him; grasshoppers sprang from hidden places in the grass, clicketing ahead of him to disappear, then lift again.

A gopher squeaked questioningly as Brian sat down upon a rock warm to the backs of his thighs. He picked a pale blue flax-flower at his feet, stared long at the stripings in its shallow throat, then looked up to see a dragonfly hanging on shimmering wings directly in front of him. The gopher squeaked again, and he saw it a few yards away, sitting up, watching him from its pulpit hole. A suave-winged hawk chose that moment to slip its shadow over the face of the prairie.

And all about him was the wind now, a pervasive sighing through great emptiness, unhampered by the buildings of the town, warm and living against his face and in his hair.

Then for the second time that day he saw a strange boy—one who came from behind him soundlessly, who stood and stared at him with steady grey eyes in a face of remarkable broadness, with cheekbones circling high under a dark and freckled skin. He saw that the boy's hair, bleached as the dead prairie grass itself, lay across his forehead in an all-round cowlick curling under at the edge. His faded blue pants hung open in two tears just below the knees. He was barefooted.

Brian was not startled; he simply accepted the boy's presence out here as he had accepted that of the gopher and the hawk and the dragonfly.

"This is your prairie," Brian said.

The boy did not answer him. He turned and walked as silently as he had come, out over the prairie. His walk was smooth.

After the boy's figure had become just a speck in the distance, Brian looked up into the sky, now filled with a soft expanse of cloud, the higher edges luminous and startling against the blue. It stretched to the prairie's rim. As he stared, the grey underside carded out, and through the cloud's softness was revealed a blue well shot with sunlight. Almost as soon as it had cleared, a whisking of cloud stole over it.

For one moment no wind stirred. A butterfly went pelting past. God, Brian decided, must like the boy's prairie.

JIMMY

by Jacques Poulin
translated by Sheila Fischman

Jacques Poulin was born in 1937 in Saint-Gédéon, in the Beauce region of Quebec. He worked for a number of years as a commercial translator. He is the author of several critically acclaimed novels, including Les grandes marées, *which won a Governor General's Award in 1978. In 1995, Jacques Poulin received the Athanase-David prize, the highest distinction awarded by the Quebec government for an artist's body of work. Jacques Poulin lived in Paris for fifteen years and has now returned to Quebec City.*

IN THE FOLLOWING EXTRACT from *Jimmy* (1969), the narrator is a young boy who lives with his father (Papou) and mother (Mamie) near Quebec City. His mother is emotionally disturbed after losing a child, and his father is often shut up in his attic study, working on a biography of Hemingway. Jimmy spends much time alone and is kept company by his cat, Chanoine. He has a rich imaginative life, in which his favourite words—*catshit* and *zouave*—figure prominently. One of Jimmy's worries is that the pilings on which their house is constructed are rotten. He likes to discuss the pilings, and other issues, with his next-door neighbour, the Commodore.

C hanoine is clinging to the back of the sofa, his tail as big around as my arm, his nose against the window and his fur as stiff as a porcupine's.

We're being invaded, inundated, submerged, taken by storm. We've closed the front windows and the back ones. Papou's gone up to the attic with a case of Molson's and Mamie's shut herself in her room. The Commodore hadn't even got to his cottage before Trixie, Dixie and Flixie had jumped out the car window and took off at a hundred miles an hour as though their asses were on fire. They ran around their cottage twice, then made a mad dash for the beach and came and took us by storm. We've barricaded ourselves inside; we can hold out for a week with the food and everything.

They climb up the iron ladder and run along the gallery of our cottage, barking and crashing into one another; they come and stick their noses against the glass, standing up on their back feet with their tongues hanging out between yellow teeth, ears pointed, tails stiff, slobbering. Then they go away again, howling like the devil, jump down the ladder without touching a single rung and go back home, taking detours to avoid the trees and jumping in the air to catch butterflies. Chanoine buried himself under the sofa; I pulled him out by the tail, grabbed him by the scruff of his neck and sat him at the window to give him a detailed view of the invasion. Every time the assault began again he'd start snarling and spitting.

I go out on the gallery with the helicopter. From Dufferin Terrace you get a good view of the helicopter taking off from the icebreaker "d'Iberville" and then flying over the river between Quebec and Lévis.

They come down the road and climb up the back stairs. I swoop down on them, propeller whirling. They've never seen a helicopter in their lives and they get the jitters; they retreat and I pursue them down the stairs and on to the road. I push my motor as far as it will go and with my propeller blades I swipe at the grasshoppers, horseflies, butterflies, grass, flowers and branches in my way. Trixie, Dixie and Flixie jump off the road, moaning plaintively, and scurry off across the fields with their bellies to the ground and their tails between their legs. Catshit! I just broke a blade on a tree and I'm crumpling into the ditch. The main blade, catshit, my rotor! It's fine to make a helicopter with a mop in front and a poker in the back, but then you break your rotor on a goddamn spruce tree and you land in the ditch on your hands and knees, with your poker and half of the mop handle, head first in the mud, to tell the truth.

The pilot doesn't hear the dogs or anything; he's a bit stunned and he wonders if anybody's seen the whole business: his main blade that broke on the spruce tree and his helicopter that dived into it, and as a matter of fact somebody puts a hand on his shoulder.

"The dogs aren't bothering you too much?"

It's the Commodore. He's wearing his Commodore's cap and everything.

"We had enough rations for a week!"

"Did they attack you?"

"Took us by storm."

The Commodore sits on the edge of the ditch, pushes back his Commodore's cap and wipes his forehead on his sleeve.

"I see, you launched a counter-attack."

"No."

"No?"

"I tried to get out."

"I see. An accident?"

"Broke my rotor."

He whistles between his teeth and says, "The birth tree?"

"The goddamn spruce."

"A squall, I suppose?"

He stands, picks up the other half of the mop and examines it in silence, like an expert.

"No, I was flying low," I say.

"No way to fix your rotor. Anything else broken?"

"Fractured skull."

"Oh!"

"Could have been worse."

"Can you stand up?"

I manage to get to my feet. He holds out his red handkerchief so I can wipe the mud off my face. He examines the fracture thoroughly while I explain.

"It could have been worse. I could have landed in the river."

"You think you can walk?"

"No choice, with a broken propeller."

"Unless I lend you another rotor?"

"Thanks, I'll walk because of the fracture."

He extends his hand to help me out of the ditch. I watch him walk towards their cottage to unload the rest of the baggage from the trailer. He really would have lent me another propeller blade for my helicopter. Halfway there he turns around and says:

"All the same, you shouldn't fly over the river too often."

Mamie is half-lying in the living-room, her head on a pillow, and Chanoine is stretched out on top of her.

The two comrades glance at the pilot just as he goes past them to hang the poker by the fireplace and put the broken mop away in the cupboard. They don't look directly at him; they simply give him a sideways glance and don't ask any questions. It's the pilot's favourite moment, to tell the truth. When he walks past them, he stops for a minute, puts down his propellers and takes the time to tie his shoelace so the comrades can get a better idea of the whole business: the broken blade, the fracture and everything. They pretend they aren't looking and don't feel like asking any questions. Out of discretion or something they act as if nothing has happened, and you'd do exactly the same thing in their place.

The pilot draws himself up before his comrades, whistles a few notes very softly, almost absentmindedly, picks up the little blade and the other one that was broken, staggers slightly because of the fracture, and goes to put his things away. That's discipline: the wounded pilot doesn't think of himself. The equipment comes first. All the comrades do the same when they return from a mission; they're well trained and they do what they have to do, mechanically, because discipline's stronger than being tired or hurt. The pilot hangs the poker on the nail to the right of the fireplace and puts the two halves of the mop in the kitchen cupboard between the broom and the dustpan. Everything in its place.

Only then does the pilot think of himself. He heads calmly for the bathroom, takes off his muddy, sweaty clothes, puts in the plug, turns on the water and pours in bath salts. The pilot checks the temperature of the water with the toes of his right foot, puts his other dirty foot in the tub and crouches down, almost stretched out. At the base of the falling water, perfumed foam bubbles up, spreading out as the tide rises.

Mamie opens the door.

She picks up the pilot's clothes, examines them and sticks them in the laundry basket without a word. Just then Chanoine comes in, swishing his tail from side to side; he jumps on the edge of the bathtub and stretches out his paw to catch the chain that's holding the plug. Mamie sits beside Chanoine.

"Want me to help you?"

"No."

I give two or three rapid orders—clear the decks for action, everybody down, close the hatch, periscope, and things like that; the submarine starts to dive and I put the washcloth over it. On the surface, the foam begins to disappear. The sea is calm. The submarine slides under the water. Mamie throws an underwater grenade; water sprays Chanoine in the face.

"Rub hard," she says.

I pursue her soap which slips between my fingers and down my back, then gets stuck between my legs just under the submarine. Mamie strokes Chanoine.

"Rub! Rub!"

I must look like a real Egyptian mummy in a sarcophagus. She made me put soap all over, even in my hair and ears. She's laughing like a loony. Then she asks, "Have you seen Thierry?"

"Soap in the eyes!"

She holds out the towel. You take your bath, wash your face—and you always get soap in your eyes. And you can't use the washcloth because of the submarine.

"Is that better?" Mamie asks.

"*Twenty Thousand Leagues Under the Sea.*"

"Have you seen Thierry?"

"Captain Nemo doesn't answer questions."

She picks up the chain that holds the plug.

"Answer me or I'll pull it out!"

The river will empty, the submarine will run aground. I answer at a hundred miles an hour.

"Not seen Thiers!"

She drops the chain. Chanoine holds out a paw to pick it up. But I add, "I'm not sure."

"Explain."

"Amnesia or something."

All at once she pulls out the plug. The tide starts going out. I explain the whole business.

"Fractured skull!"

And as I dig my heel into the hole to stop the water I point to where I was hurt. Without even looking at the fracture she abruptly turns on the shower taps. A flood! Blinded, inundated, drowned, I capitulate, ask her to pardon me, stop playing.

"Catshit!"

With a jerk she turns off the shower. Everything's drifted away: soap, suds, sponge, washcloth. And the submarine's capsized, periscope pointing down. I want to answer everything, really lay it on, everything she wants to know.

"Did you or didn't you see Thierry?"

"No, I swear!"

"Is he coming?"

"Yes!"

"When? Who told you? The Commodore?"

"The Commodore brought Trixie, Dixie and Flixie and the baggage in the trailer and he said Thiers would be coming at a hundred miles an hour with the girls, he asked if you were better and how was Papou and if the pilings seemed to be holding up and he said not to fly over the river and he's going to give me a new propeller blade."

"A propeller blade?"

"I swear! Put the plug back, please."

She puts the plug in the hole. Chanoine took off when the flood began. She comes closer to examine the fractured skull; I replace the washcloth over the submarine which has straightened up, with the periscope pointing to the surface. It seems as if Papou hasn't come down from the attic or anything. Mamie runs her hand through my hair to take an account of the damage. I warn her, "The skull's split in two."

"Tell me what happened."

The wounded pilot tells the whole story: the assault, the attempted getaway, the helicopter, the broken rotor, the Commodore.

Anyway, there's another love story between I and Mamie: we both love Thiers, the Commodore's son.

Thiers is a boat pilot. He pilots boats in the channel of the St. Lawrence from Quebec to Les Escoumins and back. He just pilots boats, to tell the truth. I mean, I'm a pilot myself: helicopters, boats and racing cars. But he sticks to boats. He's the best boat pilot you've ever met in your whole life. You'd think he'd surveyed the channel at the bottom of the river in a diving suit and lead-soled boots with a waterproof electric lamp and an underwater camera, from Quebec to Les Escoumins and back. He's an expert and he's the one who gives me advice about everything that has to do with piloting boats. But after Les Escoumins you have to manage on your own if you feel like heading for the Gulf.

Every summer they all come and move into the cottage next door: the Commodore, Trixie, Dixie and Flixie, Thiers and the long-distance swimmer and their six daughters— Patsy, Ingrid, Kathy, Mary, Lucy and Jenny. I named them in descending order. Mary's the same age as me but she's smaller. She doesn't know one goddamn word of French. Neither does Thiers's wife. He met her in South Africa back in the days when he was in the Merchant Marine, in some kind of cottage at the Cape of Good Hope where they could see the Atlantic Ocean and the Indian Ocean at the same time. You might think that Thiers is as good a liar as me, but he isn't. Mamie calls him Thierry because he makes her think of Thierry la Fronde on television.

What I like about Mamie, she isn't too zouave. Most zouaves make you wash your ears, but not Mamie. Yesterday, though, she cleaned out Chanoine's ears with some cotton batting on a toothpick and when Chanoine started getting impatient she looked him in the eyes and said, "I know it's no fun, but. You can't go around with one ear dirty and one ear clean!"

For once she was zouave.

Papou bought it at Latulippe Surplus de Guerre and I always sleep in it.

It's khaki for camouflage, and inside it's white with red and blue flowers all over it. You could turn it inside out and put the flowers on the outside, but. I mean, I've tried everything and here's what I think about the whole business: the best thing to do is pull the zipper all the way up and pull down your pillow so your head doesn't stick out and go to sleep naked in the flowers, lying curled up with your feet on Chanoine who's at the bottom, purring, his eyes shining from time to time, yellow or green.

Today's the day they're coming.

I remember a long time before the Hôtel-Dieu, Mamie took me in a corner and asked me three questions.

"What's your mother's name? What's your father's name? What's your name?"

If you answered the three questions correctly she'd let you go, convinced you could go on living. I mean, you really felt as if you were going to die all of a sudden if you missed one answer.

They're coming today, Thiers and the whole family.

I pull down the zipper. Chanoine gets out of the sleeping bag as he does every morning and stretches.

The fresh air envelops me; I turn over on my stomach and close my eyes for a second, but Chanoine comes and licks my cheeks and then, purring, he rubs his wet nose against my neck. Only one way to have any peace with Chanoine; you get up, give him his breakfast and open the cottage door for him.

I put on my jeans and my grey sweatshirt with the hood. I don't wear the hood very often, but. You like to know that the hood's there on your back. Sometimes I put Chanoine inside when I take him for a walk but he doesn't really like it, especially in the helicopter. I have to tie the cord around the hood otherwise he'll parachute down first chance he gets. He thinks he's a flying squirrel or something.

It's a problem, Chanoine's breakfast. You take one step, he brushes against your legs, you lift your feet really high so you won't step on his paws and you end up looking just like a ballet dancer; you look weird, to tell you the truth. He loves fish: his favourite breakfast is a dish of fish and a bowl of milk. I won't say anything about the milk but I've tasted his fish a few times: usually I go and spit it down the john at a hundred miles an hour. Mamie tasted it, I swear, and she spit it out too, in the same place. Good thing the john didn't decide to spit it out too.

The floor's cold. I almost forgot my moccasins. If you forget your moccasins in the morning you can hurt yourself on the bamboo points.

It's an old story. You've been shipwrecked, you grab hold of some flotsam and all the rest and you end up on a desert island in the Pacific. You don't know it's deserted yet, to tell the truth; you land there in the pitch dark with just enough moonlight so you can make out the jungle with the monkeys and the parrots and the vines and the bamboo. With your bone-handled hunting knife you cut one-foot-long bamboo stems with the ends pointed like an arrow and you stick them deep in the sand with the point on top, in circles that get broader and broader. You lie down in the middle under the stars, protected by your circles of pointed bamboo. You've hollowed out a little hole in the sand for your hips that they call the camper's hole and you fall asleep thinking it would have been a good idea to paint the bamboo points with curare. You're safe from wild animals though: even if a black panther was attracted by your smell during the night he'd hurt himself and stay there all night long, moaning. In the morning you could approach him slowly, give him something to drink, take the pointed stems out of his paws, look after his sores and feed him something; he'd get his strength back and he'd end up being your friend, as gentle and faithful as Chanoine.

It's an old story, the one about the chief scout whose totem is the Tiger; the tame panther saves his life when he's stealthily attacked by a real tiger in the jungle and he finally dies in a circus, fighting against an elephant that's furious because some zouave put a lighted cigarette up his trunk.

I put on my moccasins and give Chanoine his breakfast so I'll have some peace. I put the can of Puss 'n Boots on the kitchen floor and start to take off the top with the can-opener. We're both down on our hands and knees. The fish smell gets stronger. Chanoine rubs his chin against the edge of the can, then he licks my fingers, weaves between my legs, jumps up on my back and sticks his tail right in my face, purring like a helicopter that's about to take off. I fill his pink plastic dish with fish and his yellow bowl with milk. The milk's in a cardboard carton but I prefer glass bottles because of the sound they make when you knock them together like the milkmen do early in the morning when they put them down on your steps; they do it on purpose, the milkmen, to let you know the day's begun. It's a signal, like the beadle who rings the church bells.

Chanoine crouches down, eyes closed, to attack his fish, and you'd think he hadn't eaten for a week. I go out, propping the cottage door open with an empty pint cream bottle so Chanoine can go out too. When he's got his fish down he races out at a hundred miles an hour and nobody inside the cottage has any peace till he's outside.

The Commodore's walking along the beach by himself, with his hands behind and his pipe in front. He's wearing his Commodore's cap and he's put on his great white sweater with the kind of Indian totem on the back.

I yell at him:

"Ship ahoy!"

He isn't really in a ship, but. To tell you the truth I just wanted to see the Indian heads. He turns towards me.

"Ahoy young man!"

You can clearly see Hawk Eye and Sitting Bull on either side of the zipper, with their feathers and war paint and everything, exactly the way you wanted to see them.

"They coming today?"

"At noon," the Commodore replies. "How's the helicopter?"

"Catshit on the helicopter!"

"That bad?"

"Chanoine's coming. We sleep in the flowers. He ate his fish."

"I see."

"You should have a talk with the dogs."

Without taking out his pipe or anything the Commodore spits on a rock. I spit too, two rocks closer. He's luckier because he's bigger; if he got down on his knees we'd probably spit on the same rock. I ask him if he wants to try.

"Okay young mate."

He gets down in the sand on one knee and I come closer so I'm on exactly the same line as he is. I say "un deux trois go" and I spit first: my spit takes off and disappears in a hole between two rocks. Then he spits, in exactly the same hole, I swear. I wipe off my chin. Apparently if you've got a stitch in your side from running too much you just have to lift a stone, spit in the hole, put the stone back on top of it and your stitch is gone. The Commodore gets up, tries to light his pipe and says:

"Don't you like dogs?"

"Yes, but Chanoine doesn't. Do you like raccoons?"

"Of course."

"I don't like dogs when I'm flying in my helicopter."

"You can have the new propeller whenever you want."

He tries again to light his pipe; he puts his lighter flame in a little shelter made by curving his hands so they form a hut. If Papou smoked a pipe he'd shield his flame with a book. Papou doesn't smoke a pipe.

"You should ask if Mamie's better."

"Why?"

"Because."

"Is Mamie feeling better?"

"She's very well, thanks. She nearly drowned me."

"In the river?"

"In the bathtub. Do you have to be able to swim to be a good boat pilot?"

"Not necessary."

"You should ask about Papou."

"How is he?"

"Don't know, he spends all his time in the attic."

"Sick?"

"No, he's writing or something. You should ask if the pilings seem to be holding out."

"Why?"

"Because."

He takes off his Commodore's cap with one hand and with the other he scratches his ideas with the tips of his fingers. The two Indians turn towards me.

"They aren't holding out?"

"Don't know, they're rotten."

"Let's go have a look."

One thing I like about the Commodore is his great white sweater with the totem on the back and the two Indian heads on the chest, on either side of the zipper like on either side of a river, Hawk Eye and Sitting Bull. I mean, you get out of your sleeping bag with the little red and blue flowers, you put on your jeans and your grey sweatshirt with the hood, and your moccasins so you won't hurt yourself on the bamboo points, you give Chanoine his Puss 'n Boots to get some peace, you go outside and there's the Commodore with his sweater like I explained, and right away he's ready to come and see if the pilings seem to be holding out.

He walked around the twelve pilings, taking a long time to look at each one of them. He knocked his pipe against the last one to empty it. We sat down in the sand with our backs against a piling and I asked him, "Do you know the song?"

"The song?"

I start singing Mamie's song: "Mamma, I see boats sailing past in the water. Do they have legs or do they have wings?"

I take away a stone that was digging into my bum and I sing all the verses right to the end. The Commodore declares coldly, "I know all the sailor songs that are sung on every sea in every port in the world."

"You're talking through your hat!"

"'Valparaiso,' for instance."

"Sing it and see."

He unscrews his pipe and then, with his head cocked to one side, he blows hard into the stem. Good thing he turned his head: all the puke would have landed on his legs. Finally he answers, "You ask Thiers, he sings better than me."

"They get here at noon?"

"Yes. Didn't you already ask me?"

"Time?"

He looks at the sun above Saint-Nicholas.

"Nine o'clock."

"And the pilings?" I ask.

The Commodore doesn't answer. His eyebrows are grey and I swear they're an inch thick. He's got grey eyes, too, with wrinkles in the corners whenever he's thinking like an expert. Finally he asks, "You worried about them?"

I frown like him and I scrunch up my left eye by twisting my mouth on that side. I'm not an expert when it comes to pilings. I'm an expert in racing cars, boats and helicopters; I'm also an expert at making up stories and I'm the best liar in the whole city. But pilings, that's beyond me. The Commodore's the only expert in that area. At first you might not think there's any similarity between a pilot and a piling, but the Commodore used to be a pilot and he's an expert in pilings. He's the only expert on pilings but he doesn't say anything.

Jimmy Clark won the World Driving Championship in nineteen hundred and sixty-three and sixty-five in a Lotus and he missed the Championship by a hair in sixty-four because of the goddamn Grand Prix race in Mexico. I mean, CATSHIT, WHEN YOU KNOW SOMETHING YOU SAY IT! Jimmy won more Grand Prixs than Fangio, the best driver of all time. A zouave idea goes through your head: maybe it isn't just the pilings that are rotten. What comes out of the Commodore's pipe when he unscrews it and blows in the stem isn't very pretty. What I mean is, catshit— maybe the cottage is rotten too!

AND GODDAMNIT WHEN SOMETHING'S ROTTEN I GET FURIOUS!

I climb up the iron ladder at a hundred miles an hour. Jimmy leaps into his Lotus, makes the motor roar and the single-seater charges on to the first curve of the Monaco Grand Prix. When it comes out of the curve, the Lotus is leading and the driver steps on the accelerator, right down to the floor, and outstrips the compact class—the midnight blue Eagle, the green and orange BMW, the bright red Ferrari, the green Cooper-Maserati with white stripes, the green and bronze Brabham, the Japanese Honda and the rest of the Formula Ones that

are desperately trying to stick with their class. Jim
Clark's still in the lead after one lap and he's widening
the gap! The throbbing of the motors operating at top
capacity reverberates off the walls of the houses, the
gearboxes and brakes moan as they go into each turn,
the tires squeal and a revolting smell of burned oil
spreads through the air and gets in your throat in spite
of the handkerchief protecting your mouth and nose.
All along the streets, behind the barricades and at the
windows of the houses, the spectators' faces rush past at
a frantic rate. It's a hell of a course and when you drive it
you have to keep switching from the accelerator to the
brake and step on the clutch every three seconds. But
the other cars are coming closer, they gain a few seconds
at every lap and now Jimmy's starting to feel the red
Ferrari breathing hotly on his neck. Suddenly the
yellow-striped red flags snap out: oil on the track! The
driver lets up on the accelerator a little and starts to slow
down, one eye on the rear-view mirror to check whether
the other competitors are doing the same thing. They're
slowing down. Jimmy Clark looks over the track
carefully.

Standing on the gallery near the door that goes into
the cottage, strangely wrapped up in his long yellow
bathrobe with the letter C where his heart is, Papou is
standing, motionless. Mamie's beside him.

Jimmy applies the brakes, brings the good old Lotus
to a stop with its oval nose and its long yellow band,
breaks the contact.

The Commodore, leaning against the railing, takes
his old pipe and his tobacco pouch out of his pocket.
Mamie and Papou, frozen in the persistent smell of

burned oil, watch Jim Clark—nicknamed the Flying Scot—slowly extract himself from the cockpit and push his rubber goggles over the visor of his protective helmet.

Papou's wearing glasses on the end of his nose and carrying a book. He asks, "May I know what's going on here?"

The Flying Scot feels as though he's all wet. It's hard to explain; I mean, you get out of the cockpit where you were half lying between the gas tanks, an overheated gearbox and a boiling motor and it can be over a hundred inside your bloody fireproof coverall that you're wrapped in from heels to neck, but it isn't that. Jimmy feels soft and wet and a little bit sticky.

The Commodore pushes back his Commodore's cap with his pipe and explains, "We came to have a look at the pilings. How are you?"

Mamie smiles without saying a word. Her arms are folded. She's barefoot.

"Fine, thanks," says Papou. "How about you?"

"Not too bad."

"And the pilings?"

The Commodore shakes his head, sucks on his pipe and mutters, "Hard to say."

"We'll have to take a good look at them. You're an earlybird!"

The Commodore jerks his chin towards Jimmy.

"We ran into each other on the beach."

The burnt oil smell's been replaced by tobacco and the driver feels a little bit zouave; he isn't really in the mood for talking, to tell the truth. He's in another world, in his long white coverall with the red stripes that sticks to him from the ankles to the neck, with the various zippers encrusted in the fabric, the white silk handkerchief over his mouth and nose like the cowboys in the Far West and the black helmet with the white visor. Thoughts go whirling around under his helmet like the multicoloured single-seaters following each other at a wild speed down the streets of Monaco.

Mamie's happy just to walk around the Hôtel-Dieu. She's convalescing or something. It's a good day: we've just seen a little Lotus on rue des Remparts. She walks slowly, looking at everything. She says, "The Quartier Latin has a soul."

"Why?"

"Because it's old."

"So I don't have a soul then."

"Why?"

I'm talking to the deaf, obviously. Must speak to the Commodore about it. What's a soul anyway? I mean, I and the Commodore will have to take some time and sit on a rock; he'll be wearing his great sweater with the Indian heads and we'll have a serious talk about the whole business. I'll start with the pilings.

"They're rotten—yes or no?"

"Depends. What do you think?"

"They're rotten, it's obvious."

"Why?"

I won't answer his why. I'll start thinking about Mamie and Papou and then I'll ask, "Has the cottage got a soul?"

"Hard to say. Why do you ask?"

"It's got a soul—yes or no?"

"Depends."

"On Mamie and Papou?"

"And you."

"And Chanoine too?"

"Maybe, yes."

"I and Chanoine haven't got a soul."

"Why?"

Finally I'll spit as far as possible and just drop the whole business.

"The cottage has got the soul of a boat!"

The sky is reflected in one of the cottage windows and the sparrow crap on the glass seems to be floating in the clouds. Beneath the protective helmet of the Flying Scot, world champion in sixty-three and sixty-five, the single-seaters are jostling with ideas in a kind of Noah's Ark filled with people who don't have souls, like dogs, Chanoine, raccoons, black panthers, tigers and Puss in Boots.

Mamie, her arms still folded, makes up her mind and says, "Would you like some coffee?"

"We woke you up," the Commodore apologizes.

Smiling, she opens the door.

"Come in!"

"I'll let you twist my arm."

When the Commodore walks past Mamie he lifts his cap. One thing I like about the Commodore, he'll lift his cap but he never takes it off. The Flying Scot goes behind him and Papou, holding his book, comes in last.

"Have a seat," Mamie says.

She goes into the kitchen. Papou in his yellow bathrobe and the Commodore with his Indian heads sit at either end of the table.

"What are you reading?" the Commodore asks politely.

"*Across the River and Into the Trees.*"

Jimmy hangs around in the room for a while before taking off his driver's coverall, his silk handkerchief and his protective helmet with the goggles pushed up over the visor.

"Do you know Hemingway?" Papou asked.

"I know the face."

"Didn't you read *The Old Man and the Sea*?"

"I saw the movie."

"I'm writing a book about Hemingway," Papou explains.

The racing driver crawls under the table on his hands and knees and sits down in the middle; the red checked tablecloth falls on either side. Mamie comes in from the kitchen, puts some things on the table and goes back.

The Commodore crosses his legs. "You're writing a book?" he asks.

"A study."

Papou's legs are as hairy as Chanoine's. Mamie comes back once more and says, "It's instant, sorry."

You can hear the water pouring into the cups and the sounds of the spoons. Papou scratches his knee with a fingernail. "I suppose you liked old Santiago."

"It's one of the most beautiful cities in Chile, if you ask me, and the old palace at La Monedad is magnificent!"

"Of course. But what did you think of the old fisherman in *The Old Man and the Sea*?"

Mamie comes and sits between them, her legs folded under her chair. The Commodore takes his time, then replies: "Very good sailor and no complaints about the kind of fisherman he was either."

"Yes, but…."

"The old man knew where to find the fish, how to catch it, play it. Nobody could have done any better; sharks are terribly voracious."

I'm going to have to ask the Commodore to tell me everything from the start and how the story ended; we'll take the time to sit down and talk about the whole business. He knows a lot about the history of boats and sailors because he used to be a boat pilot himself.

"It's symbolic," Papou said, "don't you think?"

"Sorry?"

Jim Clark has been stealthily attacked from the rear; Far West bandits slammed him on the skull with the butt of a revolver, stuffed a handkerchief into his mouth, tied his wrists and ankles and threw him under the table. Jimmy was about to suffocate at any moment.

Papou scratches his other knee; his knees are like the knots on an old tree trunk.

"The story means that we spend our lives looking for happiness but if we find it we can't hold on to it. Do you know Hemingway?"

"No, but he must know his way around boats and fish."

"He liked hunting too, and swimming, boxing, baseball, horses, dogs …"

"… cats," Mamie adds.

"But the most important," Papou begins.

Jimmy Clark is about to have a fit.

"Did you know that for several days Hemingway was impotent?"

The racing driver suddenly has the feeling that the pilings aren't really sunk into the sand but that they're sunk into his stomach, as deep as Mamie's song in his memory.

Jimmy snaps the cords that bind his wrists and ankles and grabs a fold of the tablecloth. All the dishes come crashing to the floor. He runs to the door at full speed. The yellow flags with red stripes are down: there's no more oil on the track. The Flying Scot leaps into his Lotus, turns on the motor, and presses the accelerator to the floor, one eye on the tachometer and the other on the side of the track so he can steer out of the skids. The tachometer needle was in the red zone, the driver stepped on the clutch without lifting the accelerator one hair and dropped into second gear; the motor howled and the single-seater sprang ahead.

Jimmy turns his head and in a glance he takes in the red Ferrari, the green and bronze Brabham and the midnight blue Eagle, all breathing down his neck, noses to the ground like hunting dogs. He slips his glasses, which he'd forgotten on the visor of his helmet, back down over his eyes, abandons the accelerator, steps firmly on the brake and shifts back into first just as he enters a hairpin curve. As he comes out of the turn he opens the throttle out full, a little too abruptly; the Lotus skids; he straightens it out with one turn of the wheel, grazing the bales of hay lined up along the sidewalk, lets out the clutch and slams into second gear, but the goddamn Ferrari has gained during that wasted moment. Faster on the straight, the Ferrari clings to the rear of the Lotus, taking advantage of the suction like a goddamn leech, lets himself be carried along and waits for some awkwardness or sign of mechanical failure. Jimmy negotiates each turn at the outer limit of adherence and pushes the single-seater as far as he can on the straightaway.

The first cars from the back appear: the world champion starts weaving between the slow cars; slipping to left and right, passing even the dawdlers on the curves, he gradually makes gains on the Ferrari, which lacks flexibility. Jim Clark forces the speed, pushes the accelerator to the floor on the second last straightaway, then slams on the brake for a tenth of a second before placing the Lotus inside the last curve, shifts into second, accelerates as he goes into the turn, steadily increasing his speed; the Lotus skids but the tires grip well and the single-seater comes out of the curve at full speed, passes in third and crosses the finish line at the peak of its power. They wave the checkered flag; it's the first victory for the Flying Scot in the Grand Prix de Monaco! Jimmy comes back to the pit and makes the victor's circuit with the famous checkered flag, pulls the Lotus to the side of the track and turns off the engine.

The driver takes off his glasses and helmet, unties the white handkerchief protecting his mouth and nose. A blonde girl with very short hair drapes a wreath of flowers around his neck and kisses him on the cheeks. Dead tired but proud of his Lotus and himself, the driver thinks of a nice warm bath and tells himself that all the same, he and the Commodore should take the time to sit down on a rock and have a good talk about the Hemingway business and all that stuff about impotence.

KAPUSITCHKA

by A.M. Klein

A.M. Klein is one of Canada's great poets. He was born in the Ukraine in 1909. His family emigrated to Montreal shortly thereafter. He practised law from 1934 to 1956. He ran for Parliament as a CCF candidate in 1949. Klein's work is heavily influenced by his Jewish heritage. His only novel, The Secret Scroll *(1951), is regarded as a Canadian classic. A.M. Klein died in 1972.*

"KAPUSITCHKA" IS FROM *A.M. Klein: Short Stories*, published in 1983.

I don't want a cent. I don't want a nickel. I want my cat. In the yard he is lying with his front feet stretched forward, and his mouth wide open, and his lips pulled down below his teeth. Like that. Flies are buzzing around him.

I'll stop crying. If you make him alive again, I'll stop crying.

He was such a beautiful cat. All black. With green eyes. In the dark they shone like marbles, no, like allees. And he had so much fun in our house. In the summer, he would sleep on the window-sill in the sun, all curled up. When he woke up, he would stretch himself, and would seem so long, and he would yawn, and his nice red tongue would show. His teeth would stick out, too, but not like they do now. At me he always smiled.

We always played together. We were friends, me and Kapusitchka. I would make a piece of cord twirl like a snake on the floor, and he would try and catch it. He would try and hit it down with his paws. It's a lie when they say he scratched. He never did. His paws had no nails. Whenever I took his paw in my hand, it was soft, like the green, green grass that grows on stones. He was a good cat. He ate up all the rats, but he never ran after birds on the roof, like other cats do.

If he was so terrible, why was he such friends with Grandma? She doesn't like bad things. She is always praying; she goes to see holy men who come from Europe. She wears a perruque. Always, in winter, when Grandma sits near the stove and knits socks—in winter Grandma knits socks—Kapusitchka would lie at her feet. He would sleep, with one eye open. Just a little bit open, like looking through a keyhole. Sometimes he would play with the ball of wool, but when Grandma said, Kapusitchka! like that, he would always go to sleep again.

She used to bring him his milk in a special plate, and he would lap it up with his tongue, his tongue making a nice, licking noise, and the plate would be all clean. He never spilled the milk, like I did once.

He and Grandma were friends, also. Whenever he would be left outside, and be jumping at the door-knob to be let in, Grandma, even though she is a little deaf, would hear him, or she would see the door shaking, and let him in. At night, she would kitzu-kitzu him into the shed, and spread out empty coal-sacks for him to lie on, and close the door. She said it was never dark for a cat. In the morning, when Grandma would get up the first, Kapusitchka would hear her, and begin to meow.

Always when I went to the table, Grandma would say that you have to feed the cat first, because there is nobody to look after cats, they have no father and no mother.

Grandma liked the cat, because he always gave her news about guests coming to the house. Whenever Kapusitchka would lie in a corner, and begin to lick himself, wetting his paw, and with his paw wiping his sides, his head, and his ears, Grandma would say: The cat is washing himself; we are going to have guests.

Kapusitchka had whiskers like the French doctor on the square. When he began to stroke these with his paw, licking his tongue this way and that, we knew for sure that we were going to have guests.

How he knew, nobody told me, even though I asked. But it always came true. Before our cousin came from Russia, the one who brought pollyseeds for all the children, and wore her hair, that was golden, shooting in and out in braids on her head, like a Sabbath bread, Kapusitchka washed himself. Before the old rabbi, who stayed at our house for a long time, and used to ask me all kinds of questions from the Bible, came from Palestine, the cat washed himself. Before my uncle, the one my father called a good-for-nothing when he went away, came from New York with his violin, the cat washed himself.

Sometimes the cat washed himself, and we waited and waited, and looked at the door for somebody to come with baggage, and nobody came. But always when somebody came, the cat washed himself before.

At the beginning of summer, when the baseball games begin on the field, Kapusitchka washed himself, and after that, a guest came. A baby: I don't know where it came from. Everybody tells me lies. Father says a bird dropped it down the chimney, mother says she bought it in the fifteen cent store. Grandma says God gave it to us. Becky—my sister—says she heard them talking—it came from the belly.

Anyway, everybody was having a lot of fun, laughing and everything, making a fuss about him. What a nice baby, they said. And a boy, too, they said. Such big blue eyes, they said.

And all the time the baby bawled, and made a lot of noise, and everybody fussed about it, and rocked it, and called it baby names. They even made a big party for it, when a lot of men with beards came, and they sang, and drank ginger ale and beer, and ate peanuts. Everybody forgot about me, and I played with Kapusitchka, and both of us watched and nobody said anything to me, except one man who said: Such a big boy to play with a cat. Shame. You'll forget everything that you learn if you play with cats. Then that man gave me some peanuts, and a glass of beer, and said, Drink, drink. It was bitter, and I went away from the party to the yard, and Kapusitchka followed me, and rubbed himself against my stockings.

After that, uncles and aunties, and cousins and friends were bringing presents for the baby, blue sweaters, and blue covers for the carriage, and little shirts, and tiny shoes, and a lot of things like that. And everybody hugged the baby, carefully, and then asked me how I liked my new little brother. I didn't answer, because I didn't know what to say, and then everybody laughed, and said I was jealous. I am not jealous. I hate him.

All the time Kapusitchka watched them hugging the baby, and didn't know who it was.

Then one day my mother went away to the market to buy a chicken for Saturday. The baby was alone with Becky, and then Becky went out on the gallery because a friend was calling to her to show off how clean she looked in her Saturday dress after a bath.

Then Kapusitchka jumped up on the bed, and began hugging the baby, and playing with it, like all the other people.

When my mother came back, the baby was bawling its head off, and there was blood on his face and neck. My mother made a whole fuss, and began to scream on everybody, but especially on Becky.

Kapusitchka ran away in a corner, and was sleeping with one eye open.

Then when my father came from work, my mother told him all about it, how Becky was minding the baby, and she went away, and how when my mother came back, the baby was crying, and there was blood on him, and she said, Me for his little head. She blamed it all on the cat, because he was playing with the baby. Then my father got good and sore, and began to shout, Where is that cat? And when he found Kapusitchka he took it into the yard, and with a piece of wood he hit him, and now Kapusitchka is lying there with his mouth wide open.

Grandma was not around, because she went out to talk to another Grandma up the street, and I was crying, but my father said for me to shut up. Then he went and killed Kapusitchka.

Now he is lying there in the sun, with his teeth showing, and flies buzzing all around him.

I hate my brother. I hate my father. I only want my Kapusitchka.

Make him alive again, and I'll stop crying. Only make him alive again.

THE SMELL OF SULPHUR

by Marian Engel

*Marian Engel was born in 1933 in Toronto.
She was the author of journalism, children's books,
two collections of short stories and many novels, the most
famous of which is* BEAR, *winner of the Governor General's
Award in 1976. Marian Engel died in 1985.*

"THE SMELL OF SULPHUR" is from the story collection entitled *The Tattooed Woman*, published posthumously in 1985.

There were two girls in that family, Tess and Janie, six years apart. Tess was the little one, named after her mother's cousin Maria Theresa Brown, who worked at *The Toronto Star* and gave her namesake a silver locket. Only Theresa was a Catholic name and wouldn't do, so she was called Tessa Marie. She was six that summer and Janie was twelve. Janie called her Tillie the Toilet, after the comic character and her own feelings.

What happened was that when their father went to his ulcer doctor in Brantford in March, the doctor said, "Frank, you've still got that house-on-wheels thing of yours, and when school lets out in June, I tell you what you're going to do and it isn't a suggestion, it's an order. There's a place called Star Bay about five miles from my cottage up the Bruce. All the land there is owned by a family named Ellis and I know them well. Nobody much is going up there now because of gas rationing, and what you're going to do is save up your gas ration, drive up there and park your trailer where the hotel used to be and spend two months fishing."

Frank went back later and was told that a man who taught boys to fix cars wouldn't have a hard time laying hands on a boat: they'd needed a mechanic up there the last ten years. The two men talked bass and pickerel and glowed.

Maudie got out the sewing machine and started running up seersucker outfits for Tessa. Janie ordered hers from Eaton's catalogue, she was that age.

Tessa had few talents, and her greatest one was being sick in the car. Once it was over with, Janie was the one who suffered. Tessa sat high in the back seat of the Studebaker Commander, Queen of the World as the landscape rushed by her, changing at her command. The trailer had, her father said, the best hitch in Christendom, and, her mother said, this made them snails with their house on their back. Tessa looked and smiled and babbled and nobody listened. Janie practised her Deanna Durbin imitations.

It took a long time to get there, and where was that? First the road was all farms, then it was cottages with bits of lake glistening between them, but that wasn't where they were going. They entered a flat, desolate landscape, where there were grey stones and sheep and scrubby bushes. The road was very straight. There wasn't any traffic: they were the only ones who had been provident enough to save their whole gas ration. You had to hand over a coupon the way you had to for butter, but they were a different colour and shape. It was about the war, but Tessa didn't care: the day the King came on everyone had looked serious and told her not to talk in competition with the radio.

"Now girls, look out," their mother, Maudie, said from the front seat. She had black hair and she looked happy with a kerchief around her neck. "We're turning at a place called Mar, and the first one to see the sign gets a nickel."

"I do," Tessa shouted, "right up there."

"Moth—er!" Janie groaned. "You're going to have to turn this kid in to the cops."

"No, Jane, she's right, there it is," said Frank. "We turn left and in about two miles we drive over a causeway over Sky Lake."

"It's a hot day," said Maudie, "and a long drive for you, Frank."

Mar, Mar, Mars, thought Tessa. Mars and Sky take us to Star Bay.

"I see Sky Lake!" Jane shouted, straining through her spectacles. And she did. And it was full of lily pads. And the causeway rumbled as they drove over it.

They had hung over Dr. Arnold's map night after night at home, and Tessa, who was put to bed long before Janie, lay sleepless, dreaming of it: up the Peninsula to Mar, to Sky Lake, down a road through the bush to Star Bay. And Dr. Arnold had promised them the perfect place, and he would know, because he was special: he was curing her father. He'd even made him stop smoking, and that other time they went away he sent huge bottles of thick pink medicine in wooden boxes with dovetailed ends, lined like chocolate boxes with padding, that would have made good doll beds, only they had to send them back. That was when she was four, and they sat watching the men carve the Presidents on Mount Rushmore, looking like ants on irritated faces (she kept waiting for the noses to twitch).

The Snail Family at Large, she thought. She was already a reader.

After the boggy lake, the road turned south. It was narrow and twisting, and the woods shouldered in at them on either side. Father blew the horn before every little rise and turning: they had a big car and a big trailer, and everyone needed to be warned.

"It looks like nothing," the doctor had warned. "It takes a while to find out it's heaven."

It was the last day of June, and hot, though somewhat cooler as they proceeded through the woods. The road turned from gravel to sand and they had to turn right—"towards the lake," Frank said to Maudie, who never knew where she was. They went through scrubby cedar bush hedged by snake fences, past a tumbledown farm. "That'll be Ellis's, we'd better stop."

"No!" cried Tessa. "I want to get there."

"Shuddup, kid," said Janie, because her parents were already out of the car. She got out too, and Tessa was going to, but when she went to open her door, there was a big sort of duck there staring at her and hissing. The sound was dreadful, dry and angry. The creature had a thick yellow tongue but it didn't stick out, it curved meanly up. It took Tessa a long time to learn to hiss like that.

They found her cowering. "Oh, I know what you mean, Tess," said Maudie. "I always hated geese. And did I tell you about the time my brother Will found me down in the barnyard and the turkey cock was pecking at me?"

"Not exactly friendly," the father said.

"No, but she likes to rule her own roost."

"I thought she was very interesting," said Janie.

"She has a boy about your age," Maudie said.

Janie huffed and puffed.

It was only a little way now: the lake was already there, looking grey because the sun was so bright. There wasn't a road along the beach, they just turned and humped along a track, past two cottages, big ones, and then two little ones, and over a log bridge. "There it'll be," Frank said.

"Oh," said Maudie, because she was looking at nothing. A dump of old cans, a half-fallen chimney. "You can get out, girls," she said.

Janie got out her side, and went into conference at once with the adults. Tessa finally wrangled her door open, found no goose-guardian, and stepped into her world. A stony beach, thin, shallow water with well-spaced grasses growing in it and look—but nobody was there to look, they were parking and levelling and doing whatever they did with the trailer so they could open the door without having it slam right into their faces—look, there are tiny little fish, there. And then there was a big island, and further out, a paradise of little islands. Tessa took off her shoes, and then her socks. She put them neatly down on a rock, tucked her new seersucker shirt into her new seersucker shorts, and set off to find her world.

She didn't have to go far. She just lay down on the sand and began to stare into the water. Very small fish nipped from reed to reed: it was enough.

"Tessa … Tess—a."

They had done their things now, even had the two folding chairs and two folding stools in a row facing the beach and parallel to it. "It's your job to get the flowers," her mother said, "and, oh, put on your shoes."

New Sisman Scampers.

What could the flowers have been that June? Because later she remembers cinquefoil and pearly, everlasting fireweed. But they are August flowers. And when do the harebells, leafless and blue, come out?

The trailer door faces inland, and when Tessa returns with much-praised flowers the table is already set, Janie has been sent somewhere to get a pail of water, and the naphtha gas stove is lit and Maudie is scrambling eggs. Soon enough, they seal the place up against mosquitoes and they're lying in their bunks in the last glow of the Coleman lantern. If Tessa remembers that it was because she couldn't keep her fingers off the rainy tentsides that they got the trailer, she doesn't remind herself. She dreams of touching the glowing, forbidden mantle of the lamp.

Does she hear her mother whisper to her father, "But there's nothing here, Frank, nothing"? If she does, she doesn't care. Janie, who is elderly and responsible, turns heavily in her sleep.

All the years of summer in heaven run together and who can tell how many there were? Two? Three? Five? Janie got big in the summers there, and pretty enough to get the better of her glasses, and modest enough to hide with a flurry that knocked the upper bunk down on Tessa's head the night Joey Ellis came late with the ice. Tessa was never big there, never awkward (though old Mrs. Ellis kept saying, "don't send that Tessa for the milk, she's that clumsy she'll fall into the spring"), never fell out of heaven.

Because even her talent for vomiting became an asset; even the war became her ally: once they got the use of a boat, or whichever boat her father was fixing up for whichever cottage, Tessa was firmly left on shore and for what seemed a wonderful eternity she was in possession of paradise.

They got up early, slipped into their bathing suits, or their seersucker costumes. Mother went out and got their washcloths off the line and they went down to the water to wash their faces. There was drama if the Pike boys from Detroit, whose mother was supposed to be a German spy, had been along first and tied garter snakes to the clothes-line, which was a tow rope. Then Maudie had to decide whether to be merciful and untie the snakes, be sluttish and let the girls go dirty, or go in and fry the eggs. Frank was already off tinkering with something somewhere: how he spent his life.

Then suddenly everyone was gone, there was no one to call her Tillie the Toilet, there was nothing to do and everything to do. No other kids—the Pike boys weren't kids, and they only wanted to get a look at Janie and hand out snakes—no one her age: only Tess and the beach.

She ran and ran and ran. She outran sandpipers and caught their babies, holding the fuzzy balls in her hands before she let them go again, being careful not to hold too tight, because last spring on Uncle Will's farm ... She outran Popeye, Joey Ellis's black and white dog, and nobody believed her but when she threw a stick in the water for him down further by the big dock where the fishermen's boats were, threw it good and far out into the water, the dog swam after it and his green coating of fleas rose from the water and hovered over him, hopping through the air. Nobody believed her, but it happened.

There was a fair number of cottages, most empty. The two next to them belonged to the Pennypackers from Buffalo. Then there was the Crow's Nest, owned by a man named Crow who never spoke. Past the creek where the live box was, there was Sovereigns' place: they had a niece called Dorothy Crown. Over the road from there was a man called Grimes and even though his cottage was empty Janie and Tessa went mad with embarrassment when their mother sang, in her church contralto, "Old Grimes is dead, that dear old man" as they passed it when they took a stroll in the evening.

But the evenings weren't the best time: the lone mornings were: running alone on the beach, king of the castle on every rock and *no one to see!* No one to say, don't, Tessa.

There was only one rule. It all ends if you swim alone. It was like Uncle Will's farm: it all ends if you try to get on a horse. You can be, but you can't do. A bad rule for later life, it turned out, but she couldn't have known that.

Probably, they could always see her from where they fished. But she did not feel watched.

There was lunch when they got back; then a nap; then swimming. She learned to swim, but so did her mother, the very same day, and scooped her. They all except Janie, who got something prettier from the catalogue, had woollen bathing suits. Her father's had big holes in the sides. Hers took the skin off her thighs: it was pink.

If she stayed too long in the sun she got sick, disgusting them all with her vomiting. Mostly she remembered to keep on her hat.

There was much to see, and when they were swimming she lay in the shallows and felt the minnows nibbling at her with their soft puckering little mouths. One year when the water was low she and Jane swam out to the island, but she got scared when she got turned out to face the open lake and had to be rescued.

The islands out there were called the Fishing Islands and there were certainly a lot of fish. Every night they had bass for supper. Tessa went to the live box with her father and helped to pick them out, big sturdy fellows, all over eight inches because that was the rule. Among them sometimes there were beautiful little baby fish that had hatched in the creek, but it was against the law to take them home and put them in a jar, Frank said.

Then he sat in the grove of cedars by the trailer and filleted the fish with a special knife he had bought in South Dakota for trout. The nasty part came when it was Tessa's job to take the cleanings out on an aluminum plate to the seagulls. She hated it, it was a rock she played King of the Castle on she had to set the plate on, and the gulls were always expecting her and swooped down greedily. Their wings were beautiful and they looked as if they could knock your head off: they were sharp and clean as a shining knife. She never got out of the job. Or failed, later, to eat as many delicious slivers of bass as she could obtain.

She must have grown up: one summer two English children came, and she hated them, and they hated her, and that was that. She collected a whole Campbell's soup can of baby toads and fixed them in the crotch of a cedar tree, to have someone to talk to, but the wind blew it over. Her mother said. Once a week she was allowed to overturn a certain board in the clearing and watch the ants carry their Rice Krispies away. In the evenings they sat in a row outside, listening to the night-hawks boom and cry. They mewed like cats sometimes. A bat took up residence inside the window by Janie's bunk, and they didn't dare open it all summer: they lay and watched him hanging upside down. He had an evil-looking nose, but he was very shy.

When the mosquitoes got bad they went indoors and went through the ritual of watching Father light the Coleman lantern. (Father was the most important person in the world: nobody else could control naphtha gas.) Then they played rummy, trying to beat him, but he could remember the cards. Then they went to bed and lay in their beds singing "Red-wing" and "When It's Springtime in the Rockies," and (Tessa was patriotic and the war was still on, always on) "There'll Always Be an England." "The White Cliffs of Dover" was too high for Mother.

Tessa got old enough to go up to the spring house for milk, through the woods instead of up the road, because she hated, vividly and personally, the geese, who hated her, surrounded her when she tried to take a step. Once, dreaming, swinging the tin billycan, she walked straight into a cow and ran home so fast that she spilled not a drop, and it took her mother an hour to get a descrip-tion of the monster.

Janie must have had another life, but sometimes they went somewhere together. Once up to the Big Sand Pile, a strip of dunes inland towards the forest road. There were other children with them, and they threw themselves down the hillocks of fine white sand screaming and crying and rolling as if it were snow: then a rattlesnake slithered across the bottom of a dune, its tail sizzling like dried peas in a gourd and they fell silent and after it went home, they went home.

Other things happened: she took up catching baby leopard frogs for fishermen. One of them paid her in stale humbugs instead of money and her mother taught her about business. Her father made friends with a fat man from Buffalo, a cooper, who admired a mechanical man and invited them to come to his cottage for steak and ice cream from Mrs. Ellis's cows, churned in a big vessel with a crank. One of Jane's friends rubbed poison ivy on her face to see what would happen. Tessa made a friend, and then she went away.

How many summers? Who can tell? Tess has tried to ask Jane, Jane has tried to remember: neither of them knows. They lead different lives, and Star Bay wasn't important to Jane: she had no leopard frog business, she had other things on her mind, the time just went.

Once they went into the woods together, the forbidden woods, and Jane was the leader, and Jane, with her mother's gifts, got lost. "We must sit and wait, Tess, until they come and find us," she said piously. "That's what Daddy said."

Tess sat on a log as long as she could, a whole minute. "Look, Jane, the sun sets over the lake and it's afternoon and there's the sun so if we walked we get to the beach, see?"

"Tess, we are to sit and wait until we are rescued. Otherwise we will walk in circles. People die that way."

Tess, conscious as Jane that she was the great-grandchild of pioneers, extended her arm. "Look, Janie, you stick out your arm and at the end of it are your fingers, and you put them between the sun and the horizon: each one is fifteen minutes. It's only about three o'clock."

"Tess, stay there."

"Well, you can stay there. I'm going to the beach, and when I get there I'm turning left." She skittered off, leaving Janie, scared, in a mossy cathedral of a clearing, trying to decide how best to be elderly and responsible. Reluctantly, she followed Tess.

They came out somewhere they'd never been before and even Tess was scared for a minute, but she knew home was left. She danced ahead and Jane followed sulkily. "Look," she cried finally, "we're on the other side of the clearing, look!" Janie, stubborn and humiliated, looked down instead of ahead and saw that the rarest of treasures, a leaf-coloured whippoorwill on her nest. They sat down and worshipped, not daring to breathe. The bird's whiskers twitched, her eyes rolled with fear, she was as quiet as they were. When they got up and tiptoed home she flopped off, but only a little way, for a little while. When they looked back she was back with her eggs. They went home hand in hand and told their adventure.

Then something happened: their father was given a job teaching on an army base. He wouldn't turn it down: his First War service record put him in an excellent category (though he wouldn't join up and be a Captain, once was enough, he said, and civilian staff got better pay); everything about the job was advantageous, especially having a sergeant to handle the discipline. They moved. Janie set out to conquer her eleventh school. Tess was no longer thin and faster than a sandpiper. There were only two weeks' holidays, and Father's ulcers were cured.

They never went back. Frank and Maudie didn't believe in going back anywhere. And anyway, wouldn't Tess like to go to summer camp with the girl next door? They could afford it now. So Tess went to camp and her parents took the green trailer somewhere by themselves. Janie was fruit-picking.

It might even have been thirty years later that Tess and her husband were driving down the Bruce from Tobermory, arguing who had overspent on the holiday. There was a big green sign, "Mar," on the highway, and Tess, who never learned to drive said, "Oh, please." He gave her his Kismet look and sighed. "We can have lunch there." The children were asleep in the back of the car.

She began to bounce. "Sky Lake," she said. The way he looked at it, she knew it was a plain patch of swamp. The road through the bush had been widened, but he honked for her pleasure. The children didn't wake.

At Ellis's, she said, "I'll just get out and get a quart of milk."

He said he'd stay with the kids, but got out of the car and stood against the fender, not unpleased to find himself beside a tumbledown farm in a sandy wilderness.

She asked for a quart of milk in the store, which was a farm kitchen, then confessed, "We used to come in the summer. We had a trailer."

"Oh, you're the Chalmers girl, you write for the papers and you married a Jew. I heard about you. Well, it's not the same place, we sold off a lot of cottage lots. And don't you try to put up your tent or your trailer: we don't allow that now. People aren't what they used to be." She went on for a bit about how they didn't eat what was put before them, either, and how she'd married Joey's brother and taken over the store from the old lady, who died a couple of years ago, she was a hundred.

Tess, conscious of Sam out there waiting, said well, it was nice to see her, and where was the milk?

"Don't you remember? Why, it's out where it's always been, in the spring house, by the road. And don't fall in." Then she told her how her husband had had a foot cut off because of the diabetes and the other one would soon have to go, which was pity because for a while he was Township Reeve.

Tess felt guilty going down the path, as if, like Elmer Ellis, she'd eaten too many chocolate bars. Sam was still by the car, but she couldn't quite remember where the spring house was, and she was tense: then she thought, it's the geese and the old woman, I was scared of the geese and the old woman.

Right at the bottom of the path, where the wire fence with pressed iron maple leaves between its scallops left off, there was a wooden shed. It was open to the road, so she had only one gate to go through. She walked in: it was new inside, all concrete, but there was a funny smell. There was a concrete floor, and it had certainly been earth before, and there were wire baskets containing waxed-paper cartons of milk, not billycans or bottles or whatever there were before, and she half closed her eyes and reached forward.

Then she remembered: because around each carton there was a garter snake coiled. And the smell was sulphur because it was a sulphur spring. She took her milk and half ran to the car.

"Home?" Sam laughed.

"Sort of. Oh, look, two rows of cottages, like a subdivision. That was the Little Sand Pile. It was always full of cow pies."

"Glamorous." He wasn't particularly urban, but he had gone to more expensive camps: he expected his wilderness to be up to a certain standard.

They got down to the lake. There was a new dock, but not a very good one. The ice house had collapsed. Sovereigns' and Grimes' and Crows' cottages were exactly as they had been before. "That's Sunset Island," she said, pointing at it. It looked terrible: a mud blob in a mercury pool. The day was so hot everything had flattened out.

She got out the food box and set about making some sandwiches. The children woke up and were so overheated she set them down in their shorts in the shallow water. Nobody wanted any milk. The children paddled in the water and pronounced it yucky. Sam told her to go for a walk: he would baby-sit.

She set out. Mrs. Ellis had told her the Blue Cottage was for sale. She went past it and Pennypackers' and came to their own clearing: it was exactly the same. The cedar grove was still the shape of a woodshed or a living-room. She might find the aluminum plate for the fish cleanings if her parents had been the sort of people who ever left an object behind. But they had littered with memories, and she had become the sort of person who picked them up after them. And if she went looking for a board with the ants under it, or the can of toads, or the scars of the tow-rope against the tree, or the whippoorwill's nest, what wouldn't happen. Anyway, she was too big to be king of the castle any more. She heard her mother's voice, "You won't remember, but that first day up there, I thought, what's happening to us now, what is this place, how can we bear it?"

She turned back towards Sam and the children and saw in the distance because she was still long-sighted a tall athletic woman walking, and remembered a certain woman, another non-Canadian, a minister's daughter from California who used to organize games on the beach. She pelted back to Sam. "Let's pack up. There's someone coming."

Ten years after that, she thought, would it have helped if I had said something artistic like "Od und leer das Meer"? And laughed, and plunged her hand in again among the cold bottles and the cold snakes and smelled sulphur.

WAR

by Timothy Findley

Timothy Findley was born in Toronto in 1930. He was an actor before turning to writing full-time. The Wars, which won the Governor General's Award, established him as one of Canada's most celebrated writers at home and abroad. His many books and plays have won numerous awards. He has also been named to the Order of Canada and the Order of Ontario, and in France he was made a Chevalier de l'Ordre des Arts et des Lettres. Timothy Findley died in 2002.

"WAR" IS FROM the short-story collection *Dinner Along the Amazon*, published in 1984.

That's my dad in the middle. We were just kids
then, Bud on the right and me on the left. That
was taken just before my dad went into the army.
Some day that was.

It was a Saturday, two years ago. August, 1940. I can
remember I had to blow my nose just before that and I
had to use my dad's hankie because mine had a worm in
it that I was saving. I can't remember why; I mean, why
I was saving that worm, but I can remember why I had
to blow my nose, all right. That was because I'd had a
long time crying. Not exactly because my dad was going
away or anything—it was mostly because I'd done
something.

I'll tell you what in a minute, but I just want to say
this first. I was ten years old then and it was sort of the
end of summer. When we went back to school I was
going into the fifth grade and that was pretty important,
especially for me because I'd skipped grade four. Right

now I can't even remember grade five except that I didn't like it. I should have gone to grade four. In grade five everyone was a genius and there was a boy called Allan McKenzie.

Anyway, now that you know how old I was and what grade I was into, I can tell you the rest.

It was the summer the war broke out and I went to stay with my friend, Arthur Robertson. Looking back on it, Arthur seems a pretty silly name for Arthur Robertson because he was so small. But he was a nice kid and his dad had the most enormous summer cottage you've ever seen. In Muskoka, too.

It was like those houses they have in the movies in Beverly Hills. Windows a mile long—pine trees outside and then a lake and then a red canoe tied up with a yellow rope. There was an Indian, too, who sold little boxes made of birch-bark and porcupine quills. Arthur Robertson and I used to sit in the red canoe and this Indian would take us for a ride out to the raft and back. Then we'd go and tell Mrs. Robertson or the cook or someone how nice he was and he'd stand behind us and smile as though he didn't understand English and then they'd have to buy a box from him. He certainly was smart, that Indian, because it worked about four times. Then one day they caught on and hid the canoe.

Anyway, that's the sort of thing we did. And we swam too, and I remember a book that Arthur Robertson's nurse read to us. It was about dogs.

Then I had to go away because I'd only been invited for two weeks. I went on to this farm where the family took us every summer when we were children. Bud was already there, and his friend, Teddy Hartley.

I didn't like Teddy Hartley. It was because he had a space between his teeth and he used to spit through it. Once I saw him spit two-and-a-half yards. Bud paced it out. And then he used to whistle through it, too, that space, and it was the kind of whistling that nearly made your ears bleed. That was what I didn't like. But it didn't really matter, because he was Bud's friend, not mine.

So I went by train and Mr. and Mrs. Currie met me in their truck. It was their farm.

Mrs. Currie got me into the front with her while Mr. Currie put my stuff in the back.

"Your mum and dad aren't here, dear, but they'll be up tomorrow. Buddy is here—and his friend."

Grownups were always calling Bud "Buddy." It was all wrong.

I didn't care too much about my parents not being there, except that I'd brought them each one of those birch-bark boxes. Inside my mother's there was a set of red stones I'd picked out from where we swam. I thought maybe she'd make a necklace out of them. In my dad's there was an old golf ball, because he played golf. I guess you'd have to say I stole it, because I didn't tell anyone I had it—but it was just lying there on a shelf in Mr. Robertson's boathouse, and he never played golf. At least I never saw him.

I had these boxes on my lap because I'd thought my mum and dad would be there to meet me, but now that they weren't I put them into the glove compartment of the truck.

We drove to the farm.

Bud and Teddy were riding on the gate, and they waved when we drove past. I couldn't see too well because of the dust but I could hear them shouting. It was something about my dad. I didn't really hear exactly what it was they said, but Mrs. Currie went white as a sheet and said: "Be quiet," to Bud.

Then we were there and the truck stopped. We went inside.

And now—this is where it begins.

After supper, the evening I arrived at the Curries' farm, my brother Bud and his friend Teddy Hartley and I all sat on the front porch. In a hammock.

This is the conversation we had.

BUD: (to me) Are you all right? Did you have a good time at Arthur Robertson's place? Did you swim?

ME: (to Bud) Yes.

TEDDY HARTLEY: I've got a feeling I don't like Arthur Robertson. Do I know him?

BUD: Kid at school. Neil's age. (He said that as if it were dirty to be my age.)

TEDDY HARTLEY: Thin kid? Very small?

BUD: Thin and small—brainy type. Hey, Neil, have you seen Ted spit?

ME: Yes—I have.

TEDDY HARTLEY: When did you see me spit? (Indignant as hell) I never spat for you.

ME: Yes, you did. About three months ago. We were still in school. Bud—he did too, and you walked it out, too, didn't you?

BUD: I don't know.

TEDDY HARTLEY: I never spat for you yet! Never!

ME: Two yards and a half.

TEDDY HARTLEY: Can't have been me. I spit four.

ME: Four YARDS!!

TEDDY HARTLEY: Certainly.

BUD: Go ahead and show him. Over the rail.

TEDDY HARTLEY: (Standing up) Okay. Look, Neil ... Now watch ... Come on, WATCH!!

ME: All right—I'm watching. (Teddy Hartley spat. It was three yards-and-a-half by Bud's feet. I saw Bud mark it myself.)

BUD: Three yards and a half a foot.

TEDDY HARTLEY: Four yards. (Maybe his feet were smaller or something.)

BUD: Three-and-foot. Three and one foot. No, no. A *half*-a-one. Of a foot.

TEDDY HARTLEY: Four.

BUD: Three!

TEDDY HARTLEY: Four! Four! Four!

BUD: Three! One-two-three-and-a-half-a-foot!!

TEDDY HARTLEY: My dad showed me. It's four! He showed me, and he knows. My dad knows. He's a mathematical teacher—yes, yes, yes, he showed me how to count a yard. I saw him do it. And he knows, my dad!!

BUD: You dad's a crazy man. It's three yards and a half a foot.

TEDDY HARTLEY: (All red in the face and screaming) You called my dad a nut! You called my dad a crazy-man-nut-meg! Take it back, you. Bud Cable, you take that back.

BUD: You dad is a matha-nut-ical nutmeg tree.

TEDDY HARTLEY: Then your dad's a ... your dad's a ... your dad's an Insane!

BUD: Our dad's joined the army.

That was how I found out.

They went on talking like that for a long time. I got up and left. I started talking to myself, which is a habit I have.

"Joined the army? Joined the army? Joined the ARMY! Our dad?"

Our dad was a salesman. I used to go to his office and watch him selling things over the phone sometimes. I always used to look for what it was, but I guess they didn't keep it around the office. Maybe they hid it somewhere. Maybe it was too expensive to just leave lying around. But whatever it was, I knew it was important, and so that was one thing that bothered me when Bud said about the army—because I knew that in the army they wouldn't let my dad sit and sell things over any old phone—because in the army you always went in a trench and got hurt or killed. I knew that because my dad had told me himself when my uncle died. My uncle was his brother in the first war, who got hit in his stomach and he died from it a long time afterwards. Long enough, anyway, for me to have known him. He was always in a big white bed, and he gave us candies from a glass jar. That was all I knew— except that it was because of being in the army that he died. His name was Uncle Frank.

So those were the first two things I thought of: my dad not being able to sell anything any more—and then Uncle Frank.

But then it really got bad, because I suddenly remembered that my dad had promised to teach me how to skate that year. He was going to make a rink too, in the back yard. But if he had to go off to some old trench in France, then he'd be too far away. Soldiers always went in trenches—and trenches were always in France. I remember that.

Well, I don't know. Maybe I just couldn't forgive him. He hadn't even told me. He didn't even write it in his letter that he'd sent me at Arthur Robertson's. But he'd told Bud—he'd told Bud, but I was the one he'd promised to show how to skate. And I'd had it all planned how I'd really surprise my dad and turn out to be a skating champion and everything, and now he wouldn't even be there to see.

All because he had to go and sit in some trench.

I don't know how I got there, but I ended up in the barn. I was in the hayloft and I didn't even hear them, I guess. They were looking all over the place for me, because it started to get dark.

I don't know whether you're afraid of the dark, but I'll tell you right now, I am. At least, I am if I have to move around in it. If I can just sit still, then I'm all right. At least, if you sit still you know where you are—but if you move around, then you don't know where you are. And that's awful. You never know what you're going to step on next and I always thought it would be a duck. I don't like ducks—especially in the dark or if you stepped on them.

Anyway, I was in that hayloft in the barn and I heard them calling out—"Neil, Neil"—and "Where are you?" But I made up my mind right then I wasn't going to answer. For one thing, if I did, then I'd have to go down to them in the dark—and maybe I'd step on something. And for another, I didn't really want to see anyone anyway.

It was then that I got this idea about my father. I thought that maybe if I stayed hidden for long enough, then he wouldn't join the army. Don't ask me why— right now I couldn't tell you that—but in those days it made sense. If I hid then he wouldn't go away. Maybe it would be because he'd stay looking for me or something.

The trouble was that my dad wasn't even there that night, and that meant that I either had to wait in the hayloft till he came the next day—or else that I had to go down now, and then hide again tomorrow. I decided to stay where I was because there were some ducks at the bottom of the ladder. I couldn't see them but I could tell they were there.

I stayed there all night. I slept most of the time. Every once in a while they'd wake me up by calling out "Neil! Neil!"—but I never answered.

I never knew a night that was so long, except maybe once when I was in the hospital. When I slept I seemed to sleep for a long time, but it never came to morning. They kept waking me up but it was never time.

Then it was.

I saw that morning through a hole in the roof of the hayloft. The sunlight came in through cracks between the boards and it was all dusty; the sunlight, I mean.

They were up pretty early that morning, even for farmers. There seemed to be a lot more people than I remembered—and there were two or three cars and a truck I'd never seen before, too. And I saw Mrs. Currie holding on to Bud with one hand and Teddy Hartley with the other. I remembered thinking, "If I was down there, how could she hold on to me if she's only got two hands and Bud and Teddy Hartley to look after?" And I thought that right then she must be pretty glad I wasn't around.

I wondered what they were all doing. Mr. Currie was standing in the middle of a lot of men and he kept pointing out the scenery around the farm. I imagined what he was saying. There was a big woods behind the house and a cherry and plum-tree orchard that would be good to point out to his friends. I could tell they were his friends from the way they were listening. What I couldn't figure out was why they were all up so early— and why they had Bud and Teddy Hartley up, too.

Then there was a police car. I suppose it came from Orillia or somewhere. That was the biggest town near where the farm was. Orillia.

When the policemen got out of their car, they went up to Mr. Currie. There were four of them. They all talked for quite a long time and then everyone started going out in all directions. It looked to me as though Bud and Teddy Hartley wanted to go, too, but Mrs. Currie made them go in the house. She practically had to drag Bud. It looked as if he was crying and I wondered why he should do that.

Then one of the policemen came into the barn. He was all alone. I stayed very quiet, because I wasn't going to let anything keep me from going through with my plan about my dad. Not even a policeman.

He urinated against the wall inside the door. It was sort of funny, because he kept turning around to make sure no one saw him, and he didn't know I was there. Then he did up his pants and stood in the middle of the floor under the haylofts.

"Hey! Neil!"

That was the policeman.

He said it so suddenly that it scared me. I nearly fell off from where I was, it scared me so much. And I guess maybe he saw me, because he started right up the ladder at me.

"How did you know my name?"

I said that in a whisper.

"They told me."

"Oh."

"Have you been here all night?"

"Yes."

"Don't you realize that everyone has been looking for you all over the place? Nobody's even been to sleep."

That sort of frightened me—but it was all right, because he smiled when he said it.

Then he stuck his head out of this window that was there to let the air in (so that the barn wouldn't catch on fire)—and he yelled down, "He's all right—I've found him! He's up here."

And I said: "What did you go and do that for? Now you've ruined everything."

He smiled again and said, "I had to stop them all going off to look for you. Now,"—as he sat down beside me—"do you want to tell me what it is you're doing up here?"

"No."

I think that sort of set him back a couple of years, because he didn't say anything for a minute—except "Oh."

Then I thought maybe I had to have something to tell the others anyway, so I might as well make it up for him right now.

"I fell asleep," I said.

"When—last night?"

"Yes."

I looked at him. I wondered if I could trust a guy who did that against walls, when all you had to do was go in the house.

"Why did you come up here in the first place?" he said.

I decided I could trust him because I remembered once when I did the same thing. Against the wall.

So I told him.

"I want to hide on my dad," I said.

"Why do you want to do that? And besides, Mrs. Currie said your parents weren't even here."

"Yes, but he's coming today."

"But why hide on him? Don't you like him, or something?"

"Sure I do," I said.

I thought about it.

"But he's … he's … Do you know if it's true, my dad's joined the army?"

"I dunno. Maybe. There's a war on, you know."

"Well, that's why I hid."

But he laughed.

"Is that why you hid? Because of the war?"

"Because of my dad."

"You don't need to hide because of the war—the Germans aren't coming over here, you know."

"But it's not that. It's my dad." I could have told you he wouldn't understand.

I was trying to think of what to say next when Mrs. Currie came into the barn. She stood down below.

"Is he up there, officer? Is he all right?"

"Yes, ma'am, I've got him. He's fine."

"Neil dear, what happened? Why don't you come down and tell us what happened to you?"

Then I decided that I'd really go all out. I had to, because I could tell they weren't going to—it was just obvious that these people weren't going to understand me and take my story about my dad and the army and everything.

"Somebody chased me."

The policeman looked sort of shocked and I could hear Mrs. Currie take in her breath.

"Somebody chased you, eh?"

"Yes."

"Who?"

I had to think fast.

"Some man. But he's gone now."

I thought I'd better say he was gone, so that they wouldn't start worrying.

"Officer, why don't you bring him down here? Then we can talk."

"All right, ma'am. Come on, Neil, we'll go down and have some breakfast."

They didn't seem to believe me about that man I made up.

We went over to the ladder.

I looked down. A lot of hay stuck out so that I couldn't see the floor.

"Are there any ducks down there?"

"No, dear, you can come down—it's all right."

She was lying, though. There was a great big duck right next to her. I think it's awfully silly to tell a lie like that. I mean, if the duck is standing right there it doesn't even make sense, does it?

But I went down anyway and she made the duck go away.

When we went out, the policeman held my hand. His hand had some sweat on it but it was a nice hand, with hair on the back. I liked that. My dad didn't have that on his hand.

Then we ate breakfast with all those people who'd come to look for me. At least, *they* ate. I just sat.

After breakfast, Mr. and Mrs. Currie took me upstairs to the sitting-room. It was upstairs because the kitchen was in the cellar.

All I remember about that was a vase that had a potted plant in it. This vase was made of putty and into the putty Mrs. Currie had stuck all kinds of stones and pennies and old bits of glass and things. You could look at this for hours and never see the same kind of stone or glass twice. I don't remember the plant.

All I remember about what they said was that they told me I should never do it again. That routine.

Then they told me my mother and my dad would be up that day around lunch time.

What they were really sore about was losing their sleep, and then all those people coming. I was sorry about that—but you can't very well go down and make an announcement about it, so I didn't.

At twelve o'clock I went and sat in Mr. Currie's truck. It was in the barn. I took out those two boxes I'd put in the glove compartment and looked at them. I tried to figure out what my dad would do with an old box like that in the army. And he'd probably never play another game of golf as long as he lived. Not in the army, anyway. Maybe he'd use the box for his bullets or something.

Then I counted the red stones I was going to give my mother. I kept seeing them around her neck and how pretty they'd be. She had a dress they'd be just perfect with. Blue. The only thing I was worried about was how to get a hole in them so you could put them on a string. There wasn't much sense in having beads without a string—not if you were going to wear them, anyway— or your mother was.

And it was then that they came.

I heard their car drive up outside and I went and looked from behind the barn door. My father wasn't wearing a uniform yet like I'd thought he would be. I began to think maybe he really didn't want me to know about it. I mean, he hadn't written or anything, and now he was just wearing an old blazer and some grey pants. It made me remember.

I went back and sat down in the truck again. I didn't know what to do. I just sat there with those stones in my hand.

Then I heard someone shout, "Neil!"

I went and looked. Mr. and Mrs. Currie were standing with my parents by the car—and I saw Bud come running out of the house, and then Teddy Hartley. Teddy Hartley sort of hung back, though. He was the kind of person who's only polite if there are grownups around him. He sure knew how to pull the wool over their eyes, because he'd even combed his hair. Wild-root-cream-oil-Charlie.

Then I noticed that they were talking very seriously and my mother put her hand above her eyes and looked around. I guess she was looking for me. Then my dad started toward the barn.

I went and hid behind the truck. I wasn't quite sure yet what I was going to do, but I certainly wasn't going to go up and throw my arms around his neck or anything.

"Neil. Are you in there, son?"

My dad spoke that very quietly. Then I heard the door being pushed open, and some chicken had to get out of the way, because I heard it making that awful noise chickens make when you surprise them doing something. They sure can get excited over nothing—chickens.

I took a quick look behind me. There was a door there that led into the part of the barn where the haylofts were and where I'd been all night. I decided to make a dash for it. But I had to ward off my father first—and so I threw that stone.

I suppose I'll have to admit that I meant to hit him. It wouldn't be much sense if I tried to fool you about that. I wanted to hit him because when I stood up behind the truck and saw him then I suddenly got mad. I thought about how he hadn't written me, or anything.

It hit him on the hand.

He turned right around because he wasn't sure what it was or where it came from. And before I ran, I just caught a glimpse of his face. He'd seen me and he sure looked peculiar. I guess that now I'll never forget his face and how he looked at me right then. I think it was that he looked as though he might cry or something. But I knew he wouldn't do that, because he never did.

Then I ran.

From the loft I watched them in the yard. My dad was rubbing his hands together and I guess maybe where I'd hit him it was pretty sore. My mother took off her handkerchief that she had round her neck and put it on his hand. Then I guess he'd told them what I'd done, because this time they all started toward the barn.

I didn't know what to do then. I counted out the stones I had left and there were about fifteen of them. There was the golf ball, too.

I didn't want to throw stones at all of them. I certainly didn't want to hit my mother—and I hoped that they wouldn't send her in first. I thought then how I'd be all right if they sent in Teddy Hartley first. I didn't mind the thought of throwing at him, I'll tell you that much.

But my dad came first.

I had a good view of where he came from. He came in through the part where the truck was parked, because I guess he thought I was still there. And then he came on into the part where I was now—in the hayloft.

He stood by the door.

"Neil."

I wasn't saying anything. I sat very still.

"Neil."

I could only just see his head and shoulders—the rest of him was hidden by the edge of the loft.

"Neil, aren't you even going to explain what you're angry about?"

I thought for a minute and then I didn't answer him after all. I looked at him, though. He looked worried.

"What do you want us to do?"

I sat still.

"Neil?"

Since I didn't answer, he started back out the door—I guess to talk to my mother or someone.

I hit his back with another stone. I had to make sure he knew I was there.

He turned around at me.

"Neil, what's the matter? I want to know what's the matter."

He almost fooled me, but not quite. I thought that perhaps he really didn't know for a minute—but after taking a look at him I decided that he did know, all right. I mean, there he was in that blue blazer and everything—just as if he hadn't joined the army at all.

So I threw again and this time it really hit him in the face.

He didn't do anything—he just stood there. It really scared me. Then my mother came in, but he made her go back.

I thought about my rink, and how I wouldn't have it. I thought about being in the fifth grade that year and how I'd skipped from grade three. And I thought about the Indian who'd sold those boxes that I had down in the truck.

"Neil—I'm going to come up."

You could tell he really would, too, from his voice.

I got the golf ball ready.

To get to me he had to disappear for a minute while he crossed under the loft and then when he climbed the ladder. I decided to change my place while he was out of sight. I began to think that was pretty clever and that maybe I'd be pretty good at that war stuff myself. Field Marshal Cable.

I put myself into a little trench of hay and piled some up in front of me. When my dad came up over the top of the ladder, he wouldn't even see me and then I'd have a good chance to aim at him.

The funny thing was that at that moment I'd forgotten why I was against him. I got so mixed up in all that Field Marshal stuff that I really forgot all about my dad and the army and everything. I was just trying to figure out how I could get him before he saw me—and that was all.

I got further down in the hay and then he was there.

He was out of breath and his face was all sweaty, and where I'd hit him there was blood. And then he put his hand with my mother's hankie up to his face to wipe it. And he sort of bit it (the handkerchief). It was as if he was confused or something. I remember thinking he looked then just like I'd felt my face go when Bud had said our dad had joined the army. You know how you look around with your eyes from side to side as though maybe you'll find the answer to it somewhere near you? You never do find it, but you always look anyway, just in case.

Anyway, that's how he was just then, and it sort of threw me. I had that feeling again that maybe he didn't know what this was all about. But then, he had to know, didn't he? Because he'd done it.

I had the golf ball ready in my right hand and one of those stones in the other. He walked toward me.

I missed with the golf ball and got him with the stone.

And he fell down. He really fell down. He didn't say anything—he didn't even say "ouch," like I would have—he just fell down.

In the hay.

I didn't go out just yet. I sat and looked at him. And I listened.

Nothing.

Do you know, there wasn't a sound in that whole place? It was as if everything had stopped because they knew what had happened.

My dad just lay there and we waited for what would happen next.

It was me.

I mean, I made the first noise.

I said: "Dad?"

But nobody answered—not even my mother.

So I said it louder. "*Dad?*"

It was just as if they'd all gone away and left me with him, all alone.

He sure looked strange lying there—so quiet and everything. I didn't know what to do.

"Dad?"

I went over on my hands and knees.

Then suddenly they all came in. I just did what I thought of first. I guess it was because they scared me—coming like that when it was so quiet.

I got all the stones out of my pockets and threw them, one by one, as they came through the door. I stood up to do it. I saw them all running through the door, and I threw every stone, even at my mother.

And then I fell down. I fell down beside my dad and pushed him over on his back because he'd fallen on his stomach. It was like he was asleep.

They came up then and I don't remember much of that. Somebody picked me up, and there was the smell of perfume and my eyes hurt and I got something in my throat and nearly chocked to death and I could hear a lot of talking. And somebody was whispering, too. And then I felt myself being carried down and there was the smell of oil and gasoline and some chickens had to be got out of the way again and then there was sunlight.

Then my mother just sat with me, and I guess I cried for a long time. In the cherry and plum-tree orchard—and she seemed to understand because she said that he would tell me all about it and that he hadn't written me because he didn't want to scare me when I was all alone at Arthur Robertson's.

And then Bud came.

My mother said that he should go away for a while. But he said: "I brought something" and she said: "What is it, then?" and now I remember where I got that worm in my handkerchief that I told you about.

It was from Bud.

He said to me that if I wanted to, he'd take me fishing on the lake just before the sun went down. He said that was a good time. And he gave me that worm because he'd found it.

So my mother took it and put it in my hankie and Bud looked at me for a minute and then went away.

The worst part was when I saw my dad again.

My mother took me to the place where he was sitting in the sun and we just watched each other for a long time.

Then he said: "Neil, your mother wants to take our picture because I'm going away tomorrow to Ottawa for a couple of weeks, and she thought I'd like a picture to take with me."

He lit a cigarette and then he said: "I would, too, you know, like that picture."

And I sort of said: "All right."

So they called to Bud, and my mother went to get her camera.

But before Bud came and before my mother got back, we were alone for about ten hours. It was awful.

I couldn't think of anything and I guess he couldn't, either. I had a good look at him, though.

He looked just like he does right there in that picture. You can see where the stone hit him on his right cheek—and the one that knocked him out is the one over the eye.

Right then the thing never got settled. Not in words, anyway. I was still thinking about that rink and everything—and my dad hadn't said anything about the army yet.

I wish I hadn't done it. Thrown those stones and everything. It wasn't his fault he had to go.

For another thing, I was sorry about the stones because I knew I wouldn't find any more like them—but I did throw them, and that's that.

They both got those little boxes, though—I made sure of that. And in one there was a string of red beads from Orillia and in the other there was a photograph.

There still is.

THE JADE PEONY

by Wayson Choy

Wayson Choy was born in 1939 in Vancouver.
His bestselling debut novel, The Jade Peony *(1995), won*
the Trillium Book Award and the Vancouver Book Award.
His haunting memoir, Paper Shadows *(1999), was*
nominated for the Governor General's Award.
His second novel, All That Matters *(2004), also won the*
Trillium Book Award and was shortlisted for the
Scotiabank Giller Prize. Wayson Choy lives in Toronto
where he teaches at the Humber School for Writers.

"THE JADE PEONY" TELLS THE STORY of a Chinese family living in Vancouver in the thirties and early forties. There are four children in the family: brothers Kiam, Jung and Sek-Lung, and sister Liang. In this excerpt, eight-year-old Sek-Lung, the youngest child, describes his life after his beloved grandmother's death, when the boy, sickly to this point in his life, is finally given the go-ahead to attend school.

After the family had decided to respect Grandmama's spirit, to bow three times, burn joss sticks, and pray before the Old One's gilt-framed photograph—that is, to bai sen—the Old One no longer haunted us. Now, when I picked up the coin-sized jade peony, remembering how Grandmama used to hold it up to the light and tell me stories, the carved semitranslucent stone was a reminder that she was gone.

A few days later, Father had Kiam hammer in three nails on the parlour wall facing the front windows. In between two elegant scrolls of memorial calligraphy, Father hung up Grand-mama's portrait. The front room, however, and her upstairs room, which was now more or less Liang's bedroom, never quite lost the smell of myrrh. Mrs. Lim said the lingering fragrance was a good sign, and Jung said he liked the smell, because the scent reminded him of the Tong Association assembly hall where on special days, rows of incense and thick red candles burned before warrior gods.

A kind of peace settled over the household.

That summer, seven months after Grandmama's death, a long time for a young boy, I flung myself into life without her.

I wanted to grow up fast, to have my chance to fly a teeth-baring Fighting Tiger over the skies of China, to storm over Europe and bomb and strafe as many of the enemy as possible, to mow down as many Nazis and Japanese as my older brothers and their grown-up pals vowed to kill.

I imagined Stepmother and Father, even Liang, and brothers Kiam and Jung, standing at the Vancouver docks to wave me off while a military band with trumpets and drums and bagpipes played on and on. And I, handsome in my military uniform, would promise to stay healthy and never wheeze again.

That year, 1941, I had my first outdoor summer, with my two older brothers packing me off to soccer games and football practice, encouraging me to be as physical and as robust as they were.

All that summer, whenever he had time off from his work at Third Uncle's warehouse, Kiam had me chasing and kicking soccer balls on the school grounds, sometimes goodnaturedly laughing at my awkwardness. Jung took me to the Hastings Gym, where he and his pals taught me how to put up my fists to defend myself.

All the foot-stomping, jumping, pushing and shoving I had been forbidden to do because I would choke and wheeze, all the pent-up physical energies inside my bony frame, suddenly exploded. I was a new boy.

When my two brothers were working, or when they were too busy to bother with me, I hitched up with a half-dozen or so bloodthirsty boys—boastful eight-, nine- and know-it-all ten-year-old comrades. We were constantly bending down our shorn heads in a football huddle to plot out endless movie-inspired war games.

We were, of course, all "good guys" fighting the dirty Nazis and Japanese. We broke into threes and fours and soared into snarling, arm-stretching, attack-and-dive flight patterns, loudly dropping brick and concrete bombs down the grassy slopes of MacLean Park. We roared through clouds of playground dust in oversized shipping cartons devised by Joe Eng to look like Sherman tanks, setting cardboard towns and cities on fire with stolen matches. We slammed together ear-crunching, dented garbage-can lids, and cheerfully yelped ourselves dry with the cheap thrill of murderous victories as we sent smaller children scrambling and screaming out of the range of our howling gunsights. And one late afternoon Alfred Stevorsky, the oldest of all of us, jumped over a garbage pile and plucked out a discarded bakelite doll the size of a real baby. He sat it up against a pile of bricks.

"Watch this," he snarled.

He poured out some liquid from a small paint can, took out a match from his shirt pocket, and set the half-dressed doll on fire.

We all watched with fascinated horror as the baby-sized head began to melt. Its rose-coloured cupid mouth twisted into a wide gaping grimace. Its two large glassy eyes burst from their wired sockets and, slowly, one after another, drooled down the distorting flaming cheeks.

"That's what real bombs do," one of the Han boys said. "That's what my Uncle Bing told me."

Alfred Stevorsky unbuttoned his fly and pulled out his show-off cock. A long stream of urine splashed over the mess.

The enemy was everywhere. The *Vancouver Sun* newspaper said so. Newsreels said so. Hollywood and British movies said so. All of Chinatown said so, out loud.

On June 20, 1941, at 10:15 p.m., shelling from a Japanese submarine hit Estevan Point on Vancouver Island; then, a day later, shells hit the Oregon coast. An unidentified submarine was spotted in the Strait. It's true, I thought. The enemy is everywhere.

Every household along the West Coast was ordered by the government to hang thick blackout cloth over each window. Air raid sirens screamed practice warnings and frightened birds flew into the air. On certain clear days at noon, foghorns and sirens tested Warning and All-Clear patterns. Kiam and Father agreed with the series of editorials in the *Sun*: the Japanese along the coast were potential spies and traitors. Letters in the newspapers demanded that something be done with the "infiltrating treacherous" Japanese in B.C. Gangs of older, jobless boys roamed back streets hunting for Japanese. Fights broke out. There were knifings on some streets, and on Fourth Avenue and Alberta, a Japanese boy, trying to protect his mother, was shot dead. Stepmother told Father to write something about that, to protest the killing.

"They're killing Chinese boys in China," Father said, in Stepmother's dialect. "I lost three cousins, the youngest seven years old. You lost your Mission Church friend when they bombed Canton. What the hell am I supposed to write about?"

Our war games went on unabated, fed by movies, spy comics, drum-beating parades, trading cards, fund-raising drives, recruiting posters and war toys of every kind. I had a dozen tin American pursuit bombers and British fighter planes. I remember how pleased I was to trade away an early Curtiss B-24 and a chipped-wing Hurricane (it had a broken tail as well) for three chunky Sherman tanks for much-needed ground support.

The gang treasured bits and pieces of army and navy surplus military clothing salvaged from the First War. Alfred Stevorsky had the best outfit. His older brother gave him a patched-up U.S. Army coat, with what the brother swore was a real bullet hole in the left arm, and Alfred's mother opened up a trunk and gave him an RAF captain's hat with a stiff brim. Some of us, like the Han boys, got our stuff from second-hand clothing stores along Hastings Street. I had Father buy me from the Army and Navy Store's clear-out sale a British-made leather aviator's cap, with its genuine cracked flight goggles and authentic earflaps and a mysterious number inked inside the right flap. The world was full of secrets.

When September came, the school doctor put his cold stethoscope on my chest and pronounced the slight wheezing to be some kind of allergy. I nervously passed the rest of the medical exam; then I confidently completed a six-page English reading test, matching cartoon pictures with English words, wrote a paragraph of my choice, passed everything—and was allowed to start at Strathcona in Advanced Grade Three. I was joyful: it would be as if I had not missed a single day of school.

Grandmama had kept her promise. No longer would those towering red-bricked Strathcona School buildings along Pender and Keefer Streets be a mystery to me: I was starting school in five days. Kiam and Jung gave me some new pencils and three blank exercise books. Even Liang gave me things: a stick-pen holder with an unlicked nib and a large ink eraser she hardly ever used. Stepmother stitched a brown corduroy carrying case for me. Father showed me a new Waterman fountain pen he said would be mine as soon as I learned to write properly.

I might even start Chinese School.

Advanced Grade Three at Strathcona was a class for immigrant kids who knew too little English, or who could understand English but not read or speak it well, or who for whatever reason were starting late and needed extra attention, like me.

Jung had taught me to use my fists, so I even-stevened in two recess fights and lost one. It was worth it; I learned to spit blood, just like the elders spit out tobacco. I didn't really enjoy the fights, but I enjoyed the attention. Except for a few scrapes, plus a few name-calling sessions during the first two weeks of recesses—*Sick-kee Sekkk-kee!*—everything was going A-okay.

In Miss E. Doyle's classroom, at least, there was no name-calling; in class, no pushing, no kicking. Not even whispering. Her commands were simple, and simply barked: "Sit." "Eyes front." "Feet flat on the floor." And all the boys and girls obeyed.

"I am the General of this class," she said, looking particularly at a front row of tall boys whom she had placed there on purpose, including my friends Alfred Stevorsky and Joe Eng.

Big Miss Doyle waved a steel-edged ruler just like the one my Grade One teacher, Miss MacKinney, had waved. With her large palms, Miss Doyle brushed the stiff lapels of her brass-buttoned tartan jacket.

"All of you are my soldiers, and some of you, like Joseph Piscatella here, need more English before you are finally marched out of my care. Some of you need pro-nun-ci-a-tion lessons."

She looked at the tall boy in the front row.

"I can tell your *spoken* English is much improved this year, Joseph."

Miss Doyle looked around and nodded at one or two familiar faces. She noticed my aviator's cap folded neatly on my lap.

"Next time, Sek-Lung," she said, "that stays in the cloakroom."

"The boys at recess called him Sekky, Miss Doyle." A red-haired girl with braces on her legs smiled at the teacher.

"Thank you, Darlene," Miss Doyle smiled back, "but you remember from last year how you should raise your hand and wait for permission before speaking out in class."

"Yes, Miss Doyle."

After the daily roll call, rain or shine, warm or cold, Miss Doyle assigned one of the bigger boys, like Joseph, to pry open a window. She asked for other volunteers to water the row of flower pots she carefully seeded at the beginning of every school term. The seeding was part of her nature lesson. At the end of June, the best students were awarded plants bursting with blooms.

"Perhaps, Sek-Lung," Miss Doyle said, looking directly at me, "you might like to help Darlene with the watering jug on Mondays."

"Yes, Miss Doyle."

Joe Eng snickered.

"—and Joe Eng will help on Thursdays and dust the windows as well ... yes, Joe?"

"Yes, Miss Doyle."

No one snickered.

In Miss Doyle's class, we sat with our backs straight "like soldiers," with our hands folded in front of us. Our hands sat pressed against a book opened to the correct page, its number chalked on the blackboard; and our feet, for Miss Doyle's inspection, were to be flat as an iron against the floor.

Miss Doyle, with her loud gravel voice, was the guardian of our education. With hawk-eyed precision, she reined in her Third Graders with a kind of compassionate terror, blasting out a delinquent's full name as if she were God's avenging horn: each vowel of any name, however multisyllabled, whether it was Japanese, East Asian or Eastern European, Italian or Chinese, was enunciated; each vowel cracked with the clarity of thunder. She walked so heavily that the floor boards squeaked with stress. And if you pleased her, she would seem to be amused, and sharply pulled her opened red jacket tightly about her thick body so that her large breasts poked up. Alfred Stevorsky always liked that.

Most of us, like Darlene or Joseph, liked to please Miss Doyle, but she was, like a mother, easier to annoy than please and, like a father, careful to display authority, in her case, the strap hanging next to the large Neilson Chocolate Map of the World at the front of the classroom. She used the leather strap to point out the latest battles in the British Empire—which was all the red colour on the map—or the battle in England itself.

Each afternoon, we waited with excitement for Miss Doyle's descriptions of the day's battles and victories. No matter how small the conflicts or how great the number of casualties, Miss Doyle rarely talked of people killing each other, but always mentioned "rescue" and "courage" and "kindness."

She also regularly read aloud letters from her brother, whose name she enunciated clearly for us: "John Wil-lard Hen-ry Doyle." He was a fire marshal for his district of St. Martin's, London.

"A fire marshal," the General said, "is someone assigned to take charge of putting out fires caused by the bombing. But his main job, boys and girls, is to save lives, not buildings."

She repeated her only and older brother's full name so that we would not think, she said, that our own variety of names was any more unusual.

"A name is a name," Miss Doyle emphasized. "Always be brave enough to be proud of yours."

Bravery was a central theme in her class. I saw her brother in a fireman's outfit climbing ladders and walking through flames.

In his world, bombs fell night and day, injured people were pulled out from under collapsed buildings, children were hurt but brave. Miss Doyle kept her brother's picture in a small silver frame on her desk. He looked very young in the picture, very tall, and the small girl beside him, looking up at John Willard Henry's big smile, was Miss Doyle herself.

Miss Doyle read us sections of her brother's vivid letters, which thrilled us all.

I remember listening to how the smoke rose in furious clouds over a place called *Pick-a-dill-lee* Square; how in a place called Kensington Gardens, a statue of a boy named Peter Pan was not disturbed even an inch by the concussion bombs. There were ghastly smells coming from burning factories and houses, the awful weight of collapsed walls and twisted steel girders, the cries and screams from the mysterious dust-choking darkness beneath trembling beams. There was rescue and valour, and unending hope for the nightmare to end. "We will never surrender," John Willard Henry wrote, quoting a man named Churchill, who, Miss Doyle emphasized, was a loyal friend of the King and Queen.

"When I was a little girl," Miss Doyle said to the class, "my brother John used to read the story of Peter Pan to me. It is a book written by whom, Darlene?"

"Mr. J. M. Barrie."

The letters inspired everyone in the class to believe in "the just cause" and bravery. We saved our pennies to help our families buy more war bonds. One day, when John Doyle noted that the bombs were coming closer and closer to St. Martin's, I noticed the red-haired Darlene dropping her head to her desk, as if she were afraid. Joe Piscatella tensely bit his bottom lip, following every word of the brave John Doyle.

"*Adventurous times, my dear Tinker*," he wrote in one letter, using a pet name for Miss Doyle, "*but we'll pull through.*"

At night, in bed, I prayed to Grandmama to keep John Willard Henry safe from the bombs. Some nights I dreamed of a tall man wearing a fireman's hat, standing with the Old One, safely. I would learn to be as brave as Miss Doyle's wonderful brother. Sometimes the gang would play rescue war games, but it never seemed as much fun as sky diving, blowing apart cities and torpedoing ships.

We pleased Miss Doyle when we were brave; that is, when we raised our hands to answer her questions, or ventured to speak aloud. Most of us knew the humiliation and the mockery—"Me wan'nee fly lice! Lot-see lice!"— the tittering, brought on by our immigrant accents. On streetcars and in shops where only English was spoken, people ignored you or pretended they didn't hear you or, worse, shouted back, "WHAT? WHAT'S THAT YOU SAY? CAN'T YOU SPEAK ENGLISH!?!"

Miss Doyle never ignored us, never tittered; she stood strictly at attention as if to compliment our valiant efforts when we spoke or read out loud, daring anyone to mock us.

We were brave, she said, just as the King and Queen, their framed portraits hanging separately above us, encouraged us to be. Miss Doyle pinned up on the cork board by the back cloakroom a newspaper picture of King George and his Queen talking to a group of British people; they were all standing in front of a bombed-out building as if it were an ordinary day for a chat.

"Their Majesties always enunciate perfectly," Miss Doyle informed us, loudly.

Day after day, we absorbed her enunciated syllables, the syllables of a King and Queen. Without our fully realizing what was happening, our English vocabulary multiplied and blossomed. When I prayed to Grandmama, asking her again and again to help Miss Doyle's brother, the fire marshal, I prayed more and more with English words, pronounced perfectly. Grandmama, in the other world, somehow could understand all languages.

Though every girl and boy found out quickly enough what irritated the General, no one was ever certain what, besides bravery, would really specifically please her.

There weren't that many chances for anyone living in Canada to be truly brave. Murderous bombs were not falling down on Vancouver as they were in London, though they fell down every day in Miss Doyle's brother's succinct, suspense-filled stories about rescue and valour.

Reading aloud from those three-folded onionskin pages, Miss Doyle told us about the darkest days of the Battle of Britain in the gentle light of her brother's rescue stories. As she carefully folded each letter and returned it to its heavily stamped envelope, we could feel our backs stiffen with courage.

One of her brother's rescue stories was so exciting that I told it to Jung. There were struggling baby noises coming from a dark bombed-out section of a hospital building, and John Willard Henry's team of five men and a woman named Grace risked everything to reach the trapped child. When Grace poked her hand through a small cleared-out space to reach for the whimpering infant, the woman screamed, jumped back. The child was covered with hair. Finally, John Willard Henry reached in and pulled out a small frightened terrier.

"*I have the nipped finger to prove it,*" he wrote. "*Damn odd business, this risking your life for a puppy!*"

Miss Doyle even said the word *damn*, just like her brother wrote it.

Jung laughed, then waited until I finished laughing, too.

"Want to know something?" he asked me, carefully.

I nodded yes, thinking that he was going to tell me that story was probably made up, but I was ready to let him know that it was all in a real handwritten letter sent from England.

"You don't know, do you, Sekky?"

"Know what?"

"Last Christmas—Miss Doyle's brother—blown to bits."

My mouth dropped open. I refused to believe Jung, who years ago had been in Miss Doyle's class and hated her because she strapped him for pulling the fire alarm.

"Everyone knows he's dead, Sekky," Jung persisted. "His picture was in the *Sun*. Ask Kiam."

I dared not ask Kiam, nor did I ask anybody in the class, not even Alfred Stevorsky or Joe Eng. After all, if John Willard Henry was really dead, why didn't someone in the class say so? Why didn't Miss Doyle say so?

Tormented all week, I did not even say a prayer to the Old One. No one knew I still talked to her. Grandmama should have warned me.

I waited after school to ask Miss Doyle about her brother. She had just put another of his airmail letters away and dismissed the class. We could hear Mr. Barclay's class next door stampeding out like cattle, but everyone in Miss Doyle's class left in the usual orderly fashion. Miss Doyle was busy cleaning off the blackboard.

I could hear Darlene's braces clunking away.

"Sekky," Miss Doyle said, turning around. "You're still here."

"Miss Doyle," I began, "was Mr. Doyle blown to bits?"

She looked puzzled, then her eyes glazed over. Her face registered shock, betrayal.

I wanted to get out of the room. I abruptly turned and rushed to the cloakroom to get my jacket and hat.

"Sek-Lung," Miss Doyle thundered my name, "come here."

With my coat and hat in my hand, I walked slowly back to her. She had used me, tricked me, made me care for someone, made me pray for the safety of someone who was already dead.

Miss Doyle gave me a wide-eyed YOU'D BETTER PAY ATTENTION look.

"That first day," Miss Doyle began, speaking to me as if I had forgotten to help Darlene with the water jug, "that day when I started to read my brother's letters, you must *remember* that I ... *oh, my God ...*" she took my hand. "You were away that day."

It was true. I had been away from her class one afternoon.

"Oh, Sekky, you went to the nurse's office!" Miss Doyle's voice suddenly went soft, as if she were once again the little girl in the picture. "I did. I told the class of John's death. Yes ... he is ... dead ..." And then Miss Doyle used Jung's words, my words, a child's words, in a whisper I could barely make out, "... *blown to bits.*"

In uneasy silence, I let Miss Doyle lift my arms and push them through my jacket; I let her half guide me to the front of the room. Passing her desk, however, I pushed against her and stopped to study the picture in the small silver frame.

In the picture, I could see how brightly the little girl's blonde hair shone; her smiling face said, *Nothing in the world can ever go wrong.*

I took my pilot's cap from her hand and walked out the door. I knew I still liked Miss E. Doyle.

Miss E. Doyle made it a rule never to tolerate interruptions or careless behaviour in her class.

Not only did she prefer to stand at attention for most of the time she spent with us, she expected every boy and girl in her class to adopt her military bearing, her exact sense of decorum.

We were an unruly, untidy mixed bunch of immigrants and displaced persons, legal or otherwise, and it was her duty to take our varying fears and insecurities and mould us into some ideal collective functioning together as a military unit with one purpose: to conquer the King's English, to belong at last to a country that she envisioned including all of us.

After morning prayer, in a carefully modulated stage whisper, Miss Doyle told us to open our eyes and keep our bowed heads before her, then "carefully and quietly" to put our fingers under our desktop ledges and lift. A single whoosh sound filled the room as the tops of desks moved upward, like so many wings. Books and pencil boxes came clattering out, and desktops fell back down. We were now to remember to keep our feet flat on the floor.

When we were all ready, she would say, "Excellent." That was the signal to be "at ease."

In training us, she never hesitated to use her desk ruler repeatedly on our burning backsides, nor was she slow to engage the leather strap on our stinging bare hands. And few of our poverty-raised, war-weary parents or guardians expected a teacher, male or female, to do any less.

Once, from the back of the room in the unnatural silence that was the miracle of her careful training of her troops, we heard a delinquent pencil box crash to the hardwood floor like a bomb.

We all turned to look: on the floor, in the middle of the back aisle, sat an absurdly large *Grand Dutch Coronas* cigar box the size of Miss Doyle's Holy Bible. The lid was held tightly shut by thick-knotted yellow twine.

Some of us stared straight at the leather strap hanging on the wall, afraid even to blink. Some of us turned to see Tammy Okada in a grubby flowery dress, pale with fear, her dirty knees shaking.

Tammy Okada, of mixed parentage, had tightly braided brownish pigtails and wore obvious hand-me-downs; her English was terrible. None of the girls wanted to play with her, not even those who were more or less her own kind, the Japanese girls. Tammy Okada was a stupid girl, thick-waisted from a poor diet, not much blessed with looks. She always had to borrow someone else's pencils because she could never untie her own twine-knotted box. Yet she was too proud to let anyone help her undo the twine.

For some reason, Miss Doyle had never forced Tammy to open her pencil box; instead she always commanded one of the other students to lend Tammy a ruler or an eraser or whatever. And now the cigar box had slipped off her desktop and banged on to the floor.

The eagle-eyed General could see right away whose stupid makeshift pencil box it was.

Miss Doyle walked straight up the aisle, bent down and snatched up the cigar box. The box immediately broadcast a rolling noise, as if it held no more than a tiny solitary item: a single steel marble, perhaps, or maybe a small round ball of foil, rolling inside ... round, round, round. We could all hear the loud rolling hiss coming from the box as it was held in mid-air, frozen in Miss Doyle's surprised grip. Now everyone knew: a box almost ten inches square and three inches high, and it was practically empty!

Empty! This absurd discovery caused three or four of the girls in the class to trade smirks across the aisles. Florence Chan giggled. Elizabeth Brown threw her head back. Alfred Stevorsky snorted. Joe Eng started to guffaw, but thought better of it when the General's blonde head did not move. The classroom grew still, waiting, watching. Tammy Okada instinctively held her hands over her scalp as if she expected Miss Doyle, her grey eyes glistening, to take the box and break it over her head.

For a long, long moment, the big woman did nothing. Miss Doyle's stillness also warned the rest of us

that her uncanny radar was *O-N*. The slightest hint of
another giggle or snort, or even a misplaced sigh, would
mean the strap. We held our breath.

The General loudly cleared her throat: *Ahem!*

In three seconds, like disciplined soldiers, we sat up,
hands folded, feet flat on the floor, eyes front, staring at
the Map of the World. Still, I couldn't resist turning my
head a little, straining the corner of my eyes to sneak a
look: General Doyle, unsmiling, still held the knotted
box in her enormous grip. She focussed her steel-cold
eyes on Tammy Okada.

"Take out your books and put them in a pile," she
said to Tammy, each word clear and sharp as a warning
bell. She stood silently watching, as the brownish-haired
girl, eyes edged with tears, dropped her shaking hands
and nervously emptied her desk.

Miss Doyle put her hand out, gripped Tammy's
shoulder, walked up the aisle and stopped before the one
remaining empty front seat.

"*Here*, Tammy Okada," Miss Doyle carefully enunciated each syllable, "you will be able to pay much better
attention, *yes?*"

From my seat in the middle of the room, I could see
Tammy Okada's braided pigtails visibly trembling.

"You will become my best student, *yes?*"

Tammy Okada's back, in spite of herself, seemed to
straighten a little.

"Sit."

Miss Doyle walked away with Tammy's cigar box still
clutched in her hand. We figured this was the last anyone
would ever see of that pathetic dirty box. We all waited
to see if Miss Doyle would throw it into her desk drawer

of confiscated stuff, or if she would toss it into the wastepaper basket; after which, she would slowly dust off her big hands and walk over to the hanging strap.

I thought Tammy Okada must feel like a leaky submarine. I was feeling a little sorry for her when Miss Doyle walked past the wastepaper basket and strode directly to the front of her own cabinet-style desk. She reached down into a bottom drawer out of everyone's sight. There were snipping noises. Miss Doyle threw away cut pieces of knotted twine and rummaged noisily, but we could not see what she was doing. Then we heard the smart *Snap! Snap!* of elastic bands.

Still unsmiling, Miss Doyle walked back to Tammy Okada's front row seat and placed the big cigar box on the desktop. The whole class could hear a weighty load of contents shifting and rattling with what every boy and girl suddenly knew to be the best possible pencil-box paraphernalia anyone could ever dream of owning: stuff from the General's own hidden cave of seized treasures.

I imagined the years and years of confiscated collectibles—coloured pencils of every hue and length, mechanical pencils, pen nibs, holders, crayons, jacks, pencil sharpeners, paper cutouts, elastics, marbles, stencils, erasers, fold-away rulers, Crackerjack miniatures, maybe even a *compass*—all poured into that single box. Tammy Okada, unbelieving, ran a shy finger over the criss-crossed rubber bands.

"Tammy Okada," Miss Doyle's crisp enunciation did not falter, "your pencil box, *yes?*"

"Yes," Tammy said, in a voice so soft we barely heard it.

"*Jeez*," Elizabeth Brown breathed.

The rest of us sighed.

Miss Doyle picked up a chalk, tapped the blackboard for attention and began to teach us how to use the letter *S* to show possession. The General printed in big letters: *Alfred's book ... Sekky's cap ... Tammy's pencil box ...*

"You're all paying attention, *yes?*"

"*Yes*, Miss Doyle," we sang in unison, like soldiers.

We had learned to answer the General's tone-dipping *Yes?* or deeper *No?* with "*Yes*, Miss Doyle" or "*No*, Miss Doyle."

Jung, who had been in Miss Doyle's class many years ago, advised me not to raise my hand to answer a single question, not even if I knew the answer.

"It'll work in your favour if the General hollers your name and you surprise her with the answer."

Then up would go her ample breasts.

The girls in the class grew to admire Miss Doyle and would hold themselves high like her, chin back, sweater buttoned to the absolute top. The oldest boy, aged twelve, just arrived from Poland, would widen his eyes at Miss Doyle. "Denny"—his real name was too easy to make fun of and too hard to pronounce—liked to please Miss Doyle, too, though he, like Tammy Okada, only fitfully spoke half a dozen English phrases. Miss Doyle strapped him once, and at recess he muttered, "I kill that bitch ... I kill!" But by the next day, Denny only wanted to copy a straight line of words, neatly spaced and correctly spelled, line after tidy line. Like the rest of us, he wanted to earn the General's gold star stuck on the top of the page.

At recess, our dialects and accents conflicted, our clothes, heights and handicaps betrayed us, our skin colours and backgrounds clashed, but inside Miss E. Doyle's tightly disciplined kingdom we were all—lions or lambs—equals.

We had glimpsed Paradise.

CAT'S EYE

by Margaret Atwood

*Margaret Atwood was born in Ottawa in 1939 and
grew up in northern Quebec and Ontario. She is the
award-winning author of over forty books—novels,
short stories, poetry, literary criticism, social history,
and books for children. Atwood's work is acclaimed
internationally and has been published around the world.
She currently lives in Toronto.*

IN THIS EXTRACT FROM *Cat's Eye* (1988), the narrator's
family has recently moved from the remote countryside
to Toronto, where the father works at the University, in
a place his children call "the building." Here, eight-year-
old Elaine describes her first year at her new school.

The school we are sent to is some distance away, past a cemetery, across a ravine, along a wide curving street lined with older houses. The name of it is Queen Mary Public School. In the mornings we walk across the freezing mud in our new winter overshoes, carrying our lunches in paper bags, and down through the remains of an orchard to the nearest paved road, where we wait for the school bus to come lurching towards us, up the hill and over the pot-holes. I wear my new snowsuit, my skirt wrapped around my legs and stuffed down into the bulgy legs of the snowpants, which whisk together as I walk. You can't wear pants to school, you have to wear skirts. I'm not used to this, or to sitting still at a desk.

We eat our lunches in the chilly dimly lit cellar of the schoolhouse, where we sit in supervised rows on long scarred wooden benches under a festoon of heating pipes. Most of the children go home for lunch, it's only the school-bus ones that have to stay. We're issued small bottles of milk which we drink through straws stuck in through a hole in the cardboard bottle tops. These are my first drinking-straws, and they amaze me.

The school building itself is old and tall, made of liver-coloured brick, with high ceilings, long ominous wood-floored hallways, and radiators that are either on full blast or not at all, so that we're either shivering with cold or too hot. The windows are high and thin and many-paned, and decorated with cut-outs made of construction paper; right now there are snowflakes, for winter. There's a front door which is never used by children. At the back are two grandiose entranceways with carvings around them and ornate insets above the doors, inscribed in curvy, solemn lettering: GIRLS and BOYS. When the teacher in the yard rings her brass handbell we have to line up in twos by classrooms, girls in one line, boys in another, and file into our separate doors. The girls hold hands; the boys don't. If you go in the wrong door you get the strap, or so everyone says.

I am very curious about the BOYS door. How is going in through a door different if you're a boy? What's in there that merits the strap, just for seeing it? My brother says there's nothing special about the stairs inside, they're plain ordinary stairs. The boys don't have a separate classroom, they're in with us. They go in the BOYS door and end up in the same place we do. I can see the point of the boys' washroom, because they pee differently, and also the boys' yard, because of all the kicking and punching that goes on among them. But the door baffles me. I would like to have a look inside.

Just as there are separate doors for boys and girls, there are also separate parts of the schoolyard. At the front, outside the teachers' entrance, is a dirt field covered with cinders, the boys' playing field. At the side of the school facing away from the street is a hill, with wooden steps going up it and eroded runnels worn down the side, and a few stunted evergreens on top. By custom this is reserved for the girls, and the older ones stand around up there in groups of three or four, their heads bent inwards, whispering, although boys sometimes make charges up the hill, yelling and waving their arms. The cement-paved area outside the BOYS and GIRLS is common territory, since the boys have to cross it in order to go in their door.

Lining up is the only time I see my brother at school. At home we've rigged up a walkie-talkie with two tin cans and a piece of string, which runs between our two bedroom windows and doesn't work very well. We push messages under each other's doors, written in the cryptic language of the aliens, which is filled with X's and Z's and must be decoded. We nudge and kick each other under the table, keeping our faces straight above the tablecloth; sometimes we tie our shoe-laces together, for signalling. These are my main communications with my brother now, these raspy tin-can words, sentences without vowels, the Morse of feet.

But in the daytime I lose sight of him as soon as we go out the door. He's up ahead, throwing snowballs; and on the bus he's at the back, in a noisy whirlpool of older boys. After school, after he's gone through the fights that are required of any new boy at any school, he's off helping to wage war on the boys from the Catholic school nearby. It's called Our Lady of Perpetual Help, but the boys from our school have re-named it Our Lady of Perpetual Hell. It's said that the boys from this Catholic school are very tough and that they conceal rocks inside their snowballs.

I know better than to speak to my brother during these times, or to call his or any boy's attention to me. Boys get teased for having younger sisters, or sisters of any kind, or mothers; it's like having new clothes. When he gets anything new my brother dirties it as soon as possible, to avoid having it noticed; and if he has to go anywhere with me and my mother, he walks ahead of us or crosses to the other side of the street. If he's teased about me, he will have to fight some more. For me to contact him, or even to call him by name, would be disloyal. I understand these things, and do my best.

So I am left to the girls, real girls at last, in the flesh. But I'm not used to girls, or familiar with their customs. I feel awkward around them, I don't know what to say. I know the unspoken rules of boys, but with girls I sense that I am always on the verge of some unforeseen, calamitous blunder.

A girl called Carol Campbell makes friends with me. In a way she has to, because she's the only school-bus girl in my grade. The children who come on the school bus, who eat their lunches in the cellar instead of going home, are considered a little foreign, and are in danger of finding themselves without a partner when the bell rings and it's time to line up. So Carol sits beside me on the school bus, holds my hand in line, whispers to me, eats her lunch beside me on the wooden bench in the cellar.

Carol lives in one of the older houses on the other side of the abandoned orchard, closer to the school, a yellow brick house with two storeys and green-painted shutters framing the windows. She's a stubby girl with a frequent laugh. She tells me her hair is honey-blonde, that her haircut is called a pageboy, that she has to go the hairdresser's every two months to get it done. I haven't known there are such things as pageboys and hairdressers. My mother doesn't go to the hairdresser's. She wears her hair long, pinned up at the sides, like the women in wartime posters, and my own hair has never been cut.

Carol and her younger sister have matching outfits for Sundays: fitted brown tweed coats with velvet collars, round brown velvet hats with an elastic under the chin to hold them on. They have brown gloves and little brown purses. She tells me all this. They are Anglicans. Carol asks me what church I go to, and I say I don't know. In fact we never go to church.

After school Carol and I walk home, not the way the school bus goes in the morning but a different way, along back streets and across a decaying wooden footbridge over the ravine. We've been told not to do this alone, and not to go down into the ravine by ourselves. There might be men down there, is what Carol says. These are not ordinary men but the other kind, the shadowy, nameless kind who do things to you. She smiles and whispers when saying *men,* as if they are a special, thrilling joke. We cross the bridge lightly, avoiding the places where the boards have rotted through, on the lookout for men.

Carol invites me to her house after school, where she shows me her cupboard with all her clothes hanging in it. She has a lot of dresses and skirts; she even has a dressing-gown, with fuzzy slippers to match. I have never seen so many girls' clothes in one place.

She lets me look at her living-room from the doorway, although we aren't allowed to go into it. She herself can't go in except to practise the piano. The living-room has a sofa and two chairs and matching drapes, all of a flowered rose and beige material Carol says is chintz. She pronounces this word with awe, as if it's the name of something sacred, and I repeat it silently to myself: *chintz*. It sounds like the name of a kind of crayfish, or of one of the aliens on my brother's distant planet.

Carol tells me that her piano teacher hits her fingers with a ruler if she gets a note wrong, and that her mother spanks her with the back of a hairbrush or else a slipper. When she's really in for it she has to wait until her father comes home and whacks her with his belt, right on the bare bum. All of these things are secrets. She says her mother sings on a radio program, under a different name, and we do overhear her mother practising scales in the living-room, in a loud quavery voice. She says her father takes some of his teeth out at night and puts them into a glass of water beside his bed. She shows me the glass, although the teeth aren't in it. There seems to be nothing she won't tell.

She tells me which boys at school are in love with her, making me promise not to tell. She asks me which ones are in love with me. I've never thought about this before, but I can see that some sort of an answer is expected. I say I'm not sure.

Carol comes to my house and takes it all in—the unpainted walls, the wires dangling from the ceilings, the unfinished floors, the army cots—with incredulous glee. "This is where you *sleep*?" she says. "This is where you *eat*? These are your *clothes*?" Most of my clothes, which are not many in number, are pants and jersey tops. I have two dresses, one for summer and one for winter, and a tunic and a wool skirt, for school. I begin to suspect that more may be required.

Carol tells everyone at school that our family sleeps on the floor. She gives the impression that we do this on purpose, because we're from outside the city; that it's a belief of ours. She's disappointed when our real beds arrive from storage, four-legged and with mattresses, like everybody else's. She puts it around that I don't know what church I go to, and that we eat off a card-table. She doesn't repeat these items with scorn, but as exotic specialties. I am, after all, her lining-up partner, and she wants me to be marvelled at. More accurate: she wants herself to be marvelled at, for revealing such wonders. It's as if she's reporting on the antics of some primitive tribe: true, but incredible.

On Saturday we take Carol Campbell to the building. When we walk into it she says, wrinkling up her nose, "Is this where your father works?" We show her the snakes and the turtles; she makes a noise that sounds like "Ew," and says she wouldn't want to touch them. I'm surprised by this; I've been discouraged from having such feelings for so long that I no longer have them. Neither does Stephen. There's not much we won't touch, given the chance.

I think Carol Campbell is a sissy. At the same time I find myself being a little proud of her delicacy. My brother looks at her in an odd way: with contempt, true, and if I myself said such a thing he would make fun of me. But there's an undertone, like an invisible nod, as if something he wants to suspect has come true after all.

By rights he should ignore her after this, but he tries her out on the jars of lizards and ox eyeballs. "Ew," she says. "What if they put one down your *back*?" My brother says how would she like some for dinner? He makes chewing and slurping noises.

"Ew," says Carol, screwing up her face and wriggling all over. I can't pretend to be shocked and disgusted too: my brother wouldn't be convinced. Neither can I join in the game of making up revolting foods, such as toadburgers and leech chewing-gum, although if we were alone or with other boys I would do it without a second thought. So I say nothing.

After we get back from the building I go to Carol's house again. She asks me if I want to see her mother's new twin set. I don't know what this is, but it sounds intriguing, so I say yes. She takes me stealthily into her mother's bedroom, saying that she'll really get it if we're caught, and shows me the twin set, folded on a shelf. The twin set is just two sweaters, both the same colour, one with buttons down the front, the other without. I've already seen Mrs. Campbell wearing a different twin set, a beige one, her breasts pronging out, the buttoned sweater draped over her shoulders like a cape. So this is all twin sets are. I'm disappointed, because I was expecting something to do with twins.

Carol's mother and father don't sleep in one big bed, the way mine do. Instead they sleep in two little beds, exactly alike, with matching pink chenille bedspreads and matching night-tables. These beds are called twin beds, which makes more sense to me than the twin set. Still, it's strange to think of Mr. and Mrs. Campbell lying in them at night, with different heads—his with a moustache, hers without—but nevertheless twin-like, identical, under the sheets and blankets. It's the matching bedspreads, the night-tables, the lamps, the bureaus, the doubleness of everything in their room, that gives me this impression. My own parents' room is less symmetrical, and also less neat.

Carol says her mother wears rubber gloves while washing the dishes. She shows me the rubber gloves and a spray thing attached to the water tap. She turns on the tap and sprays the inside of the sink, and part of the floor by accident, until Mrs. Campbell comes in, wearing her beige twin set and frowning, and says hadn't we better go upstairs to play. Possibly she isn't frowning. She has a mouth that turns slightly down even when she's smiling, so it's hard to tell whether she's pleased or not. Her hair is the same colour as Carol's, but done in a cold wave all over her head. It's Carol who points out that this is a cold wave. A cold wave has nothing to do with water. It's like doll hair, very tidy and arranged, as if sewn into place.

Carol is more and more gratified the more bewildered I am. "You don't know what a *cold wave* is?" she says, delighted. She's eager to explain things to me, name them, display them. She shows me around her house as if it's a museum, as if she personally has collected everything in it. Standing in the downstairs hall, where there is a coat-tree—"You've never seen a *coat-tree*?"—she says I am her best friend.

Carol has another best friend, who is sometimes her best friend and sometimes not. Her name is Grace Smeath. Carol points her out to me, on the bus, the same way she's pointed out the twin set and the coat-tree: as an object to be admired.

Grace Smeath is a year older and in the next grade up. At school she plays with the other girls in her class. But after school and on Saturdays she plays with Carol. There are no girls in her class on our side of the ravine.

Grace lives in a two-storey shoebox-shaped red brick house with a front porch that has two thick round white pillars holding it up. She's taller than Carol, with dark thick coarse hair done into two braids. Her skin is extremely pale, like a body under a bathing-suit, but covered with freckles. She wears glasses. Usually she wears a grey skirt with two straps over the shoulders, and a red sweater pebbled with little balls of wool. Her clothes smell faintly of the Smeaths' house, a mixture of scouring powder and cooked turnips and slightly rancid laundry, and the earth under porches. I think she is beautiful.

On Saturdays I no longer go to the building. Instead I play with Carol and Grace. Because it's winter, we play mostly inside. Playing with girls is different and at first I feel strange as I do it, self-conscious, as if I'm only doing an imitation of a girl. But I soon get more used to it.

The things we play are mostly Grace's ideas, because if we try to play anything she doesn't like she says she has a headache and goes home, or else tells us to go home. She never raises her voice, gets angry, or cries; she is quietly reproachful, as if her headache is our fault. Because we want to play with her more than she wants to play with us, she gets her way in everything.

We colour in Grace's movie star colouring books, which show the movie stars in different outfits, doing different things: walking their dogs, going sailing in sailor suits, swirling around in evening dresses at parties. Grace's favourite movie star is Esther Williams. I have no favourite movie star—I've never been to a movie—but I say mine is Veronica Lake, because I like the name. The Veronica Lake book is paper-doll cutouts, with Veronica Lake in her bathing-suit and dozens of outfits you can stick on to her with tabs that fold around her neck. Grace won't let us cut out these outfits, although we can put them on and take them off once she's done it, but we're allowed to work away at her colouring books as long as we stay inside the lines. She likes to get these books all coloured in. She tells us what colours to use, on which parts. I know what my brother would do—green skin for Esther, with beetle antennae, and hairy legs for Veronica, eight of them—but I refrain from doing it. Anyway I like the clothes.

We play School. Grace has a couple of chairs and a wooden table in her cellar, and a small blackboard and chalk. These are set up underneath the indoors clothes-line where the Smeath underwear is hung up to dry when it rains or snows. The cellar isn't a finished cellar: the floor is cement, the pillars holding up the house are brick, the water pipes and wires are showing, and the air smells of coal dust because the coal bin is right beside the blackboard.

Grace is always the teacher, Carol and I the students. We have to do spelling tests and sums in arithmetic; it's like real school, but worse, because we never get to draw pictures. We can't pretend to be bad, because Grace doesn't like disorder.

Or we sit on the floor in Grace's room with piles of old Eaton's Catalogues. I've seen lots of Eaton's Catalogues before: up north they're hung in outhouses for use as toilet paper. Eaton's Catalogues remind me of the stench of such outhouses, the buzzing of the flies down the hole underneath, the box of lime and the wooden paddle for dumping the lime down, on to the piles of old and recent droppings, of all shapes and colours of brown. But here we treat these catalogues with reverence. We cut the small coloured figures out of them and paste them into scrapbooks. Then we cut out other things—cookware, furniture—and paste them around the figures. The figures themselves are always women. We call them "My lady." "My lady's going to have this refrigerator," we say. "My lady's getting this rug." "This is my lady's umbrella."

Grace and Carol look at each other's scrapbook pages and say, "Oh, yours is so good. Mine's no good. Mine's *awful*." They say this every time we play the scrapbook game. Their voices are wheedling and false; I can tell they don't mean it, each one thinks her own lady on her own page is good. But it's the thing you have to say, so I begin to say it too.

I find this game tiring—it's the weight, the accumulation of these objects, these possessions that would have to be taken care of, packed, stuffed into cars, unpacked. I know a lot about moving house. But Carol and Grace have never moved anywhere. Their ladies live in a single house each and have always lived there. They can add more and more, stuff the pages of their scrapbooks with dining-room suites, beds, stacks of towels, one set of dishes after another, and think nothing of it.

I begin to want things I've never wanted before: braids, a dressing-gown, a purse of my own. Something is unfolding, being revealed to me. I see that there's a whole world of girls and their doings that has been unknown to me, and that I can be part of it without making any effort at all. I don't have to keep up with anyone, run as fast, aim as well, make loud explosive noises, decode messages, die on cue. I don't have to think about whether I've done these things well, as well as a boy. All I have to do is sit on the floor and cut frying pans out of the Eaton's Catalogue with embroidery scissors, and say I've done it badly. Partly this is a relief.

For Christmas, Carol gives me some Friendship's Garden bath-salts and Grace gives me a colouring book of Virginia Mayo. I open their presents before anyone else's.

I also get a photo album, to go with my camera. The pages and covers are black, tied together with something that looks like a big black shoe-lace; there's a package of black triangles with glue on them to stick the photos in with. So far I have taken only one roll of film with my camera. I think about what each picture will look like as I press the button. I don't want to waste any. When the pictures come back from being developed, the negatives come too. I hold them up to the light: everything that's white in the real picture is black in the negative. Snow for instance is black, and people's eyeballs and teeth.

I stick my photos into the album with the black triangles. Some of the pictures are of my brother, making threatening gestures with snowballs. Some are of Carol, some of Grace. There's only that one picture of me, standing in front of the motel door with 9 on it, long ago, a month ago. Already that child seems much younger, poorer, farther away, a shrunken, ignorant version of myself.

Another thing I get for Christmas is a red plastic purse, oval in shape, with a gold-coloured clasp and a handle at the top end. It's soft and pliable inside the house, but hardens outside in the cold, so that things rattle in it. I keep my allowance in it, five cents a week.

By this time we have a living-room floor, hardwood, waxed by my mother down on her knees, polished with a long-handled weighted brush that she pushes back and forth, making a sound like waves. The living-room has been painted, the fixtures installed, the baseboards added on. There are even curtains; drapes, they're called. The public, visible parts of the house have been finished first.

Our bedrooms remain in a rawer state. The windows there do not yet have drapes. Lying in bed at night, I can look out of my window at the snow falling, illuminated by the light from my brother's bedroom window beside mine.

It's the darkest time of the year. Even in the daytime it seems dark; and at night, when the lights are on, this darkness pervades everything, like a fog. Outside there are only a few streetlights, and they're far apart and not very bright. The lamps in people's houses cast a yellowish light, not cold and greenish but a buttery dim yellow with a tinge of brown. The colours of things in houses have darkness mixed into them: maroon, mushroom beige, a muted green, a dusty rose. These colours look a little dirty, like the squares in a paint box when you forget to rinse the brush.

We have a maroon chesterfield which has come out of storage, with an oriental-style maroon and purple rug in front of it. We have a tri-light floor lamp. The air in the evening lamplight is coagulated, like a custard thickening; heavier sediments of light collect in the corners of the living-room. The drapes are kept closed at night, folds and folds of cloth drawn against the winter, hoarding the dim heavy light, keeping it in.

In this light I spread the evening paper out on the polished hardwood floor and rest on my knees and elbows, reading the comics. In the comics there are people with round holes for eyes, others who can hypnotize you instantly, others with secret identities, others who can stretch their faces into any shape at all. Around me is the scent of newsprint and floor wax, the bureau-drawer smell of my itchy stockings mingled with that of grimy knees, the scratchy hot smell of wool plaid and the cat-box aroma of cotton underpants. Behind me the radio plays square-dance music from the Maritimes, Don Messer and His Islanders, in preparation for the six o'clock news. The radio is of dark varnished wood with a single green eye that moves along the dial as you turn the knob. Between the stations this eye makes eerie noises from outer space. Radio waves, says Stephen.

Often, now, Grace Smeath asks me over to her house after school without asking Carol. She tells Carol there's a reason why she isn't invited: it's because of her mother. Her mother is tired, so Grace can only have one best friend over that day.

Grace's mother has a bad heart. Grace doesn't treat this as a secret, as Carol would. She says it unemotionally, politely, as if requesting you to wipe your feet on the mat; but also smugly, as if she has something, some privilege or moral superiority that the two of us don't share. It's the attitude she takes towards the rubber plant that stands on the landing halfway up her stairs. This is the only plant in Grace's house, and we aren't allowed to touch it. It's very old and has to be wiped off leaf by leaf with milk. Mrs. Smeath's bad heart is like that. It's because of this heart that we have to tiptoe, walk quietly, stifle our laughter, do what Grace says. Bad hearts have their uses; even I can see that.

Every afternoon Mrs. Smeath has to take a rest. She does this, not in her bedroom, but on the chesterfield in the living-room, stretched out with her shoes off and a knitted afghan covering her. That is how she is always to be found when we go there to play after school. We come in through the side door, up the steps to the kitchen, trying to be as quiet as possible, and into the dining-room as far as the double French doors, where we peer in through the glass panes, trying to see whether her eyes are open or closed. She's never asleep. But there's always the possibility—put into our heads by Grace, in that same factual way—that on any given day she may be dead.

Mrs. Smeath is not like Mrs. Campbell. For instance, she has no twin sets, and views them with contempt. I know this because once, when Carol was bragging about her mother's twin sets, Mrs. Smeath said, "Is that so," not as a question but as a way of making Carol shut up. She doesn't wear lipstick or face-powder, even when she goes out. She has big bones, square teeth with little gaps between them so that you can see each tooth distinctly, skin that looks rubbed raw as if scrubbed with a potato brush. Her face is rounded and bland, with that white skin of Grace's, though without the freckles. She wears glasses like Grace too, but hers have steel rims instead of brown ones. Her hair is parted down the middle and greying at the temples, braided and wound over her head into a flat hair crown crisscrossed with hairpins.

She wears print housedresses, not only in the mornings but most of the time. Over the dresses she wears bibbed aprons that sag at the bosom and make it look as if she doesn't have two breasts but only one, a single breast that goes all the way across her front and continues down until it joins her waist. She wears lisle stockings with seams, which make her legs look stuffed and sewn up the backs. She wears brown Oxfords. Sometimes, instead of the stockings, she has thin cotton socks, above which her legs rise white and sparsely haired, like a woman's moustache. She has a moustache too, though not very much of one, just a sprinkling of hairs around the corners of the mouth. She smiles a lot, with her lips closed over her large teeth; but, like Grace, she does not laugh.

She has big hands, knuckly and red from the wash. There's a lot of wash, because Grace has two younger sisters who get her skirts and blouses and also her underpants passed down to them. I'm used to getting my brother's jerseys, but not his underpants. It's these underpants, thin and grey with use, that hang dripping on the line over our heads as we sit in Grace's cellar pretending to be schoolchildren.

Before Valentine's Day we have to cut out hearts of red construction paper at school and decorate them with pieces of paper doily to stick on the tall thin windows. While I am cutting mine I think about Mrs. Smeath's bad heart. What exactly is wrong with it? I picture it hidden, underneath her woollen afghan and the billow of her apron bib, pumping in the thick fleshy darkness of the inside of her body: something taboo, intimate. It would be red, but with a reddish-black patch on it, like rot in an apple or a bruise. It hurts when I think about it. A little sharp wince of pain goes through me, as it did when I watched my brother cut his finger once on a piece of glass. But the bad heart is also compelling. It's a curiosity, a deformity. A horrible treasure.

Day after day I press my nose against the glass of the French doors, trying to see if Mrs. Smeath is still alive. This is how I will see her forever: lying unmoving, like something in a museum, with her head on the antimacassar pinned to the arm of the chesterfield, a bed pillow under her neck, the rubber plant on the landing visible behind her, turning her head to look at us, her scrubbed face, without her glasses, white and strangely luminous in the dim space, like a phosphorescent mushroom. She is ten years younger than I am now. Why do I hate her so much? Why do I care, in any way, what went on in her head?

The snow erodes, leaving the pot-holes in the roads near our house filled with muddy water. Thin bubbles of ice form across these puddles overnight; we shatter them with the heels of our boots. Icicles crash down from the eaves of roofs, and we pick them up and lick them like popsicles. We wear our mittens dangling. On the lawns, as we walk home from school, we can see damp pieces of paper under the hedges, old dog turds, crocuses poking up through the grainy, soot-coloured snow. The gutters run with brownish water; the wooden bridge over the ravine is slippery and soft and has regained its smell of rot.

Our house looks like something left over from the war: all around it spreads rubble, devastation. My parents stand in their backyard, hands on their hips, looking out over the expanse of raw mud, planning their garden. Already clumps of couch-grass are beginning to thrust up. Couch-grass can grow in anything, my father says. He also says that the contractor, the same one that flew the coop, took the dense clay from where our cellar went in and spread it around the house, over what should have been the topsoil. "An idiot as well as a crook," says my father.

My brother watches the water level in the giant hole next door, waiting for the hole to dry up so he can use it for a bunker. He would like to roof it over, with sticks and old planks, but he knows this isn't possible because the hole is too big and also he wouldn't be allowed. Instead he plans to dig a tunnel down there, into the side of the hole, and to get up and down to it by a rope ladder. He has no rope ladder, but he says he'll make one, if he can get some rope.

He and the other boys run around in the mud; large extra feet of clay stick to the soles of their boots, leaving tracks like monsters. They crouch behind the trees in the old orchard, sniping at one another, shouting:

"You're dead!"

"I am not!"

"You're dead!"

At other times they crowd into my brother's room, lying on their stomachs on his bed or on the floor, reading his huge piles of comic books. I sometimes do this too, wallowing among the pages of coloured paper, surrounded by the fuggy scent of boys. Boys don't smell the same as girls. They have a pungent, leathery, underneath smell, like old rope, like damp dogs. We keep the door closed because my mother doesn't approve of comics. The reading of comics is done in reverential silence, with now and then a few monosyllables of trade.

Comic books are what my brother is collecting now. He's always collected something. Once it was milk-bottle tops, from dozens of dairies; he carried sheaves of them around in his pockets, held together with rubber bands, and stood them up against walls and threw other milk-bottle tops at them to win more. Then it was pop-bottle tops, then cigarette cards, then sightings of licence plates from different provinces and states. There is no way of winning comic books. Instead you trade them, one good one for three or four of lesser value.

At school we make Easter eggs out of construction paper, pink and purple and blue, and stick them on to the windows. After that it's tulips, and soon there are real tulips. It seems to be a rule that the paper things always appear before the real ones.

Grace produces a long skipping rope, and she and Carol teach me how to turn it. As we turn, we chant, in monotonous minor-key voices:

Salome was a dancer, she did the hoochie kootch;
And when she did the hoochie kootch, she didn't
wear very mooch.

Grace puts one hand on her head, the other on her hip, and wiggles her bum. She does this with perfect decorum; she's wearing her pleated skirt with the straps over the shoulders. I know Salome is supposed to be more like the movie stars in our paper-doll books. I think of gauzy skirts, high heels with stars on the toes, hats covered with fruit and feathers, lifted eyebrows, pencil-thin; gaiety and excess. But Grace in her pleats and woollen straps can wipe out all that.

Our other game is ball. We play it against the side wall of Carol's house. We throw our rubber balls up against the wall and catch them as they come down, clapping and twirling in time to the chant:

Ordinary, moving, laughing, talking, one hand,
the other hand, one foot, the other foot, clap front,
clap back, back and front, front and back,
tweedle, twydle, curtsy, salute, and roundabout.

For *roundabout* you throw the ball and twirl all the way around before catching it. This is the hardest thing, harder even than the left hand.

The sun lasts longer and longer and goes down golden-red. The willow trees drop yellow catkins over the bridge; the maple keys fall twirling to the sidewalks and we split the sticky seed part and pinch the keys on to our noses. The air is warm, humid, like invisible mist. We wear cotton dresses to school, and cardigans, which we take off walking home. The old trees in the orchard are in flower, white and pink; we climb up into them, breathing in their hand-lotion smells, or we sit in the grass making chains of dandelions. We unbraid Grace's hair, which falls down her back in coarse brown ripples, and wind the chains around her head like a crown. "You're a princess," says Carol, stroking the hair. I take a picture of Grace and stick it into my photo album. There she sits, smiling primly, festooned with blossoms.

The field across from Carol's house is sprouting new houses, and in the evenings groups of children, boys and girls alike, clamber about inside them, in the fresh wood smell of shavings, walking through walls that don't yet exist, climbing ladders where there will soon be stairs. This is forbidden.

Carol won't climb to the higher floors because she's afraid. Grace won't climb either, but not because of fear: she doesn't want anybody, any boy, to see her underpants. No girl can wear slacks to school, but Grace never wears them at any time. So the two of them stay on the ground floor while I climb, up and along the beams with no ceiling covering them, up again to the attic. I sit on the top floor where there is no floor, among the rafters in this house of air, basking in the red-gold sunset, looking down. I don't think about falling. I am not yet afraid of heights.

One day someone appears in the schoolyard with a bag of marbles, and the next day everyone has them. The boys desert the boys' playground and throng into the common playground in front of the BOYS and GIRLS doors; they need to come to this side of the playground, because marbles have to be played on a smooth surface and the boys' yard is all cinders.

For marbles you're either the person setting up the target or the person shooting. To shoot you kneel down, sight, and roll your marble at the target marble like a bowling ball. If you hit it you keep it, and your own marble too. If you miss, you lose your marble. If you're setting up, you sit on the cement with your legs spread open and put a marble on a crack in front of you. It can be an ordinary marble, but these don't get many shooters, unless you offer two for one. Usually the targets are more valuable: cat's eyes, clear glass with a bloom of coloured petals in the centre, red or yellow or green or blue; puries, flawless like coloured water or sapphires or rubies; waterbabies, with undersea filaments of colour suspended in them; metal bowlies; aggies, like marbles only bigger. These exotics are passed from winner to winner. It's cheating to buy them; they have to be won.

Those with target marbles call out the names of their wares: *purie, purie, bowlie, bowlie*, the two-syllable words drawn out into a singsong, the voice descending, the way you call dogs, or children when they're lost. These cries are mournful, although they aren't meant to be. I sit that way myself, the cold marbles rolling in between my legs, gathering in my outspread skirt, calling out cat's eye, cat's eye, in a regretful tone, feeling nothing but avarice and a pleasurable horror.

The cat's eyes are my favourites. If I win a new one I wait until I'm by myself, then take it out and examine it, turning it over and over in the light. The cat's eyes really are like eyes, but not the eyes of cats. They're the eyes of something that isn't known but exists anyway; like the green eye of the radio; like the eyes of aliens from a distant planet. My favourite one is blue. I put it into my red plastic purse to keep it safe. I risk my other cat's eyes to be shot at, but not this one.

I don't collect many marbles because I'm not a very good shot. My brother is deadly. He takes five common marbles to school with him in a blue Crown Royal Whisky bag and comes back with the bag and his pockets bulging. He keeps his winnings in screw-top Crown preserving jars, donated by my mother, which he lines up on his desk. He never talks about his skill though. He just lines up the jars.

One Saturday afternoon he puts all his best marbles—his puries, his waterbabies and cat's eyes, his gems and wonders—into a single jar. He takes it down into the ravine somewhere, in under the wooden bridge, and buries it. Then he makes an elaborate treasure map of where it's buried, puts it in another jar, and buries that one too. He tells me he's done these things but he doesn't say why, or where the jars are buried.

BODY
AND SOUL

by Barbara Gowdy

*Barbara Gowdy was born in 1950 in Windsor, Ontario,
but has lived in Toronto since the age of four. She is an
internationally bestselling author and the winner of the
Marian Engel Award (1996) and the Trillium Book
Award (2007). She has also been a finalist for the
Commonwealth Writers' Prize and a repeat finalist for the
Giller Prize, the Governor General's Award, and the Rogers
Writers' Trust Fiction Prize. Barbara Gowdy was made a
Member of the Order of Canada in 2006.*

"BODY AND SOUL" IS TAKEN FROM the collection of short
stories *We So Seldom Look On Love*, published in 1992.

In the apartment building across from theirs, six storeys above the ground, a cat walks along a balcony railing.

"Cat," Julie announces, then stretches open her mouth in a pantomime of her mother screaming when there was a cat in their toilet.

"What colour is it?" Terry asks.

"Black and white."

"Oh, black and *white*." Terry's disdain is her second foster mother's disdain for black-and-white movies.

"Black and white and black and white and black and white," Julie shouts, hitting her doll on the window-ledge.

"I heard you," Terry says primly. As she turns from the window there is a sound from outside like a siren starting up. She is about to ask what was that? but instead she screams, "Aunt Bea!" because Julie has begun to make the sink-draining noise in her throat. "Aunt Bea!"

"I'm coming," Aunt Bea says, her sandals clicking into the room. Terry is bumped aside by her big hip, while Julie, who isn't having an epileptic seizure, pushes away Aunt Bea's arm.

"Now," Aunt Bea chides, but Julie slaps the pencil out of Aunt Bea's hand, then abruptly shuts up, providing a moment of dreamlike silence that signals to Aunt Bea the presence of the Lord. She feels her blood pressure draining from her temples like mercury down a thermometer. She smiles into Julie's pearl-coloured eyes and says, "I guess we had a false alarm."

Julie's features contort into an expression of ugly, inconsolable, private and measureless grief.

"You're all right now?" Aunt Bea says. She can never be sure, but she assumes that Julie is smiling back at her.

"Penny—" Julie points her doll at the window.

"Yes?" Terry says. "Penny" is what Julie calls Terry, nobody knows why.

Julie forgets what she was going to say. She begins hitting her doll on the window-pane.

"Hold your horses, I'm looking," Aunt Bea says, inserting her hand between Julie's doll and the window. She clutches the knob of the doll's head. "Good heavens," she says.

"What?" Terry cries.

Aunt Bea dips her chin to see out the top of her bifocals. "Well," she says, "there seems to be a cat lying out there in the parking lot."

"Fell," Julie says in an anguished voice.

"Oh, did it," Aunt Bea says. "Oh, dear."

"Dead," Julie says.

"No, no, I don't think so," Aunt Bea says, although

from the pool of blood and the unnatural angle of the cat's head she's thinking, Dead as a doornail.

"Is it bleeding?" Terry cries.

Aunt Bea hears, "Is it *breathing?*" and her heart constricts. It never fails to constrict Aunt Bea's heart how eagle-eyed this little blind girl imagines everybody is. "Yes," she says slowly, as if she is scrutinizing, "yes, you know, I think its chest is moving up and down."

"Is it *bleeding?*" Terry repeats. She holds her hand out.

"It is *not* moving up and down," Julie says in a severely reproachful voice.

Aunt Bea would swear that the only time Julie speaks in complete sentences is to catch her in a lie. "It's hard to tell, of course," she says.

"But is it *bleeding?*" Terry cries. The faint emanation of heat that she senses in her extended hand is Aunt Bea's blood pressure going back up.

"Nobody seems to be coming down," Aunt Bea observes to change the subject.

"You better phone the Humane's Society," Terry cries.

"I guess so," Aunt Bea says. She snatches Terry's hand and squeezes it to calm the child. "All right, I'll go call them," she says, and leaves the room.

"Is it bleeding?" Terry asks Julie. Blood concerns Terry. Eyes, she was disturbed to learn, can bleed.

"Dead," Julie says.

"*But is it bleeding, I asked.*" Terry is on the verge of tears. She wants an answer to this question even though she never relies on what Julie says. Whenever Julie answers the phone and it's a woman, she always says, "It's my mother."

"Black and white and black and white," Julie says.

Terry sighs. "I know *that*," she says, giving up.

Julie, however, is referring to the checkered dress of a woman who has run across the parking lot and is now kneeling over the cat. Mommy! Julie thinks, ecstatic, and then she knows that it is not her mother, and she chews thoughtfully on her doll's foot.

"Bleeding doesn't mean you die, though," Terry says, making her way over to her dresser. With the palm of her hand she taps the bristles of her hairbrush for the tingling sensation that reminds her of drinking Coke. Julie believes that Coke *looks* bristly. Milk, being smooth, she thinks of as round. The only thing she cannot imagine, the only thing she is prepared to be surprised by, is colour.

Terry was born nine years ago to an eighteen-year-old migrant corn detassler who left the abortion too late, mostly out of curiosity as to who the father might be. By the colour of the baby's hair, she'd know. But Terry came into the world bald and blind and with a birthmark covering most of the left side of her face, and Terry's mother walked out of the hospital that same evening. To the nurse who tried to stop her, she hollered, "I coulda had her at home and thrown her in a dumpster, ya know!"

The nurses adored Terry. She hardly ever cried; in fact, she smiled most of the time. (Some of the nurses held this up as proof that a baby's smile indicated gas; others said it proved that smiling was innate and not learned.) During the day they kept her in a bassinet at their station, on a table next to the photocopier, where it was discovered that the rhythm of the cartridge moving back and forth sent her to sleep. When she was teething, the head nurse left written orders that the copier was to be kept going for as long as Terry fretted. The head nurse, a collector and exhibitor of ethnically dressed dolls, made outfits for Terry in her spare time. Crocheted gowns, elaborately frilled, embroidered and aproned dresses, matching bows backed with tape so they could be stuck to her bald head. The other nurses bought her toys and sleepers. If an adoption agency was coming by to take her picture, they dressed her up and dabbed make-up on her birthmark to give her a fighting chance.

No couples wanted her, though. It took two years for Children's Aid to come through with just a foster mother, and even *she* was obviously reluctant. Her name was Mrs. Stubbs. "Terry won't be getting any special treatment," she informed the nurses. "My own son's asthmatic, and I treat him exactly like my daughter." She refused to take the dresses because they had to be washed by hand and ironed. "I've got better things to do than that," she said.

Such as housecleaning. In Mrs. Stubbs's house the plastic was still on the lampshades, and Terry was taught to eat cookies with a hand cupped under her chin to catch the crumbs. There were two other children—the woman's daughter, who eloped when Terry was six, and the asthmatic son, who was devoted to goldfish. Once, he let Terry put her hand in the tank to feel fish swim by. She was startled by how soft and slimy they were; she had expected the cold hardness of her foster mother's wedding band. Her foster mother admired the glass-cleaning snails but was disgusted by the goldfish going to the bathroom in the very water that passed through their gills. The bathroom in her house smelled like pine cones. Terry was slapped for leaving the top off the toothpaste, for wearing her shoes in the house, for spilling anything—those were the worst offences. Living with this foster mother, she became a high-strung child with fingers like antennae. She could extend her hand and sense if another person was in the room. By the air currents passing through her fingers, she could tell if somebody was breathing in her direction.

Terry cried her heart out when she had to leave that home for a home closer to the school for the blind, but within a few days she loved her second foster mother to death. They spent most of their time together on the couch in front of the TV, one of the foster mother's arms around Terry, the other holding the channel changer, which she used every two minutes because she wouldn't watch commercials and because "Andy of Mayberry" was the only program that didn't drive her crazy.

"Oh, right, give us a break," she'd say to the newscaster, then eliminate him. "Christ," she'd say, tapping her long nails on the wooden armrest next to Terry, "who comes *up* with this shit?"

Terry squirmed at the bad language, but the "us" flattered and enthralled her.

Her second foster mother's husband was a jolly, long-distance truck driver. He came home once a week, then left early the next morning before Terry woke up. Terry's foster mother groaned at the sound of his rig pulling into the driveway. She made him pork and beans and sat smoking and sighing at the dinner table while he relayed with his mouth full the hilarious things that he and his buddies had said to each other over their short-wave radios. Terry rarely understood the joke, but she laughed because of his infectious laugh, and then he would mess her hair and say, "You liked that, eh, Orphan Annie?" When he stopped coming home at all, she wasn't surprised. If he'd been a man on their TV, he wouldn't have lasted five seconds.

But she *was* surprised—and so distressed she began pulling out her baby-fine hair in her sleep; nests of it in her clenched fist every morning—when she learned that his disappearance meant she would have to leave.

Her third foster mother lived two blocks away. In a voice very familiar to Terry she said, "Mrs. Brodie is too formal. I don't want you calling me that. How about if you just call me Aunt Joyce."

"How about if I call you Aunt Bea?" Terry said.

"Aunt Bea?" Mrs. Brodie's dead sister was named Bea, so she was taken aback.

"From 'Andy of Mayberry.'"

Mrs. Brodie smiled. "Well, you know, I have to admit there's a resemblance. She's got a bun, though, as I recall. And I've got glasses, which I don't think she has. Plus I'm about fifty pounds fatter. But our faces are kind of the same, you know, kind of …" She touched her face.

"Old," Terry offered. She took it for granted that everybody had the same face.

"Old!" Mrs. Brodie laughed. "That's right! Old! How would you like to help me bake a pie?"

The only bad thing about living with Aunt Bea was when her granddaughter, Marcy, came to visit. The first time she came she didn't speak until she and Terry were outside in the playground, and then she said, "Everybody hates you" and pinched Terry's arm.

Until then Terry had thought Marcy was a mute. There was a mute who used to play with her first foster mother's son. Despite the fact that Marcy's breath hit Terry at face level, Terry had pictured a soft, little mute you could hold in your hand. The pinch burst Marcy into the spiky shape of a scream. "Go home!" Terry cried.

"She's *my* grandmother!" Marcy shouted. "You're the one that better go home before I kill you!"

Terry began to run. But since she had a poor sense of direction and no concept of space, "far away" meaning simply that it took longer to get there than "nearby" did, she ran in a large circle and didn't realize until a split second before Marcy shrieked in her ear that she had ended up back where she started.

"They're getting along like a house on fire," Aunt Bea said.

She and her daughter, who was Marcy's mother, were keeping watch from the apartment. The daughter was trying to unlatch the window. She glanced over at Aunt Bea and thought, Jesus Christ, she's as deaf as a post. When she got the window open, she stuck her head out and yelled, "Marcy! Don't chase her out on to the road! Marcy! Do you hear me?"

"Yes!" Marcy hollered without looking up. She was racing to get a stick she had spotted in the sandbox. Terry stood very still and oblivious, like somebody waiting for a bus.

Sighing, Aunt Bea's daughter closed the window. She could hardly blame Marcy. Suddenly there was this stray living in her granny's apartment, sleeping in the bed that used to be reserved for *her*, playing with her Barbie doll. "I wish you'd talked this over with me first," she said.

"You don't have to shout," Aunt Bea said gently.

Marcy speared the stick straight at Terry, missing her by inches. "Oh, God," Aunt Bea's daughter said. She glanced at Aunt Bea's placid face. "They say you shouldn't make any big decisions for at least a year," she said. "Now you're tied down again."

Thank the Lord, Aunt Bea thought.

"Just don't get too attached to her," her daughter said. "She could be taken away at any time."

Aunt Bea crossed her arms over the ledge of her bosom and said, "Yesterday I made meringues, and when I gave her one, you know what she said?"

"I have no idea."

Aunt Bea chuckled. "She said, 'This is good styrofoam.'"

"I can't get it out of my mind that time I came here and you'd left the burner on," her daughter said. "I'm going to worry myself sick when we're living in Saskatoon."

The idea was to get somebody full of beans like Marcy but a little older, eleven or twelve, maybe, somebody who could play with Terry and walk her to and from the school for the blind. That walk was the hardest part for Aunt Bea. The school wasn't far, just a couple of blocks, but in the mornings, until she'd been up and around for a while, her ankles were so swollen they hardly fit into her shoes.

Out of some mixup, however, the social worker brought over Julie. It was a weekday afternoon, and Terry was at school. At the social worker's recommendation Aunt Bea was waiting until she and the new girl—Esther, she had been told her name was—had met each other before she said anything to Terry. The visit was a trial. If Esther took a strong dislike to Aunt Bea (or vice versa, although Aunt Bea couldn't imagine disliking a child), then Children's Aid would come up with somebody else.

While she sat in the dining-room window keeping an eye out for the social worker's old blue Chevy, Aunt Bea busied herself with knitting a skating sweater that was gradually, in her mind, changing from Terry's to Esther's. When she saw the car, she quickly folded the knitting up and put it in the sideboard drawer, then turned to the window again. The social worker was striding around as if to open the passenger door, but it opened before she got there. Aunt Bea adjusted her bifocals to get a good look.

"Oh, my," she said out loud.

It was the name, Esther, that had misled her. She had pictured a Jewish girl—dark, undernourished ... haunted Anne Frank eyes. She had pictured a cardigan sweater several sizes too small. The girl who climbed out of the car was fat—Lord, as fat as Aunt Bea herself—and she had short white-blond hair in some kind of crazy brushcut. She headed in a beeline for the wrong apartment building. When the social worker called her back, she turned on her heel and took up a new beeline. Like a remote-control car, Aunt Bea thought. There was something else funny about that walk, though ... a looseness in the legs and torso, a struggle for co-ordination that didn't seem at all right.

"Poor thing," Aunt Bea said to herself. This was not so much sympathy as a resolute summoning of sympathy. "Poor little motherless thing."

She scarcely had the door open when the girl said, "Hi." She said it suddenly and loudly, as if to frighten Aunt Bea. Then she rolled her eyes as if she were about to black out.

"Hi! Come in! Come in!" Aunt Bea said enthusiastically, but she was thinking, "A retard," and now she really was thrown for a bit of a loop. "Don't sweat the petty things!" she said, reading the girl's sweatshirt.

"Believe me," the social worker said. "It was not *my* idea that she wear that." She took the girl's arm and turned her around.

"Pet the sweaty things," Aunt Bea read. She didn't get it.

"It belonged to her mother," the social worker said, giving Aunt Bea a confidential look.

"Oh?" Aunt Bea said.

"Come on, Julie, don't do that," the social worker said. The girl was bunching up the shirt with her fists, revealing a belly like a mound of virgin snow.

Julie? Aunt Bea thought.

"Should we take off our shoes?" the social worker asked.

"No, no," Aunt Bea said, blinking herself back into action. "Sit down anywhere. I've got shortbreads and chocolate milk, and coffee's made. Would you like some chocolate milk?" she asked. She looked at the girl and added, "Julie?"

"Coffee," Julie said loudly.

"Julie's been drinking coffee for years," the social worker said, falling into a chair. "*And* beer, *and* I shudder to think what else." The social worker was a homely, frizzy-haired woman in dungarees and work boots. "Actually *I* wouldn't mind a glass of chocolate milk," she said.

Don't sweat the petty things, Aunt Bea said to herself as she poured the coffee. Pet the sweaty things. Speaking of sweat, her body was soaked in it. "Everything's fine," she told herself. "Everything's just fine and dandy." She hummed a hymn:

> *A charge to keep I have,*
> *A God to glorify,*
> *A never-dying soul to save*
> *And fit it for the sky.*

The first thing she would do was give that crazy jailbird hair a perm.

Coming out of the kitchen, she asked Julie how old she was. Fifteen was her guess.

"Five," Julie answered.

"Five?" Aunt Bea looked at the social worker.

"Eleven," the social worker said with mild exasperation.

Aunt Bea nodded. At least Children's Aid had got *that* right. She handed Julie her coffee, and Julie immediately gulped half of it down.

"There isn't sugar in here," Julie said, holding up her mug.

Aunt Bea was startled. She cast back to a moment ago. "No, there's sugar."

"It's *not* sugar," Julie said. She looked infuriated.

"Oh!" Aunt Bea laughed. "Yes, you're right! It's Sweet'n Low!" She beamed at the social worker. "I can't tell the difference."

"Just drink it," the social worker said.

"No, no. I've got sugar." Aunt Bea hurried over to retrieve Julie's mug. She smiled into Julie's suddenly blank eyes. Pale, pale pupils, almost white. Aunt Bea had never seen eyes like that.

The social worker seemed to assume that everything was settled. "I'll bring her back Monday morning," she said after Aunt Bea had given Julie a tour of the apartment, showing her the bed she'd share with Terry, the empty dresser drawers where her clothes would go, the chair that would be hers at the dining-room table. Julie exposed her belly and rolled her eyes.

At the front door the social worker handed over a file, saying, "You might as well keep this."

"Oh, good," Aunt Bea said, as if the contents were familiar but she'd better have them just in case. When she was alone, she sat on the couch with a cup of coffee and the rest of the cookies and opened the file. How she would end up explaining Julie to people (to her daughter) was that she was floored by the coincidences, especially the coincidence of Julie's last name—Norman. "That was the clincher," Aunt Bea would say.

To see or hear her husband's name still threw weight on Aunt Bea's heart, but to see his name written next to that poor, forsaken girl's fogged up Aunt Bea's glasses. She touched under one eye, and she was crying all right. Before Norman died she wouldn't have believed it was possible to cry unbeknownst to yourself. Before Norman died she wouldn't have said that her glasses fogged from crying, although she didn't doubt that they had and she just couldn't remember. The most startling and depressing news in her life these days was what she was capable of forgetting. Well, she wouldn't forget the girl's last name, she could guarantee that. She removed her glasses, wiped them on her blouse and lifted her feet on to the coffee table.

The report was handwritten, hard to read. Under "Mother" it said either "Sally" or "Sandy" and then "38." Then there was a short, tragic biography. Sally or Sandy had an honours BA in English Literature but she also had a drug habit and a long history of arrests for possession and trafficking. She was currently serving a five- or an eight-year jail sentence. Her only other child had been born addicted to heroin and had lived just a day.

As she read, Aunt Bea shook her head in pity and amazement. It so happened that she had a cousin named Sally, who used to teach school but who lost her husband and her job due to addiction to alcohol. She died at age forty, a broken old woman.

"Heaven help her," Aunt Bea prayed for Julie's mother.

Under "Father," all it said was "Michael, 111."

"Good heavens!" Aunt Bea said. He must be a stepfather, she thought. Or maybe he was the mother's father. But still ... 111. And then she let out a whoop of laughter as she realized that what it actually said was "Ill." She laughed and laughed and had to remove her glasses and wipe them again. When she settled down she got a little irritated. What did they mean by "Ill"? Crazy? Dying? Dying from AIDS which they didn't want to say in case people were afraid to take Julie? Aunt Bea clicked her tongue to imagine so much ignorance.

She turned the page, and there was another coincidence—Julie suffered from epileptic fits. Aunt Bea's younger sister, dead thirty-four years now, had suffered from epileptic fits. Aunt Bea was handy, therefore, with a pencil. Get the tongue out of the way first, tilt back the head. Nothing to be alarmed about, so long as there were unsharpened pencils all over the house.

"Prone to temper tantrums," Aunt Bea read. "Domineering." She thought of her daughter and felt herself well prepared. "Behavioural and intellectual age," she read, "five or six." "Well …," she said dubiously. She had been very impressed by Julie's detection of Sweet'n Low.

She told Terry the news that afternoon, on their walk home from school. It wasn't until she was actually describing Julie that she recognized what a burden she was asking Terry to share. This wasn't how she had planned it at all. The brain-damaged girl she found herself bracing Terry for was a far cry from the helpful and spirited older sister she'd had in mind. She tried to brighten up the picture. "We'll have a whale of a time, though," she said, "the three of us."

"Doing what?" Terry asked.

"Oh, I don't know …" Aunt Bea thought back to when her daughter was small. "We'll take the ferry to the island," she said, although being on boats gave her heart palpitations.

Terry swept her white cane in scrupulous arcs.

"And we'll go the zoo," Aunt Bea said, although the zoo was a good fifty miles away, and Aunt Bea no longer drove a car.

"Where will she sleep?" Terry asked.

"With you. If that's all right. It's a big enough bed."

"What if she wets her pants? A boy at school who is five, he wets his pants."

"In that department, I'm sure she's eleven," Aunt Bea said, although she thought, Good point, and wondered if she shouldn't lay some plastic garbage bags under the sheet.

"Will she go to school?"

"She already goes. That school on Bleeker. You know, where the sidewalk's all cracked?"

"Will she go by herself?"

"No, I don't think so. We'll both walk her there, and then I'll take you to school."

Terry came to a stop and lifted her thin face in Aunt Bea's direction. "Your feet will kill you!" she cried, as if delivering the punch line.

"Lord," Aunt Bea said. "Lord, you're right."

Julie is holding Aunt Bea's left hand. Terry is holding Aunt Bea's right hand. The three of them take up the whole sidewalk, and oncoming people have to step out on to the road. Julie is thrilled by this, believing, as she does, that it is happening because she does not smell afraid. "Bastards and dogs can smell it when you're afraid," her mother told her. So Julie is walking with her head lowered to butt. Whenever somebody veers off the sidewalk she murmurs, "Bastard."

Eventually Aunt Bea asks, "Where's the fire?" She thinks that Julie is saying, "Faster."

"Dog," Julie says quietly—this time it's a dog that has trotted on to the road. She laughs and pulls up her dress.

"No!" Aunt Bea says.

"No!" Terry echoes, recognizing the familiar sound of Aunt Bea slapping Julie's clothing down.

"Oh-kay, oh-kay," Julie says.

"Not now," Terry says. Sometimes Julie and Terry play a game that Julie made up, where Julie chants oh-kay, oh-kay while she and Terry hold hands and swing their arms back and forth, just a bit at first, and then higher and higher until they swing them right around over their heads. Terry isn't crazy about this game, but she plays it to calm Julie. She thinks that Julie is probably blue with lines. Aunt Bea is green. Blood is red.

Aunt Bea gives them each a Life Saver, then takes their hands. The sweeps of the white cane along the sidewalk strike Aunt Bea as a blessing, a continuous sanctification of their path. "I want you both to be angels in church," she says. "It's a special day."

"I know," Terry says importantly.

Julie sucks her Life Saver and rubs Aunt Bea's wrist against her cheek.

"Do you know what?" Terry says.

"What?" Aunt Bea says.

"Julie poked the eyes out of her doll." The hole in her Life Saver has reminded her.

"Yes, I saw that," Aunt Bea says.

Julie isn't paying attention. She is remembering her mother's phone call and is daydreaming about her mother singing "Six Little Ducklings." Julie smiles at her mother, which provokes Aunt Bea, who after a year still gets Julie's smiles and grimaces confused, to say, "Listen, *I* don't give a hoot. It's *your* doll. If you want to destroy it, that's up to you."

"Just don't expect a new one!" Terry cries.

"That's right," Aunt Bea says.

"My mother has left the jail," Julie says.

"What?" Aunt Bea comes to a stop.

"She phoned yesterday. She told Penny."

"No, she didn't!" Terry cries. Her shrill laugh shoots a pain through Aunt Bea's eyes.

"Yes, she did," Julie says slowly and murderously.

"It's so funny!" Terry cries. She yanks her hand from Aunt Bea's and pats the air in an excited manner. She is wearing white felt gloves. "You know how she always says it's her mother on the phone? Well, do you know what? Yesterday the phone rang when you were in the laundry room, and I answered it, and it was a woman, and she said, 'This is Sally, is Marge ...' or somebody ... yes, it was Marge. She said, 'This is Sally, is Marge there?' And I said she had the wrong number, and then I told Julie, and she said that her mother's name is Sally."

"That's right," Aunt Bea says. "It is."

"It is," Julie says, scowling at Terry.

"But it's so funny!" Terry cries. The strap of her white plastic purse falls down her shoulder. She reaches for it and drops her cane. "No!" she screams, imagining that the dog Julie mentioned a minute ago is racing to retrieve it.

Aunt Bea picks the cane up. "Honey, that was *another* woman named Sally," she says to Julie.

Julie bunches the skirt of her dress and rolls her eyes.

"I *told* her," Terry says.

"But your mother will be out of jail one day," Aunt Bea says, tugging down Julie's dress. "And until then Penny and I want you to live with us."

Julie's face empties. She has been dazed, suddenly, by a recollection of the woman who knelt over the cat that fell from the balcony, by a recollection of the woman's black-and-white dress, exactly like her mother's. She reasons that the woman was in jail before and is now out.

"Okie dokie?" Aunt Bea says.

Julie covers her mouth with both hands, the way the woman did.

"Okie dokie," Aunt Bea answers for her.

In the middle of the sermon Aunt Bea is visited by the notion that the reason Julie calls Terry "Penny" might be that somebody, her educated mother for instance, told her about the pennies that used to be put on the eyes of the dead who, of course, can no longer see.

She gives Julie a ruminating look. Julie looks blankly back at her and begins to jerk. Before Aunt Bea understands what is happening, she kicks the pew. She swings her arm and knocks Aunt Bea's glasses off.

"Stop it!" Terry says to Julie. Aunt Bea's glasses have landed in her lap. She holds them over Julie, who has gone stiff and is slipping off the pew. Aunt Bea snatches her glasses back. "She pretending!" Terry says. "She's jealous."

"Shush!" Aunt Bea snaps. Julie begins jerking again. Aunt Bea pours out the contents of her purse but she

can't find the pencil. Finally she shoves a hymnal into
Julie's mouth, then throws her leg up and over Julie's to
stop her kicking the pew, at which point she becomes
aware that Hazel Gordimer is leading Terry into the
aisle, and that Tom Alcorn, the minister, is asking if
there's a doctor in the congregation.

"It's all right," Aunt Bea calls out. "This happens all
the time! It'll be over in a jiffy!" She smiles at the
stricken faces turned toward her. She knows it looks
worse than it is. Luckily, though, it's a short fit. With a
mighty heave, Julie relaxes her body, and Aunt Bea calls
out to Tom Alcorn, "All finished! You can carry on
now!" She looks around for Terry, but she's not there—
Hazel must have taken her outside. So she throws everything back in her purse, tugs the hymnal from Julie's
mouth and coaxes her to her feet. "Sorry," she says to
the people along the pew. "Thank you so much," she
says, referring to their prayers for Terry.

The last man in the aisle, a big man about her age,
takes her arm and walks her and Julie to the back of the
church. In the silence can be heard, clear as a bell, the
Sunday school children down in the basement singing
"All Things Bright and Beautiful." Normally, Terry and
Julie would be down there, but the topic of this
Sunday's service, "Suffer Little Children," was dedicated
to Terry, and Aunt Bea wanted her to hear it. Well, she
heard most of it. She heard her name mentioned in two
prayers. Aunt Bea runs a hand over her pounding
forehead, and the man, whose name she wishes she
could remember, gives her arm a squeeze. Oh, the
consolation of big, church-going men! Aunt Bea allows
herself to lean into him a little. Julie leans into her.

Aunt Bea looks down at her and sees what she knows in her bones is a smile.

At the door the man draws his arm away, and the three of them go outside and descend the steps toward Hazel Gordimer and Terry. Terry's eyelids are pink from crying. Suddenly Aunt Bea can't bear it that those tender lids will feel the scalpel. Letting go of one child, she goes up to the other and hugs her.

"She didn't make the sink-draining noise," Terry says coldly. "She always makes it first."

Aunt Bea is unable to recall whether Julie made that noise or not. "It was bad timing, I'll grant you that," she says. Terry wrenches free and begins to sweep the sidewalk with her cane. "Where are you going?" Aunt Bea asks. Terry approaches the man, who makes way, and then Julie, who doesn't. Terry has anticipated this, however, and she steps on to the grass one sweep before her cane would have touched Julie's shoe.

"Bastard," Julie murmurs.

"I *heard* that!" Terry says. At the stairs to the church she stops, confused—she thought she was heading in the other direction.

"Are you going back in?" Aunt Bea asks.

Terry doesn't know. She starts crying again—high, puppy-like whimpers that plunge Julie into grief and start her crying, too.

"Here we go," Aunt Bea sighs, walking over to Terry.

"Julie is stupid," Terry says.

"Oh, now," Hazel Gordimer admonishes.

"Julie has rocks in her head," Terry says.

Two days later Terry goes into the hospital. She is supremely confident. At the admission desk she asks if anyone knows a blind girl who needs an almost brand-new cane.

Aunt Bea is confident, too. The same doctor has been monitoring Terry ever since she was born, and he says she is the optimum age for the operation. He calls it a delicate but routine procedure with an extremely high success rate. "The only real worry I have," he says, "is how Terry will react to suddenly being able to see. There are always adjustment problems."

"You mean the birthmark," Aunt Bea says, getting down to brass tacks. Even though the doctor has explained to Terry how next year a plastic surgeon is going to erase the birthmark with a laser beam ("erase"—that's the word he used, as if somebody had spilled purple ink on her cheek), Aunt Bea doesn't exactly expect Terry to jump for joy the first time she looks in a mirror.

But the doctor says, "Spacial problems. An inability, in the beginning anyway, to judge depth and distances."

"Oh, well," Aunt Bea says. She has spacial problems herself, if that's the case. When she used to drive she had an awful time pulling out into traffic.

The church has arranged for a private hospital room, and members of the congregation have already filled it with flowers. Terry is exhilarated, Aunt Bea is touched, but when Aunt Bea has to go home, and Terry is lying down waiting for her dinner tray, all those bouquets surrounding that little body on the bed make Aunt Bea uneasy. Right after supper, leaving the dirty dishes on the table, she rushes back. She brings Julie this time, plus a big bag of chocolate-chip cookies, which, despite the flowers, Terry immediately smells. "I can't eat those!" she cries.

"You can't?" Aunt Bea says.

Terry gives her head the single nod that, for her, means absolutely not. "I can't eat anything till the operation. I have to have an empty stomach."

"Oh, that's right," Aunt Bea says, annoyed with herself. You'd have thought that after all of Norman's operations she'd have remembered.

Julie is still in the doorway. Although she hasn't said anything yet, Terry is aware of her. "Why are you just standing there?" she asks.

"Come on, honey, come over here and help me wolf some of these down," Aunt Bea says, dropping on to the chair and digging into the bag of cookies.

"Can Penny see?" Julie asks in her loud voice.

"Of course not!" Terry cries. "I haven't even had the operation yet!"

"In a week, Penny will be able to see," Aunt Bea says. She hoists her sore feet on to the radiator.

Julie scowls and sticks a finger in her ear. She pushes so hard that she groans.

"What's the matter?" Aunt Bea says. "Come on over here."

Julie stays where she is. She is mentally scanning Aunt Bea's apartment. She sees the hammer and nails in an apple basket on the broom-closet floor. She sees the two screwdrivers in a juice can. She moves to the bedroom and sees the hangers in the bedroom closet, and she lingers there as she remembers her mother straightening out a hanger and poking it up a hash pipe once.

Despite her bandage, Terry is sure that she is already detecting the colour red. "It's very bright," she says. "It could hurt you, even."

Colours are all she talks about. For the first time in her life she wonders what colour writing is.

"Black," Aunt Bea says. "Nine times out of ten."

Terry can't understand how it is visible in that case—she can't grasp the idea of black against white, and Aunt Bea finally gives up trying to explain. "You'll see," she says.

"*I'll* see!" Terry loves saying this. She thinks it's the cleverest joke. *She'll* see—everything will become clear to her in a few days. She takes it for granted that she will know how to read as soon as she opens a book.

She also takes it for granted that people will want to adopt her, now that she's "normal." Aunt Bea is wounded by the eagerness in her voice. In a cautiously optimistic tone she says, "They probably will." Aunt Bea realizes, of course, that more couples will be interested, but there are still the adjustment problems that the doctor mentioned. And there's the birthmark, not just the first, startling sight of it, but having to deal with the laser-beam operation and *its* aftermath—expensive lotions or infections or whatever. In Aunt Bea's experience, there's always something. She can't help feeling the faintest breath of relief when she takes into account the birthmark. She hugs Julie and says, "Don't you worry. Penny will be back home before you know it."

Julie says, "Can Penny see yet?"

She asks every ten minutes. She is also suddenly obsessed by Terry's mother. Whenever they pass a woman in the hall of their apartment building—even a woman she knows—she asks, "Is that Penny's mother?"

"How many times have I told you?" Aunt Bea says, and this becomes another worry, not Julie's questions (who can hope to fathom what goes on in that child's damaged head?) but her own impatience with them. To strengthen herself she sings "Onward, Christian Soldiers." One night she falls into such a swamp of pity over Julie's childhood that she gets out of bed and sews her a dress out of the green velvet and white silk she'd intended to make Terry a dress out of. But when she presents the dress to Julie the next morning, Julie plants her fists on her hips and says, "Throw it in the garbage." So Aunt Bea cuts the threads and turns the dress into Terry's after all. She takes it to the hospital, her intention all along being that when the bandage is removed Terry should see the colour she has decided will be her favourite.

The doctor leads Terry to a chair and asks her to sit. Aunt Bea sits at the edge of the sofa.

"I just hope the blinds are closed," Terry says.

"They are." The doctor laughs.

"She doesn't miss a trick, that one," Aunt Bea says, leaning forward to smooth Terry's dress. She regrets the white sash and trim—she thinks they give the impression that she had bandages on the brain. She startles herself by letting out an explosive sob.

"It's so gloomy in here," the nurse says sympathetically.

"Are you crying?" Terry asks. "What are you crying for?"

Aunt Bea extracts a wad of kleenex from the sleeve of her sweater. "I always cry at miracles," she says. She squeezes Terry's bony knee. Terry is so keyed up that her legs are sticking straight out like a doll's. She tucks them in fast, however, when the doctor asks if she's all set. He moves a stool in front of her, sits, then signals to the nurse, who turns a dial on the wall.

The room darkens. Everything white seems to leap out—his gown, the silk, the bandage, the moons of his fingers touching the bandage. Aunt Bea looks at the moons in her own fingers, at the kleenex. She glances up at the light, wondering if it has a special bulb. On the far wall are staves of light from the gaps between the venetian blinds.

"Oh," Terry says.

The bandage is off.

The whites of her eyes are so white.

"Do your eyes hurt?" the doctor asks.

Terry blinks. "No," she whispers. The doctor waits a moment, then raises his hand a fraction and the nurse turns the dial.

"Angels," Terry says. All she can see are dazzling slashes and spots.

Aunt Bea is overcome. "Oh, dear Lord," she sobs.

"That is light," the doctor says.

"I know," Terry agrees. Now the slashes and spots aren't so brilliant, and she is beginning to make out shapes filled in with what she realizes must be colour. Between the coloured shapes there is black.

"What else do you see?" the doctor asks.

"You," she whispers, but it is an assumption.

"What did she say?" Aunt Bea asks, wiping her fogged-up glasses.

"She sees me."

"I see you," Terry says, and now she does. That is his face. It grows, it comes closer. He is staring into one of her eyes and then the other. He is pulling down on her bottom lids. She stares back at his eyes. "An eye is greasy," she says.

When he moves his hand away, she looks down at her dress, then over at Aunt Bea, who isn't green. More startling than that, Aunt Bea's face is different from the doctor's. Men must have different faces from women, she thinks, but when she looks at the nurse, *her* face is different, too. The nurse is very tiny, only an inch high. Terry looks back at Aunt Bea and considers the gleaming lines between her eyes and her mouth. "I see your tears," she says.

"Oh, honey," Aunt Bea says.

Terry extends her hand, and though it seems to touch Aunt Bea, it doesn't. She waves it, and it brushes the doctor's face. "But—" she says, confused.

"That's what I was telling you about," the doctor says to Aunt Bea. "It's going to take her a while to judge distances." He turns to the nurse. "Let's open the blinds."

The nurse goes over to the window. Terry watches her. She expands as she approaches Terry, shrinks as she moves to the other side of the room. This is no surprise—Terry has always figured that certain people are big close up and little far away. But she had no idea that you could see behind you, that what was behind you remained visible. She twists back and forth to try to catch the space behind her in blackness.

"Stand up, why don't you," the doctor says.

Terry comes to her feet and faces the window.

"That's sky and clouds at the top part," the doctor says. "Blue sky, white clouds, and trees underneath, the green leaves of trees. These windows are tinted, so it's all a bit darker than it is really."

Terry takes a step. She stops, certain that she has reached the window. She holds out her hand, and Aunt Bea jumps up and grabs it. "Oh, honey," she says. It's all she can say.

"No," Terry says sharply, shaking Aunt Bea away. She feels better with her hand out in front of her. She takes two more steps, but she is still not at the window. Two more steps, two more. The nurse moves aside. Two more steps, and Terry's fingers hit the glass.

It is her hand that arrests her, pressed flat against the pane. "What are those cracks?" she says, referring to the wrinkles on her knuckles.

Aunt Bea is beside her. She scans the view outside. "On the building?" she asks, wondering if Terry means the lines between the bricks. "Over there?"

"No!" Terry slaps the window. She is suddenly panicky. "Where is Julie?" she says.

"At school," Aunt Bea says, putting an arm around her. "You know that, honey. You'll see her at home."

"Where's my face?" Terry says, and starts to cry.

"Okay," the doctor says. "It's a little overwhelming, isn't it, Terry?" He tells her to sit down and close her eyes. Whenever she is overwhelmed, he says, she should close her eyes for a few moments.

Terry targets the couch. She waves her hands to keep Aunt Bea from helping. She has the impression that she is walking into a picture of flat shapes and that the heat she senses radiating from Aunt Bea's body is what's causing the shapes to gradually melt from view.

Terry's hand is on her reflection in the bathroom mirror.

"That's coming off, remember," Aunt Bea says. "It'll be the same colour as the rest of your skin."

Terry's hand moves from the mirror to the fair side of her face. With the tips of her fingers she dabs herself, making what strike Aunt Bea as oddly haphazard leaps from cheekbone to jawbone to eyebrow, nose, mouth and then to the other side of her face—her cheek— where she halts for a moment.

She begins to smooth the skin there—she is testing if the birthmark wipes off. "You know what?" she says.

"What?"

"I love purple," she says wistfully.

"So do I!" Aunt Bea exclaims.

"But I thought purple would be green," Terry says. She turns her head as if her eyes were in danger of falling out. Her eyes look completely different since the operation. They seem smaller ... and older—they have the vague intensity that reminds Aunt Bea of old people listening to something difficult and new.

"Would you like to see more purple?" Aunt Bea asks.

Terry's eyes fix on Aunt Bea's left hand. "Do you know what?" she says. "I thought veins would be red."

On the bus ride home, behind oversized sunglasses to eliminate glare, Terry had studied the veins in Aunt Bea's hands. Every few minutes she carefully lifted her head to look at the other passengers and at the ads above the windows, but she didn't look out the windows, although once or twice she caught sight of her dim reflection, she recognized the movement of her own head, and the first time this happened she said, alarmed, "That's a mirror!"

Between these investigations, she had returned to her real interest—examining the back of Aunt Bea's hand. As they were walking from the bus Aunt Bea showed her how when she held her hand up for a few moments all the veins disappeared, then when she brought it back down they re-emerged and made it seem as if she were ageing fifty years in five seconds. Terry loved that. "Again," she said. "Again."

As soon as they entered the apartment, however, she impatiently pushed away Aunt Bea's hand, looked down the hall and said, "The mirror over the sink, that's a real one, isn't it?"

"Yes," Aunt Bea said warily. In the hospital, despite asking where her face was, Terry had closed her eyes every time the doctor had tried to get her to look in a mirror. "Yes," Aunt Bea said. "That's a real mirror."

"Will you hold these?" Terry asked, taking off her sunglasses. Then she made her way down to the bathroom.

Now she comes out into the hall, stops and shuts her eyes. This is how she walks—stopping every five or six steps to close her eyes and assume an expression of beseeching concentration. Aunt Bea tries to get her to put the sunglasses back on, but she says they turn off the lights. Everywhere she sees lights. In the benjamina plant, in Aunt Bea's hair, strips of light on a vase, squares and spills of light that take Aunt Bea a moment and some wilful hallucinating to discern.

Terry switches on the television. There is a face not unlike the doctor's. It upsets her when Aunt Bea says it's not him. Every time the picture changes she cries, "What's that?" although she usually figures it out before

Aunt Bea answers. After about a quarter of an hour she switches the TV off, saying, "It's too crowded." She wants to see Julie, who is being walked home from school by a neighbour.

"She'll be home at four o'clock," Aunt Bea says.

So she wants to see the kitchen clock. Aunt Bea removes it from the wall and lets her hold it. "But where's the time?" she cries, distressed.

It's the same with the Bible. "But I can't see what it says," she cries. They are sitting on Aunt Bea's bed, the Bible opened on Terry's lap to a page of all-red words, which is Jesus speaking.

Aunt Bea says, "Of course you can't, honey."

Terry closes the Bible. With an air of respectful but absolute dismissal she sets it on the bedside table. She looks down at Aunt Bea's hands. "Show me your veins," she says.

They are still in the bedroom when the apartment door opens. "In here!" Aunt Bea calls, and suddenly Julie is standing in the doorway, with Anne Forbes, from down the hall, behind her.

"Hi!" Terry says in a dreamlike voice. She knows which one is Julie, and Julie so rivets her that Anne Forbes, a tall, horse-faced woman wearing gold hoop earrings and two green combs in her red hair, is nothing but an unfocused mass of colours.

"Can Penny see yet?" Julie asks.

"I see you," Terry says. "You have blue on."

"Well," Julie sighs. She glances back at Anne Forbes. "Your mother is here."

"Oh, my goodness!" Anne Forbes trills.

"That's Mrs. Forbes," Terry says. She recognizes the voice.

"Oh-kay, oh-kay," Julie says loudly.

"For heaven's sakes, Julie, you know that's Mrs. Forbes." Clutching the edge of the dresser, Aunt Bea pulls herself to her feet.

Julie throws her head back so that she is gaping into Anne Forbes's face. "Oh-kay, oh-kay," she shouts and rolls her eyes.

"Is it a fit?" Anne Forbes asks with a jittery laugh, stepping back.

"No, no," Aunt Bea says, "she's just a bit upset." She starts to go over to Julie, but Terry stands up and begins making her way there, so Aunt Bea stays where she is.

Terry crosses to the door without a halt. Her fingers hit Julie's shoulder, and Julie, who seemed to be ignoring her, now looks at her and says, softly for Julie, "Oh-kay, oh-kay." She and Terry appear very engrossed, very dutiful as they clutch each other's hands and proceed to swing them back and forth.

There is no convincing Julie that the specialist who visits twice a week to help Terry adjust—a black woman no less—is not Terry's mother. She also can't seem to get it through her head that Terry no longer needs her to relate what's going on in the parking lot and playground next door.

"Red car," she says, and Terry glances out and says, "I know, I see it." In fact, Terry, who is making what the specialist calls astounding progress, adds, "It's a hatch-back."

"Hatch-back! Hatch-back!" Julie shouts, and continues shouting it and exposing her stomach and breasts until Terry bursts into tears.

"Julie feels abandoned," Aunt Bea explains to the woman from the newspaper, who happens to witness one of Julie's tantrums. "Of course," she adds, "Terry is high-strung."

"I can see that," the woman says. But in her "Everyone's Children" column, which advertises a different foster child each day, she decides that all she saw in terms of Terry's character was a "quick-witted, independent charmer ... a friendly and cheerful chatterbox." After a morning of arguing with herself, Aunt Bea phones the columnist up and gives her a piece of her mind. "It's only fair to paint the whole picture," she says. "I mean, it's not like there's a money-back guarantee."

"At this early stage," the columnist says, "the strategy is to stir up interest."

The interest of three couples is stirred up. For one reason or another, though, they all change their mind before even paying Terry a visit. Aunt Bea's heart breaks over these near misses, and yet she also feels as if she's been granted an eleventh-hour reprieve, and consequently she experiences attacks of guilt, such bitter attacks that she writes Ann Landers a letter signed "Possessive in Port Credit." Since she asks for a confidential response she doesn't really expect an answer—it was just a case of getting a load off of her chest. Just the same, she checks the newspaper every day, and a month later, lo and behold, there's a two-sentence response for "Possessive in P.C.," which Aunt Bea assumes must be her despite the fact that the message doesn't really add up. "Get the egg off your face, yokel," it says. "Do yourself a favour and seek counselling pronto."

What Aunt Bea does instead—what she's been doing all along—is get down on her knees and pray, three and four times a day, dimpling her forearms on the chenille coverlet she hasn't washed since Norman died because she believes she can still detect his body odour in it. Also she gives herself a penance—grateful dedication to Julie. When Terry is glued to the television or leafing through the piles of magazines the specialist brings over, Aunt Bea and Julie go down to the swings. Aunt Bea has to laugh at the two of them flailing their legs like beetles on their backs, a pair of fatsos in danger of bringing the whole set crashing down on to their heads. After a few minutes, though, Julie squirms off her swing to give Aunt Bea a push. She'd rather push than be pushed, and Lord knows she's as strong as an ox, and as dogged. If she could, she'd stand there pushing Aunt Bea all day. She pushes her so high that the chains buckle and Aunt Bea cries out.

It is always a surprise to Julie every time the specialist leaves without taking Terry with her. Then she remembers that there is a bad man over at Terry's mother's house, that's why. He's the same man who punched Julie's mother and drowned the cat in the toilet.

"When the man goes to jail," she assures Terry, "your mother will take you home."

"I don't have a mother!" Terry cries.

"When the man goes ...," Julie says, nodding. Her faith in this is invincible.

She waits for her own mother to show up. She rushes to answer the phone and the buzzer, often persuading herself that it is her mother in the lobby, so that when it's only Anne Forbes, or the specialist, or somebody else, she is incredulous. She hurries over to the window, hoping to catch sight of her mother walking away. She thinks that what happened was, her mother changed her mind. She throws herself into a fit. She swats at Aunt Bea. One day, while Aunt Bea is talking to someone out in the hall, she snatches Aunt Bea's blue sweater from the back of her chair and drops it out the window. A minute later Terry emerges from the bathroom, leans out the window and cries, "There's a little lake down there!"

"Lake! Lake!" Julie mocks her. It enrages her when Terry makes these errors. A sweater is not a lake! Terry's mother will get mad! With her shirt up around her neck, Julie struts around the living-room, enraged and growing brave. Before Aunt Bea manages to get away from her visitor, Julie has gone into the kitchen, taken a chopstick out of the cutlery drawer and stabbed it through a plastic placemat.

"No!" Terry screeches.

Julie holds the placemat up. "Oh-kay, oh-kay," she says, disappointed. The hole is so small she can't even poke her finger through.

Terry sees things that Aunt Bea has never seen before or has forgotten having seen. When the subway is leaving the station, Terry thinks it's the platform not the subway that is moving. She sees the spokes of bicycle wheels rotating in the opposite direction than they actually are. She sees faces in the trunks of a tree. The bark of a tree she compares to the back of Aunt Bea's hand. She says, "The sky comes right down to the ground"—they are

standing on the shore of the lake at the time—and Aunt
Bea thinks, It's true, the sky isn't up there at all. It is all
around us. We are *in* the sky.

"You are the Lord's little visionary," she tells Terry.

Sometimes she is happy just to be alive and a witness.
Sometimes she wants to run off with both girls to a
desert island. "Why aren't I adopted yet?" Terry
occasionally asks, not so much wounded as puzzled. "It
takes time" is Aunt Bea's lame answer, but as the weeks
pass and no more couples make inquiries, she begins to
suppose that it really does take time. She begins to lose
some of her awful anxiety and guilt.

The days settle around her, each blessed, hard-won
day. She believes she is reaping the reward of prayer—
she can sense the Lord in the apartment, keeping tabs
on her blood pressure. She tugs down Julie's shirt and
slaps down Julie's slapping hands and is no more upset
than if she was hanging laundry on a windy day and
the sheets were pelting her head. She remembers her
own daughter's tantrums at this age, her cruel tongue,
and she tells Terry, "This is nothing. This won't hurt
you."

One day, though, when Julie is stomping around the
living-room, the picture over the couch—an oil painting
of two Scotty dogs exactly like Angus and Haggis, the
litter-mates she and Norman used to have—comes
crashing down, ripping away a chunk of plaster and
missing Terry, who is looking at a magazine on the floor,
by a fraction of an inch.

After the first seconds of silence following Terry's
scream, Aunt Bea turns to Julie and says, "Bad girl." She
is so angry that her jaw trembles.

Julie throws herself on the floor and begins to punch herself in the head.

"Bad," Aunt Bea says. A sob leaps to her throat.

Terry is kneeling over the painting. It has landed face down and she seems to be trying to dig her fingers under the frame.

"Don't do that!" Aunt Bea snaps.

"But where's their backs!" Terry cries. "Where's the back of them?"

Aunt Bea has no choice except to call Fred, the superintendent, to fix the plaster. She hates doing this because Fred always acts rudely interrupted and because the first time Terry saw him after the operation, she said, "I thought you would have hair." But Fred says, "Christ, I guess I better take a look at it," and arrives with powdered plaster, which he mixes in Aunt Bea's cut-glass salad bowl. When he's done he makes Aunt Bea come out of the bathroom so that he can hold the nail up before her eyes. "You mean to tell me you were using this?" he says.

Aunt Bea fails to understand.

"You can't hang a picture that size with a half-inch nail. You got to use a screw. Drill a hole, stick in a wall plug."

"Oh, I see." Aunt Bea pats her heart. "Could you do that for me, Fred?" She doesn't own a drill. She has palpitations and gas. She has just remembered that it's her wedding anniversary. She can't get Julie, who is still lying on the floor, grimacing wildly, to so much as glance at her.

"The plaster's wet," Fred says, as if she's an idiot.

"When it's dry then," Aunt Bea says.

"I haven't got all day," he says. "I'll do it now, a couple of inches over from where you had it. Doesn't look like it was centred on the wall anyway."

He comes back with a drill. Terry covers her ears when he turns it on, but Julie scrambles to her feet and stands right next to him, so close that he lifts his elbow and orders her to back up. A few seconds later he says, "Christ, now look what you made me do." He's drilled a hole too big for the plugs he has in his pocket.

He goes back down to the basement. Terry accompanies him to the elevator so that she can press the button. Aunt Bea goes into the bathroom to take more antacid.

Julie picks up the drill.

She doesn't scream, she doesn't make a peep. When Aunt Bea hears the whirring, all she thinks is, That was fast. She comes out of the bathroom just as Terry disappears into the living-room.

Terry's scream is as high and clean as a needle.

"Oh, dear," Aunt Bea says, because she doesn't know yet what she is seeing. Julie's head jerks, as if she is sneezing. Red paint drips from her forehead. She holds the drill in both hands. Fred's drill—that's what's upsetting to Aunt Bea. Fred's paint.

Terry screams again. Right into Julie's head the scream goes, right into the hole where Julie's finger is going. Aunt Bea brings down the knick-knack holder on her way to the floor.

Everybody reassures Aunt Bea. The doctor pokes rods into a rubberized brain to demonstrate the harmless route the drill bit took and the dozen other harmless routes it might have taken. The child psychologist says that nothing short of boring the hole and sticking her finger in it was probably going to convince Julie there weren't rocks in her head. The social worker says that Julie's mother has been stunned into realizing that her parental responsibilities don't end at a cell door. Another social worker, the one who takes Julie to the group home, says that Julie should have been living with mentally disabled children all along.

But Aunt Bea doesn't let herself off the hook. When Terry leaves for school she starts remembering things that Julie said and did. Every gesture, every word seems to be a clue. Aunt Bea is appalled by the multitude of clues.

She is resigned to having Terry taken away from her as well. She is almost glad. Her daughter is right—she is too old for this, and it could have been a lot worse. When a social worker she doesn't know phones to ask if she is interested in another girl, she suspects it's a mixup and starts explaining who she is and what happened. But the social worker has heard all about it and blames Children's Aid.

"This new girl is bright," the social worker says. "The only thing is, she's missing both arms just above the elbow. She's in the process of being fitted with new artificial arms, though, and very sophisticated mechanical hands."

At supper that night, Aunt Bea tells Terry. "We don't have to have her," she says. "I'm happy enough just with you."

"I'd love to see a girl without arms!" Terry cries.

"If she lived here," Aunt Bea says, "it would involve more than just seeing her arms."

"Would her artificial arms come off?"

"I imagine so." Aunt Bea strokes the purple side of Terry's face. The birthmark is being "erased" in a month.

Terry takes Aunt Bea's hand and lifts it up. "Show me your veins," she says.

Aunt Bea holds her hand over her head for a minute, then puts it on the table. The blue rivulets emerge as if the hand is under an evil maiden-to-crone spell.

"Too bad I can't go around with my hands up in the air all the time," Aunt Bea says.

"You know what?" Terry cries. Her feverish, old-woman gaze still startles Aunt Bea a bit when it fixes on her.

"What?"

"Too bad you can't go around with your whole body up in the air!"

The girl's name is Angela; she is twelve years old. She is perky, pretty (long black hair, flirtatious brown eyes), and she performs a tap-dance routine to "Singing in the Rain," which she has on a cassette tape.

Terry is enraptured. Aunt Bea is too, but not so much because of the dance—her daughter took tap-dancing lessons. What wins Aunt Bea's heart is the sight of those two little wing-like arms flapping at one of her artificial arms (she insists on putting them on her herself), flapping and failing to grasp it, flapping and failing, and at last lining it up, slipping the stump into the socket, and clicking it in.

THE HOCKEY
SWEATER

by Roch Carrier

Roch Carrier was born in Sainte-Justine-de-Dorchester, in the Beauce region of Quebec, in 1937. He is the author of many books enjoyed by children and adults, in their original French and in English translation. Roch Carrier is a Fellow of the Royal Society of Canada, an Officer of the Order of Canada, and the holder of many honorary doctorates. He lives in Westmount, Quebec.

"THE HOCKEY SWEATER" IS TAKEN FROM *The Hockey Sweater and Other Stories*, translated by Sheila Fischman and published in 1979.

The winters of my childhood were long, long seasons. We lived in three places—the school, the church and the skating-rink—but our real life was on the skating-rink. Real battles were won on the skating-rink. Real strength appeared on the skating-rink. The real leaders showed themselves on the skating-rink. School was a sort of punishment. Parents always want to punish children and school is their most natural way of punishing us. However, school was also a quiet place where we could prepare for the next hockey game, lay out our next strategies. As for church, we found there the tranquillity of God: there we forgot school and dreamed about the next hockey game. Through our daydreams it might happen that we would recite a prayer: we would ask God to help us play as well as Maurice Richard.

We all wore the same uniform as he, the red, white and blue uniform of the Montreal Canadiens, the best

hockey team in the world; we all combed our hair in the
same style as Maurice Richard, and to keep it in place
we used a sort of glue—a great deal of glue. We laced
our skates like Maurice Richard, we taped our sticks like
Maurice Richard. We cut all his pictures out of the
papers. Truly, we knew everything about him.

On the ice, when the referee blew his whistle the two
teams would rush at the puck; we were five Maurice
Richards taking it away from five other Maurice
Richards; we were ten players, all of us wearing with the
same blazing enthusiasm the uniform of the Montreal
Canadiens. On our backs, we all wore the famous
number 9.

One day, my Montreal Canadiens sweater had
become too small; then it got torn and had holes in it.
My mother said: "If you wear that old sweater people
are going to think we're poor!" Then she did what she
did whenever we needed new clothes. She started to leaf
through the catalogue the Eaton company sent us in the
mail every year. My mother was proud. She didn't want
to buy our clothes at the general store; the only things
that were good enough for us were the latest styles from
Eaton's catalogue. My mother didn't like the order forms
included with the catalogue; they were written in
English and she didn't understand a word of it. To order
my hockey sweater, she did as she usually did; she took
out her writing paper and wrote in her gentle school-
teacher's hand: "Cher Monsieur Eaton, Would you be
kind enough to send me a Canadiens' sweater for my
son who is ten years old and a little too tall for his age
and Docteur Robitaille thinks he's a little too thin? I'm
sending you three dollars and please send me what's left

if there's anything left. I hope your wrapping will be better than last time."

Monsieur Eaton was quick to answer my mother's letter. Two weeks later we received the sweater. That day I had one of the greatest disappointments of my life! I would even say that on that day I experienced a very great sorrow. Instead of the red, white and blue Montreal Canadiens sweater, Monsieur Eaton had sent us a blue and white sweater with a maple leaf on the front—the sweater of the Toronto Maple Leafs. I'd always worn the red, white and blue Montreal Canadiens sweater; all my friends wore the red, white and blue sweater; never had anyone in my village ever worn the Toronto sweater, never had we even seen a Toronto Maple Leafs sweater. Besides, the Toronto team was regularly trounced by the triumphant Canadiens. With tears in my eyes, I found the strength to say:

"I'll never wear that uniform."

"My boy, first you're going to try it on! If you make up your mind about things before you try, my boy, you won't get very far in this life."

My mother had pulled the blue and white Toronto Maple Leafs sweater over my shoulders and already my arms were inside the sleeves. She pulled the sweater down and carefully smoothed all the creases in the abominable maple leaf on which, right in the middle of my chest, were written the words "Toronto Maple Leafs." I wept.

"I'll never wear it."

"Why not? This sweater fits you … like a glove."

"Maurice Richard would never put it on his back."

"You aren't Maurice Richard. Anyway, it isn't what's

on your back that counts, it's what you've got inside your head."

"You'll never put it in my head to wear a Toronto Maple Leafs sweater."

My mother sighed in despair and explained to me:

"If you don't keep this sweater which fits you perfectly I'll have to write to Monsieur Eaton and explain that you don't want to wear the Toronto sweater. Monsieur Eaton's an *Anglais*; he'll be insulted because he likes the Maple Leafs. And if he's insulted do you think he'll be in a hurry to answer us? Spring will be here and you won't have played a single game, just because you didn't want to wear that perfectly nice blue sweater."

So I was obliged to wear the Maple Leafs sweater. When I arrived on the rink, all the Maurice Richards in red, white and blue came up, one by one, to take a look. When the referee blew his whistle I went to take my usual position. The captain came and warned me I'd be better to stay on the forward line. A few minutes later the second line was called; I jumped on to the ice. The Maple Leafs sweater weighed on my shoulders like a mountain. The captain came and told me to wait; he'd need me later, on defence. By the third period I still hadn't played; one of the defencemen was hit in the nose with a stick and it was bleeding. I jumped on the ice: my moment had come! The referee blew his whistle; he gave me a penalty. He claimed I'd jumped on the ice when there were already five players. That was too much! It was unfair! It was persecution! It was because of my blue sweater! I struck my stick against the ice so hard it broke. Relieved, I bent down to pick up the debris. As I straightened up I saw the young vicar, on skates, before me.

"My child," he said, "just because you're wearing a new Toronto Maple Leafs sweater unlike the others, it doesn't mean you're going to make the laws around here. A proper young man doesn't lose his temper. Now take off your skates and go to the church and ask God to forgive you."

Wearing my Maple Leafs sweater I went to the church, where I prayed to God; I asked him to send, as quickly as possible, moths that would eat up my Toronto Maple Leafs sweater.

TO EVERYTHING THERE IS A SEASON

by Alistair MacLeod

Alistair MacLeod was born in North Battleford, Saskatchewan, in 1936 and moved to Cape Breton, the birthplace of his parents, when he was ten. He is the author of three collections of short stories and one novel, No Great Mischief, *which won the International IMPAC Dublin Literary Award, the Dartmouth Book Award for Fiction, the Thomas Raddall Atlantic Fiction Award, and the Trillium Award, among others. He has lived in Windsor since 1969.*

"TO EVERYTHING THERE IS A SEASON" IS TAKEN FROM *As Birds Bring Forth the Sun.*

I am speaking here of a time when I was eleven and lived with my family on our small farm on the west coast of Cape Breton. My family had been there for a long, long time and so it seemed had I. And much of that time seems like the proverbial yesterday. Yet when I speak on this Christmas 1977, I am not sure how much I speak with the voice of that time or how much in the voice of what I have since become. And I am not sure how many liberties I may be taking with the boy I think I was. For Christmas is a time of both past and present and often the two are imperfectly blended. As we step into its nowness we often look behind.

We have been waiting now, it seems, forever. Actually, it has been most intense since Halloween when the first snow fell upon us as we moved like muffled mummers upon darkened country roads. The large flakes were soft and new then and almost generous and the earth to which they fell was still warm and as yet unfrozen. They fell in silence into the puddles and into the sea where they disappeared at the moment of contact. They disappeared, too, upon touching the heated redness of our necks and hands or the faces of those who did not wear masks. We carried our pillowcases from house to house, knocking on doors to become silhouettes in the light thrown out from kitchens (white pillowcases held out by whitened forms). The snow fell between us and the doors and was transformed in shimmering golden beams. When we turned to leave, it fell upon our footprints and as the night wore on obliterated them and all the records of our movements. In the morning everything was soft and still and November had come upon us.

My brother Kenneth, who is two and a half, is unsure of his last Christmas. It is Halloween that looms largest in his memory as an exceptional time of being up late in magic darkness and falling snow. "Who are you going to dress up as at Christmas?" he asks. "I think I'll be a snowman." All of us laugh at that and tell him Santa Claus will find him if he is good and that he need not dress up at all. We go about our appointed tasks waiting for it to happen.

I am troubled myself about the nature of Santa Claus and I am trying to hang on to him in any way that I can. It is true that at my age I no longer *really* believe in him; yet I have hoped in all his possibilities as fiercely as I can, much in the same way, I think, that the drowning man waves desperately to the lights of the passing ship on the high sea's darkness. For without him, as without the man's ship, it seems our fragile lives would be so much more desperate.

My mother has been fairly tolerant of my attempted perpetuation. Perhaps because she has encountered it before. Once I overheard her speaking about my sister Anne to one of her neighbours. "I thought Anne would *believe* forever," she said. "I practically had to tell her." I have somehow always wished I had not heard her say that as I seek sanctuary and reinforcement even in an ignorance I know I dare not trust.

Kenneth, however, believes with an unadulterated fervour, and so do Bruce and Barry who are six-year-old twins. Beyond me there is Anne who is thirteen and Mary who is fifteen, both of whom seem to be leaving childhood at an alarming rate. My mother has told us that she was already married when she was seventeen, which is only two years older than Mary is now. That too seems strange to contemplate and perhaps childhood is shorter for some than it is for others. I think of this sometimes in the evenings when we have finished our chores and the supper dishes have been cleared away and we are supposed to be doing our homework. I glance sideways at my mother, who is always knitting or mending, and at my father, who mostly sits by the stove coughing quietly with his handkerchief at his mouth. He has "not been well" for over two years and has difficulty breathing whenever he moves at more than the slowest pace. He is most sympathetic of all concerning my extended hopes and says we should hang on to the good things in our lives as long as we are able. As I look at him out of the corner of my eye, it does not seem that he has many of them left. He is old, we think, at forty-two.

Yet Christmas, in spite of all the doubts of our different ages, is a fine and splendid time, and now as

we pass the midpoint of December our expectations are
heightened by the increasing coldness that has settled
down upon us. The ocean is flat and calm and along the
coast, in the scooped-out coves, has turned to an icy
slush. The brook that flows past our house is almost
totally frozen and there is only a small channel of
rushing water that flows openly at its very centre. When
we let the cattle out to drink, we chop holes with the axe
at the brook's edge so that they can drink without
venturing on to the ice.

The sheep move in and out of their lean-to shelter,
restlessly stamping their feet or huddling together in
tightly packed groups. A conspiracy of wool against
the cold. The hens perch high on their roosts with
their feathers fluffed out about them, hardly feeling it
worthwhile to descend to the floor for their few scant
kernels of grain. The pig, who has little time before
his butchering, squeals his displeasure to the cold and
with his snout tosses his wooden trough high in the
icy air. The splendid young horse paws the planking of
his stall and gnaws the wooden cribwork of his
manger.

We have put a protective barricade of spruce boughs
about our kitchen door and banked our house with
additional boughs and billows of eel grass. Still, the pail
of water we leave standing in the porch is solid in the
morning and has to be broken with the hammer. The
clothes my mother hangs on the line are frozen almost
instantly and sway and creak from their suspending
clothespins like sections of dismantled robots: the stiff-
legged rasping trousers and the shirts and sweaters with
unyielding arms outstretched. In the morning we race

from our frigid upstairs bedrooms to finish dressing around the kitchen stove.

We would extend our coldness half a continent away to the Great Lakes of Ontario so that it might hasten the Christmas coming of my oldest brother, Neil. He is nineteen and employed on the "lake boats," the long flat carriers of grain and iron ore whose season ends any day after December tenth, depending on the ice conditions. We wish it to be cold, cold on the Great Lakes of Ontario, so that he may come home to us as soon as possible. Already his cartons have arrived. They come from different places: Cobourg, Toronto, St. Catharines, Welland, Windsor, Sarnia, Sault Ste. Marie. Places that we, with the exception of my father, have never been. We locate them excitedly on the map, tracing their outlines with eager fingers. The cartons bear the lettering of Canada Steamship Lines, and are bound with rope knotted intricately in the fashion of sailors. My mother says they contain his "clothes" and we are not allowed to open them.

For us it is impossible to know the time or manner of his coming. If the lakes freeze early, he may come by train because it is cheaper. If the lakes stay open until December twentieth, he will have to fly because his time will be more precious than his money. He will hitchhike the last sixty or hundred miles from either station or airport. On our part, we can do nothing but listen with straining ears to radio reports of distant ice formations. His coming seems to depend on so many factors which are out there far beyond us and over which we lack control.

The days go by in fevered slowness until finally on the morning of December twenty-third the strange car rolls into our yard. My mother touches her hand to her lips and whispers "Thank God." My father gets up unsteadily from his chair to look through the window. Their longed-for son and our golden older brother is here at last. He is here with his reddish hair and beard and we can hear his hearty laugh. He will be happy and strong and confident for us all.

There are three other young men with him who look much the same as he. They too are from the boats and are trying to get home to Newfoundland. They must still drive a hundred miles to reach the ferry at North Sydney. The car seems very old. They purchased it in Thorold for two hundred dollars because they were too late to make any reservations, and they have driven steadily since they began. In northern New Brunswick their windshield wipers failed but instead of stopping they tied lengths of cord to the wipers' arms and passed them through the front window vents. Since that time, in whatever precipitation, one of them has pulled the cords back and forth to make the wipers function. This information falls tiredly but excitedly from their lips and we greedily gather it in. My father pours them drinks of rum and my mother takes out her mincemeat and fruitcakes she has been carefully hoarding. We lean on the furniture or look from the safety of sheltered doorways. We would like to hug our brother but are too shy with strangers present. In the kitchen's warmth, the young men begin to nod and doze, their heads dropping suddenly to their chests. They nudge each other with their feet in an attempt to keep awake. They will not stay and rest because they have come so far and tomorrow is Christmas Eve and stretches of mountains and water still lie between them and those they love.

After they leave we pounce upon our brother physically and verbally. He laughs and shouts and lifts us over his head and swings us in his muscular arms. Yet in spite of his happiness he seems surprised at the appearance of his father whom he has not seen since March. My father merely smiles at him while my mother bites her lip.

Now that he is here there is a great flurry of activity. We have left everything we could until the time he might be with us. Eagerly I show him the fir tree on the hill which I have been watching for months and marvel at how easily he fells it and carries it down the hill. We fall over one another in the excitement of decoration.

He promises that on Christmas Eve he will take us to church in the sleigh behind the splendid horse that until his coming we are all afraid to handle. And on the afternoon of Christmas Eve he shoes the horse, lifting each hoof and rasping it fine and hammering the cherry-red horseshoes into shape upon the anvil. Later he drops them hissingly into the steaming tub of water. My father sits beside him on an overturned pail and tells him what to do. Sometimes we argue with our father, but our brother does everything he says.

That night, bundled in hay and voluminous coats, and with heated stones at our feet, we start upon our journey. Our parents and Kenneth remain at home but all the rest of us go. Before we leave we feed the cattle and sheep and even the pig all that they can possibly eat so that they will be contented on Christmas Eve. Our parents wave to us from the doorway. We go four miles across the mountain road. It is a primitive logging trail and there will be no cars or other vehicles upon it. At first the horse is wild with excitement and lack of exercise and my brother has to stand at the front of the sleigh and lean backwards on the reins. Later he settles down to a trot and still later to a walk as the mountain rises before him. We sing all the Christmas songs we know and watch for the rabbits and foxes scudding across the open patches of snow and listen to the drumming of partridge wings. We are never cold.

When we descend to the country church we tie the horse in a grove of trees where he will be sheltered and not frightened by the many cars. We put a blanket over him and give him oats. At the church door the neighbours shake hands with my brother. "Hello, Neil," they say. "How is your father?"

"Oh," he says, just "Oh."

The church is very beautiful at night with its festooned branches and glowing candles and the booming, joyous sounds that come from the choir loft. We go through the service as if we are mesmerized.

On the way home, although the stones have cooled, we remain happy and warm. We listen to the creak of the leather harness and the hiss of runners on the snow and begin to think of the potentiality of presents. When we are about a mile from home the horse senses his destination and breaks into a trot and then into a confident lope. My brother lets him go and we move across the winter landscape like figures freed from a Christmas card. The snow from the horse's hooves falls about our heads like the whiteness of the stars.

After we have stabled the horse we talk with our parents and eat the meal our mother has prepared. And then I am sleepy and it is time for the younger children to be in bed. But tonight my father says to me, "We would like you to stay up with us a while," and so I stay quietly with the older members of the family.

When all is silent upstairs Neil brings in the cartons that contain his "clothes" and begins to open them. He unties the intricate knots quickly, their whorls falling away before his agile fingers. The boxes are filled with gifts neatly wrapped and bearing tags. The ones for my younger brothers say "from Santa Claus" but mine are not among them any more, as I know with certainty they will never be again. Yet I am not so much surprised as touched by a pang of loss at being here on the adult side of the world. It is as if I have suddenly moved into another room and heard a door click lastingly behind me. I am jabbed by my own small wound.

But then I look at those before me. I look at my parents drawn together before the Christmas tree. My mother has her hand upon my father's shoulder and he is holding his ever-present handkerchief. I look at my sisters who have crossed this threshold ahead of me and now each day journey farther from the lives they knew as girls. I look at my magic older brother who has come to us this Christmas from half a continent away, bringing everything he has and is. All of them are captured in the tableau of their care.

"Every man moves on," says my father quietly, and I think he speaks of Santa Claus, "but there is no need to grieve. He leaves good things behind."

A TEMPEST IN THE SCHOOL TEAPOT

by L.M. Montgomery

L.M. Montgomery was born in Prince Edward Island in 1874 and grew up there. She taught for several years in Halifax, then lived in Ontario from 1911 until her death in 1942. She was the author of Anne of Green Gables *(1908) and seven sequels. She wrote many other novels, as well as short-story collections and poems.*

IN THIS EXTRACT FROM *Anne of Green Gables*, eleven-year-old Anne has recently been adopted by Marilla and Matthew Cuthbert, a brother and sister who live on a farm in Prince Edward Island. Here, Anne goes to school on the Island for the first time.

"What a splendid day!" said Anne, drawing a long breath. "Isn't it good just to be alive on a day like this? I pity the people who aren't born yet for missing it. They may have good days, of course, but they can never have this one. And it's splendider still to have such a lovely way to go to school by, isn't it?"

"It's a lot nicer than going round by the road; that is so dusty and hot," said Diana practically, peeping into her dinner basket and mentally calculating if the three juicy, toothsome, raspberry tarts reposing there were divided among ten girls how many bites each girl would have.

The little girls of Avonlea school always pooled their lunches, and to eat three raspberry tarts all alone or even to share them only with one's best chum would have for ever and ever branded as "awful mean" the girl who did it. And yet, when the tarts were divided among ten girls you just got enough to tantalize you.

The way Anne and Diana went to school was a pretty one. Anne thought those walks to and from school with Diana couldn't be improved upon even by imagination. Going around by the main road would have been so unromantic; but to go by Lovers' Lane and Willowmere and Violet Vale and the Birch Path was romantic, if ever anything was.

Lovers' Lane opened out below the orchard at Green Gables and stretched far up into the woods to the end of the Cuthbert Farm. It was the way by which the cows were taken to the back pasture and the wood hauled home in winter. Anne had named it Lovers' Lane before she had been a month at Green Gables.

"Not that lovers ever really walk there," she explained to Marilla, "but Diana and I are reading a perfectly magnificent book and there's a Lovers' Lane in it. So we want to have one, too. And it's a very pretty name, don't you think? So romantic! We can imagine the lovers into it, you know. I like that lane because you can think out loud there without people calling you crazy."

Anne, starting out alone in the morning, went down Lovers' Lane as far as the brook. Here Diana met her, and the two little girls went on up the lane under the leafy arch of maples—"maples are such sociable trees," said Anne; "they're always rustling and whispering to you,"—until they came to a rustic bridge. Then they left the lane and walked through Mr. Barry's back field and past Willowmere. Beyond Willowmere came Violet Vale—a little green dimple in the shadow of Mr. Andrew Bell's big woods. "Of course there are no violets there now," Anne told Marilla, "but Diana says there are millions of them in spring. Oh, Marilla, can't you just imagine you see them? It actually takes away my breath. I named it Violet Vale. Diana says she never saw the beat of me for hitting on fancy names for places. It's nice to be clever at something, isn't it? But Diana named the Birch Path. She wanted to, so I let her; but I'm sure I could have found something more poetical than plain Birch Path. Anybody can think of a name like that. But the Birch Path is one of the prettiest places in the world, Marilla."

It was. Other people besides Anne thought so when they stumbled on it. It was a little narrow, twisting path, winding down over a long hill straight through Mr. Bell's woods, where the light came down sifted through so many emerald screens that it was as flawless as the heart of a diamond. It was fringed in all its length with slim young birches, white-stemmed and lissom-boughed; ferns and starflowers and wild lilies of the valley and scarlet tufts of pigeon berries grew thickly along it; and always there was a delightful spiciness in the air and music of bird calls and the murmur and laugh of wood winds in the trees overhead. Now and then you might see a rabbit skipping across the road if you were quiet— which, with Anne and Diana, happened about once in a blue moon. Down in the valley the path came out to the main road and then it was just up the spruce hill to the school.

The Avonlea school was a whitewashed building low in the eaves and wide in the windows, furnished inside with comfortable substantial old-fashioned desks that opened and shut, and were carved all over their lids with the initials and hieroglyphics of three generations of schoolchildren. The schoolhouse was set back from the road and behind it was a dusky fir wood and a brook where all the children put their bottles of milk in the morning to keep cool and sweet until dinner hour.

Marilla had seen Anne start off to school on the first day of September with many secret misgivings. Anne was such an odd girl. How would she get on with the other children? And how on earth would she ever manage to hold her tongue during school hours?

Things went better than Marilla feared, however. Anne came home that evening in high spirits.

"I think I'm going to like school here," she announced. "I don't think much of the master, though. He's all the time curling his moustache and making eyes at Prissy Andrews. Prissy is grown-up, you know. She's sixteen and she's studying for the entrance examination into Queen's Academy at Charlottetown next year. Tillie Boulter says the master is *dead gone* on her. She's got a beautiful complexion and curly brown hair and she does it up so elegantly. She sits in the long seat at the back and he sits there, too, most of the time—to explain her lessons, he says. But Ruby Gillis says she saw him writing something on her slate and when Prissy read it she blushed as red as a beet and giggled; and Ruby Gillis says she doesn't believe it had anything to do with the lesson."

"Anne Shirley, don't let me hear you talking about your teacher in that way again," said Marilla sharply. "You don't go to school to criticize the master. I guess he can teach *you* something and it's your business to learn. And I want you to understand right off that you are not to come home telling tales about him. That is something I won't encourage. I hope you were a good girl."

"Indeed I was," said Anne comfortably. "It wasn't so hard as you might imagine, either. I sit with Diana. Our seat is right by the window and we can look down to the Lake of Shining Waters. There are a lot of nice girls in school and we had scrumptious fun playing at dinner-time. It's so nice to have a lot of little girls to play with. But of course I like Diana best and always will. I *adore* Diana. I'm dreadfully far behind the others. They're all in the fifth book and I'm only in the fourth. I feel that it's a kind of a disgrace. But there's not one of them has such an imagination as I have, and I soon found that out. We had reading and geography and Canadian History and dictation today. Mr. Phillips said my spelling was disgraceful and he held up my slate so that everybody could see it, all marked over. I felt so mortified, Marilla; he might have been politer to a stranger, I think. Ruby Gillis gave me an apple and Sophia Sloane lent me a lovely pink card with 'May I see you home?' on it. I'm to give it back to her tomorrow. And Tillie Boulter let me wear her bead ring all the afternoon. Can I have some of those pearl beads off the old pincushion in the garret to make myself a ring? And oh, Marilla, Jane Andrews told me that Minnie MacPherson told her that she heard Prissy Andrews tell Sara Gillis that I had a very pretty nose. Marilla, that is the first compliment I have ever had in my life and you can't imagine what a strange feeling it gave me. Marilla, have I really a pretty nose? I know you'll tell me the truth."

"Your nose is well enough," said Marilla shortly. Secretly she thought Anne's nose was a remarkably pretty one; but she had no intention of telling her so.

That was three weeks ago and all had gone smoothly so far. And now, this crisp September morning, Anne and Diana were tripping blithely down the Birch Path, two of the happiest little girls in Avonlea.

"I guess Gilbert Blythe will be in school today," said Diana. "He's been visiting his cousins over in New Brunswick all summer and he only came home Saturday night. He's *awf'ly* handsome, Anne. And he teases the girls something terrible. He just torments our lives out."

Diana's voice indicated that she rather liked having her life tormented out than not.

"Gilbert Blythe?" said Anne. "Isn't it his name that's written up on the porch wall with Julia Bell's and a big 'Take Notice' over them?"

"Yes," said Diana, tossing her head, "but I'm sure he doesn't like Julia Bell so very much. I've heard him say he studied the multiplication table by her freckles."

"Oh, don't speak about freckles to me," implored Anne. "It isn't delicate when I've got so many. But I do think that writing take-notices up on the wall about the boys and girls is the silliest ever. I should just like to see anybody dare to write my name up with a boy's. Not, of course," she hastened to add, "that anybody would."

Anne sighed. She didn't want her name written up. But it was a little humiliating to know that there was no danger of it.

"Nonsense," said Diana, whose black eyes and glossy tresses had played such havoc with the hearts of Avonlea schoolboys that her name figured on the porch walls in half a dozen take-notices. "It's only meant as a joke. And don't you be too sure your name won't ever be written up. Charlie Sloane is *dead gone* on you. He told his mother—

his *mother*, mind you—that you were the smartest girl in school. That's better than being good-looking."

"No, it isn't," said Anne, feminine to the core. "I'd rather be pretty than clever. And I hate Charlie Sloane. I can't bear a boy with goggle eyes. If anyone wrote my name up with his I'd *never* get over it, Diana Barry. But it *is* nice to keep head of your class."

"You'll have Gilbert in your class after this," said Diana, "and he's used to being head of his class, I can tell you. He's only in the fourth book although he's nearly fourteen. Four years ago his father was sick and had to go out to Alberta for his health and Gilbert went with him. They were there three years and Gil didn't go to school hardly any until they came back. You won't find it so easy to keep head after this, Anne."

"I'm glad," said Anne quickly. "I couldn't really feel proud of keeping head of little boys and girls of just nine or ten. I got up yesterday spelling 'ebullition.' Josie Pye was head and, mind you, she peeped in her book. Mr. Phillips didn't see her—he was looking at Prissy Andrews—but I did. I just swept her a look of freezing scorn and she got as red as a beet and spelled it wrong after all."

"Those Pye girls are cheats all round," said Diana indignantly, as they climbed the fence of the main road. "Gertie Pye actually went and put her milk bottle in my place in the brook yesterday. Did you ever? I don't speak to her now."

When Mr. Phillips was in the back of the room hearing Prissy Andrews's Latin, Diana whispered to Anne:

"That's Gilbert Blythe sitting right across the aisle from you, Anne. Just look at him and see if you don't think he's handsome."

Anne looked accordingly. She had a good chance to do so, for the said Gilbert Blythe was absorbed in stealthily pinning the long yellow braid of Ruby Gillis, who sat in front of him, to the back of her seat. He was a tall boy, with curly brown hair, roguish hazel eyes, and a mouth twisted into a teasing smile. Presently Ruby Gillis started up to take a sum to the master; she fell back into her seat with a little shriek, believing that her hair was pulled out by the roots. Everybody looked at her and Mr. Phillips glared so sternly that Ruby began to cry. Gilbert had whisked the pin out of sight and was studying his history with the soberest face in the world; but when the commotion subsided he looked at Anne and winked with inexpressible drollery.

"I think your Gilbert Blythe *is* handsome," confided Anne to Diana, "but I think he's very bold. It isn't good manners to wink at a strange girl."

But it was not until the afternoon that things really began to happen.

Mr. Phillips was back in the corner explaining a problem in algebra to Prissy Andrews and the rest of the scholars were doing pretty much as they pleased, eating green apples, whispering, drawing pictures on their slates, and driving crickets, harnessed to strings, up and down the aisle. Gilbert Blythe was trying to make Anne Shirley look at him and failing utterly, because Anne was at that moment totally oblivious, not only of the very existence of Gilbert Blythe, but of every other scholar in Avonlea school and of Avonlea school itself. With her chin propped on her hands and her eyes fixed on the blue glimpse of the Lake of Shining Waters that the west window afforded, she was far away in a gorgeous dreamland, hearing and seeing nothing save her own wonderful visions.

Gilbert Blythe wasn't used to putting himself out to make a girl look at him and meeting with failure. She *should* look at him, that red-haired Shirley girl with the little pointed chin and big eyes that weren't like the eyes of any other girl in Avonlea school.

Gilbert reached across the aisle, picked up the end of Anne's long braid, held it out at arm's length, and said in a piercing whisper:

"Carrots! Carrots!"

Then Anne looked at him with a vengeance!

She did more than look. She sprang to her feet, her bright fancies fallen into cureless ruin. She flashed one indignant glance at Gilbert from eyes whose angry sparkle was swiftly quenched in equally angry tears.

"You mean, hateful boy!" she exclaimed passionately. "How dare you!"

And then—Thwack! Anne had brought her slate down on Gilbert's head and cracked it—slate, not head—clear across.

Avonlea school always enjoyed a scene. This was an especially enjoyable one. Everybody said, "Oh," in horrified delight. Diana gasped. Ruby Gillis, who was inclined to be hysterical, began to cry. Tommy Sloane let his team of crickets escape him altogether while he stared open-mouthed at the tableau.

Mr. Phillips stalked down the aisle and laid his hand heavily on Anne's shoulder.

"Anne Shirley, what does this mean?" he said angrily.

Anne returned no answer. It was asking too much of flesh and blood to expect her to tell before the whole school that she had been called "carrots." Gilbert it was who spoke up stoutly.

"It was my fault, Mr. Phillips. I teased her."

Mr. Phillips paid no heed to Gilbert.

"I am sorry to see a pupil of mine displaying such a temper and such a vindictive spirit," he said in a solemn tone, as if the mere fact of being a pupil of his ought to root out all evil passions from the hearts of small imperfect mortals. "Anne, go and stand on the platform in front of the blackboard for the rest of the afternoon."

Anne would have infinitely preferred a whipping to this punishment, under which her sensitive spirit quivered as from a whiplash. With a white, set face she obeyed. Mr. Phillips took a chalk crayon and wrote on the blackboard above her head:

"Ann Shirley has a very bad temper. Ann Shirley must learn to control her temper," and then read it out loud, so that even the primer class, who couldn't read writing, should understand it.

Anne stood there the rest of the afternoon with that legend above her. She did not cry or hang her head. Anger was still too hot in her heart for that and it sustained her amid all her agony of humiliation. With resentful eyes and passion-red cheeks she confronted alike Diana's sympathetic gaze and Charlie Sloane's indignant nods and Josie Pye's malicious smiles. As for Gilbert Blythe, she would not even look at him. She would *never* look at him again! She would never speak to him!

When school was dismissed Anne marched out with her red head held high. Gilbert Blythe tried to intercept her at the porch door.

"I'm awfully sorry I made fun of your hair, Anne," he whispered contritely. "Honest I am. Don't be mad for keeps, now."

Anne swept by disdainfully, without look or sign of hearing. "Oh, how could you, Anne?" breathed Diana as they went down the road, half reproachfully, half admiringly. Diana felt that *she* could never have resisted Gilbert's plea.

"I shall never forgive Gilbert Blythe," said Anne firmly. "And Mr. Phillips spelled my name without an *e*, too. The iron has entered into my soul, Diana."

Diana hadn't the least idea what Anne meant, but she understood it was something terrible.

"You mustn't mind Gilbert making fun of your hair," she said soothingly. "Why, he makes fun of all the girls. He laughs at mine because it's so black. He's called me a crow a dozen times; and I never heard him apologize for anything before either."

"There's a great deal of difference between being called a crow and being called carrots," said Anne with dignity. "Gilbert Blythe has hurt my feelings *excruciatingly*, Diana."

It is possible the matter might have blown over without more excruciation if nothing else had happened. But when things begin to happen they are apt to keep on.

Avonlea scholars often spent noon hour picking gum in Mr. Bell's spruce grove over the hill and across his big pasture field. From there they could keep an eye on Eben Wright's house, where the master boarded. When they saw Mr. Phillips emerging therefrom they ran to the schoolhouse; but the distance being about three times longer than Mr. Wright's lane they were very apt to arrive there, breathless and gasping, some three minutes too late.

On the following day Mr. Phillips was seized with one of his spasmodic fits of reform and announced, before going to dinner, that he should expect to find all the scholars in their seats when he returned. Anyone who came in late would be punished.

All the boys and some of the girls went to Mr. Bell's spruce grove as usual, fully intending to stay only long enough to "pick a chew." But spruce groves are seductive and yellow nuts of gum beguiling; they picked and loitered and strayed; and as usual the first thing that recalled them to a sense of the flight of time was Jimmy Glover shouting from the top of a patriarchal old spruce, "Master's coming."

The girls, who were on the ground, started first and managed to reach the schoolhouse in time, but without a second to spare. The boys, who had to wriggle hastily down from the trees, were later; and Anne, who had not been picking gum at all but was wandering happily in the far end of the grove, waist deep among the bracken, singing softly to herself, with a wreath of rice lilies on her hair as if she were some wild divinity of the shadowy places, was latest of all. Anne could run like a deer, however; run she did with the impish result that she overtook the boys at the door and was swept into the schoolhouse among them just as Mr. Phillips was in the act of hanging up his hat.

Mr. Phillips's brief reforming energy was over; he didn't want the bother of punishing a dozen pupils; but it was necessary to do something to save his word, so he looked about for a scapegoat and found it in Anne, who had dropped into her seat, gasping for breath, with her forgotten lily wreath hanging askew over one ear and giving her a particularly rakish and dishevelled appearance.

"Anne Shirley, since you seem to be so fond of the boys' company we shall indulge your taste for it this afternoon," he said sarcastically. "Take those flowers out of your hair and sit with Gilbert Blythe."

The other boys snickered. Diana, turning pale with pity, plucked the wreath from Anne's hair and squeezed her hand. Anne stared at the master as if turned to stone.

"Did you hear what I said, Anne?" queried Mr. Phillips sternly.

"Yes, sir," said Anne slowly, "but I didn't suppose you really meant it."

"I assure you I did"—still with the sarcastic inflection which all the children, and Anne especially, hated. It flicked on the raw. "Obey me at once."

For a moment Anne looked as if she meant to disobey. Then, realizing that there was no help for it, she rose haughtily, stepped across the aisle, sat down beside Gilbert Blythe, and buried her face in her arms on the desk. Ruby Gillis, who got a glimpse of it as it went down, told the others going home from school that she'd "acksually never seen anything like it—it was so white, with awful little red spots on it."

To Anne, this was as the end of all things. It was bad enough to be singled out for punishment from among a dozen equally guilty ones; it was worse still to be sent to sit with a boy; but that that boy should be Gilbert

Blythe was heaping insult on injury to a degree utterly unbearable. Anne felt that she could not bear it and it would be of no use to try. Her whole being seethed with shame and anger and humiliation.

At first the other scholars looked and whispered and giggled and nudged. But as Anne never lifted her head and as Gilbert worked fractions as if his whole soul was absorbed in them and them only, they soon returned to their own tasks and Anne was forgotten. When Mr. Phillips called the history class out Anne should have gone; but Anne did not move, and Mr. Phillips, who had been writing some verses "To Priscilla" before he called the class, was thinking about an obstinate rhyme still and never missed her. Once, when nobody was looking, Gilbert took from his desk a little pink candy heart with a gold motto on it, "You are sweet," and slipped it under the curve of Anne's arm. Whereupon Anne arose, took the pink heart gingerly between the tips of her fingers, dropped it on the floor, ground it to powder beneath her heel, and resumed her position without deigning to bestow a glance on Gilbert.

When school went out Anne marched to her desk, ostentatiously took out everything therein, books and writing tablet, pen and ink, testament and arithmetic, and piled them neatly on her cracked slate.

"What are you taking all those things home for, Anne?" Diana wanted to know, as soon as they were out on the road. She had not dared to ask the question before.

"I am not coming back to school any more," said Anne.

Diana gasped and stared at Anne to see if she meant it.

"Will Marilla let you stay home?" she asked.

"She'll have to," said Anne. "I'll *never* go to school to that man again."

"Oh, Anne!" Diana looked as if she were ready to cry. "I do think you're mean. What shall I do? Mr. Phillips will make me sit with that horrid Gertie Pye—I know he will, because she is sitting alone. Do come back, Anne."

"I'd do almost anything in the world for you, Diana," said Anne sadly. "I'd let myself be torn limb from limb if it would do you any good. But I can't do this, so please don't ask it. You harrow up my very soul."

"Just think of all the fun you will miss," mourned Diana. "We are going to build the loveliest new house down by the brook; and we'll be playing ball next week and you've never played ball, Anne. It's tremendously exciting. And we're going to learn a new song—Jane Andrews is practising it up now; and Alice Andrews is going to bring a new Pansy book next week and we're all going to read it out loud, chapter about, down by the brook. And you know you are so fond of reading out loud, Anne."

Nothing moved Anne in the least. Her mind was made up. She would not go to school to Mr. Phillips again; she told Marilla so when she got home.

"Nonsense," said Marilla.

"It isn't nonsense at all," said Anne, gazing at Marilla, with solemn, reproachful eyes. "Don't you understand, Marilla? I've been insulted."

"Insulted fiddlesticks! You'll go to school tomorrow as usual."

"Oh, no." Anne shook her head gently. "I'm not going back, Marilla. I'll learn my lessons at home and I'll be as good as I can be and hold my tongue all the time if it's possible at all. But I will not go back to school I assure you."

Marilla saw something remarkably like unyielding stubbornness looking out of Anne's small face. She understood that she would have trouble in overcoming it; but she resolved wisely to say nothing more just then.

"I'll run down and see Rachel about it this evening," she thought. "There's no use reasoning with Anne now. She's too worked up and I've an idea she can be awful stubborn if she takes the notion. Far as I can make out from her story, Mr. Phillips has been carrying matters with a rather high hand. But it would never do to say so to her. I'll just talk it over with Rachel. She's sent ten children to school and she ought to know something about it. She'll have heard the whole story, too, by this time."

Marilla found Mrs. Lynde knitting quilts as industriously and cheerfully as usual.

"I suppose you know what I've come about," she said, a little shamefacedly.

Mrs. Rachel nodded.

"About Anne's fuss in school, I reckon," she said. "Tillie Boulter was in on her way home from school and told me about it."

"I don't know what to do with her," said Marilla. "She declares she won't go back to school. I never saw a child so worked up. I've been expecting trouble ever since she started to school. I knew things were going too smooth to last. She's so high-strung. What would you advise, Rachel?"

"Well, since you've asked my advice, Marilla," said Mrs. Lynde amiably—Mrs. Lynde dearly loved to be asked for advice—"I'd just humour her a little at first, that's what I'd do. It's my belief that Mr. Phillips was in the wrong. Of course, it doesn't do to say so to the children, you know. And of course he did right to punish her yesterday for giving way to temper. But today it was different. The others who were late should have been punished as well as Anne, that's what. And I don't believe in making the girls sit with the boys for punishment. It isn't modest. Tillie Boulter was real indignant. She took Anne's part right through and said all the scholars did, too. Anne seems real popular among them, somehow. I never thought she'd take with them so well."

"Then you really think I'd better let her stay home," said Marilla in amazement.

"Yes. That is, I wouldn't say school to her again until she said it herself. Depend upon it, Marilla, she'll cool off in a week or so and be ready enough to go back of her own accord, that's what, while, if you were to make her go back right off, dear knows what freak or tantrum she'd take next and make more trouble than ever. The less fuss made the better, in my opinion. She won't miss much by not going to school, as far as *that* goes. Mr. Phillips isn't any good at all as a teacher. The order he keeps is scandalous, that's what, and he neglects the young fry and puts all his time on those big scholars he's getting ready for Queen's. He'd never have got the school for another year if his uncle hadn't been a trustee—*the* trustee, for he just leads the other two around by the nose, that's what. I declare, I don't know what education in this Island is coming to."

Mrs. Rachel shook her head, as much as to say if she were only at the head of the educational system of the Province things would be much better managed.

Marilla took Mrs. Rachel's advice and not another word was said to Anne about going back to school. She learned her lessons at home, did her chores, and played with Diana in the chilly purple autumn twilights; but when she met Gilbert Blythe on the road or encountered him in Sunday-school she passed him by with an icy contempt that was no whit thawed by his evident desire to appease her. Even Diana's efforts as a peacemaker were of no avail. Anne had evidently made up her mind to hate Gilbert Blythe to the end of life.

As much as she hated Gilbert, however, did she love Diana, with all the love of her passionate little heart, equally intense in its likes and dislikes. One evening Marilla, coming in from the orchard with a basket of apples, found Anne sitting alone by the east window in the twilight, crying bitterly.

"Whatever's the matter now, Anne?" she asked.

"It's about Diana," sobbed Anne luxuriously. "I love Diana so, Marilla. I cannot ever live without her. But I know very well when we grow up that Diana will get married and go away and leave me. And oh, what shall I do? I hate her husband—I just hate him furiously. I've been imagining it all out—the wedding and everything—Diana dressed in snowy garments, with a veil, and looking as beautiful and regal as a queen; and me the bridesmaid, with a lovely dress, too, and puffed sleeves, but with a breaking heart hid beneath my smiling face. And then bidding Diana goodbye-e-e—" Here Anne broke down entirely and wept with increasing bitterness.

Marilla turned quickly away to hide her twitching face; but it was no use; she collapsed on the nearest chair and burst into such a hearty and unusual peal of laughter that Matthew, crossing the yard outside, halted in amazement. When had he heard Marilla laugh like that before?

"Well, Anne Shirley," said Marilla as soon as she could speak, "if you must borrow trouble, for pity's sake borrow it handier home. I should think you had an imagination, sure enough."

EXTRACT FROM

IN A GLASS HOUSE

by Nino Ricci

Nino Ricci was born in 1959 in Leamington, Ontario. He has taught in Nigeria, studied in Florence, and now lives in Toronto. Nino Ricci's first novel, the bestselling Lives of the Saints, *garnered international acclaim, winning a host of awards, including the Governor General's Award for Fiction. His following three novels have continued to bring Ricci praise, nominations, and prizes. His most recent novel is* The Origin of Species. *Nino Ricci lives in Toronto with his family.*

SEVEN-YEAR-OLD VITTORIO and his half-sister have emigrated from Valle del Sole in Italy to join Vittorio's father in southwestern Ontario. They have since been joined by Vittorio's aunt, Tsia Teresa. It is 1961.

S t. Michael's Separate School, and the church attached to it, sat on Highway 3 at the eastern edge of town, just across from the old folks' home. The school itself was a plain, two-storey rectangular building with walls of white stucco, long rows of metal-framed windows looking into the classrooms, like the ones that lined the walls of the Sun Parlour Canning Factory, and a glassed-in passageway at one side connecting it to the side steps of the church. The church was in white stucco as well, with a squat, arch-windowed bell tower, a slate roof, and a façade whose only ornament was a small circle of stained glass near the peak of its gable. In the patch of lawn in front of the rectory, on a three-stepped pedestal, stood a stone statue of the archangel Michael, his body clad in the short, girded tunic of a Roman soldier and his hands holding a rusting metal cross-staff whose tip was plunged into a strange winged serpent at his feet.

From the back of our farm the stark white walls of
the church and school were partly visible across the mile
or so of flat field that separated us from Highway 3. But
the bus that carried me there and then home again took
over an hour in each direction, winding me each way
through nearly the whole of its erratic journey, up
countless concessions and sideroads in a jagged circle
that stretched as far as Goldsmith to the north and Port
Thomas to the east. In winter the sun would just be
rising when the bus pulled up in the morning and
setting when it dropped me off in the afternoon; and on
overcast days it seemed that the world the bus passed
through was one where the sun never rose at all, where
grey-limbed trees were forever shifting in the wind like
ghosts, and the fields were always puddled over or
covered with dirty patches of snow. Through this
landscape the bus moved like a cabin ship, cut off and
separate, sealed tight; but it was pleasant then, at the
beginning or end of the bus's run, when the bus was
nearly empty, to be sitting safely inside, the heater
sending a warm shaft of air under the seats while outside
the rain poured or the ground was rimed with frost.

After I got on in the morning the bus continued up
to the 12 & 13 Sideroad and then doubled back along
the 4th Concession to the highway again, following it
for a stretch and stopping at some of the new yellow
brick houses there. But finally it swung back into the
concessions and lost itself in their maze-like grid, and it
would seem then as if we had suddenly entered a new
country, with its own different unknown customs and
average citizens. The land here stretched flat and clean,
the horizon broken only by the occasional dark island of

pines or maples sitting strangely in the middle of a field, by the red or silver curves of silos, by the tall, steep gables of wooden farmhouses that stood, far from their neighbours, like lonely watchmen, their narrow windows gazing out over the endless fields that surrounded them. Toward Port Thomas the landscape changed again—we came out on to another highway and then entered at once into the town, smaller and meaner than Mersea, with only a few false-fronted stores at the four corners and then the houses growing gradually more weather-beaten and ramshackle until we came finally to the port, where dozens of fishing boats would be moored against the dock, some small and white and new, others with their paint peeling and strange names etched in red or black on their hulls, *Silver Dollar, Mayflower, The Betty Blue*. From Port Thomas we would follow the lake down into the black farmland of Point Chippewa, where the houses were more ramshackle still, their windows covered sometimes only with gritty plastic, and old farm machinery rusting outside barns and storage sheds like the remains of rotting animals.

Our driver was a man named Schultz, a big grey-eyed German with the rough swollen hands of a peasant and the large round face of a child. In the curved mirror that gave him a view to the back of the bus we could watch his movements as he drove, the way his face screwed into a grimace each time he ground up to a higher gear, the way his tongue strained against the side of his mouth when he turned a corner or rounded a curve. The older boys did imitations of him: sometimes, on cue, six or seven of them would begin squeezing imaginary clutches and shifting imaginary gears in tandem, their voices imitating the whine of the engine. At the noise, Schultz would raise his eyes to his mirror, his face darkening.

"Hey-you-boys," he'd say, in his thick, slow monotone, and one of the grade-eight boys would call out, "Sorry about that, Schultz."

Otherwise Schultz usually didn't take much notice of what went on on the bus; though sometimes, if a girl shrieked or if someone threw something out a window, he'd pull up to the side of the road suddenly and jam his emergency brake up hard, crossing his arms and leaning them into his steering wheel with an air of finality and intention. For a moment the bus would go silent; and then the boys at the back would begin their entreaties.

"Aw, we didn't mean anything by it Schultz."

"Yeah, Schultzy, give us a break, we promise we'll knock it off."

And finally Schultz would purse his lips and shake his head slowly, and we'd set off again.

When I first began riding the bus I made the mistake once of sitting in the back seat, not knowing then that only the older boys sat there. A tall, lean, black-haired boy who got on at one of the brick houses along the highway sat beside me, flashing me an odd, exaggerated grin and whipping his head back with a practised swivel to bring a long lock of hair up out of his eyes. When he'd settled into the seat he made some comment to me that I couldn't follow, that I hoped had simply been some sort of greeting. But when I didn't respond he spoke again, his face twisted now, mocking or angry. Then suddenly he seemed to understand.

"*Deutschman?*" he said. "*Auf wiedersehen? Nederlander? Italiano?*"

"*Italiano*," I said, clutching at the familiar word.

"*Ah, Italiano!*" He thumped a hand on his chest. "*Me speak Italiano mucho mucho. Me paesano.*"

When other boys got on the bus and came to the back, the black-haired boy said they were paesani as well, and each in turn smiled broadly at me and shook my hand. They tried to talk to me using their hands and their strange half-language. One of them pointed to the big silver lunchbox Tsia Teresa had packed my lunch in.

"*Mucho, mucho,*" he said, holding his hands wide in front of him. Then he pointed to me and brought his hands closer together. "*No mucho mucho.*" The other boys laughed.

The black-haired boy took the lunchbox from me and held it before him as if to admire it. Then finally he opened it and unwrapped one of the sandwiches inside, split it open, brought it to his nose to sniff it. He screwed up his face.

"*Mu-cho, mu-cho,*" he said, thrusting the sandwich away to one of the other boys and pinching his nose.

The sandwich began to pass from hand to hand. The other boys sniffed it as well, clutching at their throats, pretending to swoon into the aisle. Finally one of them glanced quickly up to the front of the bus, then slipped the sandwich out through an open window. From where I sat I saw it flutter briefly through the air and then fly apart as it struck the road.

They began to pass the second sandwich around. I tried to leap up to pull it away, but the black-haired boy's arm shot out suddenly in front of me and pinned me to the seat, and then his fist caught the side of my head hard three times in quick succession, my head pounding against the glass of the window beside me.

"*No, no, paesano.*"

I avoided the older boys after that, but I carried my humiliation with me like an open sore, always aware of it; and that awareness, more than the humiliation itself, seemed to be what gave the persecutions by the boys on the bus their meaning, what marked me. I thought there could be a way in which what they did to me, then and after, could stay outside me, have nothing to do with the kind of person I was, that I had only to find the right way to act. But each time it was the same, I'd fill with the same anger and hate, and my humiliation seemed then no longer simply a thing they did to me but something I always carried inside. The boys who picked on me had found the right way to act—they were perfectly detached, indifferent, didn't pick on me because they hated me or were angry but only because they could see the humiliation already inside me, as if I were made of glass, and if I'd been different they'd have left me alone or been friendly.

After school the boys would stake out seats for themselves and choose who they'd let sit beside them, and often then I'd have to sit with one of the girls or with George. George lived out near Goldsmith, in a rambling, broken-down farmhouse where in the fall and spring chickens and sometimes even pigs could be seen scavenging on the front lawn and in the laneway, roaming without restraint, as if they'd taken over the farm; and he had the unkempt, wild-eyed look of an idiot, his teeth gapped and protruding and his hair always awkwardly crew-cut, some patches longer than the others, some shaved too close to the skin. From up close I could see he was strangely large and robust, his hands almost the size of man's and the muscles of his arms bulging against his sleeves; but the way he hunched himself made him seem shrivelled and deformed. When he boarded the bus in the morning he'd lurch up the aisle and fling himself into one of the centre seats with a kind of satisfied violence, then huddle up tight against the window and stare out it the whole trip like someone seeing a landscape for the first time, his head turtled down into the collar of his coat.

"Hey, Georgie," the older boys would say, "tell us about the time your face caught on fire and your father beat it out with a crowbar."

Sometimes then he'd glance furtively toward the back of the bus. But his face would be screwed up in what seemed like a grin, as if he were shyly pleased that the boys were paying attention to him, or as if he hadn't understood them at all, had only turned at the sound of his name. The girls and the younger boys made fun of him as well, crossing their fingers and drawing away from the aisle when he got on the bus and passing on Georgie-germs if he should brush against them. Usually George seemed not to notice them; but once when a girl drew away as he was coming up the aisle he lunged toward her suddenly and made a face, and afterwards he seemed strangely pleased at what he'd done, settling into his seat with an air of impish self-satisfaction.

My own feeling about George was simply that I didn't want to be like him, didn't want other people to think I was like him; but whenever I was forced to sit beside him I'd feel a kind of rage build in me at his stupidity and strangeness. When other kids had to sit with him they'd call attention to themselves by making fun of him or by touching other people in the seats around them to pass on his germs. But I couldn't do these things, didn't have the right feeling inside to do them, and I knew my failure made me seem more like George to the others, even made me, in a way, more despicable than he was, because George was protected at least by the severity of his strangeness, had no one beneath him whom the others expected him to make fun of. I'd cross my legs under the seat sometimes the way the others crossed their fingers, furtively though, so that not even George would know I'd done it. But this useless concession made me feel worse than if I'd done nothing at all, made me think that it was only fear that kept me from making fun of George, fear that George too was stronger than I was, because of the way he flung himself into his seat each morning with a force that wasn't angry or bitter but almost carefree and gay, or the way he hummed quietly to himself sometimes as he stared out the window as if even he guarded some secret place inside him, a place that was his alone and could not be touched.

At school we went from the bus to the church, a sudden shift from the bus's strange containment into the wider containment of St. Michael's, the little world it formed with its huddled white buildings, its chain-link fence, its special logic and rules. Sister Jackson, the vice-principal, presided over our arrival from the bottom of the church steps; two other sisters stood at the fonts at the foot of the aisle. The girls sat in the left-hand pews, the boys in the right, in order of class, our heads rising in a gradual slope toward the back of the church. During the service the sisters on duty hovered in the side aisles like sentries; some of them, the older ones, carried long wooden pointers, and reached out quick and silent to rap you on the back of the neck if you whispered to your neighbour or fell asleep.

The church rose up to a high, arched roof that gave it the sense of an emptiness that couldn't be filled, that hung over us during the service as if we'd made no impression in it. In the church in Valle del Sole the pews had stood so close to the altar you could see the beads of sweat on Father Nicola's upper lip as he preached; but here the chancel was raised up four steps from the nave, separated from it by the low marble rail where people knelt for communion and by the wide expanse of the transept. The altar, of green and brown marble, was flanked by two ceiling-high mosaics of sworded angels, one clad in purple and the other in blue, staring out at us each morning like stony sentinels; for a long time I thought that the purple one, his feet wrapped in the coils of a serpent, was not Michael but Lucifer, so stern did he seem, so defiant, that he was challenging Michael across from him as in the primal battle of the angels in heaven.

The services alternated between Father Mackinnon, the school principal, brisk and nimble and efficient, and Monsignor Phelan. With the monsignor the service seemed to go on forever, because he was old and spoke in a slow monotone, and because there were long pauses between each portion of the service while his finger scanned the lines of his great red missal. At the end, when he etched a sign of the cross in the air with a trembling hand, the church seemed almost to hum with suppressed energy. But I didn't mind those morning services, the crackly thin drone of the monsignor's voice over the loudspeakers, the high, arched hollowness of the church, because the church seemed the one place where my language wasn't held against me, and I could relax into the familiar sounds of the Latin responses like a fist slowly opening. Sometimes when we sang or recited together I'd feel that I'd crawled up out of myself and into the sound of our voices, that I was floating inside them above the pews as pure and unburdened as air; and then in the hush afterwards a pleasant aloneness would settle around me, make me feel for an instant as if everything inside the church existed only for me, the tall stained-glass windows that the sun lit up like candy and that dappled the pews with coloured light, the stations of the cross that hung like tiny sculpted worlds along the walls of the nave, the candle-glasses for the dead that flickered red and blue on their tiered metal stands in the transepts. There were always some candles burning there when we came in for morning service—perhaps the sisters lit them, though it was odd to think that the sisters, too, might have their own dead to remember.

Afterwards we walked single file to our classrooms, past the glass showcase in the main hall housing ribbons and silver trophies, past the portraits of Queen Elizabeth and Pope John that hung near the principal's office like a benevolent mother and father, past the big bulletin board that the sisters and the older classes did up every month with pictures and art, on religious themes or on topics like Switzerland or Christopher Columbus. It always made me feel strangely warmed to see these things, as if they could protect me somehow, and to see how the sun glinted brightly off the floor and varnished desktops of our classroom, how the blackboards had been scrubbed clean and fresh pieces of white and coloured chalk had been lined up in the ledges. There seemed a mystery in things then, a sleepy morningtime promise, beautiful and frail as the stillness that settled over the school after a bell had rung; but it teased me like a remembered smell and then passed, seeming to hold itself from the day.

I'd been put back two years, to the first grade. Every morning our teacher, Sister Bertram, stood before us as we sang "God Save the Queen" as tall and straight-backed as the angels on the chancel wall of the church, then clapped her hands twice when we'd finished to make us sit and stretched her thin lips into a smile that held no warmth in it. For the first week or so that I was in her class I spent the first lesson of the day in the corner for failing her morning inspection of ears and hands, my own hands still cracked and discoloured from working in the fields; and after that I seemed to become that first person she'd seen me as, perpetually delinquent, always the example of error. I'd track dirt into the classroom, let my attention wander, went so far once as to fall asleep at my desk; and then suddenly Sister Bertram's voice would ring out with the strange name she had for me.

"*Vic-tur!*"

And her anger would seem to focus in on me like a light beam, as if she were inviting the other children to see how different they were from me.

If I'd been more intelligent, more myself somehow, Sister Bertram might have been kinder; but everything about me proclaimed my ignorance, from my stained hands to my awkward clothes to my large hulking conspicuousness amidst the other children in the class. When I talked I couldn't get my mouth around the simplest sounds, felt my tongue stumble against my palate as if swollen and numb; when we did assignments my exercise book was always filled with the same hopeless errors, though Sister Bertram had explained a dozen times, so that sometimes she'd take a ruler in hand and simply rip out whole pages from it with a single swift jerk. And I didn't pay attention: even though I knew that Sister Bertram would catch me out, that I wouldn't learn if I didn't pay attention, still I couldn't stop my mind from wandering, because the moment Sister Bertram began to talk I'd feel the classroom slipping away from me the way a dream did in the first moments of wakefulness, and I couldn't force myself then to hold the world in focus, to try to get inside the meaning of Sister Bertram's words. I'd stare out the window sometimes at the old folks' home across the street, drawn there perhaps merely because it was different from the school, with its dying ivy and coloured leaves, its tall, spired turret like a tower in a fairy tale, the old people who came out stooped to the gazebo and benches; sometimes a face would be etched in a window against a whispery curtain and I'd imagine the lives inside, this other world going on beyond us, the old women and men stretched out on their beds with their tired faces and withered limbs.

Then in the spring Sister Bertram fell ill and was replaced by someone new to the school, Sister Mary. Sister Mary was not much taller than the grade-eight boys, with a pale round face that seemed held in the circle of her wimple like a moon; yet she gave the impression of being larger somehow than Sister Bertram, transforming the room with the simple bright force of her energy. Her first day she taught us to sing "He's Got the Whole World," coming around to each of our desks and bending to hear if we'd got the words right. When she came to my own I thought she would simply shake her head at my garbled English and move on, as Sister Bertram had always done; but instead she paused and crouched down beside me, with a smile that seemed so friendly and well-intentioned, so misdirected, that I flushed in embarrassment.

"*E di-fficile, no, parlare in-glese*," she said.

I thought she was trying to trick me in some way or that she didn't know she shouldn't speak Italian in the classroom because she was new; but the class had fallen silent.

"*Sì*," I said, still awaiting laughter that didn't come; and in the reverent silence afterwards it seemed the first time in that classroom that the air itself hadn't felt malevolent and strange, something set against me.

I began to spend lunch hours with Sister Mary studying English. With her lessons and explanations English began to open before me like a new landscape, and as it took shape in me it seemed that I myself was slowly being called back into existence from some darkness I'd fallen into, that I'd been no one till I'd had the words to be understood. Later on, when I saw how I continued to make mistakes, how my tongue still refused to form around certain sounds and how my brain still fought to make sense of the things people said, it seemed that I hadn't learned English at all, hadn't got inside it, or that I could never see any more than a part of it, would always feel lost in it the way I felt in the flat countryside that surrounded Mersea; but that initial surge of understanding was like a kind of arrival, the first sense I'd had of the possibility of me beyond the narrow world of our farm.

For reading practice Sister Mary gave me a book called *The Guiding Light* that told the story of the bible in pictures and captions. At home I'd sit with it at the kitchen table and slowly sound out the captions, its English easier for me now than the long-worded Italian of the *Lives of the Saints* I'd brought from Italy, and its stories seeming more important because they came from the bible and were in English. Scattered throughout it were colour pictures by famous painters, gloomy and strangely rendered and harsh, the beheading of John the Baptist, the blinding of Samson, the judgement of the woman who'd sinned. But I couldn't pierce their mysteries, preferred the more rustic pictures that went with the stories, the sense they gave of a world that was magical and benign. I read the stories through and then I went back to some of them, the story of creation, with its double-paged picture of Eden, the story of Jonah, of the young Christ in the temple; and I took a special furtive pleasure at making these stories my own, at entering into them as into some secret private world.

That pleasure seemed to draw something at first from the lunch hours I spent with Sister Mary, from the quiet closeness the empty classroom took on then, the warmth that lingered in my shoulder after she'd placed a hand there, the way her clothes rustled intimately when she leaned in beside me as if she were about to whisper to me some secret about herself. But after a few weeks students from other grades began to join us in these lunch-hour sessions—a yellow-haired Belgian girl kids teased because she never talked, a boy who'd failed grade three and been expelled once for smoking, a boy from grade eight, Tony Lemieux, who was taller than Sister Mary and who'd been to reform school—till finally there were more than a dozen of us, even George from my bus route, Sister Mary moving among us all with a democratic efficiency, assigning us each our separate tasks; and I began to nurse a small resentment toward Sister Mary then, angry that I'd been grouped with people like George and the Belgian girl, that Sister Mary didn't see how we all hated each other, hated having our strangeness multiplied and reflected back at us. Even Tony Lemieux, who was tall and broad-shouldered and whose nose was set back in his face so that his nostrils stared out like second eyes, appeared awkward and small among us, coming into class every day with the same defeated lope, as if being put in with us had stripped his infamy of its distinction; and I didn't understand why the other teachers thought he was bad or why he'd been to reform school when he didn't seem strong enough inside to be mean like some of the boys on the bus were, seemed merely crippled and out of place like the rest of us. Because he was too big for the grade-one desks Sister Mary had him sit up at hers while he worked; and occasionally she'd have him help her put things up on the bulletin board, standing beside him then and handing him things one by one with an odd intimacy and trust. But whenever Sister Mary was near him Tony would twist his shoulders awkwardly like an animal trying to shake off a yoke, and it seemed that Sister Mary didn't understand how things were with him, how her attention humiliated him. She'd make me think then of my Aunt Teresa, whose energy appeared to wrap her so safely in its tight space sometimes that it held other people out like a wall, and of Father Mackinnon the school principal. Father Mackinnon came to the grade-one class about once a week to talk to us and ask us questions, smiling even when we got the answers wrong, his trim greying hair and blue eyes giving him a look of infinite compassion and wisdom. But in the schoolyard I saw how he'd laugh and joke with the same boys who picked on me on the bus, because they played on the school teams he coached, and his kindness then seemed merely a sort of stupidity, something that kept him from seeing the things that were most important about people.

Or perhaps I was the one who missed what was important, the simple goodness of Father Mackinnon, of Sister Mary, a way things were that my own contamination kept me from understanding. There seemed a realm of things other people took for granted that I couldn't enter somehow, that appeared to reside in the school's ordinariness, the mystery of it, the bulletin boards, the varnished desks, the games children played at recess, some normal life unfolding there untroubled and pure that remained as foreign and unknown to me, as inaccessible, as the first dull sounds of Sister Bertram's

English; and it was my own failure to enter it that accounted somehow for the casual insults in the schoolyard, the sudden quick elbows in my ribs on the bus, the fear I carried always now that behind every simple gesture was the threat of some new humiliation. But still sometimes the same small bright hope would surge in me that everything could magically change, be different, that all these things that held me out could finally offer up their essences, reveal some secret about themselves that would take away my humiliation and hate, that would bring me up into the warm, sure sphere of their goodness the way Jesus cured the lepers in *The Guiding Light*, and brought Lazarus back from the dead.

CORNET AT NIGHT

by Sinclair Ross

*Sinclair Ross was born in 1908 on a homestead near
Prince Albert, Saskatchewan. After dropping out of high
school, Ross worked in banking, first in Saskatchewan,
then in Winnipeg and Montreal, until his retirement
in 1968. He served with the Canadian army from 1942
to 1946. Ross was the author of four novels and two
short-story collections. His novel* As for Me and
My House *(1941) is regarded as a Canadian classic.
Sinclair Ross died in 1995.*

"CORNET AT NIGHT" IS TAKEN FROM the short-story
collection *The Lamp at Noon and Other Stories.*

The wheat was ripe and it was Sunday. "Can't help it I've got to cut," my father said at breakfast. "No use talking. There's a wind again and it's shelling fast."

"Not on the Lord's Day," my mother protested. "The horses stay in the stables where they belong. There's church this afternoon and I intend to ask Louise and her husband home for supper."

Ordinarily my father was a pleasant, accommodating little man, but this morning his wheat and the wind had lent him sudden steel. "No, today we cut," he met her evenly. "You and Tom go to church if you want to. Don't bother me."

"If you take the horses out today I'm through—I'll never speak to you again. And this time I mean it."

He nodded. "Good—if I'd known I'd have started cutting wheat on Sundays years ago."

"And that's no way to talk in front of your son. In the years to come he'll remember."

There was silence for a moment and then, as if in its clash with hers his will had suddenly found itself, my father turned to me.

"Tom, I need a man to stook for a few days and I want you to go to town tomorrow and get me one. The way the wheat's coming along so fast and the oats nearly ready too I can't afford the time. Take old Rock. You'll be safe with him."

But ahead of me my mother cried, "That's one thing I'll not stand for. You can cut your wheat or do anything else you like yourself, but you're not interfering with him. He's going to school tomorrow as usual."

My father bunched himself and glared at her. "No, for a change he's going to do what I say. The crop's more important than a day at school."

"But Monday's his music lesson day—and when will we have another teacher like Miss Wiggins who can teach him music too?"

"A dollar for lessons and the wheat shelling! When I was his age I didn't even get to school."

"Exactly," my mother scored, "and look at you today. Is it any wonder I want him to be different?"

He slammed out at that to harness his horses and cut his wheat, and away sailed my mother with me in her wake to spend an austere half-hour in the dark, hot, plushy little parlour. It was a kind of vicarious atonement, I suppose, for we both took straight-backed leather chairs, and for all of the half-hour stared across the room at a big pansy-bordered motto on the opposite wall: *As for Me and My House We Will Serve the Lord.*

At last she rose and said, "Better run along and do your chores now, but hurry back. You've got to take your bath and change your clothes, and maybe help a little getting dinner for your father."

There was a wind this sunny August morning, tanged with freedom and departure, and from his stall my pony Clipper whinnied for a race with it. Sunday or not, I would ordinarily have had my gallop anyway, but today a sudden welling-up of social and religious conscience made me ask myself whether one in the family like my father wasn't bad enough. Returning to the house, I merely said that on such a fine day it seemed a pity to stay inside. My mother heard but didn't answer. Perhaps her conscience too was working. Perhaps after being worsted in the skirmish with my father, she was in no mood for granting dispensations. In any case I had to take my bath as usual, put on a clean white shirt, and change my overalls for knicker corduroys.

They squeaked, those corduroys. For three months now they had been spoiling all my Sundays. A sad, muted, swishing little squeak, but distinctly audible. Every step and there it was, as if I needed to be oiled. I had to wear them to church and Sunday-school; and after service, of course, while the grown-ups stood about gossiping, the other boys discovered my affliction. I sulked and fumed, but there was nothing to be done. Corduroys that had cost four-fifty simply couldn't be thrown away till they were well worn-out. My mother warned me that if I started sliding down the stable roof, she'd patch the seat and make me keep on wearing them.

With my customary little bow-legged sidle I slipped into the kitchen again to ask what there was to do. "Nothing but try to behave like a Christian and a gentleman," my mother answered stiffly. "Put on a tie, and shoes and stockings. Today your father is just about as much as I can bear."

"And then what?" I asked hopefully. I was thinking that I might take a drink to my father, but dared not as yet suggest it.

"Then you can stay quiet and read—and afterwards practise your music lesson. If your Aunt Louise should come she'll find that at least I bring my son up decently."

It was a long day. My mother prepared the midday meal as usual, but, to impress upon my father the enormity of his conduct, withdrew as soon as the food was served. When he was gone, she and I emerged to take our places at the table in an atmosphere of unappetizing righteousness. We didn't eat much. The food was cold, and my mother had no heart to warm it up. For relief at last she said, "Run along and feed the chickens while I change my dress. Since we aren't going to service today we'll read Scripture for a while instead."

And Scripture we did read, Isaiah, verse about, my mother in her black silk dress and rhinestone brooch, I in my corduroys and Sunday shoes that pinched. It was a very august afternoon, exactly like the tone that had persisted in my mother's voice since breakfast time. I think I might have openly rebelled, only for the hope that by compliance I yet might win permission for the trip to town with Rock. I was inordinately proud that my father had suggested it, and for his faith in me forgave him even Isaiah and the plushy afternoon. Whereas with my mother, I decided, it was a case of downright bigotry.

We went on reading Isaiah, and then for a while I played hymns on the piano. A great many hymns—even the ones with awkward sharps and accidentals that I'd never tried before—for, fearing visitors, my mother was resolved to let them see that she and I were uncontaminated by my father's sacrilege. But among these likely visitors was my Aunt Louise, a portly, condescending lady married to a well-off farmer with a handsome motor-car, and always when she came it was my mother's vanity to have me play for her a waltz or reverie, or *Holy Night* sometimes with variations. A man-child and prodigy might eclipse the motor-car. Presently she roused herself, and pretending mild reproof began, "Now, Tommy, you're going wooden on those hymns. For a change you'd better practise *Sons of Liberty*. Your Aunt Louise will want to hear it, anyway."

There was a fine swing and vigour in this piece, but it was hard. Hard because it was so alive, so full of youth and head-high rhythm. It was a march, and it did march. I couldn't take time to practise at the hard spots slowly till I got them right, for I had to march too. I had to let my fingers sometimes miss a note or strike one wrong. Again and again this afternoon I started carefully, resolving to count right through, the way Miss Wiggins did, and as often I sprang ahead to lead my march a moment or two all dash and fire, and then fall stumbling in the bitter dust of dissonance. My mother didn't know. She thought that speed and perseverance would eventually get me there. She tapped her foot and smiled encouragement, and gradually as the afternoon wore on began to look a little disappointed that there were to be no visitors, after all. "Run along for the cows," she said at last, "while I get supper ready for your father. There'll be nobody here, so you can slip into your overalls again."

I looked at her a moment, and then asked: "What am I going to wear to town tomorrow? I might get grease or something on the corduroys."

For while it was always my way to exploit the future, I liked to do it rationally, within the limits of the sane and probable. On my way for the cows I wanted to live the trip to town tomorrow many times, with variations, but only on the explicit understanding that tomorrow there was to be a trip to town. I have always been tethered to reality, always compelled by an unfortunate kind of probity in my nature to prefer a bare-faced disappointment to the luxury of a future I have no just claims upon.

I went to town the next day, though not till there had been a full hour's argument that paradoxically enough gave all three of us the victory. For my father had his way: I went; I had my way: I went; and in return for her consent my mother wrung a promise from him of a pair of new plush curtains for the parlour when the crop was threshed, and for me the metronome that Miss Wiggins declared was the only way I'd ever learn to keep in time on marching pieces like the *Sons of Liberty*.

It was my first trip to town alone. That was why they gave me Rock, who was old and reliable and philosophic enough to meet motor-cars and the chance locomotive on an equal and even somewhat supercilious footing.

"Mind you pick somebody big and husky," said my father as he started for the field. "Go to Jenkins' store, and he'll tell you who's in town. Whoever it is, make sure he's stooked before."

"And mind it's somebody who looks like he washes himself," my mother warned, "I'm going to put clean sheets and pillowcases on the bunkhouse bed, but not for any dirty tramp or hobo."

By the time they had both finished with me there were a great many thinks to mind. Besides repairs for my father's binder, I was to take two crates of eggs each containing twelve dozen eggs to Mr. Jenkins' store and in exchange have a list of groceries filled. And to make it complicated, both quantity and quality of some of the groceries were to be determined by the price of eggs. Thirty cents a dozen, for instance, and I was to ask for coffee at sixty-five cents a pound. Twenty-nine cents a dozen and coffee at fifty cents a pound. Twenty-eight and no oranges. Thirty-one and bigger oranges. It was like decimals with Miss Wiggins, or two notes in the treble against three in the bass. For my father a tin of special blend tobacco, and my mother not to know. For my mother a box of face powder at the drugstore, and my father not to know. Twenty-five cents from my father on the side for ice-cream and licorice. Thirty-five from my mother for my dinner at the Chinese restaurant. And warnings, of course, to take good care of Rock, speak politely to Mr. Jenkins, and see that I didn't get machine oil on my corduroys.

It was three hours to town with Rock, but I don't remember them. I remember nothing but a smug satisfaction with myself, an exhilarating conviction of importance and maturity—and that only by contrast with the sudden sag to embarrassed insignificance when finally old Rock and I drove up to Jenkins' store.

For a farm boy is like that. Alone with himself and his horse he cuts a fine figure. He is the measure of the universe. He foresees a great many encounters with life, and in them all acquits himself a little more than creditably. He is fearless, resourceful, a bit of a brag. His horse never contradicts.

But in town it is different. There are eyes here, critical, that pierce with a single glance the little bubble of his self-importance, and leave him dwindled smaller even than his normal size. It always happens that way. They are so superbly poised and sophisticated, these strangers, so completely masters of their situation as they loll in doorways and go sauntering up and down Main Street. Instantly he yields to them his place as measure of the universe, especially if he is a small boy wearing squeaky corduroys, especially if he has a worldly-wise old horse like Rock, one that knows his Main Streets, and will take them in nothing but his own slow philosophic stride.

We arrived all right. Mr. Jenkins was a little man with a freckled bald head, and when I carried in my two crates of eggs, one in each hand, and my legs bowed a bit, he said curtly, "Well, can't you set them down? My boy's delivering, and I can't take time to count them now myself."

"They don't need counting," I said politely. "Each layer holds two dozen, and each crate holds six layers. I was there. I saw my mother put them in."

At this a tall, slick-haired young man in yellow shoes who had been standing by the window turned around and said, "That's telling you, Jenkins—he was there." Nettled and glowering, Jenkins himself came round the counter and repeated, "So you were there, were you? Smart youngster! What did you say was your name?"

Nettled in turn to preciseness I answered, "I haven't yet. It's Thomas Dickson and my father's David Dickson, eight miles north of here. He wants a man to stook and was too busy to come himself."

He nodded, unimpressed, and then putting out his hand said, "Where's your list? Your mother gave you one, I hope!"

I said she had and he glowered again. "Then let's have it and come back in half an hour. Whether you were there or not, I'm going to count your eggs. How do I know that half of them aren't smashed?"

"That's right," agreed the young man, sauntering to the door and looking at Rock. "They've likely been bouncing along at a merry clip. You're quite sure, Buddy, that you didn't have a runaway?"

Ignoring the impertinence I staved off Jenkins. "The list, you see, has to be explained. I'd rather wait and tell you about it later on."

He teetered a moment on his heels and toes, then tried again. "I can read too. I make up orders every day. Just go away for a while—look for your man— anything."

"It wouldn't do," I persisted. "The way this one's written isn't what it really means. You'd need me to explain—"

He teetered rapidly. "Show me just one thing I don't know what it means."

"Oranges," I said, "but that's only oranges if eggs are twenty-nine cents or more—and bigger oranges if they're thirty-one. You see, you'd never understand—"

So I had my way and explained it all right then and there. What with eggs at twenty-nine and a half cents a dozen and my mother out a little in her calculations, it was somewhat confusing for a while; but after arguing a lot and pulling away the paper from each other that they were figuring on, the young man and Mr. Jenkins finally had it all worked out, with mustard and soap omitted altogether, and an extra half-dozen oranges thrown in. "Vitamins," the young man overruled me, "they make you grow"—and then with a nod towards an open biscuit box invited me to help myself.

I took a small one, and started up Rock again. It was nearly one o'clock now, so in anticipation of his noonday quart of oats he trotted off, a little more briskly, for the farmers' hitching-rail beside the lumber-yard. This was the quiet end of town. The air drowsed redolent of pine and tamarack, and resin simmering slowly in the sun. I poured out the oats and waited till he had finished. After the way the town had treated me it was comforting and peaceful to stand with my fingers in his mane, hearing him munch. It brought me a sense of place again in life. It made me feel almost as important as before. But when he finished and there was my own dinner to be thought about I found myself more of an alien in the town than ever, and felt the way to the little Chinese restaurant doubly hard. For Rock was older than I. Older and wiser, with a better understanding of important things. His philosophy included the relishing of oats even within a stone's throw of sophisticated Main Street. Mine was less mature. I went, however, but I didn't have dinner. Perhaps it was my stomach, all puckered and tense with nervousness. Perhaps it was the restaurant itself, the pyramids of oranges in the window and the dark green rubber plant with the tropical-looking leaves, the indolent little Chinaman behind the counter and the dusky smell of last night's cigarettes that to my prairie nostrils was the orient itself, the exotic atmosphere about it all with which a meal of meat and vegetables and pie would have somehow simply jarred. I climbed on to a stool and ordered an ice-cream soda.

A few stools away there was a young man sitting. I kept watching him and wondering.

He was well-dressed, a nonchalance about his clothes that distinguished him from anyone I had ever seen, and yet at the same time it was a shabby suit, with shiny elbows and threadbare cuffs. His hands were slender, almost a girl's hands, yet vaguely with their shapely quietness they troubled me, because, however slender and smooth, they were yet hands to be reckoned with, strong with a strength that was different from the rugged labour-strength I knew.

He smoked a cigarette, and blew rings towards the window.

Different from the farmer boys I knew, yet different also from the young man with the yellow shoes in Jenkins' store. Staring out at it through the restaurant window he was as far away from Main Street as was I with plodding old Rock and my squeaky corduroys. I presumed for a minute or two an imaginary companionship. I finished my soda, and to be with him a little longer ordered lemonade. It was strangely important to be with him, to prolong a while this companionship. I hadn't the slightest hope of his noticing me, nor the slightest intention of obtruding myself. I just wanted to be there, to be assured by something I had never encountered before, to store it up for the three hours home with old Rock.

Then a big, unshaven man came in, and slouching on to the stool beside me said, "They tell me across the street you're looking for a couple of hands. What's your old man pay this year?"

"My father," I corrected him, "doesn't want a couple of men. He just wants one."

"I've got a pal," he insisted, "and we always go together."

I didn't like him. I couldn't help making contrasts with the cool, trim quietness of the young man sitting farther along. "What do you say?" he said as I sat silent, thrusting his stubby chin out almost over my lemonade. "We're ready any time."

"It's just one man my father wants," I said aloofly, drinking off my lemonade with a flourish to let him see I meant it. "And if you'll excuse me now—I've got to look for somebody else."

"What about this?" he intercepted me, and doubling up his arm displayed a hump of muscle that made me, if not more inclined to him, at least a little more deferential. "My pal's got plenty, too. We'll set up two stooks any day for anybody else's one."

"Not both," I edged away from him. "I'm sorry— you just wouldn't do."

He shook his head contemptuously. "Some farmer— just one man to stook."

"My father's a good farmer," I answered stoutly, rallying to the family honour less for its own sake than for what the young man on the other stool might think of us. "And he doesn't need just one man to stook. He's got three already. That's plenty other years, but this year the crop's so big he needs another. So there!"

"I can just see the place," he said, slouching to his feet and starting towards the door. "An acre or two of potatoes and a couple of dozen hens."

I glared after him a minute, then climbed back on to the stool and ordered another soda. The young man was watching me now in the big mirror behind the counter, and when I glanced up and met his eyes he gave a slow, half-smiling little nod of approval. And out of all proportion to anything it could mean, his nod encouraged me. I didn't flinch or fidget as I would have done had it been the young man with the yellow shoes watching me, and I didn't stammer over the confession that his amusement and appraisal somehow forced from me. "We haven't three men—just my father—but I'm to take one home today. The wheat's ripening fast this year and shelling, so he can't do it all himself."

He nodded again and then after a minute asked quietly, "What about me? Would I do?"

I turned on the stool and stared at him.

"I need a job, and if it's any recommendation there's only one of me."

"You don't understand," I started to explain, afraid to believe that perhaps he really did. "It's to stook. You have to be in the field by seven o'clock and there's only a bunkhouse to sleep in—a granary with a bed in it—"

"I know—that's about what I expect." He drummed

his fingers a minute, then twisted his lips into a kind of half-hearted smile and went on, "They tell me a little toughening up is what I need. Outdoors, and plenty of good hard work—so I'll be like the fellow that just went out."

The wrong hands: white slender fingers, I knew they'd never do—but catching the twisted smile again I pushed away my soda and said quickly, "Then we'd better start right away. It's three hours home, and I've still some places to go. But you can get in the buggy now, and we'll drive around together."

We did. I wanted it that way, the two of us, to settle scores with Main Street. I wanted to capture some of old Rock's disdain and unconcern; I wanted to know what it felt like to take young men with yellow shoes in my stride, to be preoccupied, to forget them the moment that we separated. And I did. "My name's Philip," the stranger said as we drove from Jenkins' to the drugstore. "Philip Coleman—usually just Phil," and companionably I responded, "Mine's Tommy Dickson. For the last year, though, my father says I'm getting big and should be called just Tom."

That was what mattered now, the two of us there, and not the town at all. "Do you drive yourself all the time?" he asked, and nonchalant and off-hand I answered, "You don't really have to drive old Rock. He just goes, anyway. Wait till you see my chestnut three-year-old. Clipper I call him. Tonight after supper if you like you can take him for a ride."

But since he'd never learned to ride at all he thought Rock would do better for a start, and then we drove back to the restaurant for his cornet and valise.

"Is it something to play?" I asked as we cleared the town. "Something like a bugle?"

He picked up the black leather case from the floor of the buggy and held it on his knee. "Something like that. Once I played a bugle too. A cornet's better, though."

"And you mean you can play the cornet?"

He nodded. "I play in a band. At least I did play in a band. Perhaps if I get along all right with the stooking I will again sometime."

It was later that I pondered this, how stooking for my father could have anything to do with going back to play in a band. At the moment I confided, "I've never heard a cornet—never even seen one. I suppose you still play it sometimes—I mean at night, when you've finished stooking."

Instead of answering directly, he said, "That means you've never heard a band either." There was surprise in his voice, almost incredulity, but it was kindly. Somehow I didn't feel ashamed because I had lived all my eleven years on a prairie farm, and knew nothing more than Miss Wiggins and my Aunt Louise's gramophone. He went on, "I was younger than you are now when I started playing in a band. Then I was with an orchestra a while—then with the band again. It's all I've done ever since."

It made me feel lonely for a while, isolated from the things in life that mattered, but, brightening presently, I asked, "Do you know a piece called *Sons of Liberty*? Four flats in four-four time?"

He thought hard a minute, and then shook his head. "I'm afraid I don't—not by name anyway. Could you whistle a bit of it?"

I whistled two pages, but still he shook his head. "A nice tune, though," he conceded. "Where did you learn it?"

"I haven't yet," I explained. "Not properly, I mean. It's been my lesson for the last two weeks, but I can't keep up to it."

He seemed interested, so I went on and told him about my lessons and Miss Wiggins, and how later on they were going to buy me a metronome so that when I played a piece I wouldn't always be running away with it, "Especially a march. It keeps pulling you along the way it really ought to go until you're all mixed up and have to start at the beginning again. I know I'd do better if I didn't feel that way, and could keep slow and steady like Miss Wiggins."

But he said quickly, "No, that's the right way to feel—you've just got to learn to harness it. It's like old Rock here and Clipper. The way you are, you're Clipper. But if you weren't that way, if you didn't get excited and wanted to run sometimes, you'd just be Rock. You see? Rock's easier to handle than Clipper, but at his best he's a sleepy old plow-horse. Clipper's harder to handle—he may even cost you some tumbles. But finally get him broken in and you've got a horse that amounts to something. You wouldn't trade him for a dozen like Rock."

It was a good enough illustration, but it slandered Rock. And he was listening. I know—because even though like me he had never heard a cornet before, he had experience enough to accept it at least with tact and manners.

For we hadn't gone much farther when Philip, noticing the way I kept watching the case that was still on his knee, undid the clasps and took the cornet out. It was a very lovely cornet, shapely and eloquent, gleaming in the August sun like pure and mellow gold. I couldn't restrain myself. I said, "Play it—play it now—just a little bit to let me hear." And in response, smiling at my earnestness, he raised it to his lips.

But there was only one note—only one fragment of a note—and then away went Rock. I'd never have believed he had it in him. With a snort and plunge he was off the road and into the ditch—then out of the ditch again and off at a breakneck gallop across the prairie. There were stones and badger holes, and he spared us none of them. The egg-crates full of groceries bounced out, then the tobacco, then my mother's face powder. "Whoa, Rock!" I cried, "Whoa, Rock!" but in the rattle and whir of wheels I don't suppose he even heard. Philip couldn't help much because he had his cornet to hang on to. I tried to tug on the reins, but at such a rate across the prairie it took me all my time to keep from following the groceries. He was a big horse, Rock, and once under way had to run himself out. Or he may have thought that if he gave us a thorough shaking-up we would be too subdued when it was over to feel like taking him seriously to task. Anyway, that was how it worked out. All I dared to do was run round to pat his sweaty neck and say, "Good Rock, good Rock—nobody's going to hurt you."

Besides there were the groceries to think about, and my mother's box of face powder. And with his pride and reputation at stake, Rock had made it a runaway worthy of the horse he really was. We found the powder smashed open and one of the egg-crates cracked. Several of the oranges had rolled down a badger hole, and couldn't be recovered. We spent nearly ten minutes sifting raisins through our fingers, and still they felt a little gritty. "There were extra oranges," I tried to encourage Philip, "and I've seen my mother wash her raisins." He looked at me dubiously, and for a few minutes longer worked away trying to mend the egg-crate.

We were silent for the rest of the way home. We thought a great deal about each other, but asked no questions. Even though it was safely away in its case again I could still feel the cornet's presence as if it were a living thing. Somehow its gold and shapeliness persisted, transfiguring the day, quickening the dusty harvest fields to a gleam and lustre like its own. And I felt assured, involved. Suddenly there was a force in life, a current, an inevitability, carrying me along too. The questions they would ask when I reached home—the difficulties in making them understand that faithful old Rock had really run away—none of it now seemed to matter. This stranger with the white, thin hands, this gleaming cornet that as yet I hadn't even heard, intimately and enduringly now they were my possessions.

When we reached home my mother was civil and no more. "Put your things in the bunkhouse," she said, "and then wash here. Supper'll be ready in about an hour."

It was an uncomfortable meal. My father and my mother kept looking at Philip and exchanging glances. I told them about the cornet and the runaway, and they listened stonily. "We've never had a harvest-hand before that was a musician too," my mother said in a somewhat thin voice. "I suppose, though, you do know how to stook?"

I was watching Philip desperately and for my sake he lied, "Yes, I stooked last year. I may have a blister or two by this time tomorrow, but my hands will toughen up."

"You don't as a rule do farm work?" my father asked.

And Philip said, "No, not as a rule."

There was an awkward silence, so I tried to champion him. "He plays his cornet in a band. Ever since he was my age—that's what he does."

Glances were exchanged again. The silence continued.

I have been half-intending to suggest that Philip bring his cornet into the house to play it for us, I perhaps playing with him on the piano, but the parlour with its genteel plushiness was a room from which all were excluded but the equally genteel—visitors like Miss Wiggins and the minister—and gradually as the meal progressed I came to understand that Philip and his cornet, so far as my mother was concerned, had failed to qualify.

So I said nothing when he finished his supper, and let him go back to the bunkhouse alone. "Didn't I say to have Jenkins pick him out?" my father stormed as soon as he had gone. "Didn't I say somebody big and strong?"

"He's tall," I countered, "and there wasn't anybody else except two men, and it was the only way they'd come."

"You mean you didn't want anybody else. A cornet player! Fine stooks he'll set up." And then, turning to my mother, "It's your fault—you and your nonsense about music lessons. If you'd listen to me sometimes, and try to make a man of him."

"I do listen to you," she answered quickly. "It's because I've had to listen to you now for thirteen years that I'm trying to make a different man of him. If you'd go to town yourself instead of keeping him out of school—and do your work in six days a week like decent people. I told you yesterday that in the long run it would cost you dear."

I slipped away and left them. The chores at the stable took me nearly an hour; and then, instead of returning to the house, I went over to see Philip. It was dark now, and there was a smoky lantern lit. He sat on the only chair, and in a hospitable silence motioned me to the bed. At once he ignored and accepted me. It was as if we had always known each other and long outgrown the need of conversation. He smoked, and blew rings towards the open door where the warm fall night encroached. I waited, eager, afraid lest they call me to the house, yet knowing that I must wait. Gradually the flame in the lantern smoked the glass till scarcely his face was left visible. I sat tense, expectant, wondering who he was, where he came from, why he should be here to do my father's stooking.

There were no answers, but presently he reached for his cornet. In the dim, soft darkness I could see it glow and quicken. And I remember still what a long and fearful moment it was, crouched and steeling myself, waiting for him to begin.

And I was right: when they came the notes were piercing, golden as the cornet itself, and they gave life expanse that it had never known before. They floated up against the night, and each for a moment hung there clear and visible. Sometimes they mounted poignant and sheer. Sometimes they soared and then, like a bird alighting, fell and brushed earth again.

It was *To the Evening Star*. He finished it and told
me. He told me the names of all the other pieces that he
played: an *Ave Maria, Song of India*, a serenade—all
bright through the dark like slow, suspended lightning,
chilled sometimes with a glimpse of the unknown. Only
for Philip there I could not have endured it. With my
senses I clung hard to him—the acrid smell of his
cigarettes, the tilted profile daubed with smoky light.

Then abruptly he stood up, as if understanding, and
said, "Now we'd better have a march, Tom—to bring us
back where we belong. A cornet can be good fun, too,
you know. Listen to this one and tell me."

He stood erect, head thrown back exactly like a
picture in my reader of a bugler boy, and the notes came
flashing gallant through the night until the two of us
went swinging along in step with them a hundred
thousand strong. For this was another march that did
march. It marched us miles. It made the feet eager and
the heart brave. It said that life was worth the living and
bright as morning shone ahead to show the way.

When he had finished and put the cornet away I said,
"There's a field right behind the house that my father
started cutting this afternoon. If you like we'll go over now
for a few minutes and I'll show you how to stook…. You
see, if you set your sheaves on top of the stubble they'll be
over again in half an hour. That's how everybody does at
first but it's wrong. You've got to push the butts down
hard, right to the ground—like this, so they bind with the
stubble. At a good slant, see, but not too much. So they'll
stand the wind and still shed water if it rains."

It was too dark for him to see much, but he listened
hard and finally succeeded in putting up a stook or two

that to my touch seemed firm enough. Then my mother called, and I had to slip away fast so that she would think I was coming from the bunkhouse. "I hope he stooks as well as he plays," she said when I went in. "Just the same, you should have done as your father told you, and picked a likelier man to see us through the fall."

My father came in from the stable then, and he, too, had been listening. With a wondering, half-incredulous little movement of his head he made acknowledgement.

"Didn't I tell you he could?" I burst out, encouraged to indulge my pride in Philip. "Didn't I tell you he could play?" But with sudden anger in his voice he answered, "And what if he can! It's a man to stook I want. Just look at the hands on him. I don't think he's ever seen a farm before."

It was helplessness, though, not anger. Helplessness to escape his wheat when wheat was not enough, when something more than wheat had just revealed itself. Long after they were both asleep I remembered, and with a sharp foreboding that we might have to find another man, tried desperately to sleep myself. "Because if I'm up in good time," I rallied all my faith in life, "I'll be able to go to the field with him and at least make sure he's started right. And he'll maybe do. I'll ride down after school and help till supper time. My father's reasonable."

Only in such circumstances, of course, and after such a day, I couldn't sleep till nearly morning, with the result that when at last my mother wakened me there was barely time to dress and ride to school. But of the day I spent there I remember nothing. Nothing except the midriff clutch of dread that made it a long day—

nothing, till straddling Clipper at four again, I galloped him straight to the far end of the farm where Philip that morning had started to work.

Only Philip, of course, wasn't there. I think I knew—I think it was what all day I had been expecting. I pulled Clipper up short and sat staring at the stooks. Three or four acres of them—crooked and dejected as if he had never heard about pushing the butts down hard into the stubble. I sat and stared till Clipper himself swung round and started for home. He wanted to run, but because there was nothing left now but the half-mile ahead of us, I held him to a walk. Just to prolong a little the possibility that I had misunderstood things. To wonder within the limits of the sane and probable if tonight he would play his cornet again.

When I reached the house my father was already there, eating an early supper. "I'm taking him back to town," he said quietly. "He tried hard enough—he's just not used to it. The sun was hot today; he lasted till about noon. We're starting in a few minutes, so you'd better go out and see him."

He looked older now, stretched out limp on the bed, his face haggard. I tiptoed close to him anxiously, afraid to speak. He pulled his mouth sidewise in a smile at my concern, then motioned me to sit down. "Sorry I didn't do better," he said. "I'll have to come back another year and have another lesson."

I clenched my hands and clung hard to this promise that I knew he couldn't keep. I wanted to rebel against what was happening, against the clumsiness and crudity of life, but instead I stood quiet a moment, almost passive, then wheeled away and carried out his cornet to the buggy. My mother was already there, with a box of lunch and some ointment for his sunburn. She said she was sorry things had turned out this way, and thanking her politely he said that he was sorry too. My father looked uncomfortable, feeling, no doubt, that we were all unjustly blaming everything on him. It's like that on a farm. You always have to put the harvest first.

And that's all there is to tell. He waved going through the gate; I never saw him again. We watched the buggy down the road to the first turn, then with a quick resentment in her voice my mother said, "Didn't I say that the little he gained would in the long run cost him dear? Next time he'll maybe listen to me—and remember the Sabbath Day."

What exactly she was thinking I never knew. Perhaps of the crop and the whole day's stooking lost. Perhaps of the stranger who had come with his cornet for a day, and then as meaninglessly gone again. For she had been listening, too, and she may have understood. A harvest, however lean, is certain every year; but a cornet at night is golden only once.

THE HEIGHTS

by Joyce Marshall

Joyce Marshall was born in 1913 in Montreal. After graduating from McGill in 1935 with an honours B.A. in English and winning the university's English Language and Literature medal, she moved to Toronto. As well as being an acclaimed translator of many French-Canadian works, Joyce Marshall was a founding member of the Literary Translators Association and won the Canada Council Prize for Translation in 1976. She is also the author of two novels and two collections of short stories. Joyce Marshall died in 2005.

"THE HEIGHTS" IS ONE OF FIVE "Martha Stories," from *Any Time At All and Other Stories* (1993) recounting episodes in the life of a girl growing up in the Quebec of the twenties and early thirties.

All through this story (if I succeed in turning these events and speculations into a story) you'll have to imagine the occasional presence of another person, watching, weighing, adding things up in her way as Alison and I added them up in ours. The strange thing is that I don't remember her nor does she remember us, though she must often have been in the same place at the same time, since she saw many of the same things. Or so she says and I can't think of a reason why I shouldn't believe her. I'm not sure how I should handle this. Perhaps it's best simply to warn you: there is someone else present at least part of the time, a twelve-year-old shape of air whom for the purpose of this story I'll call Pauline; there is another clumsy adolescent mind trying to pull it all together. She may come into some of the scenes as I go on—into the gathering round the Stoddards' red tennis court in the Heights, for instance, the Sunday twilight we all assembled, the English part of the community, to watch the Japanese Davis-Cup players Mr. Stoddard had arranged to bring from Montreal, since she says she was there and remembers it well. Though I hadn't planned to use this scene except to show how high the Stoddards had risen at that time, the swift rise that came before their equally sudden fall.

One way to start would be with the accident, which happened some years before my family began to spend the summers on one of the English streets at the edge of the French-Canadian village on the Ottawa River. No, on second thoughts, I'll just leave it that there was an accident and that it's the key, not because I want to be mysterious but because there are things I must say about the time to establish it for you—the brief bright lovely time before everything began to fall, and fell and fell again, as it will continue to fall, I often feel, for the rest of my life. I'm sorry I didn't realize what a happy hopeful interval it was, those few years of Never Again War, of Prosperity Forever: I was too tangled in my efforts to find out how to live (a skill I feared might be beyond me) to recognize happiness or sense its brevity.

To me it was the time of beautiful older girls, all so airy and light, so simplified, heads silken-small, bodies a single smooth unbroken line. (Not true in every case this last. Some young women had to bind themselves flat under their Jantzen bathing-suits and were constantly fussing with straps.) But these were the unlucky ones. The ideal was to be as breastless as fish or ten-year-old boys with (just this year) hair pared close to the skull and shaved to a point in back.

If you weren't there in those days it would be no use your looking at old photographs. Even to me those pictured girls are hideous, dragged down by those heavy-skirted woollen bathing-suits, their heads so raw, all ears. But there are fashions in seeing and to the eyes of the time they were not only appropriate but lovely, not so much boyish or sexless as beyond sex, essences, the thing that remains when everything extraneous has been peeled off. For all so active and light-hearted, flashing about in open cars or motor-boats or canoes, with a great display of naked arms and legs, what need had they of breasts or hips or hair?

Most of them, the offspring of newly "bobbed" war-emancipated mothers (for that's how it was put in those days: it was the woman, not her hair that was "bobbed") had been short-haired since childhood—the Dutch cut first, the shingle, then the semi-boyish. The previous year only three of the most daring older girls had risked the ultimate shearing, the full "boyish," but by this summer they'd all succumbed (with one exception who is central to this story). Even two girls whose hair they'd always claimed (and rightly for it fell heavily, cloyingly to their hips) was their one beauty, went down to the village barber-shop and returned, red-eyed but triumphant, with their wadded snakes of hair in paper bags.

In the interests of coolness and my mother's impatience with combs and brushes, my sisters still had their hair trimmed nice and close (her words) each year before we left Montreal for the summer. I'd resisted these annual shearings after I met Alison and my hair was now long and tangly like hers, wet usually from swimming, a bit smelly. Alison's mother, who was older than most of the other mothers, forbade her to cut off

even an inch, and though my own mother kept threatening to "hack off that stupid mop that you can't even
keep tidy" some night while I was sleeping, I told her it
wouldn't be fair to Alison, I had to wait until she'd
talked her mother round. My mother looked at me and
it hung between us for a moment—"You wanted me to
have a friend and now when I have one"—an old
quarrel and boring to both of us. We avoided it as much
as we could. Actually I wanted, or part of me wanted, to
have "that mop" cut off, wanted it in a sensuous shivery
way I couldn't understand. I was entranced by the
purity of the little heads, the point in back that must
feel deliciously cool and tingly to the fingers and used
to daydream about the playing in and out of scissors,
coldly, cleanly, cropping and cropping. But at the same
time I felt/feared that this wasn't really for me, that it
might not change me, as I hoped, into one of those
envied fishlike laughing girls. Or might change me,
more and more essentially, than I wanted anything to
change me.

I was still in this state of dread and longing when
Alison informed me on our way down to the village one
morning that her mother had changed her mind so we
must dash right up to the barber's before she changed it
back again. I couldn't refuse. Alison would tease me for
months (and Alison knew all my cracks, she knew how
to reach them). We'd walked up one of the little side
streets past the Masonic Hall and cut across to the
barber-shop, which wasn't even a shack like most of the
village houses but an old wheel-less freight-car set more
or less level on the ground, before we realized we neither
of us had any money. Alison had two dollars and fifty

cents, it's true, to buy groceries for her mother. We could use the fifty cents, she thought, and she'd try to bargain with Mr. Honani or tell him she'd pay him when she got her allowance. This scheming, and the way she avoided my eyes, kicking at one of the whitewashed stones that edged the barber's walk, told me she'd been lying, her mother hadn't really relented. But all I could think was that I was spared, for a while longer at least.

Then a strange thing happened. Mrs. Stoddard came quickly towards us. We knew her as we knew everyone, even the rich people on the Heights—or thought we did, how many gaps were there, I wonder—though she'd never seemed to know us. Nor for that matter had we ever seen her on foot before; she was always driven about by a chauffeur. She was a thin, rather tall woman, always hurried in her movements, her face down-turned. And that's the curious thing: I don't remember her face. I seem never to have seen it. She always wore a hat pulled well down (that was part of it) and what I thought of as a city suit. Today, to our surprise, she not only greeted us, but stopped. Had we shopping to do for our mothers? She'd be going down to Honani's herself in a minute and would do the shopping for us. Even Alison was silent and we looked at each other, it was such a queer idea. We weren't feeling nervous about going to the barber's, were we? she went on. We needn't be. The short new style was so charming, she was thinking of trying it herself. So why didn't we run along in and she'd be back with the groceries when we came out?

"The trouble is we lost our money," Alison said.

Then she'd give us some. Would fifty cents be enough? It would, so Alison handed over the wadded bills, the change and her list and, rather slowly, Mrs. Stoddard separated the two quarters and handed one to each of us.

So I was caught.

"You first," Alison said after giving the barber explicit directions about how to cut and trim "le boyeesh." She usually did insist I go first—as a test or to make sure I didn't back out, I was never sure which.

I felt shaky, sick, excited by the risk I was taking (and by my hopes) but though I may have trembled a little, I didn't cry. The barber cropped the entire back of my hair off first, snipping away endlessly, then thrusting my head forward to scrape with the clippers at my neck. I didn't feel wounded or exhilarated or any of the other things I'd expected to feel, just numb and in an odd way excluded, even when, almost as an afterthought, the scissors slashed away at the sides. And there I was. As much myself as I'd ever been but apparent to everyone now, all face and stinging neck.

And there after ten minutes or so was Alison, sober for her, staring at herself in the mirror. Surprised? Disappointed? As if she too had expected change, a revealed new self? Not finding the Alison she'd always been enough? Only for an instant and then she was laughing, shaking her head from side to side.

I was laughing too a little, feeling weightless and unreal, as we went out together, after refusing the barber's offer of a paper bag "to carry our curls to home." There was no sign of Mrs. Stoddard so we walked down to the main road. Then a block or so away we saw her, coming towards us in her stooped rapid way.

We were standing, the three of us, by the side of the road—for some reason she insisted upon reading out

Alison's mother's list in a fluttery voice and taking each item out of the bag to show us—when May Ellis, the loveliest of all the lovely older girls, drove by in her little red car.

Mrs. Stoddard stepped back, started so abruptly that she almost tripped, though we weren't in any danger, and said something I couldn't quite catch about "fast," perhaps "She drives too fast," then to Alison, "Do you think murderers should be punished?"

"Sure," Alison said. "Sure they should. They should be hanged, Mrs. Stoddard."

We stood there for a moment, Mrs. Stoddard muttering still—I was thinking about my head, trying not to raise my hand to its rasp and novelty. Then Alison grabbed the bag of groceries and we ran home.

My mother was delighted and kept telling me how much better I felt, which wasn't any help since I felt worse. As punishment for her defiance Alison was to be confined to the house for a week. Her mother was in tears, she said when she came across the field to tell me, but she couldn't think of any way to glue Alison's hair back on. Then in a whisper, though we were at the back of our yard and no one could overhear us, "Mind you don't breathe a word about Mrs. Stoddard. I think there's something fishy about that whole thing. Tell your mother you got the quarter for the barber from me. I said I got mine from you." So I did and when Alison was free in a week's time we both had an extra quarter with our allowance.

I'd have liked to stay home that afternoon. I needed to think, needed to get used to the sight and feel of myself. If I went swimming, people would notice my changed unchanging self, would comment upon it and I'd have to answer. But my mother talked a great deal about my servitude to Alison, my inability to do even the smallest thing without her, so I gathered up my towel, my blue Jantzen and my bathing-cap and went down at two o'clock to the Club—the Yacht Club, it was called, though there wasn't a yacht about the place, just tennis courts and a dance pavilion, with changing-rooms, moorings for canoes and motor-boats, and a diving platform beneath. I was early so I was alone as I changed and swam out to the raft. I remember taking off my ludicrously ballooning bathing-cap after I'd pulled myself up and giving that toss of the head that used to tumble hair to my shoulders. Then, and then only, I burst into tears. Just snivelled actually for there was another person on the raft, May Ellis, my ideal.

She was leaning back against her hands, her hair, nut-coloured and glossy, the sort of hair that seems to have weight to it—for it was part of her specialness that she'd kept it long—hanging plumb from her skull to the boards. The straps of her scarlet Jantzen had been slipped down so the sun could strike full on the long slope of her chest. Hers was one of the skimpiest bodies, barely rippled at the breasts, which I imagined as quite without flesh, the skin drawn tight over tiny muscular rises. The strange thing, though I didn't find it so at the time, was that she was only three years older than I was, not yet sixteen, though she'd been an older girl for as long as I'd known her, going to the Saturday adult dances, racing about in the open roadster she shared with her brother. He was practising for the end-of-summer regatta in one of those tippy racing shells and I think she'd been watching him, continued to watch him as we talked.

I don't remember much of what we said that day. "So you've come to it too," she said or something of the sort, then added with a switch of her lovely cascade that she'd have to see about getting rid of her own silly mane, had I ever seen anything so ridiculous, so hot and tiresome, so old-fashioned? Lingering over the adjectives so I could see she didn't mean a word of it. She made me turn from side to side, put out a finger to smooth (explore?) the raspy bits above my ears, then told me I looked "cute" (or "swell" or some other word of the time). I remember her face as we talked, the wide-spaced eyebrow-hoops, so scant you could almost count the hairs, the nearly heart-shaped, very red little mouth, and the way her hair, which had been trimmed at a point where it was still thick—at about elbow-length—shifted about her as she moved. I was startled by a condescension I wouldn't have expected and by the concern (if it wasn't just the usual lazy indifference that seemed to enclose her) that made her ignore my tears. I don't know whether I told her about the transformation I'd half feared, half hoped for (unlikely in view of my shyness with her) or what if anything she said that made me think she understood. For I had (still have) a strong sense that she was telling me I shouldn't (needn't) try to be like other people. Or perhaps just showing me. For who could have looked more "different" than she did, crouching in that tent of shimmery hair? "You're quite pretty, you know." That she did say. "I noticed when I passed you this morning with poor homely little Alison. And Mrs. Stoddard."

I wanted to ask her about the woman. Why had she been so determined to do Alison's shopping that she'd actually bribed us? But something knocked against the raft. May's brother, whose name was Jonathan, a loose-hung rangy youth who'd never to my knowledge given me even a look (and didn't now), was tired of paddling, he said. And steadying his wobbly craft with one hand, he used the other to help May gather up her hair and wad it into her rubber bathing-cap. She dove in then (she was a neat, almost silent diver) and swam back beside him to the Club.

Soon after this she must have started a new romance, I can't remember with whom. Like the other older girls she already had two or three former boy friends with whom she was no longer on speaking terms. That was how it was with them—one summer part of an insepa-rable couple, the next passing the youth with eyes to the side. Or perhaps she slipped into going about with the rather plain young man who filled in the gaps for her. This was special to her also: that she could inspire such devotion without seemingly doing anything about it. At any rate she no longer sat alone on the raft, though she almost always greeted me and sometimes, to my delight, waved as she flew by in her little red car, her scarf or hair flung back.

I got into the way of going up to her house in the Heights from time to time and hanging about the gate for ten minutes or so, usually with my bicycle so I could pretend to be fussing with a tire or the chain. If she saw me and wasn't doing anything important, I thought, she might ask me to come in. This never happened but I may not have wanted it to happen, preferring to continue to believe we were on the verge, or might be, of something more. Or to catch, by closeness, something of her specialness.

I missed Alison that first week—"moped" my mother called it. After that trip over to tell me, she was forbidden to come into the field or even wave to me. (She'd told her mother I'd asked her to accompany me to the barber's but lost my nerve at the last moment, so to show me how simple it was she'd jumped into the chair herself but of course the barber didn't understand English and before she could stop him he'd chopped off one whole side.) What minefields of lies we laid for ourselves. Not only did we lie to get out of trouble (or anticipated or fancied trouble), we were incapable of doing even the smallest thing without inventing elaborate reasons for doing it. Alison was better at this than I was. I was always finding myself trapped, not knowing how I'd got to where I was. Alison's stories, though often more daring and complicated, were consistent; whatever she said she remembered and maintained.

I think my mother hoped this week would be a chance for me to become friendlier with Lucille James, who was a tagger-on of ours. No, that's not right. Lucille didn't tag after us or after anyone. She joined us for swimming or bike rides when she chose—and that week called for me two or three times on her way down to the Club. I think she already had more self than either Alison or me, which may be why I found her troubling—a tall sinewy girl with wide shoulders and strong legs that were, I seem to remember, a trifle bowed. She had pronounced bones in her face (ours were still soft) and narrow deepset eyes of some greeny grey. She found Alison a bit comical, I could tell, but despite the loyalty I felt (had to feel) to Alison, who'd chosen me and seemed not to want any other friend, it occurred to me that week that I might have known Lucille better (would have liked to know her better) if I'd tried. But I was incapable of trying with someone who said almost as little as I did but had a great deal, I sensed, that she might say. I'm glad I sensed even that much because she died a few years later of some disease of the blood, her mysteries unexplained. And perhaps that's why I feel that there was already something absent about her. Foreknowledge of absence?

Alison's week of penance ended and she came across the field to show me her new eyebrows, which she'd plucked a few hairs at a time so her mother wouldn't notice; the righthand one, she announced proudly, now had only six hairs.

Perhaps because I hadn't seen her for some days, perhaps too because so much more of her face was visible now, I realized that Alison was, as May had put it, "homely," not just ordinary plain like me, a possibly curable condition—face too long, nose a bit soft, showing the nostrils, muddy brown eyes. I wondered whether she knew this, remembering those moments when she'd stared into the barber's mirror. It occurred to me that I might have to pity Alison and the thought frightened me. Because being chosen was a new experience for me; I was still trying to believe I'd deserved it. We'd scarcely moved in that first summer when she appeared at the door and before I could begin to be shy and stiff, "Got a bike?" she'd asked. "Fine then. Get it and I'll show you the Club."

She'd used the time also, she told me now, to decide on our project for the summer. My heart missed a beat or two. Many of Alison's projects (in which I'd never yet refused to take part) were risky or sneaky—or both risky and sneaky. We were to follow Mrs. Stoddard.

Follow?

Well, find out about her. Because there was something very odd going on. Being around the house like that, Alison had managed to eavesdrop on conversations between her parents—and between her mother and the ladies with whom she played bridge. "Poor soul." Things like that they kept saying and "Well, of course it was a terrible—but it's been years now and after all it was an *accident*, don't you think it's time she tried to put it behind her?" It seemed we weren't the only kids she'd paid to do their errands for them. "Your mother'll say something about that," she warned. "Mine already has." (And she did, to all of us except the youngest of my three younger sisters, who was too small still to be trusted with even tiny errands. "She's an unhappy woman," was how my mother put it. "It's because of something tragic that happened years ago. Sometimes she does strange things. We have to make allowances. So if she offers to take the money I've given you and do the shopping I sent you out to do, you must refuse very politely." We said we would, also that if it happened we wouldn't mention it to anyone, except to her, because it wasn't nice to gossip about someone who was so unhappy. No one, not even Hilary, who could usually be counted on for a flat unequivocal question or two, asked what being unhappy had to do with wanting to do other people's shopping. She knew, as I knew, as children always know, that this was one of the things that belonged to the grownups and that they intended to keep for themselves.

As it happened, Mrs. Stoddard never approached us again. For a week or so Alison and I roamed the main road, from Honani's store, up the hill and along to the Stoddards' house, which stood appropriately on the highest point of the Heights. (I remember it as white, very high and stark, with an off-centre tower and glassed-in porches on both sides instead of the screened or open galleries most other houses had.) We didn't even see her, except once, as we lurked by the gate with our bicycles, driving out with their chauffeur. She was sitting in front with him, I noticed. Alison waved vigorously but she didn't seem to see us.

Alison decided that we'd have to "close in," in other words invite ourselves to swim with the two Stoddard girls at their beach. We knew them, though they didn't swim at the Club and were ordinarily beneath our notice, being younger than we were and decked out always in heavily smocked dresses with their hair in long stick curls that unravelled as they walked.

Alison spent some time considering what we'd say when we phoned, or rather what I'd say, because I was to do the phoning for some complicated reason having to do with my not being the one who gave the money to Mrs. Stoddard, then decided that surprise would be better. So we took my father's cedar canoe, which I wasn't supposed to use without permission, and paddled up to the little sandy beach below the Stoddards' house.

Lucille, I'm fairly but not quite sure, was with us. Or at the beach already? There were a number of people splashing about with the two Stoddard girls. Including the ghost? You haven't forgotten the twelve-year-old shape of air it was agreed I should call Pauline? Perhaps, for she remembers this or some similar occasion—Mrs. Stoddard dashing out of the house, wearing one of her hats, and running up and down the pier, wringing her hands because, urged on by Alison, the girls were swimming in the deep water. Swimming took from the strength, she kept saying, they must come in at once.

They did and she turned her attention to the rest of us, ordering us to get off her property. "Murderer, murderer," she said or something like that. Was that for Alison? I wondered as we struggled to get the canoe afloat. Did she know it was Alison who'd coaxed the girls to swim in water that was over their heads?

We scrambled into the canoe finally. Yes, Lucille must have been with us for I'm fairly sure it was she who gave the final push and jumped in when the canoe was afloat. The others ran past the house to the road.

News moved fast in that place. Two or three days later my mother took me aside after breakfast.

"What is this I hear, Martha?" she said and without waiting for an answer, "You mustn't swim at private beaches without being invited. Surely you know that."

"*Does* swimming take from the strength?" I asked.

"I suppose if you overdid it," my mother said, then "Did Mrs. Stoddard say that? As I told you, she's an unhappy woman. A bit over-anxious too." She looked at me in a measuring way, first shaking her head at my eyebrows, which I'd plucked into one-hair loops, locked in the bathroom with the tap running so no one would hear me sneezing, then said I'd understand all this better when I was older. (So I'd failed the test. I still looked like what I was, a kid.)

Alison had already pronounced Mrs. Stoddard coo-coo and decided that we wouldn't go there again, though we still snooped about, patrolled the main road, wondered and watched.

My memory of time and sequence is a bit tricky at this point. (And those summers were so long.) I'm not sure how soon after our excursion to the Stoddards' beach it was that Hilary made one of her pronounce-ments at the dinner-table. Hilary remains a mystery to me. I still don't know whether she realized the possible effect of many of her remarks, whether she was simply innocently outspoken or just pretending to be. At any rate the words came out in a cool level voice: "I saw Mrs. Stoddard going into the hotel today, Mother. She was with their chauffeur."

For "hotel" read "saloon," the quite ordinary-looking wooden house with a screen-door right on the main street where people went to get drunk: Alison and I sometimes loitered about nearby, hoping to see a real staggering drunkard sometime. A few years later it became a smart cocktail lounge but at that time there was only one place more disreputable in the whole community—the "blind pig" on one of the little side streets in the French part of the village. (We'd hung about there for a while the previous year, seeing only members of the family go in and out, till we learned that "liquor" was only sold there "after hours" and though Alison thought we might sneak out of bed some night, that was too late for us.)

My parents had stopped eating at Hilary's words. My father said "Oh my God," then was silent while my mother tried to break into Hilary's explanation of how she knew it was the chauffeur: "He was wearing one of those caps only chauffeurs wear, why would she be going there with him, Mother?"

"For God's sake, stop that at once," my father said and, to my mother, "I guess there's no point our not telling them, they're bound to find out."

My mother looked round the table so we'd know she was speaking to all four of us. "Sometimes," she said, "when people are very unhappy they drink. Mrs. Stoddard, as I explained to you once before, is very unhappy. You see, the Stoddard girls had an older brother. Years ago, before we first came here, he was run over and killed. Right in front of their house. He was only five years old. Mrs. Stoddard saw the whole thing. What made it worse was that it was someone who was just learning to drive. Someone she knew."

"Who?" Hilary asked.

"It doesn't matter who," my father said. "She's suffered enough, poor woman. It seems she panicked and lost control of the car. It really was her fault."

By then Laura, the tender-hearted, who couldn't listen unmoved to a story in which even a fly was killed, was sobbing about "the poor little boy," so things could become more normal, my mother scooped her up to soothe her, saying to Hilary (somewhat unfairly), "Now see what you've done, you silly girl."

We weren't to mention what Hilary had seen to anyone, we were told. Nor were we to worry about it, Mrs. Stoddard wasn't a bad person, just a sick person.

"Then why isn't she in the hospital?" Hilary asked.

"Yes, why?" I asked Alison after I'd spilled the whole story on our way down to swim the next morning.

Alison shrugged. She seemed not to find my news very important. Because I'd learned it on my own, without her presence or goading? (I was beginning to have a few, a very few doubts about Alison. These were the first pricks. Falling out of friendship, I was to discover, when it was as complete as my friendship with Alison, was as difficult and painful, as much against the grain, as falling out of love.) We walked in silence for a moment or two. Then (I was watching her and saw it happen) her face brightened.

"So now we have to find out who did it," she said.

"Why? Why do we have to?"

"So we'll know," she said. "Let's see now. Your father said 'she' so it must have been one of the mothers. Which of them would have learned to drive before you first came here, which was—two years ago, three?"

We quarrelled then. I quarrelled with Alison. I didn't want to snoop any more. It was mean. And I didn't like the way Alison said "So we'll know." I wanted to know too but at the same time didn't want to, because if I knew I'd have to see a real person in the car that day, feeling the bump, realizing—

I'm not sure how much of this I said, or would have been able to say, before Alison turned on her heel and, without another word, went home.

She didn't speak to me for three days. When we were at the Club at the same time, she made a point of swimming past me, keeping her head turned away and talking in a loud excited voice to other people. Alison was good at that sort of thing.

I'd have apologized eventually as I always did apologize after our quarrels. But this time Alison broke first, simply turned up while I was at breakfast and indicated with a jerk of her chin that I should accompany her to the end of the vegetable garden so we wouldn't be overheard.

"You don't deserve to hear this, you're so stupid," she said. "But yesterday when I got home from swimming Mother and those dames were playing bridge on the gallery so I hid underneath and sure enough they were talking about Mrs. Stoddard, how when Mr. Stoddard tried to stop her drinking by not giving her an allowance, just charge accounts at Honani's and the butcher's, she took money from people and charged the things they wanted so she could use the cash to buy liquor. And when that wouldn't work any more she got the chauffeur to take her to the hotel. Imagine! How disgusting! Mr. Stoddard fired him, of course, when he found out."

"Oh?" I said. Alison was examining me closely so I stopped, as if the need had just occurred to me, and pulled out a weed or two.

"Don't let me interrupt you," Alison said. She laughed. "There's more too. Much more. Do you want me to tell you or should I just go home?"

I pulled another weed from a row of carrots, shook the dirt from its roots. "You can tell me, I guess," I said.

"They went on to talk about the accident," Alison said, "and I found out who killed the Stoddard kid. It was Mrs. Ellis."

"She doesn't even drive." And now there was a face behind that wheel, a plain closed-up face rather like Jonathan's, as the car went out of control, hit, bumped. And went on, crunching? I couldn't stop imagining those slow sickening moments, some part of me didn't want to stop.

"Would *you* drive if you'd killed someone your first time out alone?" Alison said. "And Mrs. Stoddard hates May because of her mother. Remember what she said that day? 'She drives too fast too.'"

"Are you sure that's what she said? She was sort of mumbling after nearly falling into the ditch like that. I couldn't hear her."

"Well, I could. And then she asked that thing about murderers, whether they should be punished."

"But that's just something she says," I said. "She was talking about murderers too the day we went to their beach."

"Because she thinks about May all the time. She was giving her real hate looks that day. I saw her even if you didn't. I think she's put a curse on her. Someone should warn May about that."

I said I didn't believe in curses. But a day or so later I decided to go up there, to May's, not to tell her she was hated, I couldn't imagine myself doing that, just to see her, perhaps talk to her in some sympathetic way, in case she already knew, I wasn't sure.

It was twilight when I reached the Ellises' house, which was two houses down from the Stoddards', smaller and on a considerably smaller lot and less citified, definitely a country house though much grander in itself and its surroundings than the houses in our part of the community, low and white, its up-sloping lawns set about with clear-cut flower-beds and trimmed fir-trees of some sort. I decided to edge between these trees to the gallery side of the house. I didn't feel sneaky; I could explain that I wouldn't have disturbed her if she'd been busy.

She was there, very visible for the gallery light was on, seated on a stool or low-backed chair, her arms a little out from her sides so that her hair, loose-combed, hung smooth and regular as cloth. Jonathan was kneeling beside her, in one hand an enormous pair of scissors. I thought he was about to cut off her hair, slash it right off close in some ritual, even sacrificial act. But as I watched, he began to snip the ends, moving round her on his knees, his hand deftly flicking. He'd moved twice before I began to feel ashamed and, quiet as I could be, went back to the road.

It occurred to me as I took the shortcut home across the fields that May hadn't been smiling, nor for that matter had her brother, they'd both been perfectly intent, her face perhaps a little dreamy, his sealed-off as usual, sullen even, then that May never did smile or at least that I couldn't remember seeing a smile on that usually partly-hidden face. And she hadn't any friends. She drove about or sat on the raft alone, even when surrounded by other older girls, except when her brother was with her or the plain youth who filled in the gaps in her life or some new summer beau. I didn't think of this as sad or even strange, just as part of her specialness, that in herself she was complete.

This is pretty well all I have to say about that summer, the last, though we didn't know it, before the falling off began. Alison continued to watch for Mrs. Stoddard, losing interest finally when it began to seem that she never went out of the house. Once she tacked a note with BEWARE in bold, rather sinister letters to the Ellises' gate. It was gone the next day.

Though I'll change my mind, I think, and say a bit more about the evening Mr. Stoddard brought the Japanese tennis-players out from Montreal: this may be more significant than I thought (and not only because the ghost says she was there). We sat in rows around the court and after three or four sets we all went home. There were no refreshments, not even lemonade or ice cream. I remember the quick, plunging, it seemed to me insect movements of the tennis-players, the pinging of the balls in swift long acrobatic rallies. I remember the Stoddard girls in their usual smocked dresses, their ringlets newly wound, sitting one on either side of their father, a tall, freckled, rather awkward man, but not Mrs. Stoddard, though she was such a vague presence always that she may have sat in silence beside them. I can't see her there or anywhere else though the ghost insists she was somewhere about, "wearing one of her hats." May was certainly present, with her parents and her brother (which caused Alison to wave at me excitedly from the other side of the court) and Lucille with her parents and two younger sisters. For we sat in family groups. It was that sort of occasion, rather like church. That's all I have to offer—the solemn scene and the incredible nervous swiftness of the tennis-players. And the query: Why did Mr. Stoddard do it? And why did years have to pass before I saw the sadness?

Soon after that we all moved back to the city, and in October the world changed. Next summer some of us returned to live year-round in the community—my family, Alison's—because it was cheaper than living in Montreal. Some, like Lucille's family and the Ellises, still came just for the summer. Others, among them the Stoddards, didn't come back at all. Mrs. Stoddard was loonier than ever, Alison told me, and had had to be put away. (I'm not sure whether this was true. I didn't want to know or even to think about Mrs. Stoddard. And I didn't very often, except sometimes quietly when I was alone. I never saw any of the family again.)

My mother thought it was sad that poor Mr. Stoddard had been well-off for such a little while and hadn't seemed to get much pleasure from it. He'd fallen further than almost anyone else, I gathered, since the triumphant Sunday he'd brought us all together to watch the tennis, but he didn't kill himself in his garage as several of the other fathers did or die, like my own father, from exhaustion and strain.

The big house on the height of the Heights stood vacant, the wide lawn growing up round the sign that said *To rent—à louer*, quite uselessly because no one had money now. One winter day, just before the house was sold at auction with its contents, Alison and I pried the boards from one of the windows, hoisted each other in and wandered about the rooms, which in the rather mouldy dimness we saw were furnished like city rooms, with what we believed were Persian rugs, and chairs and tables they must have bought, not discards or the sort of ravelly wicker other people had. Alison kept shooing me from room to room. She was looking for the "shrine," the room she was sure Mrs. Stoddard had kept just as the little boy left it when he ran out to be killed. We didn't find it—in fact none of the rooms seemed to belong to anyone much, not even the two pink-flounced girls' rooms, though one of the girls had left a still-boxed Baby Bye-Lo doll in her cupboard and the other several of those smocked dresses in cotton and silk. (Alison took one of the silk dresses and tried to unpick the smocking so she could make it into a blouse. Because she insisted I must have a souvenir too, I chose a tea-strainer from the kitchen. I kept it for years.) We climbed out then and nailed the window-boards back in place. This was close to the end of our friendship. Alison was leaving me behind in all sorts of ways and, though I was too ignorant and troubled to know this, I was leaving her behind in other ways. I was practising for the future, though I didn't know this either, learning how unwilling I was to detach myself from a connection with another person, how prompt to see a renewal where none was.

But that doesn't belong in this story. What does belong is my first meeting with May after the falling off began. I'd heard that the Ellises were back but I didn't see her until midsummer. We could no longer afford the Club. She no longer flashed about in that little red car. So much had changed so inexplicably that it didn't surprise me when we met on the main road one day to see that her spectacular hair was gone, trimmed to a skimpy shingle that left the back of her head flat. Her face was tense and knotted-looking now, the threadlike eyebrows too niggardly, the skin coarsened by all that relentless sunning. Prodded by my mother, I'd sent her a flowery letter during the winter and received a two-sentence reply. She was quite friendly that day, but I was too shy to do more than answer her questions about what I was doing or to realize that she was trying to make things easy for me—and for herself too of course.

"I suppose cutting off her hair was a sort of mourning," I told the ghost, no longer a twelve-year-old shape of air, the day we discovered we'd both spent summers in that community. I thought of describing the lit-up gallery scene, the absorption, the delicate snipping of the enormous scissors in the brother's hand, then decided against it. "Because she didn't die, of course. It was her brother who died, of some infection they couldn't even diagnose."

I went on to say I didn't believe in curses but still it was almost too apt. As if payment had to be made. And May hadn't got off scot free, so much life at the beginning, then so little. Not marrying until she was thirty, then two divorces in five years. And the faithful swain she'd made use of only when she hadn't anyone else becoming a war hero, admired by everyone, quite dashing-looking with his red commando beret and filled-out face.

"What curse are you talking about?" the ghost asked.

"That's what we called it, my friend Alison and I. And Mrs. Stoddard certainly hated May—Jonathan too, I guess, though that didn't occur to us—for being alive when it was their mother who'd killed her own little boy. What happened to her finally? Did you ever hear?"

"Oh she dried out eventually," the ghost said. "But whatever made you think—? It wasn't Mrs. Ellis who ran over the Stoddard boy."

"It wasn't?"

"No. It was—I've forgotten her name. She had three daughters. You were friends with the oldest one, didn't you say?"

"Yes, I was quite friendly with Lucille."

And Lucille died too, a few years later, of some wasting disease of the blood.

"Are you sure?" I asked.

"I don't know whether I was ever told formally," she said. "But I was curious. I snooped around. And you know what people were like out there. I heard it all over the place."

And Alison and I were too absorbed in schemes, tracking, plotting and carrying out our plots to hear what everyone was saying. Though Alison certainly overheard those friends of her mother's—unless she made that up, studying me closely as in pretended indifference I pulled weeds from the vegetable patch. For Alison did lie, I knew that and accepted it, or at least she invented facts to keep things going as she wanted them to go. And Mrs. Stoddard was muttering about murderers the day Lucille was with us (if she really was with us) as we swam with the Stoddard girls in the deep water.

"Well, there's no one alive now, I guess, who could tell us," I said. "But does it matter really? So many people died. In those and other families."

Which is why I don't like meeting someone who knew me, or even someone who was there and didn't know me, in those days, why I cling so hard to any poor excuse for causation and order I can find. Because there was no real reason for any of it. Just death striking here and striking there.

RED DRESS–1946

by Alice Munro

Alice Munro was born in 1931 in Wingham, Ontario. She has published eleven new collections of stories and one novel. During her distinguished career she has been the recipient of many awards, including three Governor General's Literary Awards, two Giller Prizes, and the National Book Critics Circle Award. Her stories have appeared in prestigious publications around the world, and her collections have been translated into thirteen languages. Alice Munro divides her time between Clinton, Ontario, and Comox, British Columbia.

"RED DRESS—1946" APPEARED IN Alice Munro's first short-story collection, *The Dance of the Happy Shades* (1968), which won the first of Munro's three Governor General's Awards.

My mother was making me a dress. All through the month of November I would come from school and find her in the kitchen, surrounded by cut-up red velvet and scraps of tissue-paper pattern. She worked at an old treadle machine pushed up against the window to get the light, and also to let her look out, past the stubble fields and bare vegetable garden, to see who went by on the road. There was seldom anybody to see.

The red velvet material was hard to work with, it pulled, and the style my mother had chosen was not easy either. She was not really a good sewer. She liked to make things; that is different. Whenever she could she tried to skip basting and pressing and she took no pride in the fine points of tailoring, the finishing of button-holes and the overcasting of seams as, for instance, my aunt and my grandmother did. Unlike them she started off with an inspiration, a brave and dazzling idea; from that moment on, her pleasure ran downhill. In the first place she could never find a pattern to suit her. It was no wonder; there were no patterns made to match the ideas that blossomed in her head. She had made me, at various times when I was younger, a flowered organdie dress with a high Victoria neckline edged in scratchy lace, with a poke bonnet to match; a Scottish plaid outfit with a velvet jacket and tam; an embroidered peasant blouse worn with a full red skirt and black laced bodice. I had worn these clothes with docility, even pleasure, in the days when I was unaware of the world's opinion. Now, grown wiser, I wished for dresses like those my friend Lonnie had, bought at Beale's store.

I had to try it on. Sometimes Lonnie came home from school with me and she would sit on the couch watching. I was embarrassed by the way my mother crept around me, her knees creaking, her breath coming heavily. She muttered to herself. Around the house she wore no corset or stockings, she wore wedge-heeled shoes and ankle socks; her legs were marked with lumps of blue-green veins. I thought her squatting position shameless, even obscene; I tried to keep talking to Lonnie so that her attention would be taken away from my mother as much as possible. Lonnie wore the composed, polite, appreciative expression that was her disguise in the presence of grownups. She laughed at them and was a ferocious mimic, and they never knew.

My mother pulled me about, and pricked me with pins. She made me turn around, she made me walk away, she made me stand still. "What do you think of it, Lonnie?" she said around the pins in her mouth.

"It's beautiful," said Lonnie, in her mild, sincere way. Lonnie's own mother was dead. She lived with her father who never noticed her, and this, in my eyes, made her seem both vulnerable and privileged.

"It *will* be, if I can ever manage the fit," my mother said. "Ah, well," she said theatrically, getting to her feet with a woeful creaking and sighing, "I doubt if she appreciates it." She enraged me, talking like this to Lonnie, as if Lonnie were grown up and I were still a child. "Stand still," she said, hauling the pinned and basted dress over my head. My head was muffled in velvet, my body exposed, in an old cotton school slip. I felt like a great raw lump, clumsy and goose-pimpled. I wished I was like Lonnie, light-boned, pale and thin; she had been a Blue Baby.

"Well nobody ever made me a dress when I was going to high school," my mother said, "I made my own, or I did without." I was afraid she was going to start again on the story of her walking seven miles to town and finding a job waiting on tables in a boarding-house, so that she could go to high school. All the stories of my mother's life which had once interested me had begun to seem melodramatic, irrelevant, and tiresome.

"One time I had a dress given to me," she said. "It was a cream-coloured cashmere wool with royal blue piping down the front and lovely mother-of-pearl buttons, I wonder what ever became of it?"

When we got free Lonnie and I went upstairs to my room. It was cold, but we stayed there. We talked about the boys in our class, going up and down the rows and saying, "Do you like him? Well, do you half-like him?

Do you *hate* him? Would you go out with him if he asked you?" Nobody had asked us. We were thirteen, and we had been going to high school for two months. We did questionnaires in magazines, to find out whether we had personality and whether we would be popular. We read articles on how to make up our faces to accentuate our good points and how to carry on a conversation on the first date and what to do when a boy tried to go too far. Also we read articles on frigidity of the menopause, abortion and why husbands seek satisfaction away from home. When we were not doing school work, we were occupied most of the time with the garnering, passing on and discussing of sexual information. We had made a pact to tell each other everything. But one thing I did not tell was about this dance, the high school Christmas Dance for which my mother was making me a dress. It was that I did not want to go.

At high school I was never comfortable for a minute. I did not know about Lonnie. Before an exam, she got icy hands and palpitations, but I was close to despair at all times. When I was asked a question in class, any simple little question at all, my voice was apt to come out squeaky, or else hoarse and trembling. When I had to go to the blackboard I was sure—even at a time of the month when this could not be true—that I had blood on my skirt. My hands became slippery with sweat when they were required to work the blackboard compass. I could not hit the ball in volleyball; being called upon to perform an action in front of others made all my reflexes come undone. I hated Business Practice because you had to rule the pages for an account book, using a straight pen, and when the teacher looked over my shoulder all the delicate lines wobbled and ran together. I hated Science; we perched on stools under harsh lights behind tables of unfamiliar, fragile equipment, and were taught by the principal of the school, a man with a cold, self-relishing voice—he read the Scriptures every morning—and a great talent for inflicting humiliation. I hated English because the boys played bingo at the back of the room while the teacher, a stout, gentle girl, slightly cross-eyed, read Wordsworth at the front. She threatened them, she begged them, her face red and her voice as unreliable as mine. They offered burlesqued apologies and when she started to read again they took up rapt postures, made swooning faces, crossed their eyes, flung their hands over their hearts. Sometimes she would burst into tears, there was no help for it, she had to run out into the hall. Then the boys made loud mooing noises; our hungry laughter—oh, mine too—pursued her. There was a carnival atmosphere of brutality in the room at such times, scaring weak and suspect people like me.

But what was really going on in the school was not Business Practice and Science and English, there was something else that gave life its urgency and brightness. That old building, with its rock-walled clammy basements and black cloakrooms and pictures of dead royalties and lost explorers, was full of the tension and excitement of sexual competition, and in this, in spite of daydreams of vast successes, I had premonitions of total defeat. Something had to happen, to keep me from that dance.

With December came snow, and I had an idea. Formerly I had considered falling off my bicycle and spraining my ankle and I had tried to manage this, as I rode home along the hard-frozen, deeply rutted country roads. But it was too difficult. However, my throat and bronchial tubes were supposed to be weak; why not expose them? I started getting out of bed at night and opening my window a little. I knelt down and let the wind, sometimes stinging with snow, rush in around my bared throat. I took off my pajama top. I said to myself the words "blue with cold" and as I knelt there, my eyes shut, I pictured my chest and throat turning blue, the cold, greyed blue of veins under the skin. I stayed until I could not stand it any more, and then I took a handful of snow from the windowsill and smeared it all over my chest, before I buttoned my pajamas. It would melt against the flannelette and I would be sleeping in wet clothes, which was supposed to be the worst thing of all. In the morning, the moment I woke up, I cleared my throat, testing for soreness, coughed experimentally, hopefully, touched my forehead to see if I had fever. It was no good. Every morning, including the day of the dance, I rose defeated, and in perfect health.

The day of the dance I did my hair up in steel curlers. I had never done this before, because my hair was naturally curly, but today I wanted the protection of all possible female rituals. I lay on the couch in the kitchen, reading *The Last Days of Pompeii*, and wishing I was there. My mother, never satisfied, was sewing a white lace collar on the dress; she had decided it was too grown-up looking. I watched the hours. It was one of the shortest days of the year. Above the couch, on the wallpaper, were old games of Xs and Os, old drawings and scribblings my brother and I had done when we were sick with bronchitis. I looked at them and longed to be back safe behind the boundaries of childhood.

When I took out the curlers my hair, both naturally and artificially stimulated, sprang out in an exuberant glossy bush. I wet it, I combed it, beat it with the brush and tugged it down along my cheeks. I applied face powder, which stood out chalkily on my hot face. My mother got out her Ashes of Roses Cologne, which she never used, and let me splash it over my arms. Then she zipped up the dress and turned me around to the mirror. The dress was princess style, very tight in the midriff. I saw how my breasts, in their new stiff brassiere, jutted out surprisingly, with mature authority, under the childish frills of the collar.

"Well I wish I could take a picture," my mother said. "I am really, genuinely proud of that fit. And you might say thank you for it."

"Thank you," I said.

The first thing Lonnie said when I opened the door to her was, "Jesus, what did you do to your hair?"

"I did it up."

"You look like a Zulu. Oh, don't worry. Get me a comb and I'll do the front in a roll. It'll look all right. It'll even make you look older."

I sat in front of the mirror and Lonnie stood behind me, fixing my hair. My mother seemed unable to leave us. I wished she would. She watched the roll take shape and said, "You're a wonder, Lonnie. You should take up hairdressing."

"That's a thought," Lonnie said. She had on a pale blue crepe dress, with a peplum and bow; it was much more grown-up than mine even without the collar. Her hair had come out as sleek as the girl's on the bobby-pin card. I had always thought secretly that Lonnie could not be pretty because she had crooked teeth, but now I saw that crooked teeth or not, her stylish dress and smooth hair made me look a little like a golliwog, stuffed into red velvet, wide-eyed, wild-haired, with a suggestion of delirium.

My mother followed us to the door and called out into the dark, "Au reservoir!" This was a traditional farewell of Lonnie's and mine; it sounded foolish and desolate coming from her, and I was so angry with her for using it that I did not reply. It was only Lonnie who called back cheerfully, encouragingly, "Good night!"

The gymnasium smelled of pine and cedar. Red and green bells of fluted paper hung from the basketball hoops; the high, barred windows were hidden by green boughs. Everybody in the upper grades seemed to have come in couples. Some of the Grade Twelve and Thirteen girls had brought boy friends who had already graduated, who were young businessmen around the town. These young men smoked in the gymnasium, nobody could stop them, they were free. The girls stood beside them, resting their hands casually on male sleeves, their faces bored, aloof and beautiful. I longed to be like that. They behaved as if only they—the older ones—were really at the dance, as if the rest of us, whom they moved among and peered around, were, if not invisible, inanimate; when the first dance was announced—a Paul Jones—they moved out languidly, smiling at each other as if they had been asked to take part in some half-forgotten childish game. Holding hands and shivering, crowding up together, Lonnie and I and the other Grade Nine girls followed.

I didn't dare look at the outer circle as it passed me, for fear I should see some unmannerly hurrying-up. When the music stopped I stayed where I was, and half-raising my eyes I saw a boy named Mason Williams coming reluctantly towards me. Barely touching my waist and my fingers, he began to dance with me. My legs were hollow, my arm trembled from the shoulder, I could not have spoken. This Mason Williams was one of the heroes of the school; he played basketball and hockey and walked the halls with an air of royal sullenness and barbaric contempt. To have to dance with a nonentity like me was as offensive to him as having to memorize Shakespeare. I felt this as keenly as he did, and imagined that he was exchanging looks of dismay with his friends. He steered me, stumbling, to the edge of the floor. He took his hand from my waist and dropped my arm.

"See you," he said. He walked away.

It took me a minute or two to realize what had happened and that he was not coming back. I went and stood by the wall alone. The Physical Education teacher, dancing past energetically in the arms of a Grade Ten boy, gave me an inquisitive look. She was the only teacher in the school who made use of the words social adjustment, and I was afraid that if she had seen, or if she found out, she might make some horribly public attempt to make Mason finish out the dance with me. I myself was not angry or surprised at Mason; I accepted his position, and mine, in the world of school and I saw that what he had done was the realistic thing to do. He was a Natural Hero, not a Student Council type of hero bound for success beyond the school; one of those would have danced with me courteously and patronizingly and left me feeling no better off. Still, I hoped not many people had seen. I hated people seeing. I began to bite the skin on my thumb.

When the music stopped I joined the surge of girls to the end of the gymnasium. Pretend it didn't happen, I said to myself. Pretend this is the beginning, now.

The band began to play again. There was movement in the dense crowd at our end of the floor, it thinned rapidly. Boys came over, girls went out to dance. Lonnie went. The girl on the other side of me went. Nobody asked me. I remembered a magazine article Lonnie and I had read, which said *Be gay! Let the boys see your eyes sparkle, let them hear laughter in your voice! Simple, obvious, but how many girls forget!* It was true, I had forgotten. My eyebrows were drawn together with tension, I must look scared and ugly. I took a deep breath and tried to loosen my face. I smiled. But I felt absurd, smiling at no one. And I observed that girls on the dance floor, popular girls, were not smiling; many of them had sleepy, sulky faces and never smiled at all.

Girls were still going out to the floor. Some, despairing, went with each other. But most went with boys. Fat girls, girls with pimples, a poor girl who didn't own a good dress and had to wear a skirt and sweater to the dance; they were claimed, they danced away. Why take them and not me? Why everybody else and not me? I have a red velvet dress, I did my hair in curlers, I used a deodorant and put on cologne. *Pray*, I thought. I couldn't close my eyes but I said over and over again in my mind, *Please, me, please,* and I locked my fingers behind my back in a sign more potent than crossing, the same secret sign Lonnie and I used not to be sent to the blackboard in Math.

It did not work. What I had been afraid of was true. I was going to be left. There was something mysterious the matter with me, something that could not be put right like bad breath or overlooked like pimples, and everybody knew it, and I knew it; I had known it all along. But I had not known it for sure, I had hoped to be mistaken. Certainty rose inside me like sickness. I hurried past one or two girls who were also left and went into the girls' washroom. I hid myself in a cubicle.

That was where I stayed. Between dances girls came in and went out quickly. There were plenty of cubicles; nobody noticed that I was not a temporary occupant. During the dances, I listened to the music which I liked but had no part of any more. For I was not going to try any more. I only wanted to hide in here, get out without seeing anybody, get home.

One time after the music started somebody stayed behind. She was taking a long time running the water, washing her hands, combing her hair. She was going to think it funny that I stayed in so long. I had better go out and wash my hands, and maybe while I was washing them she would leave.

It was Mary Fortune. I knew her by name, because she was an officer of the Girls' Athletic Society and she was on the Honour Roll and she was always organizing things. She had something to do with organizing this dance; she had been around to all the classrooms asking for volunteers to do the decorations. She was in Grade Eleven or Twelve.

"Nice and cool in here," she said. "I came in to get cooled off. I get so hot."

She was still combing her hair when I finished my hands. "Do you like the band?" she said.

"It's all right." I didn't really know what to say. I was surprised at her, an older girl, taking this time to talk to me.

"I don't. I can't stand it. I hate dancing when I don't like the band. Listen. They're so choppy. I'd just as soon not dance as dance to that."

I combed my hair. She leaned against a basin, watching me.

"I don't want to dance and don't particularly want to stay in here. Let's go and have a cigarette."

"Where?"

"Come on, I'll show you."

At the end of the washroom there was a door. It was unlocked and led into a dark closet full of mops and pails. She had me hold the door open, to get the washroom light, until she found the knob of another door. This door opened into darkness.

"I can't turn on the light or somebody might see," she said. "It's the janitor's room." I reflected that athletes always seemed to know more than the rest of us about the school as a building; they knew where things were kept and they were always coming out of unauthorized doors with a bold, preoccupied air. "Watch out where you're going," she said. "Over at the far end there's some stairs. They go up to a closet on the second floor. The door's locked at the top, but there's like a partition between the stairs and the room. So if we sit on the steps, even if by chance someone did come in here, they wouldn't see us."

"Wouldn't they smell smoke?" I said.

"Oh, well. Live dangerously."

There was a high window over the stairs which gave us a little light. Mary Fortune had cigarettes and matches in her purse. I had not smoked before except the cigarette Lonnie and I made ourselves, using papers and tobacco stolen from her father; they came apart in the middle. These were much better.

"The only reason I even came tonight," Mary Fortune said, "is because I am responsible for the decorations and I wanted to see, you know, how it looked once people got in there and everything. Otherwise why bother? I'm not boy-crazy."

In the light from the high window I could see her narrow, scornful face, her dark skin pitted with acne, her teeth pushed together at the front, making her look adult and commanding.

"Most girls are. Haven't you noticed that? The greatest collection of boy-crazy girls you could imagine is right here in this school."

I was grateful for her attention, her company and her cigarette. I said I thought so too.

"Like this afternoon. This afternoon I was trying to get them to hang the bells and junk. They just get up on the ladders and fool around with boys. They don't care if it ever gets decorated. It's just an excuse. That's the only aim they have in life, fooling around with boys. As far as I'm concerned, they're idiots."

We talked about teachers, and things at school. She said she wanted to be a physical education teacher and

she would have to go to college for that, but her parents
did not have enough money. She said she planned to
work her own way through, she wanted to be independent anyway, she would work in the cafeteria and in the
summer she would do farm work, like picking tobacco.
Listening to her, I felt the acute phase of my unhappiness passing. Here was someone who had suffered the
same defeat as I had—I saw that—but she was full of
energy and self respect. She had thought of other things
to do. She would pick tobacco.

We stayed there talking and smoking during the long
pause in the music, when, outside, they were having
doughnuts and coffee. When the music started again Mary
said, "Look, do we have to hang around here any longer?
Let's get our coats and go. We can go down to Lee's and
have a hot chocolate and talk in comfort, why not?"

We felt our way across the janitor's room, carrying
ashes and cigarette butts in our hands. In the closet, we
stopped and listened to make sure there was nobody in
the washroom. We came back into the light and threw
the ashes into the toilet. We had to go out and cut across
the dance-floor to the cloakroom, which was beside the
outside door.

A dance was just beginning. "Go round the edge of
the floor," Mary said. "Nobody'll notice us."

I followed her. I didn't look at anybody. I didn't look
for Lonnie. Lonnie was probably not going to be my
friend any more, not as much as before anyway. She was
what Mary would call boy-crazy.

I found that I was not so frightened, now that I had
made up my mind to leave the dance behind. I was not

waiting for anybody to choose me. I had my own plans. I did not have to smile or make signs for luck. It did not matter to me. I was on my way to have a hot chocolate, with my friend.

A boy said something to me. He was in my way. I thought he must be telling me that I had dropped something or that I couldn't go that way or that the cloakroom was locked. I didn't understand that he was asking me to dance until he said it over again. It was Raymond Bolting from our class, whom I had never talked to in my life. He thought I meant yes. He put his hand on my waist and almost without meaning to, I began to dance.

We moved to the middle of the floor. I was dancing. My legs had forgotten to tremble and my hands to sweat. I was dancing with a boy who had asked me. Nobody told him to, he didn't have to, he just asked me. Was it possible, could I believe it, was there nothing the matter with me after all?

I thought that I ought to tell him there was a mistake, that I was just leaving, I was going to have a hot chocolate with my girl friend. But I did not say anything. My face was making certain delicate adjustments, achieving with no effort at all the grave absentminded look of these who were chosen, those who danced. This was the face that Mary Fortune saw, when she looked out of the cloakroom door, her scarf already around her head. I made a weak waving motion with the hand that lay on the boy's shoulder, indicating that I apologized, that I didn't know what had happened and also that it was no use waiting for me. Then I turned my head away, and when I looked again she was gone.

Raymond Bolting took me home and Harold Simons took Lonnie home. We all walked together as far as Lonnie's corner. The boys were having an argument about a hockey game, which Lonnie and I could not follow. Then we separated into couples and Raymond continued with me the conversation he had been having with Harold. He did not seem to notice that he was now talking to me instead. Once or twice I said, "Well I don't know I didn't see that game," but after a while I decided just to say "H'm hmm," and that seemed to be all that was necessary.

One other thing he said was, "I didn't realize you lived such a long ways out." And he sniffled. The cold was making my nose run a little too, and I worked my fingers through the candy wrappers in my coat pocket until I found a shabby Kleenex. I didn't know whether I ought to offer it to him or not, but he sniffled so loudly that I finally said, "I just have this one Kleenex, it probably isn't even clean, it probably has ink on it. But if I was to tear it in half we'd each have something."

"Thanks," he said. "I could sure use it."

It was a good thing, I thought, that I had done that, for at my gate, when I said, "Well, good night," and after he said, "Oh, yeah. Good night," he leaned towards me and kissed me, briefly, with the air of one who knew his job when he saw it, on the corner of my mouth. Then he turned back to town, never knowing he had been my rescuer, that he had brought me from Mary Fortune's territory into the ordinary world.

I went around the house to the back door, thinking, I have been to a dance and a boy has walked me home and kissed me. It was all true. My life was possible. I went past the kitchen window and I saw my mother. She was sitting with her feet on the open oven door, drinking tea out of a cup without a saucer. She was just sitting and waiting for me to come home and tell her everything that had happened. And I would not do it, I never would. But when I saw the waiting kitchen, and my mother in her faded, fuzzy Paisley kimono, with her sleepy but doggedly expectant face, I understood what a mysterious and oppressive obligation I had, to be happy, and how I had almost failed it, and would be likely to fail it, every time, and she would not know.

JACK OF HEARTS

by Isabel Huggan

Isabel Huggan was born in Kitchener, Ontario, in 1943 and grew up in nearby Elmira. She is the author of two volumes of short stories and Belonging, *a travel memoir that won the Charles Taylor Prize in 2004. Her work has been published around the world. In 1987, she moved with her family to Kenya, and since then has lived abroad. She now resides in France but returns annually to Canada to teach at the Humber School for Writers.*

"JACK OF HEARTS" IS ONE OF *The Elizabeth Stories*, a series of related episodes in the life of a girl growing up in small-town Ontario.

People never expect me to be good at poker, probably because I have such an open face. (My mother used to say she could read me like a book. Her mistake, my advantage.) But what people don't know is that I've been playing poker since I turned eleven, and I play the game very well. I may appear flushed and agitated, but my excitement is impersonal, abstract. How can I explain this? What I love about poker is the tension, not the actual winning or losing but the tension between random chance and changeless numbers. Slap, slap, slap, slap, cards dealt and destiny beckons, two-and-a-half million different hands in a deck. It's the chance to play around with fate a little, that's what draws me in. It's what you do with what you've got; in every encounter with pure, immutable kings and queens and their rough and tumble shuffle with luck, you get the chance to make it work for you.

There is no certainty anywhere, but in poker that's part of the game.

Sometimes strangers, especially men, are surprised by my lack of compunction in taking their money after I've bluffed my way to the pot. But as Aunt Eadie used to say, *If you can take 'em by surprise, then take 'em for everything they've got.* It was Aunt Eadie who first taught me how to play, strengthening in me a toughness that, sadly, only shows itself at cards. But then, poker isn't life, after all. I think Aunt Eadie said that, too. And of course that's what I first loved about the game. It wasn't like life at all.

Eadie was a friend of my mother's, not really an aunt. They'd worked together in Toronto when they were young, and even when they were 45 or 46 they seemed girlish when they were together. Eadie was still a secretary there, although not just any secretary, my mother was quick to point out, but an executive secretary to one of the top brokers in the whole stock exchange. I had no idea what a stock exchange was. The only exchange I knew was the one at Medley Sports where you traded in skates.

But it was easy to see that Aunt Eadie was important from the way she held herself, as if she were much taller than she actually was, and from the glamorous clothes she brought in her matching leather luggage. In winter she'd arrive in mink or fox, and those first hellos at the door were wonderful for the smells—sweet fur and perfume and smoke. "You bring the city with you, Ead," my mother would say, and it was true; there was a roar of traffic and glitter of lights just in the way she smelled. Beneath her coat there was bound to be something bright and silky, for Eadie loved passionate, tropical colours. The image still lingering in my mind is of feathers and flowers, palm leaves and hibiscus, brilliant and foreign. In her lectures to me about the importance of appearance, my mother often used Eadie as an example of someone who bought the very best quality, someone whose handbag and shoes were always the same colour. But she'd usually end with a proviso such as "although Eadie does use a trifle too much rouge" or "of course, she is a little over-fond of jewellery." Nevertheless, her friend from the city had a flair for fashion that no woman in Garten could match, and she wanted me to take note. Perhaps she hoped that I might see in Eadie what she had been, before her life required only cotton housedresses and navy crêpe for going out.

As much as my mother admired her friend, my father disparaged her. He was critical not only of the way she dressed ("flashy") and looked ("hair is never that colour in nature"), but even of the way she laughed ("she has a loose laugh, Mavis, loose!"). She was, in a word, flamboyant—the epitome of all that Frank Kessler loathed and feared.

Their mutual interest in money, rather than giving them common ground, kept them apart, for my father had such distrust of the stock market that he lumped Eadie in with "all those crooks who make their money by speculation." Banking, on the other hand, he regarded as good solid business; careful investment and guaranteed interest, twenty-year bonds and steady growth. The money in *his* bank, he said, was clean.

"She's no better than a gambler," he'd say after one of Eadie's visits in which she had described her latest killing on the market. "Never was and never will be." He'd known her nearly as long as he'd known my mother.

They had all met while working on Bay Street during the thirties. Those years of Depression influenced the course of their lives not only by changing them, but by compressing and intensifying the qualities they already had. So Frank became more heavy and solid, weighed down by the metal in his soul, and Eadie hardened under the pressure to diamond-like sharpness. Mavis stayed, as she had always been, carefully in between, but when the chips were down, her money was on solidity. The house, the husband, the child.

Eadie had never married, and that too was a flaw that incurred my father's wrath. He thought that she "ran around" and that my mother oughtn't to invite her to the house in case I, his impressionable young daughter, be corrupted. Once, when they were arguing and didn't know I was listening from behind the kitchen door, he said "She may be smart but she'd still a tart!" and I nearly gave my hiding place away by laughing out loud.

"Don't worry so much, Frank," my mother would say on these occasions. "Elizabeth has no idea what Eadie's private life entails, nor need she ever. Eadie's got a lot of goodness in her, no matter what you say. I think it's just lovely to see her with a child after all she's been through. These visits are good for them both."

In fact, I was never so fond of Aunt Eadie as either of them seemed to think. After the preliminary questions about how school was going, she didn't have the slightest notion of what to talk to me about. Not until the night she taught me how to play poker did she ever give me anything of value.

It must have been sometime in early March, for there was still snow and it was the week after my disgrace at the ballet recital. Looking back I can see how lucky I was that Eadie and her cards came along when they did, offering me salvation and self-preservation. Somehow, when you're a child, you simply accept each turn of events as it comes, as if there is no other way for the world to be. And perhaps that is the right way to look at life. But looking back you can see how coincidence created your character, like coral atolls in the Pacific, building themselves slowly, moment upon moment.

By all odds, I should have been dragged down by the life I led as a child in Garten. I should still be there, or somewhere like it, forced under by my upbringing and all the expectations around me. But luck was with me, and small pockets of defiance multiplied beneath my surface, keeping me afloat, preparing me for that final escape.

Our ballet teacher, Mrs. Verser, always chose to hold the recital in the bleak weeks of late winter because it was then, she said, that most people needed an escape, a promise of springtime. What better harbingers of spring than the daughters of Garten leaping across the stage? Along with most of my friends, I had been enrolled in Saturday morning classes at the age of seven. We were beginning that long process of instillation, the steady drip, drip, drip of Values on to our skulls and into our brains. If our parents could only control our lives long enough, we would eventually achieve grace, tidiness and frugality.

But it wasn't for the social graces alone that Mavis Kessler sent her only child to dancing class. She hoped to combat my natural inelegance. I had inherited her face but my father's shape, with such large, heavy bones it became apparent early that I would be close to six feet when I grew up. In another time or place my body might have been prized for its usefulness in the fields. Unlucky soul, I was born generations away from where I should have been; and my sturdy peasant legs, which would have been well employed plodding down the turnip rows, were instead engaged in vain exercise at the barre. "Heels down!" Mrs. Verser would cry as we'd do our *demi-pliés*, lined up along the stage at the end of the high school gymnasium. Sharon's father was manager of the ironworks factory and had produced a portable barre of pipe for the class, to which we clung white-knuckled as we tried to bend and stretch without wobbling.

Strangely, I grew to like ballet, and looked forward to those sessions of music and movement, learning to hold my arms and legs just so, as careful of my body as if it were glass. Mrs. Verser had an assistant who gave tap lessons as well, but I was in full agreement with Mavis on this point; tap was crude and showy, ballet was *élégant*. There were no French phrases in tap, it was all just brush, brush, slide, step, hop. But in ballet there was the marvellous beauty and authority of Mrs. Verser calling out, "*Battements tendus! Maintenant, ronds de jambes! Changement de pieds!*" Across the floor we would go, obedient automatons responding to her clear high voice. "*Glissade, jeté, assemblé, entrechat royale....*" She was a small woman who had been at Sadlers Wells (no one knew for what or for how long), with a straight back and a snappy manner, and a sense of mission that made it possible for her to teach dance in Garten, year after year, without ever descending into self-pity or cynicism. She was like a small bright bird chirping "*Plus haut! Plus haut!*"

The recital we worked toward was an event that beckoned with the same inviting gleam as the annual trip to the city hockey arena to see *The Nutcracker*. My mother and I always went with her friend June, whose daughter Trudy was in my ballet class. High up in the cavernous building we'd sit on wooden benches and pass my father's field glasses back and forth. I liked the music, its easy slippery flow, and I liked the predictable patterns of the dance. But best of all I liked the costumes, and would take away with me visions of velvet and satin and sparkling lace in which to clothe my own fantasies for another year. Even in the early years of our own recitals, when the junior classes only got to dress up as tulips or bunnies, I felt my heart would burst with excitement once I was zipped and buttoned into a new being. I would become, for the duration of that dance, whatever my costume dictated and thus discovered a release from the confines of Garten, transient but intense.

Ordinarily, Mrs. Verser made a big thing out of the story in each number she choreographed for us, and exhorted us to let our faces tell the tale. She made us practise various expressions—grief, joy, anticipation—along with the corresponding arm and leg movements, which we eventually interpreted as "up is happy, down is sad." But this year she put off telling us intermediate girls what our recital piece would be about, because she wasn't sure she could get the right costumes from Malabar's, and if she had to make changes at the last minute she didn't want any of us to be disappointed. So for the first few weeks of preparation she simply put us through specific drills and we learned step after step. I liked this way of doing it, having the movement clean and devoid of meaning; the purity of *des battements dégagés, des battements tendus*. I would have preferred to dance like that always, to let my own mood determine the way I rendered the steps. Often we danced without any sort of music, just Mrs. Verser on the side, steadily counting time.

There were five of us for this number—myself and Trudy, Sharon, Amy and Janet. Trudy and I kept up the pretence of liking each other for our mothers' sakes because they seemed so pleased to see their friendship extend into the next generation. But in truth we were bitterly jealous, especially in ballet class, each convinced she was better than the other. And so it was with open exultation that I noted, as we began fitting the various steps of the dance together, I was always in the middle. Trudy said it was only because I was the tallest, but I was sure I detected Mrs. Verser's subtle plan. She had been watching us practise and now it was clear to her that it was I, Elizabeth, who would be the star. I imagined what our costumes might be, and foresaw something for myself in glistening white satin and tulle. The other girls would be my handmaidens, circling around, perhaps bringing wreaths of flowers for me to wear in my hair. Twisted silk lilies would be perfect, I decided.

Still, I felt confused by some of Mrs. Verser's directions as the weeks wore on, and it became apparent that the movements required of me were much less intricate than the other girls'. And it struck me as a little odd, if I were indeed the best, that I should not be given the most difficult steps to execute, a series of *entrechats quatres*, perhaps. Nevertheless, I was completely unprepared for the letter that Mrs. Verser waved at us, that February morning, and I could barely absorb her words.

"And Malabar's have exactly what we need for our number, and in all the right sizes, at such reasonable cost I know your parents won't mind paying a little extra so that we can give a really professional show. And so this morning, girls, at long last, we can begin our rehearsal for *Jack of Hearts*, and you'll see now how all our steps go together to make a story. Quickly, let's get ourselves up on stage. Come, Elizabeth! We'll have to call you Jack from now on!" A smile, a wave of the hand, a clucking noise made to gather up the other four around me.

My heart fell like a stone. I stood there blinking, hardly able to breathe or think, with Mrs. Verser holding my elbow, ready to guide me across the stage in the opening steps.

"Now we can put our expression in, as we see what is happening in the dance. You, Jack, enter with the skipping step, a one-and-two-and-one, lightly and gaily, we must see you for what you are, a rogue, a knave, a stealer of hearts. You'll have a lovely red velvet heart, here on your arm. You must make these girls think you wear your heart on your sleeve, but really, you have no heart at all, you are the fellow who loves them and leaves them." She stopped for a moment, looking at my sad and bewildered face. She took my expression for puzzlement, and gave her tinkling, ballet-mistress laugh. "But of course, you are too young to know about the cruel ways of love. Well then, you must learn about life through the dance. You will see how, in the end, because you wouldn't choose one you are left alone by them all, broken-hearted." She made an extravagant gesture, hand to breast, head bowed.

I heard Trudy and Janet giggling, and knew they weren't laughing at Mrs. Verser the way we usually did. They were laughing at me because I was being humiliated, and they knew it, even if silly Mrs. Verser didn't. What worse shame than to play the part of a boy? It meant you were too ugly to be a girl, that's what it meant. I dreaded the mockery and teasing I knew would come as soon as we were changing in the dressing-room.

Somehow I got through the hour of rehearsal, noting at each turn how stupid I had been not to have seen before why I needed only *promenade* behind the other girls, as each one did her *pirouettes* and *arabesques*. Of course, that's why I was left alone at the end. My body had never felt so thick and lumpish, so unable to extend itself through the air. Around me danced Trudy and Janet and Sharon and Amy, more daintily than ever, making little comments whenever they came near. When we joined hands or I had to touch them in any way, they shrank away with giggles. "Don't get fresh with me," Trudy whispered as we crossed the stage in our brief *pas de deux*. "You boy, you!"

Finally, out in the cold grey noon, I ran home by myself, able to give vent at last to pent-up tears. I was still crying when I let myself in the back door. My mother heard me and came from the kitchen, holding a saucepan by its handle. "You're late, Elizabeth, your father and I went ahead with lunch. I'll just put your soup on the tab ... goodness sake, Elizabeth, what's wrong?" Her forehead furrowed with sympathetic concern. That's all I needed to start a fresh flow of tears and I sobbed out my story with emphasis on the awful injustice of it all. As we so seldom met on any level where we would communicate, I think my mother entered my crisis eagerly. Here was something she could feel too. "What a shame," she kept saying, sensing only my disappointment about the costumes and not the very thing that made it unbearable. The shame, the shame. I wanted her to hold me in her arms and stroke my hair, but she just stood there with the saucepan between us, tears filling her eyes.

My noisy grief brought my father from the living-room, the Saturday *Globe* in his hand. "I have to be a boy in the recital, Daddy," I said. "I have to be a boy just because I'm the tallest." More tears, and the waiting for his sympathy to fall down around my shoulders like silk scarves, the way my mother's had. But not a chance. No coddling from Frank Kessler.

"Nothing wrong with being a boy," he said, folding the newspaper into a narrow roll. "Be proud of it. All the other girls will look the same, you'll be different. Right, Mavis? Whoever remembers the corps de ballet, eh? No sir, you be glad, Elizabeth. A chance to show character. A chance to shine. Nothing wrong with being a boy. You be glad." He tapped his open palm with the paper for emphasis and smiled down at me. I had an excruciating opening of the heart like the wrenching up of a window. I saw clearly and absolutely how much he had wanted me to be a son. And what he had was a daughter who wasn't even very good at being a girl.

I knew all about humiliation and I coped as I always did, by clenching myself in a corner of my closet, safe in the wool-smelling dark. I tried to work out for myself what meaning there might be in what had happened, but it seemed as if there were too many things to think of at once, and my mind became more and more jumbled. The conventions of dressing up were familiar enough to me, and yet I felt so confused. What did it *mean* to be a girl or a boy, and why did I feel like such a failure? It was as if I had touched with my toe a hidden switch that suddenly made visible, as far as my eye could see, limits and lines and boundaries over which one could not transgress without great danger and pain. There it was for the first time: the minefield of sex.

The night before the recital we all met in the gymnasium for the dress rehearsal. The costumes, some made by mothers, and some ordered from Toronto, were placed on tables along the walls with crayoned signs above them. Under *Jack of Hearts* lay the Malabar boxes; I felt their unopened threat from across the room. As I crossed the floor the babble of voices around me became nightmarish, filling my head as if ten insane radio stations were screaming through at the same spot on the dial. I couldn't move, I held back as my mother went on ahead. She was determined to show me how to make the best of things.

"Ginny, stand still, the waist needs tucking." "Where are the wings, the blue wings?" "All tulips, on stage, five minutes." "Tell Susan to hitch up, her ankles are wrinkled." "Ruthie, leave Judy alone, get your slippers on." At the centre of the madness, Mrs. Verser, resplendent in sapphire silk, her small body arched with a thrilling tension. She loved the dress rehearsal, she told us, possibly even more than the actual performance night itself. This was it, the glamour of the dance in all its potential. Perhaps here she could still imagine that her girls would, with the donning of their costumes, materialize into lithe, graceful dancers. There was still a chance, there was still a hope.

Once Malabar's boxes were opened, I lost all hope. Out of the tissue paper wrappings came pastel dresses, pale green and apricot, lemon and lavender, just as Mrs. Verser had promised. And then mine: short grey velvet pants caught with an elastic band at the thigh so that they looked full and blousy, and a matching long-sleeved jacket with padded shoulders which would, as one mother noted, help to make me look "even more boyish." I was to wear high red knee socks to accent the red velvet heart, and to top it all off, a jaunty velvet hat with a red feather, to pull down over my head at one side.

"If Elizabeth's hair were just a teensie bit shorter, Mrs. Kessler, I think the whole effect would be so much more, ah, professional," suggested Mrs. Verser in that tone that implied there were no options. My hair was already bobbed at my ears, thick straight brown hair that stuck out oddly from beneath the cap. I could tell from my mother's silence, as I tried various angles, that she would have me on the high stool in the kitchen for a trim before Mrs. Verser set eyes on me again.

I went off to the dressing-room to try on the costume, and then regarded myself in the mirror above the row of sinks. I did, I looked like a big fat boy. I took off my glasses and was met by a blessed blur of grey and red. That was better. If only that was how the rest of the world would see me, I thought, a grey blur on stage. We were never allowed to wear our glasses at the recital, and dress rehearsal was usually the first time the more myopic of us danced blind. It meant there was lots of bumping and joking backstage and I could manage to avoid looking at the jeering faces of my dancing partners as we waited for our turn. But once out on the brightly lit stage, I could not help but see the glint in Trudy's eyes.

At the end of our number I was flushed with hope that once Mavis had seen her daughter being made a fool of, she would make Mrs. Verser change the dance, even at this late moment. But no, she was caught up in my father's enthusiasm for teaching me to face the challenge, and she was bound now to help me be brave. "This will help form your character," she told me on the way home, her voice all cheery. But I could tell from her expression that she was as devastated as I, and would have been much happier as the mother of Trudy, whose blond curls were perfectly set off by the apricot dress. Or Amy, who had a solo toe number to *The Surrey With the Fringe on Top* in the second half of the program. These were the daughters she should have had. For unlike Frank, she had wanted a girl; she told me she had prayed all during her pregnancy that I would be a girl.

She was 35 when I was born, as late to motherhood as she had been to marriage seven years before. She had met my father when he was starting his bank career at the Imperial's main office, long before he was near any kind of managerial level. When they wed, the Depression had the country in its grip, and perhaps they put off parenthood until they could save a little money. That's the kind of sensible move I would expect them to have made. Or perhaps they tried and tried, and I was the result of diligence and perseverance. Or perhaps she had planned to keep on working, as Eadie did, and I was a mistake that altered her expectations. I have no idea. The whole matter was so closely allied to sex that it was never possible to ask questions. It was all part of my mother's private life to which I only had secret access—rifling through her bureau drawers or eavesdropping on telephone conversations.

As soon as I wake the next morning I determine I will get out of the recital if I can. I complain of stomach cramps and a headache immediately upon rising, and later tell my mother I feel feverish. I drink hot water out of the bathroom tap before asking her to take my temperature. The thermometer registers 106 degrees, and Mavis has the presence of mind to make me lie down where she can keep an eye on me for an hour before she takes it again. Then she cuts my hair. I try to find the courage to throw myself down the cellar stairs, but each time I lunge forward my hand always goes involuntarily out to the railing. It's no good, there is no way out.

After lunch my mother announces that she and I are going to go downtown and that she is going to buy me a surprise. I feel I've had enough surprises lately but she has a spritely look that means she has decided to be nice to me and I know there's no point in resisting. In our bare feet I am as tall as Mavis, but she is wearing her high-heeled winter boots that have a ruff of black fur around the ankle, and so I feel smaller and daughter-like as we walk along. She is wearing her black persian lamb jacket with its matching hat and she looks very smart and important. My mother always dresses to go downtown, even though the shopping district is only four blocks from our house. It is a matter of pride with her to keep up her city habits; she does not expect to be in Garten forever, she says.

She tells me repeatedly not to scuff my feet and to walk properly but I keep forgetting and let my feet slide and drag along the sandy ice on the pavement. I have begun to feel curious about what she is going to buy. I know full well that her idea of a good surprise and mine are entirely different. I would like a cream-filled long-john from Bauman's Bakery, or a *Photoplay* magazine, or a box of coloured pencils, and I expect to be disappointed. We walk the full length of the street, my mother nodding and waving to several acquaintances, until we reach my father's bank standing squarely up in the corner, like a great ship anchored in the harbour.

We turn down the side street there and stop outside The Beverly Shoppe, Lingerie and Women's Apparel. My mother and her friends always call it The Beverly Shop-pay, making fun of the pretensions of its owner, a widow with whom they all play bridge on Wednesday afternoons, her half-day closing. Her name is Beverly Mutch, and she is a tall, dry stick of a woman with whom my mother loves to talk about quality. They will stand together fingering cloth and murmuring until my skin crawls and itches as I stand before the trio of mirrors in whatever sensible outfit my mother is buying for me. I loathe this store. It is where my mother buys my navy blue jumpers and bloomers, and all my wool and cotton underwear and starchy blouses. Nothing she ever buys here is beautiful or nice, it is always just good quality, meant to last.

Mavis bends toward me at the door of the shop, her voice a low, conspiratorial whisper. "Here's where we go for the surprise," she says, smiling at me in a flushed, earnest way. "I'm going to buy you a brassière. I think it's time."

She steps back and looks at me, hoping for some reaction on my part. I am stunned. She really *has* surprised me. All the blood in my body seems to be rushing to my head and I feel very hot and red around the eyes. I am still blushing when we go into the store, hating as always the little chime that rings ding-ding-dong when the door opens and closes. I would go crazy if I worked in a place where there was a bell like that, I think. No wonder Mrs. Mutch always seems so edgy and can never settle her eyes on your face.

"Ah, Elizabeth!" She comes from behind her small counter where she has been smoking a cigarette and reading a magazine. She clasps her hands and smiles at me, intimate, benevolent. "So this is the big day."

I know right away that she does not mean the ballet recital, that my mother has phoned ahead and made an appointment. It has all been plotted behind my back. I am trapped. I do not want a brassière. Nobody else in my grade has one and I do not want to be first. If I am first I will suffer for it. I would much rather be third.

"Just take off your parka, dear, and we'll go to the back for a fitting," says Mrs. Mutch. My mother gives me a little push with her hand on the place between my shoulder-blades that means "behave yourself" and so I obediently follow the other woman to the room separated from the rest of the shop by a heavy pink curtain. "Take off your blouse," Mrs. Mutch says, as she unrolls a frayed yellow tape measure, holding it out straight, ready to "do" me. The curtain moves aside and my mother's face appears, anxious to be involved in every step of the project.

"What do you think, Bev?" she asks, as Mrs. Mutch's thin fingers pull the tape rightly around my chest.

"Oh yes, Mavis, by all means," she says, appraising my breasts through the woven cotton undershirt. "Now, Elizabeth," she continues, turning back to me, "I'm going to bring you a number of bras to try on. I think you'd like to try them on yourself, wouldn't you?" She smiles, aware of how alert and sensitive she is being. "After you have each one on, your mother and I will come have a look. Like a little fashion show." A final cigarette-stained smile, and she ducks through the curtain, to join my mother in preserving my modesty.

I hear their whispered voices. "At the rehearsal," my mother is saying. "Just hadn't noticed before ... bouncing up and down ... in this costume especially ... really kind of funny, but ... I knew you could help, Bev ... probably more puppy fat than anything else, but still...."

I run my hands over the coarse undershirt and think how much I have always complained about wearing it, and how much now I don't want to part with it. There is nowhere to turn. Even my mother thinks I'm laughable.

The brassières are all stiff and unkind, digging into my skin along the edges. White cotton, pointy, harsh, unnatural. My discomfort grows with each attempt and with Mrs. Mutch's professional prodding and poking.

She and my mother are having a lovely time, laughing and reminiscing, perhaps trying to make me feel a part of their charmed circle of womanhood. I don't know.

"They really don't feel very nice," I finally say to Mrs. Mutch as she is hooking me up at the back.

"Oh dear, it's only because they're new," she says. "You'll get used to the feeling in no time. But say now, I do have a junior in satin, maybe that will be more comfy. Just a minute now."

Mutterings from behind the curtain, little murmurs and "ahs" from them both, then a blue satin brassière is thrust in. "Try this, dear," she says, and I do. It feels cool and costume-like, it is at least bearable.

"Now then, Elizabeth, isn't this a special surprise?" asks my mother as we stand at the cash register.

"Do I have to wear it all the time now?" I inquire in my most plaintive tone, hoping against hope for a no.

"Support is terribly important for big girls," Mrs. Mutch assures me, and goes on to warn of the horrors of sag and droop. "Once you get used to this one, dear, we'll get you into a nice everyday cotton and you'll feel just fine."

"You'll wear it tonight for a start," says Mavis as we head back home. She is not cross but she is very decisive. She will not have her daughter's breasts bouncing on stage, not for anything.

Right after supper I walk to the school, dreading the taunts I am sure will come. But the other girls are far too absorbed in their powdering and rouging to notice my newly short hair or the shiny blue brassière. I hunch in a corner, pulling on the heavy velvet suit. It makes me sweat before I even move. I get a little brown pancake rubbed on by one of the mothers, who tells me I look like a perfect little man, a real heartbreaker. I tell her I feel like throwing up, and she tells me to go to the washroom and be careful not to splatter the velvet. I go, but I can't make myself vomit even by sticking a finger down my throat. I wonder about falling against the porcelain toilet bowl and knocking myself out, but there's not enough room in the cubicle and I give up. I feel desperate but there are no choices. I am in a nightmare out of which I cannot awake.

Even when we have to run across the snow outside to get in the side door of the stage, the bright cold March night can't clear away the colours of the dream. We crowd together behind the curtain and make little peepholes to look out. The gymnasium is full, all of Garten seems to be there, restless on their metal folding chairs. I can't find my parents, I can't see farther than the first row where Mr. Willis, editor of the weekly *Enterprise*, sits with his camera and flash on his knee. Mrs. Verser has made him promise not to take pictures during the performance but he is there at the front just the same.

Then, lowered lights, darkness, a spotlight on Mrs. Verser introducing the junior class and *The Coming of Spring*. We mass together in the wings, waiting our turns, listening to the clatter of applause. *Spanish Dancers* follow on the heels of *Southern Belles*, and after *Anchors Aweigh* there we are, out in the warm bath of light, the phonograph needle falls down on the record and the music swells up and out of the loudspeakers and I am skipping, hands on my hips, across the stage. I think I hear a murmur from the audience but it is such an anonymous sound I have no way of judging what it means. The girls in their frothy dresses weave around me and I dance with each one, and with them all, trying to smile and wink the way Mrs. Verser showed me, putting expression in. My face is very hot from the exertion of the dance and from the effort of not crying. I am weighted down by the velvet suit, and the brassière cuts and binds along my midriff and under my arms. When I raise my arms the straps dig into my shoulders. I think no one in the world knows how unhappy I am, and somehow that helps. There is comfort in solitude.

Before I can believe it the music is over and we are joining hands for a curtain call. Trudy smiles at me in an open and friendly way and I know it is because our mothers are watching. She and Sharon and Amy and Janet all make sweeping, graceful curtsies, their heads bent low over their pointed toes, and I give my bobbing bow, then fall to one knee in the centre so that they can cluster around me. Suddenly, unrehearsed, Trudy jumps up and perches on my extended knee and fluffs her skirt, and Mr. Willis springs up and snaps a picture. The flash leaves little green explosions in my eyes, and the sound of applause is now mixed with laughter. I am feeling very odd, as if I am swelling up. But I get to my feet with the others, retreat back ten steps, and see Mrs. Verser in the wings urging us forward for one last curtain call. As we skip forward to the footlights, I can feel it, I can feel the pressure building. The summoning of the dark abyss. The others step back and I lean forward, on the edge of the stage. Into the darkness, driven.

"I'm really a girl," I shout, my voice horribly high and tinny. The noise in the gym lulls and I shout again, as loud as I can, into the startled silence. "I'm really a girl, I'm really a girl!"

My parents' scoldings that night were probably tempered by some instinctive sympathy, but it still seemed to me that my mother's major concern was *her* humiliation, not mine. My father's theme was his great disappointment at the weakness of my character. "Hysteria, Elizabeth, that's what that was! No self-control! No call for such a display, none at all!"

What could I say to explain myself? Nothing. I sat, red-faced and weeping as they reproached me, unable to tell them why I had called out, unable to understand myself why I had done it. All I knew was that I had disgraced not only myself and our household but the entire ballet school, and the next day was made to write a letter of apology to Mrs. Verser. I didn't care, I was past caring, no further punishment could equal the dance itself.

Surprisingly, the matter was never spoken of again. Mr. Willis, whether through my father's intervention or his own kindly intuition, did not publish the photo-graph in the paper, and used a full-length picture of Amy *en pointe* with his recital review. I was so relieved I felt no envy of Amy at all. She and Trudy and the others no longer called me "Jack" at school; it seemed as if everyone had set about forgetting the incident. It was almost as if I had frightened them all with the intensity of my pain.

My mother might have made more of the whole thing if there had not been the lucky diversion of a visit from Eadie, who arrived on Monday for a four-day visit.

Normally she only stayed one or two days, but this time, for some reason I was not allowed to know, Aunt Eadie needed a nice long rest away from the city. As usual, she brought gifts: a lacy slip for Mavis, silver cufflinks for Frank, and for me a box of discarded costume jewellery and scarves, last season's accessories but a gift that never failed to please me. Once, these things had all gone in my dressing-up box, but now they had a more immediate appeal. I found a ring of rhinestone chips set in red enamel, and put it on my fourth finger. A little loose, but spectacular.

My mother and her friend settled into a routine of secretive, girlish behaviour that produced in my father a more clipped and aloof manner than usual. He contrived to be out at meetings both Tuesday and Wednesday evenings, which suited my mother just fine. She and Aunt Eadie sat at the kitchen table, smoking Black Cat cigarettes and drinking tea and endlessly, endlessly talking. Sometimes they would laugh so hard they'd lean back in their chairs, gulping air and wiping away tears, and sometimes they seemed really to be crying, but in a soft, resigned sort of way. They'd barely notice my coming or going in the kitchen after supper, and if they did I was always told to get along up to my room. But my mother always said it nicely, and would slip her arm around my waist for a moment before giving me a little push off. She looked rosy and happy. She was always nicer when Eadie was there; the lines that had begun to pucker her small mouth into a tight purse seemed, suddenly, not to be there.

On the Thursday night there was a "coffee and dessert" meeting at the church, being given by the

Couples' Club for the new minister. It was the kind of social event that neither Frank nor Mavis could resist, but it was also not the sort of thing they could take Eadie to—nor would she have gone. She waved them out the door, reassuring them that she looked forward to some time alone with me. I felt nervous and embarrassed, wondering whether I was now obliged to stay down in the living-room with her all evening.

As soon as they disappeared, Aunt Eadie said, "Well, let's get out the cards, Elizabeth, we'll pass the time with a little poker."

I was relieved that she wasn't intending to talk to me, but worried because the only card games I knew were Rummy and Fish. I found the good deck my parents used at their Bridge Club, and confessed my ignorance. She had brought down her purse from her bedroom, and opened the clasp slowly as she spoke.

"Okay, then," she said. "We'll make a deal. I'll teach you how to play poker, and you'll keep a little secret." She took from her purse a flat silver flask engraved with flowers and fancy scrollwork. "Your Aunt Eadie is going to have a drink or two. God knows after three days in Garten I deserve it. And you're not going to tell a soul. How's that for an idea?" She flashed the same kind of warm smile she gave my mother when they were whispering, and I felt a terrific pleasure spreading all through me. I nodded, speechless, watching her fingers working, undoing the lid of the flask. It was a large cap, meant to be used as a measure, and she poured the amber liquid into it with a slow, steady hand. "Whisky," she said, looking at me. "Here's to you, Elizabeth."

She put the silver jigger to her lips and drained it, then poured another. She smiled and gave an enormous, happy sigh. "I'll just set this here beside the couch. You be careful now, the last thing we want to do is spill it. Now get a little table for us while I shuffle."

I could hardly move I was so fascinated by this revelation. I had never seen anyone drink openly before, and the air seemed charged with wickedness and endless possibility. Once, I had seen my father pouring drinks for a party, but he was huddled over the kitchen counter to shield my eyes from his sinning, and I was told to leave. Alcohol was a vice, to be indulged in carefully and privately, never in front of the children. I didn't have any idea that people might carry liquor with them or drink alone, and the sheer nerve of what Aunt Eadie was doing made me quiver with excitement. What if they came home and she got caught? But she seemed not even to consider that, and with each emptying of the cap grew more relaxed and easy. I could see at last what my father really hated about her—because she didn't care, she was safe.

Her painted nails flashed as she cut the deck, all the while outlining the basic rules of the game. "Get something for us to bet with, Elizabeth," she said, and I ran to the sewing closet and brought back the button jar, pleased with myself for doing something to make her laugh. And she did, she laughed and laughed, her head thrown back, her hands still busy flicking the cards out on to the table. "Okay, look sharp now," she said. "There's a lot to learn here."

Right from that moment I loved it, loved the simplicity and quickness of the game, the wonderful formality that was almost like a dance. Aunt Eadie and I were to play poker together many times in the years that followed, but I don't remember any other evening as vividly as that. I asked questions and she answered, instructing me in matters of technique and terminology. What we both sought we found in the cards—the solace of rules ("three of a kind always beats two of a kind") and the thrill of tampering with chance. Here, at last, I could exert some influence over whatever fate dealt me. My head felt as clear as if a cold wind had blown through.

By ten o'clock I had a pile of buttons in front of me and she had only a scattering. She seemed not as interested in the game as she had been, and her face had a slackness that made me feel a little uneasy. "One last hand and off to bed," she said, and dealt. I looked her straight in the eye and bluffed so that I won the whole pot, every last button she had, with a crummy pair of jacks.

"You're good," she said. "You're going to be okay, Elizabeth. Put the cards away now, and remember this is our little secret. Nighty-night." She leaned back on the couch and smiled at me, her arms spread out like wings. A bird of paradise, as out of place in that pale beige and green living-room as the joker in the deck. The wild card that meant I now had the means of escape. Even that night I began what was to become a ritual whenever I wanted to make myself feel calm. By flashlight in my closet I would lay out hand after hand, figuring out all the possibilities.

I was still in the closet when I heard my parents come in downstairs. I went to the door of my room to listen, heard a rustle of voices and then my father's heavy exclamations, and my mother's voice, all warm and forgiving. "Eadie, Eadie, what have you been doing?" And my father's, "Did the child see you like this?" Then Aunt Eadie's low laughter, and the words "bed early" and then silence. I crept away from the door and into my bed as I heard their feet on the stairs. My stomach and legs didn't stop shaking for a very long time but finally I slept, dreaming of face-cards.

At breakfast the next morning Aunt Eadie was still asleep, and all my mother said in reference to the night before was, "What time did you get to bed, Elizabeth?" And I said, "Gee, I went up to my room about 8:30, I guess. Aunt Eadie and I couldn't think of much to talk about."

When I came home for lunch she had gone. My mother's eyes were red and she let me have two bowls of fruit cocktail for dessert. At dinner that night my father told me to take off that ridiculous rhinestone ring, he didn't want to see me wearing that trash. My mother pursed her lips tightly and said, "Be a good girl, Elizabeth. Do as you're told."

HOCKEY NIGHT IN CANADA

by Diane Schoemperlen

Diane Schoemperlen was born in Fort William, Ontario, in 1954. She is the author of several novels and many story collections: The Man of My Dreams *(1990) was short-listed for both the Trillium Award and the Governor General's Award for Fiction, which she won for* Forms of Devotion *(1998). She is the recipient of the 2008 Marian Engel Award from The Writers' Trust of Canada. She lives in Kingston, Ontario.*

"HOCKEY NIGHT IN CANADA" IS TAKEN FROM *Hockey Night in Canada and Other Stories.*

We settled ourselves in our usual places, my father and I, while the singer made his way out on to the ice and the organist cranked up for "O Canada" and "The Star Spangled Banner." Saturday night and we were ready for anything, my father half-sitting, half-lying on the chesterfield with his first dark rum and Pepsi, and I in the swivel chair beside the picture window with a box of barbecue chips and a glass of 7Up.

My mother was ripping apart with relish a red and white polka dot dress she hadn't worn for years. There were matching red shoes, purse and a hat once too, but they'd already been packed or given away. Trying to interest someone in her project and her practicality, she said, "Why, this fabric is just as good as new," pulling first one sleeve, then the other, away from the body of the dress.

But the game was starting and we were already intent on the screen and each other.

"They don't stand a chance tonight," I said, shaking my head sadly but with confidence as the players skated out.

My father grinned calmly and took a drink of rum.

"Not a chance," I prodded.

"We'll see, we'll just see about that." Even when they played poorly for weeks on end, my father remained cheerfully loyal to the Chicago Black Hawks, for no particular reason I could see, except that he always had been. He must have suffered secret doubts about the team now and then—anyone would—but he never let on. I, having no similar special allegiance and wanting to keep the evening interesting, always hoped for the other team.

We were not violent fans, either one of us. We never hollered, leaped out of our chairs, or pounded ourselves in alternating fits of frustration and ecstasy. We did not jump up and down yelling, "Kill him, kill him!" Instead, we were teasing fans, pretend fans almost, feigning hostility and heartbreak, smirking and groaning gruesomely by turns, exaggerating our reactions mainly for the benefit of the other and sometimes just to get a rise out of my mother, who was by this time humming with pins in her mouth, smoothing pattern pieces on to the remains of the dress, and snipping merrily away with the pinking shears, while scraps of cloth and tissue paper drifted to the floor all around her.

The dress, I discovered, was to be reincarnated as a blouse for me, a blouse which, by the time it was finished (perfectly, seams all basted and bound, hem hand-done), I would probably hate. Between periods, she took me into the bathroom for a fitting session in front of the full-length mirror. I did not breathe, complain or look as she pinned the blouse together around me, a piece at a time, one sleeve, the other, half the front, the other half, back, collar, the cold silver pins scratching my bare skin just lightly.

By the time we got to the three-star selection after the game, my mother was off to the back bedroom with the blouse, whirring away on the Singer.

When her friend Rita was there, my mother at least played at watching the game. Whenever the crowd roared, my father groaned and Rita began to shriek, my mother would look up from her stamp collection, which she was endlessly sorting and sticking and spreading all over the card table, and smile encouragement at the TV.

"Who scored?" she asked innocently, as she put another page in her album and arranged another row of stamps across it. Russia was her favourite country for collecting, the best, because their stamps were bigger and grander than any, especially ours, which looked stingy and common by comparison. The Russians had hockey players, cosmonauts, fruits and vegetables, wild animals, trucks and ballerinas, in red, blue, green, yellow, even shiny silver and gold. We had mainly the Queen in pastels. My mother's everyday fear and loathing of Communists did not enter into the matter.

"Just guess, Violet, just you guess who scored!" Rita crowed.

"Don't ask," my father muttered.

"Most goals, one team, one game," Rita recited. "Twenty-one, Montreal Canadiens, March 3, 1920, at Montreal, defeated the Quebec Bulldogs 18 to 3."

"Ancient history," said my father. "Besides, who ever heard of the Quebec Bulldogs anyway? You're making it all up, Rita. Tell me another one."

"Fewest points, one season," Rita chanted. "Thirty-one, Chicago Black Hawks, 1953/54, won 12, lost 36, tied 4."

"Not quite what I had in mind." My father rolled his big eyes and went into the kitchen to fix more drinks, one for himself and one for Rita, who took her rum with orange juice, no ice. I said nothing, not being sure yet whether I wanted to stick up for my father or fall in love with the Canadiens too.

Rita had followed the Montreal team for years. Unlike my father and me, she was a *real* fan, a serious fan who shrieked and howled and paced around the living-room, calling the players by their first names, begging them to score, willing them to win with clenched fists and teeth. She did not consider her everyday dislike of those Frenchmen (as in, "I've got no use for those Frenchmen, no use at all") to be contradictory. Hockey, like stamp collecting, it seemed, was a world apart, immune to the regular prejudices of race, province and country—although she did sometimes berate my father for siding with a Yankee team.

When the Black Hawks lost another one, Rita and I (for I'd been won over after all by her braying) took all the credit for knowing the better team right off the bat, and heaped all the blame upon my father who was now in disgrace along with his team—a position he took rather well. When they did win, as far as he was concerned, it was all or mainly because he'd never given up on them.

After the game my father and I usually played a few hands of poker, a penny a game, with the cards spread out on the chesterfield between us. My mother and Rita were in the kitchen having coffee and maybe a cream puff. The hum of their voices came to me just vaguely, like perfume. I wanted to hear what they were saying but my father was analysing the last power play and dealing me another hand. I won more often than not, piling up my pennies. For years after this I would think of myself as lucky at cards. In certain difficult situations which showed a disturbing tendency to repeat themselves, I would often be reminded of Rita's teasing warning: "Lucky at cards, unlucky at love."

Later, after Rita had gone home, I would find the ashtray full of lipstick-tipped butts which I pored over, looking for clues.

My mother had met Rita that summer at Eaton's where Rita was working at the Cosmetics counter. Rita still worked at Eaton's, but she was in Ladies Dresses now, having passed briefly through Lingerie and Swimwear in between.

To hear Rita tell it, you'd think their whole friendship was rooted in my mother's hair.

"I just couldn't help myself," Rita said, telling me the story. "There I was trying to convince this fat lady that all she really needed was a bottle of Cover Girl and some Midnight Blue mascara and up walked your mother with her hair."

Patting her hair fondly, my mother said, "I couldn't figure out what she was staring at."

I already knew that before Rita had come to live in Hastings, she was a hairdresser in Toronto. She'd been to hairdressing school for two years and still took the occasional special course in cold waves or colouring. She was about to open her own beauty parlour just when her husband Geoffrey killed himself and everything was changed. It was not long after that that Rita gave up hairdressing and moved to Hastings to stay with her younger sister, Jeanette. Six months after that Jeanette married a doctor and moved back to Toronto. But Rita stayed on in Hastings anyway, bought herself a second-hand car and rented an apartment downtown in the Barclay Block above an Italian bakery (which was the very same building my parents had lived in when they were first married, a fact that I found significant and somehow too good to be true).

My mother always did her own hair, putting it up in pincurls every Sunday night so that it lay in lustrous black waves all around her face and rolled thickly down past her shoulders in the back. But what Rita meant was the streak, a pure white streak in front from the time she'd had ringworm when she was small. Even I had to admit it looked splendid and daring, although there were times when we were fighting and I wanted to hurt her and tell her she looked like a skunk. Rita's own hair was straggly and thin, half-dead from too many washings, a strange salmon colour, growing out blonde, from too many experiments. Her bangs hung down almost to her eyebrows. Sometimes she wore them swept back with coloured barrettes, revealing the delicate blue veins in her temples.

"Anyway," Rita said, pausing to light another cigarette with her Zippo, "I finally got rid of the fat lady and your mother and I got talking. Just seeing her hair gave me the itch again—I could just picture all the things I could do with that hair. We went up to the cafeteria for coffee—"

"And we've been friends ever since," my mother said in a pleased and final-sounding voice, the way you might say, And they all lived happily ever after.

My mother had never really had a friend of her own before. Oh, there was a neighbour lady, Mrs. Kent three doors down, who would come over once in a while to borrow things that she never returned—the angel food cake pan, the egg beater, the four-sided cheese grater. And so my mother would go over to Mrs. Kent's house occasionally too, to get the things back. But it was never what you would call a friendship, so much as a case of proximity and Mrs. Kent's kitchen being sadly ill-equipped.

I had never seriously thought of my mother as wanting or needing a friend anyway. Friends, particularly best friends, I gathered, were something you grew out of soon after you got married and had children. After that, the husband and the children became your best friends, or were supposed to.

But then she met Rita and it was as though Rita were someone she had been just waiting for, saving herself up for all those years. They told each other old stories and secrets, made plans, remembered times before when they might have met, had just missed each other, almost met, but didn't. Rita was at least ten years younger than my mother. I suppose I thought of her as doing my mother a favour by being her friend. In the way of young girls, I just naturally imagined my mother to be the needy one of the two.

When Rita was in Cosmetics, she would bring my mother make-up samples that the salesmen had left: mascara, blusher, eyebrow pencils, and sometimes half-empty perfume testers for me. And her pale face was perfect. Once she moved to Ladies Dresses, she hardly ever wore slacks any more, except when the weather turned cold. She was always trying out bold new accessories, big belts, coloured stockings, high-heeled boots. I could only imagine what she'd bought while she worked in Lingerie—the most elegant underwear, I supposed, and coloured girdles (I didn't know if there were such things for sure, but if there were, Rita would have several), and marvellous gauzy nightgowns.

On her day off during the week Rita was usually there in the kitchen when I came home from school for lunch. While my mother fixed me a can of soup and a grilled cheese sandwich, Rita sipped black coffee and nibbled on fresh fruit and cottage cheese. This was the first I knew of dieting as a permanent condition, for although Rita was quite slim and long-legged, she was always watching her weight. My mother, who was much rounder than Rita anyway, had taken up dieting too, like a new hobby which required supplies of lettuce, pink grapefruit and detailed diet books listing menus, recipes and calories. She'd begun to compliment me on my extreme thinness, when not so many years before she'd made me wear two crinolines to school so the teachers wouldn't think she didn't feed me. How was it that, without changing size or shape, I had graduated from grotesque to slender?

"How's school going this week?" Rita would ask, offering me a tiny cube of pineapple, which I hated.

She listened patiently, nodding and frowning mildly, while I told her about Miss Morton, the gym teacher who hated me because I was no good at basketball; and about my best friend Mary Yurick who was madly in love with Lorne Puhalski, captain of the hockey team and unattainable; and about everybody's enemy, Bonnie Ettinger, who'd beat up Della White on Monday in the alley behind the school.

It was easy to get carried away with such confidences in the hope that Rita would reciprocate, and I almost told her that I was in love with Lorne Puhalski too, and that Bonnie Ettinger was going around saying she'd knock my block off if she ever got the chance. But I talked myself out of it at the last minute. I wanted so much to have Rita all to myself but somehow it never was arranged.

With Rita there, my mother could listen to my problems without worrying too much or wanting to do something about them. She and I probably learned more about each other from those kitchen conversations with Rita than we ever would have any other way.

Sometimes it was as though they'd forgotten all about me. One day when I came home for lunch my mother was sitting wrapped in a sheet on the high stool in the middle of the kitchen while Rita gave her a cold wave, something she'd been threatening to do for weeks. I made my own sandwich.

My mother was saying, "I was so young then, and everybody said I was pretty. We were in love but when they found out, they shipped him off to agricultural school in Winnipeg. I still think Sonny was my own true love."

"What about Ted?" Rita asked, wrapping pieces of hair in what looked like cigarette rolling papers and then winding them nimbly on to pink plastic rods.

"Oh, Ted."

Ted was my father of course, but it was strange to hear my mother call him by his name when usually she called him "Dad" or "your Dad."

"Yes, well, Ted. That was different. I was older. I'm even older now. I didn't tell Ted about Sonny until long after we were married."

I went back to school that afternoon with a picture of my mother as another person altogether, someone I had never met and never would now. This woman, mysterious, incomplete and broken-hearted, pestered me all day long. The stink of the cold wave chemicals lingered too, bitter but promising.

At other times it was as though my mother could tell me things through Rita that she could never have expressed if we were alone.

One Saturday night after the hockey game I left my father dozing on the chesterfield and went into the kitchen.

Rita was saying, "When Geoffrey hung himself, his whole family blamed me. They said I'd driven him to it. They kept bringing up the baby who died and then Geoffrey too, as if I'd murdered them both with my bare hands. I had a nervous breakdown and they said it served me right. It was then that I realized I would have to leave town." She spoke calmly, looking down at her lap, not moving, and a sense of young tragic death wound around her like scented bandages, permanent and disfiguring, the way Japanese women used to bind their feet to keep them dainty. She was doomed somehow, I could see that now, even though I'd never noticed it before.

"You have to be strong, we all have to be strong," my mother said without looking at me. "We're the women, we have to be stronger than they think we are."

I could hear my father snoring lightly in the other room, no longer harmless. The kitchen was snug with yellow light. The window was patterned with frost like feathers or ferns and it was just starting to snow. My mother pulled the blind down so no one could see in. We could have been anywhere, just the three of us, bending in together around the kitchen table, knowing things, these sad things, that no one else knew yet.

That night Rita slept over. An odd thing for grown-ups to do, I thought, but I liked it.

After I'd gone to bed, it reminded me of Christmas: something special waiting all night long in the living-room: the tree, the unopened presents, Rita in my mother's new nightie wrapped up in an old car blanket on the chesterfield.

Around the middle of December, Rita flew to Toronto to have Christmas with her sister Jeanette and her doctor husband. My mother had somehow not considered exchanging presents with Rita and was horrified when she appeared the morning she left with three gaily-wrapped boxes, one for each of us. Even more surprising was my father, who handed Rita a little package tied up with curly red ribbons. She opened it on the spot, still standing in the doorway, and produced a silver charm of the Montreal Canadiens' crest.

On Christmas morning we opened her presents first. She'd given my mother a white silk scarf hand-painted with an ocean scene in vivid blues and greens. My father held up a red Chicago Black Hawks jersey with the Indian head on the front and the number 21 on the back. I got a leather-covered date book for the new year in which I immediately noted the birthdays of everyone I could think of. Rita's presents were the best ones that year.

After dinner, we called all our relatives in Manitoba and then my mother took some pictures of the tree, of my father in his new hockey sweater and of me eating my dessert behind the chicken carcass. My friend Mary called and we told each other everything we got. I thought Rita might call later but she didn't.

Between Christmas and New Year's my mother went out and bought a braided gold necklace to give to Rita when she got back. The silver charm was never discussed in front of me.

Not long after Rita returned from her holidays, she was moved from Ladies Dresses into Ladies Coats. Now when she came over she wore a knee-length black coat trimmed with grey Persian lamb at the collar and cuffs. She always hesitated before taking it off, caressing the curly lapels, picking invisible lint off the back, giving my mother and I just enough time to notice and admire it again. She knew a lot about mink and ermine now, how the little things were bred and raised on special farms, how vicious they were, how many tiny pelts it took to make just one coat. She lusted uncontrollably, as she put it, after one particular mink coat in her department but had resigned herself to never being able to afford it and seemed both relieved and disappointed the day it was bought by some doctor's wife.

"Just between you and I," my mother said right after Rita phoned to say she'd sold the fabulous coat, "I think mink is a waste of money. It's only for snobs. I wouldn't wear one if you gave it to me." Ten years later, my father bought her a mink jacket trimmed with ermine and she said, hugging him, "Oh, Ted, I've always wanted one."

It was an extravagant winter, with new records set for both snow and all-time low temperatures. My father seemed to be always outside shovelling snow in the dark, piling up huge icy banks all around the house. He would come in from the cold red-cheeked and handsome, trying to put his icy hands around my neck. Rita came over less and less often. She said it was because her car wouldn't start half the time, even when she kept it plugged in.

On warmer days when Rita wasn't working, my mother often took the bus downtown to her apartment. When I came home from school at three-thirty, the house would be luxuriously empty. I curled up on the chesterfield with the record player on and wrote in the date book Rita had given me or worked on the optimistic list my friend Mary and I had started: "One Thousand Things We Like." Well into its second spiral notebook, the list had passed seven hundred and was coming up quickly on eight with

> *cuckoo clocks*
> *Canada*
> *lace*
> *my mother's hair*

comfortable underwear and
having a bath without interruptions

being the most recent additions.

My mother returned just in time to start supper before my father got home from work. She was distracted then in a pleasant sort of way, all jazzed up and jingling from too much coffee or something, gabbing away gaily as she peeled the potatoes. Rita had given her some old clothes which could be made over into any number of new outfits for me. There was a reversible plaid skirt I'd always admired and wanted to wear right away but my mother said it was too old for me.

One Saturday afternoon when we had been out shopping together, my mother suggested we drop in on Rita before catching the bus home. I had never been to her apartment before and as we walked up Northern Avenue to the Barclay Block, I tried to imagine what it would be like. Small, I supposed, since Rita lived alone—and was, in fact, the only person I'd ever known who did. Such an arrangement was new to me then, a future possibility that became more and more attractive the more I thought about it. The apartment would be quite small, yes, and half-dark all the time, with huge exotic plants dangling in all the windows, shedding a humid green light everywhere. The rooms smelled of coffee and black earth. The furniture was probably old, cleverly draped with throws in vivid geometrics. The hardwood floors gleamed and in one room (which one?) the ceiling was painted a throbbing bloody red. I thought that Rita and I could have coffee there just the two of us (my mother having conveniently disappeared) and she would tell me everything I needed to know. Why did Geoffrey hang himself, what happened to the baby, do you go out with men sometimes, do you think I'm pretty, do you think I'm smart? She could tell my future like a fortune.

We climbed a steep flight of stairs up to the second floor. The smell of baking bread rose up cheesy and moist from the Italian bakery below. I'd forgotten that my parents had lived here once too, until my mother said, "I always hated that smell, we lived in 3B," and pointed to a door on the left. I could not imagine anything at all about their apartment.

My mother knocked loudly on Rita's door. Further down another door opened and a woman in her house-coat leaned out into the hall, expecting somebody, I guess, or maybe just spying. "Oh, it's you. Hi," she said and ducked back inside.

My mother knocked again, and then once more.

"Maybe she's working," I offered.

"No, she's not. She definitely told me she was off today."

"Where can she be then?" I was pretty sure I could hear a radio going inside.

"How would I know?" my mother said angrily and sailed back down the hall.

Only once did I find my father and Rita alone in the house. I came home from Mary's late one Saturday after-noon and they were drinking rum at the kitchen table, with the record player turned up loud in the living-room. They seemed neither surprised nor sorry to see me. There was something funny about Rita's eyes when she looked up at me though, a lazy softness, a shining, which I just naturally assumed to be an effect of the rum. She poured me a glass of 7Up and we sat around laying bets on the playoffs which were just starting, Montreal and St. Louis, until my mother came home from shopping. As it turned out, the Canadiens took the series four games straight that year and skated back to Montreal with the Stanley Cup.

Rita stayed for supper and then for the game. I went back to Mary's and then her father drove us downtown to the Junior A game at the arena. Rita was gone by the time I got home and I went straight to bed because I'd had one shot of rye in Lorne Puhalski's father's car in the arena parking lot and I was afraid my mother, who still liked to kiss me goodnight, would smell it.

They were arguing as they got ready for bed.

"She lost her son, Violet, and then her husband too," my father said, meaning Rita, making her sound innocent but careless, always losing things, people too. But he was defending her, and himself too, protecting her from some accusation, himself from some threat that I'd missed, something unfair.

"Well, I *know* that, Ted."

"Don't forget it then."

"That's no excuse for anything, you fool."

"I didn't say it was."

"Be quiet, she'll hear you," my mother said, meaning me.

DRUMMER

by Guy Vanderhaeghe

Guy Vanderhaeghe was born in 1951 in Esterhazy, Saskatchewan. He is the author of three collections of short stories and four novels, a body of work that has earned him wide critical acclaim and many prizes, including two Governor General's Awards. Guy Vanderhaeghe lives in Saskatoon, where he is a St. Thomas More Scholar at S.T.M. College.

"DRUMMER" IS FROM *Man Descending*, Guy Vanderhaeghe's first published volume.

You'd think my old man was the Pope's nephew or something if you'd seen how wild he went when he learned I'd been sneaking off Sundays to Faith Baptist Church. Instead of going to eleven o'clock Mass like he figured I was.

Which is kind of funny. Because although Mom is solid R.C.—eight o'clock Mass and saying a rosary at the drop of a hat—nobody ever accused Pop of being a religious fanatic by no means. He goes to confession regular like an oil change, every five thousand miles, or Easter, whichever comes first.

Take the Knights of Columbus. He wouldn't join those guys for no money. Whenever Mom starts in on him about enlisting he just answers back that he can't afford the outlay on armour and where'd we keep a horse? Which is his idea of a joke. So it isn't exactly as if he was St. Joan of Arc himself to go criticizing me.

And Pop wouldn't have been none the wiser if it wasn't for my older brother Gene, the prick. Don't think I don't know who told. But I can't expect nothing different from that horse's ass.

So, as I was saying, my old man didn't exactly take it all in stride. "Baptists! *Baptists!* I'm having your head examined. Do you hear me? I'm having it *examined!* Just keep it up and see if I don't you crazy little pecker. They roll in the aisles. Baptists, for chrissakes!"

"I been three times already and nobody rolled in an aisle once."

"Three times? *Three times?* Now it all comes out. Three, eh?" He actually hits himself in the forehead with the heel of his palm. Twice. "Jesus Christ Almighty, I'm blessed with a son like this? What's the matter with you? Why can't you ever do something I can understand?"

"Like wrecking cars?" This is a swift kick in the old fun sack. Pop's just getting over Gene's totalling off the first new car he's bought in eight years. A 1966 Chevy Impala.

"Shut your smart mouth. Don't go dragging your brother into this. Anyway, what he done to the car was *accidental*. But not you. Oh no, you marched into that collection of religious screwballs, holy belly-floppers, and linoleum-beaters under your own steam. *On purpose*. For God's sake, Billy, that's no religion that— it's *exercise*. Stay away from them Baptists."

"Can't," I says to him.

"Can't? *Can't?* Why the hell not?"

"Matter of principle."

They teach us that in school, matters of principle. I swear it's a plot to get us all slaughtered the day they graduate us out the door. It's their revenge, see? Here we are reading books in literature class about some banana who's only got one oar in the water to start with, and then he pops it out worrying about principles. Like that Hamlet, or what's his name in *A Tale of Two Cities*. Ever notice how many of those guys are alive at the end of those books they teach us from?

"I'll principle you," says the old man.

The only teacher who maybe believes all that crock of stale horseshit about principles is Miss Clark, who's fresh out of wherever they bake Social Studies teachers. She's got principles on the brain. For one thing, old Clarkie has pretty nearly wallpapered her room with pictures of that Negro, Martin Luther King, and some character who's modelling the latest in Wabasso sheets and looks like maybe he'd kill for a hamburger—Gandhi is his name—and that hairy old fart Tolstoy, who wrote the books you need a front-end loader to lift. From what Clarkie tells us, I gather they're what you call non-violent shit-disturbers.

Me too. Being a smart-ass runs in the Simpson family. It's what you call hereditary, like a disease. That's why all of a sudden, before I even *think* for chrissakes, I hear myself lecturing the old man in this fruity voice that's a halfway decent imitation of old Clarkie, and I am using the exact words which I've heard her say myself.

"Come, come, surely by this day and age everybody has progressed to the point where we can all agree on the necessity of freedom of worship. If we can't agree on anything else, at least we can agree on that."

I got news for her. My old man don't agree to no such thing. He up and bangs me one to the side of the head. A backhander special. You see, nobody in our house is allowed an opinion until they're twenty-one.

Of course, I could holler Religious Persecution. Not that it would do any good. But it's something I happen to know quite a bit about, seeing as Religious Persecution was my assignment in Social Studies that time we studied Man's Inhumanity to Man. The idea was to write a two-thousand-word report proving how everybody has been a shit to everybody else through the ages, and where did it ever get them? This is supposed to improve us somehow, I guess.

Anyway, as usual anything good went fast. Powbrowski got A. Hitler, Keller put dibs on Ivan the Terrible, Langly asked for Genghis Khan. By the time old Clarkie got around to me there was just a bunch of crap left like No Votes For Women. So I asked, please, could I do a project on Mr. Keeler? Keeler is the dim-witted bat's fart who's principal of our school.

For being rude, Miss Clark took away my "privilege" of picking and said I had to do Religious Persecution. Everybody was avoiding that one like the plague.

Actually, I found Religious Persecution quite inter-esting. It's got principles too, number one being that whatever you're doing to some poor son of a bitch— roasting his chestnuts over an open fire, or stretching his pant-leg from a 29-incher to a 36-incher on the rack— why, you're doing it for his own good. So he'll start thinking right. Which is more or less what my old man was saying when he told me I can't go out of the house on Sundays any more. He says to me, "You aren't setting a foot outside of that door [he actually points at it] of a Sunday until you come to your senses and quit with all the Baptist bullshit."

Not that that's any heavy-duty torture. What he don't know is that these Baptists have something called Prayer, Praise and Healing on Wednesday nights. My old man hasn't locked me up Wednesday nights yet by no means.

I figure if my old man wants somebody to blame for me becoming a Baptist he ought to take a peek in my older brother Gene's direction. He started it.

Which sounds awful funny if you know anything about Gene. Because if Gene was smart enough to have ever thought about it, he'd come out pretty strong against religion, since it's generally opposed to most things he's in favour of.

Still, nobody thinks the worse of my brother for doing what he likes to do. They make a lot of excuses for you in a dinky mining town that's the arsehole of the world if you bat .456 and score ninety-eight goals in a thirty-five-game season. Shit, last year they passed the hat around to all the big shots on the recreation board and collected the dough for one of Gene's liquor fines and give it to him on the q.t.

But I'm trying to explain my brother. If I had to sum him up I'd probably just say he's the kind of guy doesn't have to dance. What I mean is, you take your average, normal female: they slobber to dance. The guys that stand around leaning against walls are as popular to them as syphilis. You don't dance, you're a pathetic dope—even the ugly ones despise you.

But not Gene. He don't dance and they all cream. You explain it. Do they figure he's too superior to be bothered? Because it's not true. I'm his brother and I know. The dink just can't dance. That simple. But if I mention this little fact to anybody, they look at me like I been playing out in the sun too long. Everybody around here figures Mr. Wonderful could split the fucking atom with a hammer and a chisel if he put his mind to it.

Well, almost everybody. There's a born doubter in every crowd. Ernie Powers is one of these. He's the kind of stupid fuck who's sure they rig the Stanley Cup and the Oscars and nobody ever went up in space. Everything is a hoax to him. Yet he believes professional wrestling is on the up and up. You wonder—was he dropped on his head, or what? Otherwise you got to have a plan to grow up that ignorant.

So it was just like Einstein to bet Gene ten dollars he couldn't take out Nancy Williams. He did that while we were eating a plate of chips and gravy together in the Rite Spot and listening to Gene going on about who's been getting the benefit of his poking lately. Powers, who is a very jealous person because he's going steady with his right hand, says, oh yeah sure, maybe her, but he'd bet ten bucks somebody like Nancy Williams in 11B wouldn't even go out with Gene.

"Get serious," says my brother when he hears that. He considers himself irresistible to the opposite sex.

"Ten bucks. She's strictly off-limits even to you, Mr. Dreamboat. It's all going to waste. That great little gunga-poochy-snuggy-bum, that great matched set. Us guys in 11B, you know what we call them? The Untouchables. Like on TV."

"What a fucking sad bunch. Untouchables for you guys, maybe. If any of you queers saw a real live piece of pelt you'd throw your hat over it and run."

"Talk's cheap," says Ernie, real offended. "You don't know nothing about her. My sister says Miss High-and-Mighty didn't go out for cheerleading because the outfits was *too revealing*. My sister says Nancy Williams belongs to some religion doesn't allow her to dance. Me, I saw her pray over a hard-boiled egg for about a half-hour before she ate it in the school lunch-room. Right out where anybody could see, she prayed. No way somebody like that is going to go out with you, Simpson. If she does I'll eat my shorts."

"Start looking for the ten bucks, shitface, and skip dinner, because I'm taking Nancy Williams to the Christmas Dance," my brother answers him right back. Was Gene all of a sudden hostile, or was he hostile? I overheard our hockey coach say one time that my brother Gene's the kind of guy rises to a challenge. The man's got a point. I lived with Gene my whole life, which is sixteen years now, and I ought to know. Unless he gets mad he's useless as tits on a boar.

You better believe Gene was mad. He called her up right away from the pay phone in the Rite Spot. It was a toss-up as to which of those two jerks was the most entertaining. Powers kept saying, "There's no way she'll go out with him. No way." And every time he thought of parting with a ten-spot, a look came over his face like he just pinched a nut or something. The guy's so christly tight he squeaks when he walks. He was sharing my chips and gravy, if you know what I mean?

And then there was Gene. I must say I've always enjoyed watching him operate. I mean, even on the telephone he looks so sincere I could just puke. It's not unconscious by no means. My brother explained to me once what his trick is. To look that way you got to think that way is his motto. "What I do, Billy," he told me once, "is make myself believe, really believe, say ... well, that an H-bomb went off, or that some kind of disease which only attacks women wiped out every female on the face of the earth but the one I'm talking to. That makes her the last piece of tail on the face of the earth, Billy! It's just natural then to be extra nice." Even though he's my brother, I swear to God he had to been left on our doorstep.

Of course, you can't argue with success. As soon as Gene hung up and smiled, Powers knew he was diddled. Once. But my brother don't show much mercy. Twice was coming. It turned out Nancy Williams had a cousin staying with her for Christmas vacation. She wondered if maybe Gene could get this cousin a date? When Powers heard that, he pretty nearly went off in his pants. Nobody'll go out with him. He's fat and he sweats and he never brushes his teeth, there's stuff grows on them looks like the crap that floats on top of a slough. Even the really desperate girls figure no date is less damaging to their reputations than a date with Powers. You got to hold the line somewhere is how they look at it.

So Ernie's big yap cost him fifteen dollars. He blew that month's baby bonus (which his old lady gives him because he promises to finish school) and part of his allowance. The other five bucks is what he had to pay when Gene sold him Nancy Williams' cousin. It damn near killed him.

All right. Maybe I ought to've said something when Gene marched fat Ernie over to the Bank of Montreal to make a withdrawal on this account Powers has had since he was seven and started saving for a bike. He never got around to getting the bike because he couldn't bring himself to ever see that balance go down. Which is typical.

Already then I *knew* Ernie wasn't taking the cousin to no Christmas Dance. I'd heard once too often from that moron how Whipper Billy Watson would hand a licking on Cassius Clay, or how all the baseball owners get together in the spring to decide which team will win the World Series in the fall. He might learn to keep his hole shut for once.

The thing is *I'd* made up my mind to take the cousin. For nothing. It just so happens that, Gene being mad, he'd kind of forgot he's not allowed to touch the old man's vehicle. Seeing as he tied a chrome granny knot around a telephone pole with the last one.

Gene didn't realize it yet but he wasn't going nowhere unless I drove. And I was going to drive because I'd happened to notice Nancy Williams around. She seemed like a very nice person who maybe had what Miss Clark says are principles. I suspected that if that was true, Gene for once was going to strike out, and no way was I going to miss *that*. Fuck. I'd have killed to see that. No exaggeration.

On the night of the Christmas Dance it's snowing like a bitch. Not that it's cold for December, mind you, but snowing. Sticky, sloppy stuff that almost qualifies for sleet, coming down like crazy. I had to put the windshield wipers on. In December yet.

Nancy Williams lives on the edge of town way hell and gone, in new company housing. The mine manager is the dick who named it Green Meadows. What a joke. Nobody lives there seen a blade of grass yet nor pavement neither. They call it Gumboot Flats because if it's not frozen it's mud. No street-lights neither. It took me a fuck of a long time to find her house in the dark. When I did I shut off the motor and me and Gene just sat.

"Well?" I says after a bit. I was waiting for Gene to get out first.

"Well what?"

"Well, maybe we should go get them?"

Gene didn't answer. He leans across me and plays "Shave and a haircut, two bits" on the horn.

"You're a geek," I tell him. He don't care.

We wait. No girls. Gene gives a couple of long, long blasts on the hooter. I was wishing he wouldn't. This time somebody pulls open the living-room drapes. There stands this character in suspenders, for chrissakes, and a pair of pants stops about two inches shy of his armpits. He looked like somebody's father and what you'd call belligerent.

"I think he wants us to come to the door."

"He can want all he likes. Jesus Murphy, it's snowing out there. I got no rubbers."

"Oh, Christ," I says. "I'll go get them, Gene. It's such a big deal."

Easier said than done. I practically had to present a medical certificate. By the time Nancy's father got through with me I was starting to sound like that meatball Chip on *My Three Sons*. Yes sir. No sir. He wasn't too impressed with the horn-blowing episode, let me tell you. And then Nancy's old lady totes out a Kodak to get some "snaps" for Nancy's scrapbook. I didn't say nothing but I felt maybe they were getting evidence for the trial in case they had to slap a charge on me later. You'd have had to see it to believe it. Here I was standing with Nancy and her cousin, grinning like I was in my right mind, flash bulbs going off in my face, nodding away to the old man, who was running a safe-driving clinic for yours truly on the sidelines. Gene, I says to myself, Gene, you're going to pay.

At last, after practically swearing a blood oath to get his precious girls home, *undamaged*, by twelve-thirty, I chase the women out the door. And while they run through the snow, giggling, Stirling Moss delays me on the doorstep, in this blizzard, showing me for about the thousandth time how to pull a car out of a skid on ice. I kid you not.

From that point on everything goes rapidly downhill.

Don't get me wrong. I got no complaints against the girls. Doreen, the cousin, wasn't going to break no mirrors, and she sure was a lot more lively than I expected. Case in point. When I finally get to the car, fucking near frozen, what do I see? Old Doreen hauling up about a yard of her skirt, which she rolled around her waist like the spare tire on a fat guy. Then she pulled her sweater down to hide it. You bet I was staring.

"Uncle Bob wouldn't let me wear my mini," she says. "Got a smoke? I haven't had one for days."

It seems she wasn't the only one had a bit of a problem with the dress code that night. In the back seat I could hear Nancy apologizing to Gene for the outfit her mother had made her special for the dance. Of course, I thought Nancy looked quite nice. But with her frame she couldn't help, even though she was got up a bit peculiar. What I mean is, she had on this dress made out of the same kind of shiny material my mother wanted for drapes. But the old man said she couldn't have it because it was too heavy. It'd pull the curtain rods off the wall.

I could tell poor old Nancy Williams sure was nervous. She just got finished apologizing for how she looked and then she started in suckholing to Gene to please excuse her because she wasn't the world's best dancer. As a matter of fact this was her first dance ever. Thank heavens for Doreen, who was such a good sport. She'd been teaching her to dance all week. But it takes lots and lots of practice to get the hang of it. She hoped she didn't break his toes stepping on them. Ha ha ha. Just remember, she was still learning.

Gene said he'd be glad to teach her anything he figured she needed to know.

Nancy didn't catch on because she doesn't have that kind of mind. "That would be sweet of you, Gene," she says.

The band didn't show because of the storm. An act of God they call it. I'll say. So I drove around this dump for about an hour while Gene tried to molest Nancy. She put up a fair-to-middling struggle from what I could hear. The stuff her dress was made of was so stiff it crackled when she moved. Sort of like tin foil. Anyway, the two of them had it snapping and crackling like a bonfire there in the back seat while they fought a pitched battle over her body. She wasn't having none of that first time out of the chute.

"*Gene!*"

"Well for chrissakes, relax!"

"Don't take the Lord's name in vain."

"What's that supposed to mean?"

"Don't swear."

"Who's swearing?"

"Don't snag my nylons, Gene. Gene, what in the world are you … *Gene!*"

"Some people don't know when they're having a good time," says Doreen. I think she was a little pissed I hadn't parked and give her some action. But Lord knows what might've happened to Nancy if I'd done that.

Then, all of a sudden, Nancy calls out, sounding what you'd call desperate, "Hey, everybody, who wants a Coke!"

"Nobody wants a Coke," mumbles Gene, sort of through his teeth.

"Well, maybe we could go some place?" Meaning somewhere well-lit where this octopus will lay off for five seconds.

"I'll take you some place," Gene mutters. "You want to go somewhere, we'll go to Zipper's. Hey Billy, let's take them to Zipper's."

"I don't know, Gene ..."

The way I said that perked Doreen up right away. As far as she was concerned, anything was better than driving around with a dope, looking at a snowstorm. "Hey," she hollers, "that sounds like *fun!*" Fun like a mental farm.

That clinched it though. "Sure," says Gene, "we'll check out Zipper's."

What could I say?

Don't get me wrong. Like everybody else I go to Zipper's and do stuff you can't do any place else in town. That's not it. But I wouldn't take anybody nice there on purpose. And I'm not trying to say that Zipper and his mother are bad people neither. It's just that so many shitty things have happened to those two that they've become kind of unpredictable. If you aren't used to that it can seem pretty weird.

I mean, look at Zipper. This guy is a not entirely normal human being who tries to tattoo himself with geometry dividers and India ink. He has this home poke on his arm which he claims is an American bald eagle but looks like a demented turkey or something. He did it himself, and the worst is he doesn't know how homely that bird is. The dumb prick shows it to people to admire.

Also, I should say a year ago he quits school to teach himself to be a drummer. That's all. He doesn't get a job or nothing, just sits at home and drums, and his mother, who's a widow and doesn't know any better, lets him. I guess that that's not any big surprise. She's a pretty hopeless drunk who's been taking her orders from Zipper since he was six. That's when his old man got electrocuted out at the mine.

Still, I'm not saying that the way Zipper is is entirely his fault. Though he can be a real creep all right. Like once when he was about ten years old Momma Zipper gets a jag on and passes out naked in the bedroom, and he lets any of his friends look at his mother with no clothes on for chrissakes, if they pay him a dime. His own mother, mind you.

But in his defence I'd say he's seen a lot of "uncles" come and go in his time, some of which figured they'd make like the man of the house and tune him in. For a while there when he was eleven, twelve maybe, half the time he was coming to school with a black eye.

Now you take Gene, he figures Zipper's house is heaven on earth. No rules. Gene figures that's the way life ought to be. No rules. Of course, nothing's entirely free. At Zipper's you got to bring a bottle or a case of beer and give Mrs. Zipper a few snorts, then everything is hunky-dory. Gene had a bottle of Five Star stashed under the back seat for the big Christmas Dance, so we were okay in that department.

But that night the lady of the house didn't seem to be around, or mobile anyway. Zipper himself came to the door, sweating like a pig in a filthy T-shirt. He'd been drumming along to the radio.

"What do you guys want?" says Zipper.

Gene holds up the bottle. "Party time."

"I'm practising," says Zipper.

"So you're practising. What's that to us?"

"My old lady's sleeping on the sofa," says Zipper, opening the door wide. "You want to fuck around here you do it in the basement." Which means his old lady'd passed out. Nobody *sleeps* through Zipper on the drums.

"*Gene.*" Nancy was looking a bit shy, believe me.

My brother didn't let on he'd even heard her. "Do I look particular? You know me, Zip."

Zipper looked like maybe he had to think about that one. To tell the truth, he didn't seem quite all there. At

last he says, "Sure. Sure, I know you. Keep a cool tool."
And then, just like that, he wanders off to his drums,
and leaves us standing there.

Gene laughs and shakes his head. "What a meatball."

It makes me feel empty lots of times when I see
Zipper. He's so skinny and yellow and his eyes are
always weepy-looking. They say there's something gone
wrong with his kidneys from all the gas and glue he
sniffed when he was in elementary school.

Boy, he loves his drums though. Zipper's really what
you'd call dedicated. The sad thing is that the poor guy's
got no talent. He just makes a big fucking racket and he
don't know any better. You see, Zipper really thinks he's
going to make himself somebody with those drums, he
really does. Who'd tell him any different?

Gene found some dirty coffee cups in the kitchen sink
and started rinsing them out. While he did that I watched
Nancy Williams. She hadn't taken her coat off, in fact she
was hugging it tight to her chest like she figured
somebody was going to tear it off of her. I hadn't noticed
before she had on a little bit of lipstick. But now her face
had gone so pale it made her mouth look bright and red
and pinched like somebody had just slapped it, hard.

Zipper commenced slamming away just as the four
of us got into the basement. Down there it sounded as if
we were right inside a great big drum and Zipper was
beating the skin directly over our heads.

And boy, did it *stink* in that place. Like the sewer had
maybe backed up. But then there were piles of dirty
laundry humped up on the floor all around an old
wringer washing machine, so that could've been the
smell too.

It was cold and sour down there and we had nothing to sit on but a couple of lawn chairs and a chesterfield that was all split and stained with what I think was you know what. Nancy looked like she wished she had a newspaper to spread out over it before she sat down. As I said before, you shouldn't never take anybody nice to Zipper's.

Gene poured rye into the coffee mugs he'd washed out and passed them around. Nancy didn't want hers. "No thank you," she told him.

"You're embarrassing me, Nancy," says Doreen. The way my date was sitting in the lawn chair beside me in her make-do mini I knew why Gene was all scrunched down on that wrecked chesterfield.

"You know I don't drink, Doreen." Let me explain that when Nancy said that it didn't sound snotty. Just quiet and well-mannered like when a polite person passes up the parsnips. Nobody in their right minds holds it against them.

"You don't do much, do you?" That was Gene's two bits' worth.

"I'll say," chips in Doreen.

Nancy doesn't answer. I could hear old Zipper crashing and banging away like a madman upstairs.

"You don't do much, *do you*?" Gene's much louder this time.

"I suppose not." I can barely hear her answer because her head's down. She's checking out the backs of her hands.

"Somebody in your position ought to try harder," Doreen pipes up. "You don't make yourself too popular when you go spoiling parties."

Gene shoves the coffee mug at Nancy again. "Have a drink."

She won't take it. Principles.

"Have a drink!"

"Whyn't you lay off her?"

Gene's pissed off because he can't make Nancy Williams do what he says, so he jumps off the chesterfield and starts yelling at me. "Who's going to make me?" he hollers. "You? You going to make me?"

I can't do nothing but get up too. I never won a fight with my brother yet, but that don't mean I got to lay down and die for him. "You better take that sweater off," I says, pointing, "it's mine and I don't want blood on it." He always wears my clothes.

That's when the cousin Doreen slides in between us. She's the kind of girl loves fights. They put her centre stage. That is, if she can wriggle herself in and get involved breaking them up. Fights give her a chance to act all emotional and hysterical like she can't stand all the violence. Because she's so sensitive. Blessed are the peacemakers.

"Don't fight! Please, don't fight! Come on, Gene," she cries, latching on to his arm, "don't fight over her. Come away and cool down. I got to go to the bathroom. You show me where the bathroom is, Gene. Okay?"

"Don't give me that. You can find the bathroom yourself." Old Gene has still got his eyes fixed on me. He's acting the role. Both of them are nuts.

"Come on, Gene, I'm scared to go upstairs with that Zipper person there! He's so strange. I don't know what he might get it in his head to do. Come on, take me upstairs." Meanwhile this Doreen, who is as strong as your average sensitive ox, is sort of dragging my brother in the direction of the stairs. Him pretending he don't really want to go and have a fuss made over him, because he's got this strong urge to murder me or cripple me or something.

"You wait" is all he says to me.

"Ah, quit it or I'll die of shock," I tell him.

"Please, Gene. That Zipper person is *weird*."

At last he goes with her. I hear Gene on the stairs. "Zipper ain't much," he says, "I know lots of guys crazier than him."

I look over to Nancy sitting quietly on that grungy chesterfield, feet together, hands turned palms up on her lap. Her dress kind of sticks out from under the hem of her coat all stiff and shiny and funny-looking.

"I shouldn't have let her make me this dress," she says, angry. "We ought to have gone downtown and bought a proper one. But she had this *material*." She stops, pulls at the buttons of her coat and opens it. "Look at this thing. No wonder Gene doesn't like it, I bet."

At first I don't know what to say when she looks at me like that, her face all white except for two hot spots on her cheekbones. Zipper is going nuts upstairs. He's hot tonight. It almost sounds like something recognizable. "Don't pay Gene any attention," I say, "he's a goof."

"It's awful, this dress."

She isn't that dumb. But a person needs a reason for why things go wrong. I'm not telling her she's just a way to win ten dollars and prove a point.

"Well, kind of. That's part of it. He's just a jerk. Take it from me, I know. Forget it."

"I never even thought he knew I was alive. Never guessed. And here I was, crazy about him. Just crazy. I'd watch him in the hallway, you know? I traded lockers with Susan Braithwaite just to get closer to his. I went to all the hockey games to see him play. I worshipped him."

The way she says that, well, it was too personal. Somebody oughtn't to say that kind of a thing to a practical stranger. It was worse than if she'd climbed out of her clothes. It made me embarrassed.

"And funny thing is, all that time he really did think I was cute. He told me on the phone. But he never once thought to ask me out because I'm a Baptist. He was sure I couldn't go. Because I'm a Baptist he thought I couldn't go. But he thought I was cute all along."

"Well, yeah."

"And now," she says, "look at this. I begged and begged Dad to let me come. I practically got down on my hands and knees. And all those dancing lessons and everything and the band doesn't show. Imagine."

"Gene wouldn't have danced with you anyway. He doesn't dance."

Nancy smiled at me. As if I was mental. She didn't half believe me.

"Hey," I says, just like that, you never know what's going to get into you. "Nancy, you want to dance?"

"Now?"

"Now. Sure. Come on. We got the one-man band, Zipper, upstairs. Why not?"

"What'll Gene say?"

"To hell with Gene. Make him jealous."

She was human at least. She liked the idea of Gene jealous. "Okay."

And here I got a confession to make. I go on all the time about Gene not being able to dance. Well, me neither. But I figured what the fuck. You just hop around and hope to hell you don't look too much like you're having a convulsion.

Neither of us knew how to get started. We just stood gawking at one another. Upstairs Zipper was going out of his tree. It sounded like there was four of him. As musical as a bag of hammers he is.

"The natives are restless tonight, Giles," I says. I was not uncomfortable. Let me tell you another one.

"Pardon?"

"Nothing. It was just dumb."

Nancy starts to sway from side to side, shuffling her feet. I figure that's the signal. I hop or whatever. So does she. We're out of the gates, off and running.

To be perfectly honest, Nancy Williams can't dance for shit. She gets this intense look on her face like she's counting off in her head, and starts to jerk. Which gets some pretty interesting action out of the notorious matched set but otherwise is pretty shoddy. And me? Well, I'm none too co-ordinated myself, so don't go getting no mental picture of Fred Astaire or whoever.

In the end what you had was two people who can't dance, dancing to the beat of a guy who can't drum. Still, Zipper didn't know no better and at the time neither did we. We were just what you'd call mad dancing fools. We danced and danced and Zipper drummed and drummed and we were all together and didn't know it. Son of a bitch, the harder we danced the hotter and happier

Nancy Williams' face got. It just smoothed the unhappiness right out of it. Mine too, I guess.

That is, until all of a sudden it hit her. She stops
dead in her tracks and asks, "Where's Doreen and
Gene?"

Good question. They'd buggered off in my old man's
car. Zipper didn't know where.

The rest of the evening was kind of a horror story. It
took me a fair while to convince Nancy they hadn't gone
for Cokes or something and would be right back. In the
end she took it like a trooper. The only thing she'd say
was, "That Doreen. *That Doreen*," and shake her head.
Of course she said it about a thousand times. I was
wishing she'd shut up, or maybe give us a little variety
like, "*That Gene*." No way.

I had a problem. How to get Cinderella home before
twelve-thirty, seeing as Gene had the family chariot. I
tried Harvey's Taxi but no luck. Harvey's Taxi is one car
and Harvey, and both were out driving lunches to a
crew doing overtime at the mine.

Finally, at exactly twelve-thirty, we struck out on foot
in this blizzard. Jesus, was it snowing. There was slush
and ice water and every kind of shit and corruption all
over the road. Every time some hunyak roared by us we
got splattered by a sheet of cold slop. The snow melted
in our hair and run down our necks and faces. By the
time we went six blocks we were soaked. Nancy was the
worst off because she wasn't dressed too good with
nylons and the famous dress and such. I seen I had to be
a gentleman so I stopped and give her my gloves, and
my scarf to tie around her head. The two of us looked

like those German soldiers I seen on TV making this
death march out of Russia, on that series *Canada at War*.
That was a very educational series. It made you think of
man's inhumanity to man quite often.

"I could just die," she kept saying. "Dad is going to
kill me. This is my last dance ever. I could just die. I
could just die. *That Doreen*. Honestly!"

When we stumbled up her street, all black because of
the lack of street-lights, I could see that her house was
all lit up. Bad news. I stopped her on the corner. Just
then it quits snowing. That's typical.

She stares at the house. "Dad's waiting."

"I guess I better go no further."

Nancy Williams bends down and feels her dress
where it sticks out from under her coat. "It's soaked. I
don't know how much it cost a yard. I could just die."

"Well," I says, repeating myself like an idiot, "I guess
I better go no further." Then I try and kiss her. She sort
of straight-arms me. I get the palm of my own glove in
the face.

"What're you doing?" She sounds mad.

"Well, you know—"

"I'm not *your* date," she says, real offended. "I'm your
brother's date."

"Maybe we could go out sometime?"

"I won't be going anywhere for a long time. Look at
me. He's going to kill me."

"Well, when you do? I'm in no hurry."

"Don't you understand? Don't you understand?
Daddy will never let me go out with anybody named
Simpson again. Ever. Not after tonight."

"Ever?"

"I can't imagine what you'd have to do to redeem yourself after this mess. That's how Daddy puts it— you've got to redeem yourself. I don't even know how I'm going to do it. And none of it's my fault."

"Yeah," I says, "he'll remember me. I'm the one he took the picture of."

She didn't seem too upset at not having me calling. "Everything is ruined," she says. "If you only knew."

Nancy Williams turns away from me then and goes up that dark, dark street where there's nobody awake except at her house. Wearing my hat and gloves.

Nancy Williams sits third pew from the front, left-hand side. I sit behind her, on the other side so's I can watch her real close. Second Sunday I was there she wore her Christmas Dance dress.

Funny thing, everything changes. At first I thought I'd start going and maybe that would *redeem* myself with her old man. Didn't work. He just looks straight through me.

You ought to see her face when she sings those Baptist hymns. It gets all hot and happy-looking, exactly like it did when we were dancing together and Zipper was pounding away there up above us, where we never even saw him. When her face gets like that there's no trouble in it, by no means.

It's like she's dancing then, I swear. But to what I don't know. I try to hear it. I try and try. I listen and listen to catch it. Christ, somebody tell me. What's she dancing to? Who's the drummer?

FUGITIVE PIECES

by Anne Michaels

Anne Michaels was born in Toronto in 1958. She is the author of three highly acclaimed and award-winning poetry collections. Fugitive Pieces *(1996) was her internationally bestselling debut novel, which garnered many awards in Canada and the U.K., including the Orange Prize for Fiction, and has been made into a major motion picture. Anne Michaels lives in Toronto.*

"FUGITIVE PIECES" TELLS the interlocking stories of two men from different generations whose lives have been transformed by war. In this excerpt, one of them, Ben, the son of parents who survived the Holocaust in Poland, looks back at his childhood in 1950s Toronto.

The memories we elude catch up to us, overtake us like a shadow. A truth appears suddenly in the middle of a thought, a hair on a lens.

My father found the apple in the garbage. It was rotten and I'd thrown it out—I was eight or nine. He fished it from the bin, sought me in my room, grabbed me tight by the shoulder, and pushed the apple to my face.

> "What is this? What is it?"
> "An apple—"

My mother kept food in her purse. My father ate frequently to avoid the first twists of hunger because, once they gripped him, he'd eat until he was sick. Then he ate dutifully, methodically, tears streaming down his face, animal and spirit in such raw evidence, knowing he was degrading both. If one needs proof of the soul, it's easily found. The spirit is most evident at the point of extreme bodily humiliation. There was no pleasure, for my father, associated with food. It was years before I realized this wasn't merely a psychological difficulty, but also a moral one, for who could answer my father's question: Knowing what he knew, should he stuff himself, or starve?

> "An apple! Well, my smart son, is an apple food?"
> "It was all rotten—"

On Sunday afternoons we'd drive into the farmland bordering the city or to their favourite park at the edge of Lake Ontario. My father always wore a cap to keep his few stray hairs from flying into his eyes. He drove with both hands gripping the wheel, never violating the speed limit. I slouched in the back seat, learning Morse code from *The Boy Electrician,* or memorizing the Beaufort Scale ("Wind force 0: smoke rises vertically, sea like a mirror. Force 5: small trees sway, whitecaps. Force 6: umbrellas used with difficulty. Force 9: structural damage occurs."). Once in a while my mother's arm would appear over the front seat, a roll of candy dangling from her hand.

My parents would unfold their lawnchairs (even in winter) while I scrambled out alone, collecting rocks or identifying clouds or counting waves. I lay on grass or sand, reading, sometimes falling asleep in my heavy jacket under a clay sky with *The Moonstone* or *Men Against the Sea* with its waterspouts and volcanoes ("I cannot recall the hours that followed without experiencing something of the horror I felt at the time. Wind and rain, rain and wind, under a sky that held no promise of relief. In all that time, Mr. Bligh did not leave the tiller, and he seemed to have an exhilaration of mind that grew greater as our peril increased ..."). In good weather my mother set out the lunch she'd prepared, and they sipped strong tea from a thermos while the wind searched through the cold lake and cumulus chuffed across the horizon.

Early Sunday evenings, while my mother made dinner, I listened to music with my father in the living-room. Watching him listen made me listen differently. His attention dissolved each piece to its theoretical components like an X-ray, emotion the grey fog of flesh. He used orchestras—other people's arms and hands and breath—to signal me; a wordless entreaty, all meaning pressed into chords. Leaning against him, his arm around me—or, when I was very young, lying with my head on his lap—his hand on my hair absentmindedly but, for me, feral. He stroked my hair to Shostakovich, Prokofiev, Beethoven, Mahler's lieder: "Now all longing wants to dream," "I have become a stranger in the world."

Those hours, wordless and close, shaped my sense of him. Lines of last light over the floor, the patterned sofa, the silky brocade of the curtains. Once in a while, on summer Sundays, the shadow of an insect or bird over the sun-soaked carpet. I breathed him in. The story of his life as I knew it from my mother—strange episodic images—and his stories of composers, merged together with the music. Cow breath and cow dung and fresh hay on Mahler's muddy night road home, moonlight a spiderweb over the fields. Under the same moonlight, marching back to the camp, my father's tongue a thong of wool; unbearably thirsty as he walked at gunpoint, past a bucket of rainwater, its small circular mirror of stars. Praying for rain so they could swallow what fell on their faces, rain that smelled like sweat. How he ate the centre of a cabbage in a farmer's field, leaving it hollow but looking whole so no one would trace his escape from the soldiers in the grove.

I looked up from my father's lap to his concentrating face. He always listened with his eyes open. Beethoven with the storm of the Sixth in his face, pacing in the forest and fields of Heiligenstadt, the real storm at his back, at my father's back, mud weighing down his feet like overshoes, the shrill, desperate cry of a bird in the rainy trees. My father concentrating, during one long march, on a sliver in his hand, to keep his thoughts from his parents. I felt my skull under his fingers as he combed through my short hair. Beethoven frightening oxen with his windmill-waving arms, then stopping stock-still to look at the sky. My father staring at a lunar eclipse beside the chimneys, or staring at the sun's dead light like scum on the potholes. The gun in my father's face, how they kept nudging with their boots the cup of water from his reach.

As long as the symphony lasted, the song cycle, the quartet, I had access to him. I could pretend his attention to the music was attention to me. His favourite pieces were familiar, finite journeys we took together, recognizing signposts of ritardando and sostenuto, key changes. Sometimes he played a recording by a different conductor and I experienced the acuity of his ears as he compared interpretations: "Ben, do you hear how he rushes the arpeggios." "Listen to how he draws it out ... but if he emphasizes here, he'll ruin the crescendo later on!" And the following week we'd go back to the version we knew and loved like a face, a place. A photograph.

His absent fingers combing through my short hair. Music, inseparable from his touch.

Feeling the lines of my father's thin legs under his trousers, barely believing they were the same legs that walked those distances, stood those hours. In our Toronto apartment, images of Europe, postcards from another planet. His only brother, my uncle, whose body vanished under a squirming skin of lice. Instead of hearing about ogres, trolls, witches, I heard disjointed references to kapos, haftlings, "Ess Ess," dark woods; a pyre of dark words. Beethoven, wandering in old clothes, so shabby his neighbours nicknamed him Robinson Crusoe; the shifting wind before a storm, leaves cowering before the slap of rain, the Sixth, Opus 68; the Ninth, Opus 125. All the symphony and opus numbers I learned, to please him. That grew in my memory, under his fingers as he stroked my hair; the hair on his arm, his number close to my face.

Even my father's humour was silent. He drew things for me, cartoons, caricatures. Appliances with human faces. His drawings offered the glimpse: how he saw.

> "Is an apple food?"
> "Yes."
> "And you throw away food? You—my son—you throw away food?"
> "It's rotten—"

"Eat it.... Eat it!"
"Pa, it's rotten—I won't—"

He pushed it into my teeth until I opened my jaw. Struggling, sobbing, I ate. Its brown taste, oversweetness, tears. Years later, living on my own, if I threw out leftovers or left food on my plate in a restaurant, I was haunted by pathetic cartoon scraps in my sleep.

Images brand you, burn the surrounding skin, leave their black mark. Like volcanic ash, they can make the most potent soil. Out of the seared place emerge sharp green shoots. The images my father planted in me were an exchange of vows. He passed the book or magazine to me silently. He pointed a finger. Looking, like listening, was a discipline. What was I to make of the horror of those photos, safe in my room with the cowboy curtains and my rock collection? He thrust books at me with a ferocity that frightened me, I would say now, more than the images themselves. What I was to make of them, in my safe room, was clear. You are not too young. There were hundreds of thousands younger than you.

I dreaded my piano lessons with my father and never practised when he was home. His demand for perfection had the force of a moral imperative, each correct note setting order against chaos, a goal as impossible as rebuilding a bombed city, atom by atom. As a child I did not feel this as evidence of faith or even anything as positive as a summoning of will. Instead I absorbed it as kind of futility. All my sincere efforts only succeeded in displeasing him. My fugues and tarantellas unravelled

in the middle, my bourrées clumped along, so aware was
I of my father's uncompromising ear. Eventually his
abrupt dismissals of me in the middle of a piece, my
unhappiness, and my mother's pleading at us both,
convinced my father to give up instructing me. Not
long after our final lesson, on one of our Sundays at the
lake, my father and I were walking along the shore when
he noticed a small rock shaped like a bird. When he
picked it up, I saw the quick gleam of satisfaction in his
face and felt in an instant that I had less power to please
him than a stone.

When I was eleven, my parents rented a cottage for the
last two weeks of the summer. I'd never before experienced absolute darkness. Waking at night, I thought I'd
gone blind in my sleep—any child's terror. But made
palpable by the dark was another old fear. I lowered my
legs and thrust my arms into the dangerous air until I
found the lamp. This was a test. I knew it was essential
to be strong. After nights of sleeping with a flashlight in
my fist, I made a decision. I forced myself out of bed,
put on my sneakers, and went outside. My task was to
walk through the woods with the flashlight off until I
reached the road, about a quarter of a mile away. If my
father could walk days, miles, then I could walk at least
to the road. What would happen to me if I had to walk
as far as my father had? I was in training. My flannel
pajamas were clammy with sweat. I walked with useless
eyes and heard the river, modest knife of history, carving
its blade deeper into the earth; rusty blood seeping
through the cracked face of the forest. A fine mesh of
insects on the heavy breath of the night, the slap of ferns

weirdly cold against my ankles—nothing alive could be so cold on such a hot night. Slowly the trees began to emerge from the differentiated dark, as if embossed, black on black, and the dark itself was a pale skin stretched across charred ribs. Above, the far surf of leaves, a dark skirt of sky rustling against skeletal legs. Strange filaments from nowhere, the hair of ghosts, brushed my neck and cheeks and would not be rubbed away. The forest closed around me like a hag's embrace, all hair and hot breath, bristly skin and sharp fingernails. And just as I felt overwhelmed, sick with terror, suddenly I was in clear space, a faint breeze over the wide road. I turned on the flashlight and followed, running, its white tunnel back along the path.

In the morning I saw my legs were smeared with mud and tea-coloured blood from bites and branches. The rest of the day I discovered scratches in strange places, behind my ears, or along the inside of my arm, a thin line of blood as if drawn by red pen. I was certain that the ordeal had purged my fear. But I woke again that night in the same state, my bones cold as steel. Twice more I repeated the journey, forcing myself to face the darkness of the woods. But I still couldn't bear the darkness of my own room.

When I was twelve, I befriended a Chinese girl not much taller than me, though considerably older. I admired her leather cap, her dark skin, her elaborately twisted hair. Imagine a strand of hair four thousand years old! I also befriended an Irish boy and a Dane. I had discovered the perfectly preserved bog people in *National Geographic*, and derived a fascinated comfort from their preservation. These were not like the bodies in the photos my father showed me. I drew the aromatic earth over my shoulders, the peaceful spongy blanket of peat. I see now that my fascination wasn't archaeology or even forensics: it was biography. The faces that stared at me across the centuries, with creases in their cheeks like my mother's when she fell asleep on the couch, were the faces of people without names. They stared and waited, mute. It was my responsibility to imagine who they might be.

Like a musical score, when you read a weather map you are reading time. I'm sure, Jakob Beer, that you would agree one could chart a life in terms of pressure zones, fronts, oceanic influences.

The hindsight of biography is as elusive and deductive as long-range forecasting. Guesswork, a hunch. Monitoring probabilities. Assessing the influence of all the information we'll never have, that has never been recorded. The importance not of what's extant, but of what's disappeared. Even the most reticent subject can be—at least in part—posthumously constructed. Henry James, who might be considered coy regarding his personal life, burned all the letters he received. If anyone's interested in me, he said, let them first crack "the invulnerable granite" of my art! But even James was rebuilt, no doubt according to his own design. I'm sure he kept track of the story that would emerge if all the letters to him were omitted. He knew what to leave out. We're stuffed with famous men's lives; soft with the habits of our own. The quest to discover another's psyche, to absorb another's motives as deeply as your own, is a lover's quest. But the search for facts, for places, names, influential events, important conversations and correspondences, political circumstances—all this amounts to nothing if you can't find the assumption your subject lives by.

Any details of my parents' lives before they came to Canada I learned from my mother. Afternoons, before my father came home from the music conservatory, the grandmothers and my mother's brothers, Andrei and Max, congregated in the kitchen, where all the ghosts like to gather. My father was unaware of these revenant encounters under his roof. Only once do I remember mentioning any member of my father's vanished family in his presence—someone we were talking about at the dinner table was "just like Uncle Josef"—and my father's gaze jolted up from his plate to my mother; a terrifying look. The code of silence became more complex as I grew older. There were more and more things to keep from my father. The secrets between my mother and me were a conspiracy. What was our greatest insurrection? My mother was determined to impress upon me the absolute, inviolate necessity of pleasure.

My mother's painful love for the world. When I witnessed her delight in a colour or a flavour, the most simple gratifications—something sweet, something fresh, a new article of clothing, however humble, her love of warm weather—I didn't disdain her enthusiasm. Instead, I looked again, I tasted again, noticing. I learned that her gratitude was not in the least inordinate. I know now this was her gift to me. For a long time I thought she had created in me an extreme fear of loss—but no. It's not in the least extreme.

Loss is an edge; it swelled everything for my mother, and drained everything from my father. Because of this, I thought my mother was stronger. But now I see it was a clue: what my father had experienced was that much less bearable.

As a boy, twisters transfixed me with their bizarre violence, the random precision of their malevolence. Half an apartment building is destroyed, yet an inch away from the vanished wall, the table remains set for dinner. A chequebook is snatched from a pocket. A man opens his front door and is carried two hundred feet above the treetops, landing unharmed. A crate of eggs flies five hundred feet and is set down again, not a shell cracked. All the objects that are transported safely from one place to another in an instant, descending on ascending air currents: a jar of pickles travels twenty-five miles, a mirror, dogs and cats, the blankets ripped from a bed leaving the surprised sleepers untouched. Whole rivers lifted—leaving the riverbed dry—and then set down again. A woman carried sixty feet then deposited in a field next to a phonograph record (unscratched) of "Stormy Weather."

Then there are the whims that are not merciful: children thrown from windows, beards torn from faces, decapitations. The family quietly eating supper when the door bursts open with a roar. The tornado prowls the street, it seems to stroll leisurely, selecting its victims, capricious, the sinister black funnel slithering across the landscape, whining with the sound of a thousand trains.

Sometimes I read to my mother while she made dinner. I read to her about the effects of a Texan tornado, gathering up personal possessions until in the desert it had collected mounds of apples, onions, jewellery, eyeglasses, clothing—"the camp." Enough smashed glass to cover seventeen football fields—"Kristallnacht." I read to her about lightning—"sign of the Ess Ess, Ben, on their collars."

From conversations with my mother, when I was eleven or twelve, I learned that "those with a trade had a better chance of survival." I went to the library and found Armac's *The Boy Electrician* and set about acquiring a new vocabulary. Capacitors, diodes, voltmeters, induction coils, long-nosed pliers. I raided the "Pageant of Knowledge" series, *Electronics for Beginners, The Living World of Science*. Then I realized that knowing the right words might not be enough. Hesitantly I asked my father for money for my first circuit board and a soldering iron. Though he knew little about such things, I wasn't surprised that he saw the use of it and he encouraged my interest for a while. We went together to Esbe Science Supply for toggles and switches and various knobs and dials. For my birthday he bought me a microscope and slides. The rest of my equipment I acquired myself: my wet- and dry-bulb hygrometer, Bunsen burner, Z-tubes and funnels, pipettes, conical flasks. My mother generously cleaned out a closet to make room for my laboratory, where I spent hours alone. Even the lab coat she sewed for me from a torn sheet didn't deter me. I wasn't very good at any of it and had to follow a book at all times, having no instinct for electricity or chemistry, but I loved the smell of solder and was amazed when my first circuit lit a bulb in that dim closet.

One summer afternoon a neighbour from down the hall knocked on our door and handed me a Classics Illustrated comic book. My mother was particularly shy of Mr. Dixon, who worked in a men's clothing store and was always immaculately dressed. Mr. Dixon had bought the comic for his grandson, who, it turned out, already had that issue—#105, Jules Verne's *From the Earth to the Moon*. My mother tried to pay him, insistent, until it was clear Mr. Dixon wouldn't accept any money. Then she pressed him with thanks. Meanwhile I was on my way to the balcony, already reading: "When a man is nearly doomed to a lifetime of circling the moon, then survives the plunge of 200,000 odd miles into the Pacific, he learns not to be afraid."

After that, I wrenched money from my mother in order to collect the illustrated versions of literary masterpieces. I devoured each one from the dramatic cover to the last nagging entreaty: "Now that you've read the Classics Illustrated edition, don't miss the added enjoyment of reading the original." After consuming the pulp, I even chewed up the rind: edifying essays on a variety of topics filled the final pages. Brief biographies ("Nicholas Copernicus—Key Man in Study of Solar System"), the plots of famous operas, and arcana I've never forgotten. For example, at the back of *Caesar's Conquests*: "There are 6,000 men in a legion"; "Greek ships had eyes painted on their bows so the ships could see"; "Caesar always wrote of himself in the third person."

There was also a series on "Dog Heroes": Brandy, the quick-thinking setter who saved a young boy from a bull. Foxy, Hero of the Resistance, whose master was hiding from the Hun.

The first comic I bought was a sea adventure by Nordhoff and Hall. I followed the narrator through encounters with hurricanes and mutinies ("'We've seized the ship….' 'What, are you mad, Mr. Churchill?'"). I chose *Men Against the Sea* because I opened it and read: "I have asked for pen and paper to write this account of all that has happened … to ward off the loneliness already upon me…."

After weeks of importuning, when I was fourteen, my mother agreed to let me go with some school friends to the Canadian National Exhibition, an annual fair. I'd never felt such exhilaration, such unmediated, anonymous belonging as that day in the crowd. Our T-shirts were stained, our hands and the soles of our shoes were sticky—and the whole glutinous throng bubbled over energetically in the August sun. We gaped at colour television, watches that didn't require winding, and were galvanized by the wonders of circuit board technology in the Better Living Building. We toured the midway, shrieked to earth on the Flyer and the Wheel of Fire. When we needed to rest we slung over fences in the agriculture pavilions and watched the sheep-shearing and the milking machines in action. I collected glossy brochures on the latest domestic gadgets to please my mother—floor polishers, electric drink mixers, electric can openers. My shopping bag bulged with cardboard pennants and hats, pens advertising various companies and products, Beehive Corn Syrup scribblers, miniature samples of aftershave and stain remover, boxes of cereal and packets of teabags. We opened our satchels indiscriminately to anything offered to us.

When I came home I excitedly spilled everything on to the table for my mother's inspection. She looked at my bounty, then anxiously crammed it back into the bag. She couldn't believe the things I'd taken were free; she thought I must have made a mistake. She held up a handful of pens and pencils. I shouted, "They gave them away! I swear it! They're called 'free samples' because they're free!..." I was hysterical.

My mother made me promise not to show my father, to hide the bag in my room. Early the next morning, I walked to the corner and threw my treasure into a public trash can.

Now we had another kind of bond between us. My mother referred to the incident slyly from time to time. Though she was certain I'd taken these things improperly—admittedly by accident—she would protect me. My fault. Our secret.

From then on I began to extend my boundaries, to make detours on my way home from school. I began to learn about the city. The ravines, the coal elevators, the brickyard. Although I wouldn't have been able to put it into words then, aftermath fascinated me. The silent drama of abandonment of the empty factories and storage bins, the decaying freighters and industrial ruins.

I thought I was encouraging my mother to stop waiting for me by the window or on the balcony, to give me my freedom, not to expect me until late. I'd like to think I didn't know at the time how cruel this was. When my father and I left the apartment in the morning, my mother never felt sure we'd return at all.

I learned not to bring school friends home. I worried that our furniture was old and strange. I was ashamed by my mother's caution and need as she hovered. "What is your last name … what do your parents do … where were you born …?" My mother begged my father and me for news from our world; news of teachers and classmates, my father's piano students, the personal lives of whom we knew frustratingly little. When she left the apartment for groceries, or in summer to admire the gardens in the neighbourhood (she loved gardening and watched over a window box and trellis on our balcony), my mother prepared carefully. She carried our passports and citizenship papers in her purse "in case of a robbery." She never left a dirty dish in the sink, even if she were just walking to the corner store.

To my mother, pleasure was always serious. She celebrated the aroma each time she unscrewed the lid of the instant coffee. She stopped to inhale each fragrant fold of our freshly washed linens. She could spend half an hour eating a slice of store-bought pastry as if God had baked it with His Own Hands. Every time she purchased something new, usually a necessity (when an article of clothing had been mended too many times), she fondled it like the First Blouse or the First Pair of Stockings. She was a sensualist of proportions you, Jakob Beer, could never even estimate. You looked at me that night and placed me in your human zoo: another specimen with a beautiful wife; just another academicus dejecticus. But it was you who were embalmed! With your calmness, your expansive satiety.

The truth is you didn't acknowledge me at all that night. But I saw Naomi open like a flower.

I was about to start my second year of university and was determined to be on my own, a fact my mother had refused to accept all summer. One sun-worn August morning I carried my boxes of books down to the damp coolness of the cement parking garage and loaded up the car. My mother retreated behind the closed door of her bedroom. Only when I'd carried out the last box and was really leaving did she emerge. Grimly she prepared a parcel of food, and something was lost between us, irrevocably, the moment that plastic bag passed from her hand to mine. Over the years, the absurd package— enough for a single meal, to stop hunger for a second— was handed to me at the threshold at the end of each visit. Until it hurt less and less and the bag was simply like the roll of candy my mother passed to me from the front seat on our Sunday drives.

The first night in my own apartment, I lay in bed only a few miles across town and let my mother's phone calls ring into the dark. I didn't call for a week, then weeks at a time, though I knew it made them ill with worry. When I finally did visit, I saw that, though my parents continued in their separate silences, my defection had given them a new intimacy, a new scar. My mother still bent towards me with confidences, but only in order to withdraw them. At first I thought she was punishing me for her need of me. But my mother wasn't angry. My efforts to free myself had created a deeper harm. She was afraid. I believe that for moments my mother actually distrusted me. She would begin a story and then fall silent. "It's nothing that would interest you." When I protested, she suggested I go into the living-room and join my father. This happened even more frequently once Naomi entered our lives.

My father's behaviour remained unchanged. When I visited, I still found him either impatient, looking at his watch with desperation, or immobile, staring at a book in his room—another survivor account, another article with photographs. Afterwards, in my apartment on the upper floor of an old house near the university, I stared at the weave of my bedspread, at the bookshelf. At the dry cleaner's, flower shop, and drug store across the street. I knew my parents were awake too, our insomnia an old agreement to keep watch.

On weekends I took long self-pitying walks across the city and back again; at night, ascending into books. I spent most of my undergraduate years alone except for classes and working part time in a bookstore. I had a romance with the assistant manager. We kept on after our first embrace, just to be sure it was as joyless as it seemed. Her form was wondrously full, a firmness to everything, but especially her politics. Under her black caftan she wore shirts with slogans on them past which I never ventured: "The left hand giveth what the right taketh away." Sometimes I joined a few classmates for a meal or a movie, but I made no real effort at friendship.

For a long time I felt I had expended all my energy walking out my parents' front door.

EXTRACT FROM

Jericho's Brick Battlements

by Margaret Laurence

*Margaret Laurence was born in 1926 in
Neepawa, Manitoba, which provided the model for the
"Manawaka" of her novels and short stories.
She lived in Africa from 1950 to 1957, in Vancouver from
1957 to 1962, and in England from 1962
to 1972, then settled in Ontario. She served as chancellor
of Trent University in Peterborough, Ontario, in the
1980s. Margaret Laurence died in 1987.*

THE FOLLOWING IS AN EXTRACT FROM "Jericho's Brick
Battlements," which is from a series of related stories that
make up *A Bird in the House* (1970), which tells of the
early life of Vanessa MacLeod. Vanessa lives in the Brick
House, in the town of Manawaka, Manitoba, with her
mother, her grandfather, and her younger brother Roddie.
Grandfather Connor is a terrifying figure, who tyrannizes
the household and has tried to scare a number of potential suitors for Vanessa's Aunt Edna, who is now married
to Wes Grigg.

I had gone out with boys on rare occasions, but I had
never had what might be termed a boyfriend. The
boys who had taken me to a movie or walked me
home after skating at the Manawaka Rink on a Saturday
night were far from prepossessing. They were either
shorter than I, or dandruff-ridden, or of a stunning
stupidity. I was embarrassed at being seen with them,
but I never turned down an invitation, for reasons of
status. I would willingly have gone out with the village
idiot, had there been one, rather than not go out at all.
Mavis Duncan, my closest friend, was slender and short
and had naturally wavy auburn hair. Anyone tall,
washed, witty and handsome in the vicinity asked her
out. I was five-foot seven and had naturally poker-
straight black hair which I tortured excruciatingly and
unsuccessfully into a limp pageboy style with aluminum
rollers every night. I had decided early that I must do
the best I could with what I had, which at that time did

not seem to be much. During the war, when I was seventeen, the social situation in town altered beyond belief. The R.C.A.F. built an elementary training camp at South Wachakwa, only a few miles away, and on weekends Manawaka was miraculously descended upon by scores of airmen, for South Wachakwa had a school, a church and one store, and that was all. Manawaka, on the other hand, had the Flamingo Dance Hall, the beer parlour at the Queen Victoria Hotel, the Regal Café, and numerous high school girls, of whom I was one.

I used to go with Mavis Duncan and Stacey Cameron to the Saturday night dances at the Flamingo. All the girls would go this way, in groups of three or four, for moral support. The girls congregated at one side of the small slippery dance floor, and the boys jostled around at the other side. When the music began for each dance, Mavis and Stacey and I would be engaged in gay lighthearted chatter, with panicky hearts and queasy stomachs. What if no one asked us to dance? The girls who had not been asked usually whipped upstairs to the Powder Room and stayed there for as long as possible, applying and re-applying makeup, smoking, talking in our gay lighthearted fashion to other sufferers. But when we were asked to dance, despair melted like ice cubes in July, and we would go slithering and swooping across the floor in whomever's arms, suddenly fearless and lovely.

The music seemed the only music that ever was or ever would be. I had no means of knowing that it was being set into the mosaic of myself, and that it would pass away quickly and yet remain always as mine. "Chattanooga Choo-Choo." "Skylark." "I'll Be Seeing

You." "I'm a Little on the Lonely Side." "Don't Get Around Much Any More."

It was at the Flamingo that I met Michael. He was twenty-three, taller than I, with sandy hair, and he had developed a mocking smile to camouflage his seriousness. He came from British Columbia, where he had worked in his father's lumber business before he joined up. He told me about the lumber camps, and I could see the donkey-engines and the high-riggers and the gigantic Douglas firs pluming and plummeting down like the fall of titans, out there in the ferned forests where the air was always cool blue and warm with sun, and where the black-spined trees stood close with the light lacing through.

"I'd like to take you there, Vanessa," Michael said.

He took me home to the Brick House instead, and kissed me, and told me he'd see me next weekend. After that, I saw him every time he could get to Manawaka. Sometimes he would manage to get over just for an hour or so in the evening, hitching a lift. In order to be alone we would walk down into the Wachakwa Valley, where the brown creek pelted shallowly over the stones, and the prairie poplars grew, their leaves now a translucent yellow with autumn. The grass was thick and high, and we could make a nest and lie there and hold one another. I never actually made love with him. I was afraid. He did not try to persuade me, although he knew I wanted to as much as he did. He accepted the fear which I could not accept myself, for I despised it but could not overcome it.

Like me, Michael wrote stories and poems, a fact which he did not divulge to his Air Force friends. When we were together, there was never enough time, for we had everything to talk about and discover. I tried not to remember that in a few months he would be going away. I had never met anyone before who was interested in the same things as I was. We read Stephen Spender's "I Think Continually of Those Who Were Truly Great."

> *The names of those who in their lives fought for*
> *life,*
> *Who wore at their hearts the fire's centre.*
> *Born of the sun they travelled a short while towards*
> *the sun,*
> *And left the vivid air signed with their honour.*

"It's one of my favourite poems," I said, "and yet it shouldn't be, maybe. There's something about it that isn't true, not for me, anyway."

"How do you mean, Nessa?"

"I don't know. It sounds fine to say you think continually of those who were truly great. But you don't. You forget them. Most of the time you don't think of them at all. That's the terrible thing. I guess I was thinking of Dieppe."

The war had not affected Manawaka very much until then. Most of the Manawaka boys had joined the Queen's Own Cameron Highlanders, and when the casualty lists came in from Dieppe, half the town's families were hit. MacDonald. Gunn. Kowalski. Macalister. Lobodiak. MacIntosh. Chorniuk. Kamchuk. MacPherson. All the Scots and Ukrainian names of the boys a couple of years older than I was, the boys I had known all my life. When it happened, I had remembered that my father's brother

Roderick had been killed in the First World War. He, too, had been eighteen, like most of these. It was then that war took on its meaning for me, a meaning that would never change. It meant only that people without choice in the matter were broken and spilled, and nothing could ever take the place of them. But I did not think of them continually. Even at this relatively short distance, I already thought of them only from time to time. It was this that seemed a betrayal.

"I know," Michael said. "And they weren't truly great, either. They just happened to be there. Hardly any poetry that I've seen says it the way it really is. You know what I think? Writing's going to change a lot after the war. It did after the First War and it will even more after this one. There aren't any heroes any more."

"I don't believe there ever were," I said. "Not in that way. I could be wrong. Spender's talking about the Battle of Britain pilots, partly anyway, isn't he? Maybe they were different. Why would they be, though? They were just there, too, and before they knew it, there wasn't any way to get out. Like the clansmen at Culloden. Or Ulysses' spearmen. Maybe even Ulysses, if he ever existed."

Michael looked up at the sky, where even now the training planes were skimming around like far-off bluebottle flies.

"I don't know whether you're wrong or not," he said. "I don't know how other guys feel. It isn't what you call a topic for conversation. I only know how I feel. Every damn time I go up in one of those little Tiger Moths I can't stop sweating. What an admission, eh? If I'm like that on training planes, what the hell will I be like on bombers?"

He turned to me then and I held him tightly. There was nothing I could say to him. Too much had been said already, but perhaps it had not harmed him to speak the words. All I could do was hold him and hope that the force of my love would get through to him and have some value. What I really wanted was to marry him before he went away, but I was not yet eighteen, and we both knew my mother would not give her consent for me to marry anyone at my age. After the war seemed a time too distant and indefinite to contemplate, a time that would never arrive.

When Michael had a weekend pass he would stay at the Brick House, sleeping in Aunt Edna's old room. He got on well with my mother, and she always welcomed him and did her best to shield him from Grandfather Connor. This was not always possible. At meals, my grandfather would make muttering remarks about people who freeloaded on other people's food. The rocking chair trick was used fairly often, and when my mother and Michael and I were doing the dishes we would hear the reproachful *screee-scraaaw* coming from Grandfather's cavern.

"Just like old times," I remarked one evening. "Remember how he was with Aunt Edna?"

"Now, now, dear," my mother said, torn between a desire to sympathize with me and a feeling that family skeletons were never to be paraded in front of outsiders. "Well, if you must know, I do remember—who could ever forget it? But we mustn't forget that he's an old man."

"Heck, he was never any different that I can recall," I said.

"Well, just try," my mother said, and I was reminded, as I often was with her, of Grandmother Connor, who could not bear scenes either.

That evening was different from other evenings which Michael had spent in the Brick House. Roddie was in bed, my mother was writing letters at the mahogany desk in the dining-room, and Michael and I were sitting on the huge shell-shaped chesterfield in the living-room. My grandfather emerged from the basement, winding his watch with obvious intent.

"Aren't you folks ever going to sleep?" he demanded. "You plan on sitting up all night, Vanessa?"

"It's only eleven," I countered. "That's not late."

"Not late, eh?" Grandfather Connor said. "You're still going to school, you know. You need your rest. These late hours won't do you no good. No good at all."

He glared at Michael, who edged a little away from me.

"If Mother doesn't mind, I don't see why you should," I said.

"Your mother's got no sense," Grandfather Connor declared.

I had argued away at my mother over every possible facet of our existence, but I did not recall any of this now.

"She's got plenty of sense," I cried furiously. "She's got a darned sight more than you've ever had!"

My grandfather looked at me with dangerous eyes, and all at once, I was afraid of what he might say.

"You ought to know better than run around with a fellow like this," he said, his voice even and distinct and full of cold rage. "I'll bet a nickel to a doughnut hole he's married. That's the sort of fellow you've picked up, Vanessa."

I jumped to my feet and faced him. Our anger met and clashed silently. Then I shouted at him, as though if I sounded all my trumpets loudly enough, his walls would quake and crumble.

"That's a lie! Don't you dare say anything like that ever again! I won't hear it! I won't!"

I ran upstairs to my room and locked the door. My mother went into the living-room and quieted my grandfather somehow. I could hear her apologizing to Michael, and I felt the enormity of the task she was having to try to deal with. Then Grandfather Connor came stamping upstairs to his bedroom, and I went down again.

"It's okay, Nessa," Michael said, putting an arm around me. "Don't worry. It's all right. It doesn't matter."

Nevertheless, the next time he had a weekend leave, he did not come to the Brick House. He did not write or phone that week, either.

"It's just the same as it used to be with Aunt Edna," I stormed to my mother. "Remember the men he drove away from her? Until Wes, nobody kept coming around for long."

"It wasn't really that way," my mother said. "A man isn't driven away that easily, Vanessa. Don't worry. Maybe Michael's got flu or something."

It was December by this time, and flu was rampant. I told myself this was the reason I hadn't heard from him. Then I got flu myself. I got it at the worst possible time, for there was a dance at the South Wachakwa camp, and two buses were taking girls from Manawaka, suitably chaperoned. Mavis would be going, and all the others, but not me. I coughed and felt nauseated and wept with self-pity.

The next day Mavis came to see me after school.

"Don't go too close, dear," I could hear my mother saying in the front hall. "She may still be infectious."

"Oh, it's okay, Mrs. MacLeod," Mavis said. "I'm not very susceptible."

She came up to my room and sat down on the chair beside my dressing-table. She did not look like herself. She looked anxious and—what?

"Mavis—what's the matter? How was the dance? Did you see Michael?"

"Yeh," she said. "I saw him, Nessa."

Then she told me.

Michael had been with a fairly pretty brunette with a fancy hair-do. When Mavis said *Hi* to him, the girl asked to be introduced, and then she introduced herself. She was Michael's wife. She had come from Vancouver to visit him, a surprise visit. Michael's parents had paid her train fare. She couldn't stay at the camp, so she was staying at the Queen Victoria Hotel in Manawaka for a week. Michael was getting over as often as he could, which wasn't half often enough, she had said, laughing. He seemed to have to sneak in and out of Manawaka like a criminal, she had said, and wasn't the Air Force crazy? Mavis had replied yes, very crazy, and had walked away.

"Nessa—I'm sorry," Mavis said. "I mean it."

I did not tell my mother what had happened. From my general demeanour and from the disappearance of Michael she gathered enough.

"Vanessa," she said hesitantly one day, "I know you won't believe me, honey, but after a while it won't hurt so much. And yet in a way I guess it always will, to some extent. There doesn't seem to be anything anybody can do about that."

As it happened, she was right on all counts. I did not at the time believe her. But after a while it did not hurt so much. And yet twenty years later it was still with me to some extent, part of the accumulation of happenings which can never entirely be thrown away.

In those months that followed, I hated my grandfather as I had never hated him before. What I could not forgive was that he had been right, unwittingly right, for I did not believe for one moment that he had really thought Michael was married.

I was frantic to get away from Manawaka and from the Brick House, but I did not see how it was going to be possible. To take a business course would not have been too expensive, but I thought I would make a rotten secretary. When I applied to the women's Air Force, they told me they had enough recruits and advised me to continue my education. How? On what money? When I had finished high school, however, my mother told me that I would be able to go to university after all.

"Now don't fuss about it, Nessa," she said, "and for mercy's sake let us not have any false pride. I've gone to Patrick Irwin at the jewellery store and he says the MacLeod silver and Limoges will fetch about three hundred dollars."

"I won't," I said. "It's not right. I can't."

"Oh yes you can," my mother said blithely, "and you will. For my sake, if nothing else. Do you think I want you to stay here for ever? Please don't be stubborn, honey. Also, Wes and Aunt Edna can contribute something, and so can your Aunt Florence and Uncle Terence."

"What have you done?" I cried. "Canvassed the entire family?"

"More or less," my mother said calmly, as though the tigress beneath her exterior was nothing to be surprised about. "Father is also selling some bonds which he's been hanging on to all these years."

"Him! How did you do that? But I'm not taking a nickel of his money."

My mother put a hand on my shoulder.

"When I was your age," she said, "I got the highest marks in the province in my last year high school. I guess I never told you that. I wanted to go to college. Your grandfather didn't believe in education for women, then."

So I went. The day I left for Winnipeg, Wes and Aunt Edna drove me to the bus station. My mother did not come along. She said she would rather say goodbye to me at home. She and my brother stood on the front steps and waved as Wes started the car. I waved back. Now I was really going. And yet in some way which I could not define or understand, I did not feel nearly as free as I had expected to feel.

SILVER BUGLES, CYMBALS, GOLDEN SILKS

by Hugh Hood

Hugh Hood was born in 1928 in Toronto. He studied at the University of Toronto, then moved to Montreal in 1961, where he continued to live. He taught English literature at the Université de Montréal and was the author of seventeen novels, several volumes of short fiction, and five of non-fiction. He died in August 2000.

THIS STORY IS FROM Hugh Hood's first published work, the short-story collection *Flying a Red Kite* (1962).

When I was a child of six, in the summer of 1934, my parents sent me to a camp on the south shore of Lake Simcoe, at the upper end of the Trent Canal system, wonderful trolling and cruising waters in those days, and nowadays just about fished-out. The camp was run by a religious community of men, teaching Brothers who also conducted several Toronto schools, and I remember seeing their brochure around the house for several days before my agonized and unwilling departure. It quoted Whittier, as I recall:

> *Health that mocks the doctor's rules,*
> *Knowledge never learned in schools.*

There was a certain amount of truth in the second line. There were little line drawings in a green ink, in this brochure, of boys fishing, diving, running races, gashing their knees on rocks, the whole myth, overnight hikes, nature lore. I was still practically an infant. I hadn't gone

to nursery school—it wasn't the fashion in those days—
or to kindergarten, as the Catholic School System in the
city didn't provide them. So I was still an inhabitant of
the warm intimate world of post-babyhood, defined by
the length of one's block. I was allowed to cross streets,
but I wasn't venturesome about it. I suppose that my
parents wanted to get me out of the house for a
summer, a motive I would have questioned then, with
the fierce possessiveness of the young child, but which I
can fully appreciate now that I've two of my own.

The camp seemed enormous to me that first season.
Last summer I drove past it, and you wouldn't believe
how small and shrunken it seemed. In 1934 it seemed
limitless and wild, the wood growing right up behind
the straggling line of tents inhabited by the older
campers—the littlest kids slept in neat wooden cabins
and were very grateful for the added touch of civiliza-
tion; it meant something to graduate into a row of tents.

In front of the Administration Building stood a tall
flagpole, where a flag-raising ceremony was enacted each
morning, and where two buglers blew *retreat* at
sundown. I had never heard the *retreat* before, and I
haven't heard it blown for fifteen years, but I can still
whistle it note for note.

Two different boys served as duty-buglers each week.
I didn't understand how it was, having learned nothing
of the great world as yet, that so many of the older boys
at the camp could play this beguiling instrument, on
which I longed to be able to execute myself. After I had
been there two weeks my parents drove up for the
weekend to see how I was getting along, and I can see
now that they had been as affected by my absence as I

had been by theirs. I had missed them unutterably, though in different ways, my slim pretty mother with her comfortable big French-Canadian nose, her "proboscis" she called it, a funny word which always made me gurgle when she said it, and my handsome excitable father whom I adored and whom I longed to understand. He made a lot of remarks which I knew must be very funny because my mother laughed and laughed at them, and I wished I knew what was funny in what he said. I found out later on: he had a desperate streak of defensive irony. He was a man of position but no education, and it strained him dreadfully to hide this.

I asked them about all these buglers. "Why can Paul and Harold Phelan, and all the Juniors and Seniors, play the bugle? Do you think I could play the bugle sometime?"

It happened unluckily that the Phelan boys were the sons of a dentist in our parish whom my father particularly despised for his jumped-up ways. He raised an expressive eyebrow at my mother, as one who regrets an ill-considered action.

"Bog-Irish!" he exclaimed. It was a favourite phrase for he was a man of many prejudices, none of them violent but all irritating to him. He also disliked French-Canadians, which made things difficult with his in-laws, who all had names like Esdras, Telesphore, Onesime, Eugenie, and the like. My mother smiled at him shushingly.

"They're all in the Band," she said, and it was the first time I ever heard about the Band, the famous Oakdale Boys Band, an organization whose structure was to pre-occupy me for a dozen years. The Brothers conducted parish schools in Toronto but also, and pre-eminently, a private high school, Oakdale, "in a park in the centre of the city" as their advertisements had it. It was an institution that one paid to attend which in those Depression years meant that it was exclusive, if only in the sense that you had to be employed to send your sons there. The chief ornament of Oakdale was its famous hundred-piece drum and bugle Band which took part in all the major Toronto parades, the Garrison Parade in June, the Armistice Day Parade, the Argonauts' half-time shows, and ever so many more. The Band travelled all over the province making paid appearances at religious and civil functions. I had never heard of it before and at six years had no suspicion that such marvellous institutions even existed.

"Perhaps you'll go to Oakdale and be in the band," said my mother, off the end of her tongue, making my father glance at her in some perturbation. He didn't say it in front of me but he was likely thinking "yes, and perhaps you won't."

But my fate was sealed, and the sealing was confirmed on Dominion Day weekend when, to my intense gratification, the dozen or more boys at camp who were buglers, and another dozen who were drummers, suddenly blossomed forth early in the morning in gorgeous uniforms, a dress of an absolutely inconceivable splendour. They wore navy blue officers' caps with gold metal cap-badges and white naval cap covers, white covers, navy blue high-necked tunics with brass buttons, and red, white, and green trimmings at the wrists, and gold-trimmed collars, a golden rope-lanyard across the chest and around the left shoulder, navy blue trousers with a rich gold stripe at the seam and, most bewitching of all, long navy blue capes fastened around the neck and depending in soft folds below the waist.

These capes were lined with golden silk, and the most distinctive mark of the Band uniform was the bright glitter of the silk. It was regimental to make three precise folds in the cape, so that two broad bands of gold hung from the shoulders to the waist. I had never been so captivated in my life and at this revelation would willingly have exchanged my home, my cozy family life, my brother and sister, for the chance to live with these marvellous boys and dress like that. We soon heard that the rest of the Band would appear in the early afternoon for the patriotic ceremonies.

A few of the biggest boys wore *medals*.

At one-thirty three fat old buses appeared at the gates with seventy other bandsmen, the two bandmasters, Mr. James and Mr. Thompson, the bass drums and tenor drums, and wonder of wonders the mascot, a boy smaller than myself though older, named Jimmy Phillips, who marched in front of the bandmasters and swung a small baton. I have never since seen anything to compare with it for glitter.

Jimmy Phillips was the son of a man who owned a house on the lowest corner of the Oakdale property in Toronto. He had in some way been a benefactor of the school and still lived in the house on the grounds with his family, and his boy was the Band mascot until he outgrew the job. I don't know just what Mr. Phillips' connection with the Brothers was, but it was certainly a matter of money and/or property. And because of it,

Jimmy Phillips marched in front of the Band and carried a silver baton ... it was my first faint intimation of the uses of influence and wealth.

When he grew out of the job, he was succeeded by Fred Crawley, the son of a wealthy Catholic stockbroker whose benefactions to the school must have been indeed munificent because Fred wore a special white and gold uniform (which the Phillips' boy hadn't) and held the post of mascot long after he had ceased to be as wonderfully small (isn't he *darling*!) as a mascot should be. At last he was succeeded by the Bandmaster's son, little Billy Thompson, who lasted out my tenure with the Band. This time, the Brothers had to pay for the white and gold mascot's uniform.

That first wonderful day I saw the Band, wheeling and counter-marching in intricate patterns in front of the Administration Building, I noticed many things. For example, the two Bandmasters were of slightly unequal rank. Mr. James was Drum-Major, and Mr. Thompson was merely Sergeant-Major, and the former's gold was shinier and less brassy. There didn't seem to be any animosity or competition between them.

I noticed as well that there were some strutting little boys, scarcely bigger than myself, marching in the cymbal section. I call it the cymbal section, but the line of eight included three awfully small boys who played triangles. As far as I could tell, playing the triangle demanded no musical skill beyond the ability to keep time with a striker, loud enough to be heard in the uproar. I decided right then and there that as soon as I should be sent to Oakdale I would try out for the triangle.

It's singular how sharply the child's mind will calculate. I could foretell at six a course of action I would follow exactly over four years later; and in the interval I forgot not one detail of my plan.

At ten years, having completed the sixth grade, I was finally allowed to quit parochial school and begin at Oakdale. This was a considerable step for my parents to take, because it implied seven years of fees for me, and the like for my brother later on. In 1938 Toronto was by no means fully recovered from the Depression. The parish schools and the public high schools were free whereas my father had to pay for me to go to Oakdale. The fee wasn't outrageous but it was something, and as my father's affairs were at this time not uninvolved, it was a damned decent thing for him to do. To tell the truth, he couldn't afford it, then or long after, but he tried his best to manage the thing gracefully.

So I went, and on one of the first of a series of tender sleepy fall days, hardly fall at all, the soft gold end of September, a meeting for Band recruits was announced for after school in the Cafeteria. I was there with bells on, already clutching my triangle in rapt anticipation. The senior N.C.O. in regular school attendance, a full-grown man of nineteen, spoke briefly. That was Sergeant-Drummer Johnny Delancey, killed two years afterwards in a burning Wellington bomber, over the railway yards at Hamburg. He spoke of the Band's traditions and its reputation.

"You won't see any of us with ten medals on our tunics," he said, with a certain heat. He had a posthumous D.F.C. later on, the only medal he ever won. He was making a dig at the Saint Ursula's Boys Band, also conducted by the Brothers at a parish school way downtown in a slum district. Saint Ursula's school went through the tenth grade, so they were able to maintain a band almost as big as ours, and there was a sharp rivalry between us. Saint Ursula's went each year to the Band Competition at Waterloo, Ontario; and every year they won their class competition, so that everyone in their outfit had a medal for every year he'd been in the competition.

The Oakdale Band disdained the competition as a rather plebeian thing. Only those very senior N.C.O.s who had been awarded an Efficiency Medal at the annual inspection of the Band and Cadet Corps wore anything on their chests. We Oakdale bandsmen gave out that we were above competition, and we regarded the Saint Ursula's medals as an unseemly display, or at least we were tacitly encouraged so to regard them. A medal in our Band meant something. Johnny Delancey never won one.

"You'll find me conducting practices after school," said Johnny Delancey, "but 'Tommy' Thompson runs the Band, and don't ever forget it. He's the best Drum-Major in Canada, he used to play with a British Army Band, and everybody at the Armouries—even the Queen's Own and the Army Service Corps—wants him. But he's staying right here and we want you to appreciate him."

I pondered this. There had been two Bandmasters up at camp. Where was the other one?

"Now we'll take your names and the instruments you mean to learn. We need some tall fellows for the Tenor-Drums. You there, you're big enough." He pointed at a gangling boy near me, named George Rait.

"I was going to try out for the bugles."

"Tenor-drums," said Johnny Delancey peremptorily, determining forever the shape of George Rait's Band career. "Corporal McGarry will take that side of the room and I'll take this." They began to move along the lines of recruits. I was way down at the end, and I grew more and more overawed as big Ted McGarry came nearer. A Corporal! Finally he looked down at me and smiled.

"What would you like to be, sonny, mascot?"

"No," I said indignantly. After all, I was ten, and going into Junior Fourth (Grade Seven as it is now) and I couldn't quite allow "sonny."

"I want to try out for the triangles," I said, abashed, but outspoken, the way I've always been.

Ted McGarry was very decent. "Triangles it is!" he said, writing down my name. "One of the most important sections in the Band." He passed on to the end of the line. Afterwards they announced the hours of the recruit practices, telling us that we would have to learn our instruments, how to march, the meaning of the various commands, and how to care for a uniform, before we were accepted. Those who didn't co-operate with their instructors, and those who couldn't maintain a decent standard of drill, would be rejected and would have to join the Cadet Corps. Then they let us go and I ran all the way home to tell my mother.

Toronto is not a beautifully built city by and large, though you can find good-looking buildings if you know where to look. But the natural situation of the city is attractive, the long gentle slope of the hill rising off the lake. And the light can be superb, especially in the spring and fall, a clear but oddly smoky light softening and enriching the raw green of spring and especially grateful to the mellow browns and yellows of early fall. All through late September and early October of that year the weather held on beautifully, the air soft and clear, and the lovely Toronto light—something nobody in the city ever talks about, as though they hadn't noticed it or took it for granted or were afraid to praise lest it should disappear—the faintly smoky hazy yellow light ran on and on as we little kids drilled and practised our rhythmic noises on the campus, under the direction of the junior N.C.O.s.

Just before Armistice Day we were told whether or not we would be accepted, so that the successful candidates might march in the big memorial parade to the Cenotaph. One Friday afternoon we were admitted to the Bandroom, a cubby-hole on the ground floor of the Cafeteria, where the sixty-four bugles could be racked up line on line in a glass case, to draw our uniform issue. Brother Willibald was there, the teacher in charge of Band activities, and he presided as chief outfitter as one by one we were herded in and matched to tunics and trousers and, best of all, our capes. None of the uniforms was quite new and the gold on some of the capes was a little greenish when you saw it close to; but if anybody noticed it, nobody said anything, we were all too excited.

They had a little trouble fitting me, I was small for my age and for a moment I was terrified that I might be turned down. But kind Brother Willibald, seeing my desperation, rummaged at the very back of the closet and came out with an old discarded uniform of Jimmy Phillips, the ex-mascot.

"Have your mother adjust the cuffs," he advised, "and be sure you have the whole uniform cleaned and pressed before Armistice Day." I nodded mutely, frozen with excitement. "Are you sure you know how to clean your buttons?" I nodded again, afraid that at the last minute he might change his mind and not give me the uniform. But then he smiled and handed it to me, and told me to pick a triangle and striker off the rack. I did as he said and left the Bandroom as quickly as I could for fear somebody might take it into his head to shout after me, "You're too small!" I was always hearing that.

But no one did, and in common with the other recruits I appeared at Band Practice the following Wednesday night for our first formal practice with the Band. When the weather was clement we practised outdoors on the lower campus, and the sound of the music could be heard rolling across the city a good three miles and more. After I left the Band years later, when I was living down on Sussex Avenue, over two miles from the school, I used to hear the music of the evening practices as clearly as if it were coming from the next room. God only knows what the apartment dwellers next to the parade ground thought of these practices, for the music was indeed cacophonous; they made constant efforts to have them stopped, or at least muted in some degree, but nothing ever came of it.

As it was now early November and the yellow light had gone blandly grey, the late fall rains setting in, we practised that night upstairs in the Cafeteria, the tables and chairs shoved to the wall, and you can imagine the impression made upon the nerves of the recruits by the noise of thirty-two snare drums, eight tenor drums, two bass drums, sixty-four bugles, and eight cymbals and triangles. It was Homeric in scope, at least as far as volume was concerned; musically it was constricted. We were then using the conventional British Army brass bugle on which an ordinary bugler could produce five notes, or if he were better than average, six. To these bugles could be fitted a "crook" which changed the key of the instrument by lengthening the air column. Another four to six notes could be produced with the crook, in the key of the dominant, and these ten to twelve notes constituted the whole musical range of the Band, the drums and percussion being tuned to no key. And yet we had a repertoire at that time of over sixty marches from the simplest, "Cry Baby," to a pretty jazzy number called "Susan Jane," which Mr. Thompson had just put into the book, and which we supposed him to have composed himself. As a matter of fact he hadn't for he got his new material out of British Army manuals, or by attending other band practices at the Armouries, but we didn't know this and we regarded him as an accomplished musician and composer. He used to teach us new marches by humming them to us, first the open and then the crook parts:

> *Dee-dickety-dee, dee-dee, dee-dee,*
> *Dee-dickety-dickety-dee, dee-dee.*

If there were any special effects for the drums he would illustrate them until the N.C.O.s caught on; then they taught them to the other drummers in the afternoon. Our repertoire seemed almost illimitable to us, but to the uninstructed listener it must have seemed as though we were always playing the same tune, just as Corelli, Torelli, Boyce, Vivaldi and Handel sound alike to the ignorant.

"Tommy" Thompson—the very senior N.C.O.s called him "Tommy" but to the rest of us he was always "Mr. Thompson"—was a remarkable man in his way, though not a musician. He had formerly been second-in-command with the rank of Sergeant-Major, and people sometimes forgot and referred to him as "Sergeant-Major Thompson." The Brothers sometimes did this, whether accidentally or to keep him in his place I'm not certain. But his former superior, Drum-Major James, had quarrelled with the Brothers of "Oakdale" in some obscure way, and had left the Oakdale Band and gone over to Saint Ursula's where he now fed the flames of his resentment by attempting to bring the Saint Ursula's Band to the same pitch of reputation and excellence as that of his former command. When I found out about this it explained much of the attitude towards Saint Ursula's of the older boys and men (there were some grown men) in our outfit. It was a romantic feud and conflict of loyalties which impressed me powerfully.

Mr. Thompson was at this time securely in the saddle at Oakdale. In fact he was one of the most universally liked and respected men I've ever known. I guess he was then about thirty-eight, he must have been the same age as the century or thereabouts, because he had been a bandsman with the rank of Boy at the outbreak of the first war. He had served right through it, three years as a drummer and the last year-and-a-half as an infantryman. He was very, very short, not more than five feet one or two, but he didn't seem small because he had a solid square head and a big chest and a perfect, very striking, military carriage, shoulders well back, chest up and out. One never thought of him as small; I considered him enormous during my first years in the Band. He had a firm tanned red impassive face, and neatly clipped brown hair beginning to grizzle. Looking back, I would guess that he was not a highly intelligent man but he was purposeful and disciplined and so got by, which is all anybody can hope for.

In his other, less romantic, daytime life he was a salesman for Canada Packers, a moderate to good one but not the best or most productive. Away from the Band he had a pleasing natural diffidence that would have held down his sales. He was economical; the year I joined the Band he bought a new car, a compact Willys sedan, and he maintained this car superbly and was still driving it a decade later. Once a year without fee the Band put on a demonstration at the main Canada Packers warehouse out past St. Clair and Keele streets, in a sort of plaza bounded by loading platforms and railway sidings and dominated by a monumental stench. All the employees and, I suppose, some of the managers, maybe even J.S. McLean himself, used to watch leaning out of windows. It must have proved annually to his superiors that there were places where Mr. Thompson too was admired and obeyed without question. His uniform was always particularly regimental on these occasions.

He was buying a home in one of those Toronto districts where lower middle-class English people used to congregate. It might have been in lower Parkdale, or a few blocks west of Dufferin north of Bloor. But in fact, as I remember, his house was on Belsize Drive or one of the shorter streets parallel to it between Mount Pleasant and Yonge. Could it have been Davisville? No. Too much traffic, and he would have lived on a quiet street and a modest one. It was one of those five-room brick houses with a veranda and a wooden railing painted white, with Gothic cutouts in it, the veranda floor painted a sturdy battleship grey. There were shrubs and geraniums in front of the veranda and a big maple tree and a neat cement walk. We used to ride past his house on our bikes on Saturdays; it made us oddly confident to know that he lived there.

Mr. Thompson had at this time a great and overmastering ambition. He wanted to obtain new instruments for the Band and had been after the Brothers to buy them. Our old bugles, dating from before the war, were full of dents which impaired their tone. And the drums, though impressive in appearance, were the type which you tighten by adjusting ropes around the side of the shell. They were old and the ropes would not stay taut, which caused a lot of broken drumheads.

The Brothers were most reluctant to spend the several thousand dollars needful for the new equipment, and were looking around quietly for somebody to donate it to them. The high spot of my first few months with the Band was the evening at a practice just before Christmas when Brother Willibald made a great announcement. The well-known public figure Senator Frank J. Mulhearne had agreed to donate half the purchase price if the Band itself would contribute the remainder from the earnings of its engagements. There was much cheering and noise and Mr. Thompson's face was a picture of joy and delight.

Band outfitters' catalogues were passed around for us
to stare at and of course the proposition was accepted
by unanimous vote and the Senator's generous offer
taken up.

The new instruments were months and months
coming from England. One of the major department
stores jobbed the order. I don't remember whether it was
Eaton's or Simpson's, but I have the feeling that it was
the latter. During January and February of 1939, an
individual picture was taken of each bandsman in his
uniform with his instrument, and then these pictures
were hand tinted and cut out and mounted on little
stands, providing an entire miniature band. When the
instruments were at last delivered, the department store
set up an enormous window display, with a dummy
bugler in full Sergeant's uniform, pyramids of the new
drums, great sweeping files of the silver bugles, their
bells plated with fine gold, the regimental colours of the
Oakdale Cadet Corps and Band, and in the centre the
cutout miniature Band in the act of executing a right
wheel, so that each bandsman was plainly visible. The
display was featured repeatedly in newspaper advertisements and was instrumental in obtaining the publicity
which decided the Brothers to accept an engagement at
the New York World's Fair, just about to open for its
first season in Flushing Meadows.

The New York trip, which we actually took with
huge success, was the second great event of my first year.
My father used to go to New York two or three times a
year, spending a great deal more than he could afford
while there. It made him laugh, he said, to think that I
was getting a free trip to the Fair by playing the triangle;

by then I was almost old enough to catch the full inner sense of his joke.

"Wait until they hear you play 'The Star-Spangled Banner,'" said my father jovially. He had heard us practising and knew whereof he spoke. You couldn't really play a tune on our bugles, even the marvellous new ones—there just weren't enough notes to go round. We could eke out "God Save the King" because its intervals are easy; anything more recondite taxes our musicality excessively. But Mr. Thompson was determined that we should play the American anthem at the Fair, so he pieced out an arrangement using what notes we could command, and where we couldn't get the required tone he settled for a loud, positive, self-assertive BLAAATTT from all buglers together, thus:

> *Da-da-da, da, da, dee,*
> *Dee-dee-dee, da, da,* BLAAATTT.

It was a direful strain, and when we executed the number, bang in the middle of the Plaza of Nations at the Fair, there were shocked stares of horror and surprise from our hearers. Next day in two of the New York papers there were heated remonstrances; nobody seemed quite sure whether a joke or slight had been intended—the Americans are notoriously touchy about such things. Anyway wiser heads prevailed. Brother Willibald persuaded Mr. Thompson to drop the offending piece. He did so with reluctance, substituting "There'll Always Be An England," a tune just out and by no means as famous as it was shortly to become—for we were in the summer of 1939. We couldn't play "There'll Always Be An England" either,

without disfiguring it with weird atonal—almost
Schoenbergian—effects:

Da, da, da, da, da, da-da,
Da, dee-dee, dee-dee, BLAAATTT.

But this song had no political, national, or warlike
overtones as yet, and nobody at the World's Fair was
offended by our rendering, so that the excursion went
unmarred by further incident.

If we'd been so foolhardy as to use the same arrangement at the Canadian National Exhibition, say, next
summer or any time in the next five years, we'd have been
execrated and consigned to obloquy by our hearers, for
the war was coming on, came on, engulfed us, and the
Gracie Fields recording of the tune, unmistakable in its
clear, true, unmusical clang, became the anthem of
Toronto patriotism and remained so until the advent of
the Bomb.

We had to give up playing it.

Mr. Thompson was not, you must understand, a
man given to the frivolous adoption of novelties for
their own sake:

Be not the first by whom the new is tried,
Nor yet the last to lay the old aside,

as Mr. Pope so beautifully says. If anything he erred in
the direction of conservatism, and in the end it undid
him. He would now and then introduce an outlandish
and unplayable tune but he would never consider transforming the group into a brass band, for two reasons.
One: he couldn't so far as I'm aware read music. Two:

the Band had always been a drum and bugle corps; it was the best of its kind; he could see no reason for change.

Once or twice in the years at the end of, and just after, the second war, he did make certain concessions to modernity. He got the notion somewhere, I believe from an American newsmagazine, that the Band should acquire what he called "bugle bells." I think he made up that term himself. I've never heard anybody else refer to them as "bugle bells." They're often called glockenspiels and sometimes bell lyres, but they remained "bugle bells" to Mr. Thompson.

It must have been late in 1944 when he began to talk about them at our post-practice N.C.O. councils. I was by then a lance-corporal in the bugles having outgrown (or rather outlived, I hadn't grown more than an inch, I was under five feet until my last year with the Band) the triangle and cymbal section.

"We've got to move with the times," he would say anxiously, casting an uneasy glance upon Brother Linus, who had succeeded Brother Willibald at the latter's death, "we can't get them from England on account of the war, but I believe I can get them made up locally." Ten years before, he had introduced leopard skins for the bass and tenor drummers and still thought of this as a greatly novel *coup*. He had the reverence for history that I admire, and no itch for the sensational.

He did get the new instruments made up in Toronto, and when we finally introduced them they looked lovely. If you think of a glockenspiel you'll know what I'm describing, a lyre-shaped, xylophone-type of instrument with a dozen metal bars which the player struck with a knobbed wooden hammer. Ours had a fatal flaw when we first got them. The bars were made of the wrong sort of metal; they gave the correct sequence of notes, but only very softly, having neither ring nor resonance. You couldn't hear them even when they played solo, and it was over two years before they were finally reworked into playable condition. Meanwhile they were carried on parade, the way band-singers in the thirties used to hold guitars with rubber strings, for the look of the thing. By the time the bugs were out of our glockenspiels everybody else had them, the war was over, we had failed to move with the times quite fast enough.

I grew through adolescence to young manhood during the last years of the war, being seventeen when it ended, too young to have served and probably just old enough to miss the next one on grounds of age, which won't make much difference, I'm afraid. While I was growing up, the complexion of the Band altered drastically, somewhat undermining it as an institution. In the late thirties there had been several young men in their twenties in the Band as senior N.C.O.s. During the war they all disappeared, many of them were killed, like Johnny Delancey and Morgan Phelan, and the rest were almost middle-aged when they came back and wanted nothing to do with bugles and drums.

A whole new generation of bandsmen grew up, boys my age and younger, during the first half of the forties. None of us had any close touch with British Army traditions; we leaned if anything closer to the style of the University of Michigan Marching Band; there was a movement afoot to step up our marching pace from the conservative British step but Mr. Thompson wouldn't hear of it, and he had two powerful supporters, Perce McIlwraith the Bugle-Major, a man almost his own age, and George Delvecchio the Quartermaster-Sergeant, only slightly younger and a family man who had not gone to war. These two chaps were the last of the veterans who had been in on the Band's first years and who had stayed with it out of loyalty to "Tommy" long after they had grown up. Perce McIlwraith in particular retained the enthusiasm of a child right into his forties. I can see him still—as Bugle-Major he marched at the right of the first rank of buglers—raising his arm at the end of a long drum section to signal us to put our bugles to our lips as one man. He was a tirelessly energetic second-in-command and a man of perfect, admirable, unquestioning loyalty. He used to lecture us at N.C.O. Council when the Drum Major was out of the room.

"I don't know if you realize how much 'Tommy' Thompson has done for you fellows. Who got us the Lindsay parade, the trip to New York, the new bugles? By God, there isn't a better man alive than 'Tommy' and see you remember it." I think that even then poor Perce had an inkling that an older order was passing away. He must have been close to fifty when he left the Band. His company transferred Perce to Windsor, and it nearly broke his heart.

As second-in-command, Perce McIlwraith was senior N.C.O. and presided, ex officio, over our N.C.O. Council, the strategic and disciplinary assembly of the Band. Before I became an N.C.O. I often came before this body on various minor charges. I fell in with a crowd of older boys who congregated in the last rank of the bugles and horsed around during practice. Evil communications corrupt good manners. Mr. Thompson never appeared to notice our carryings-on but he knew perfectly how to squelch them; he gave us responsibility and finally gave most of us a stripe, that first treasured stripe, the lance-corporal's.

After I became an N.C.O. I grew sober and mature at practice—we all did—we were all hoping for another promotion and then a third, if you made corporal you would likely make Sergeant before you left the Band. A Sergeant had the right to wear a broad red sash over his right shoulder and down across the chest, it was the ultimate accolade, only one or two men in the Band's history had risen higher. I finally obtained the long-coveted Sergeancy in my last year in high school, in January 1945. I remember it vividly because the promotion came through suddenly and unexpectedly just before the annual Battalion Ball, the major dance of the year at Oakdale. As it happened, there wasn't an extra sash in the stores at the time, and I had to travel halfway across the city to borrow one from an unfortunate Sergeant-Drummer who was down with mumps and would therefore not appear at the dance. I had had mumps and wasn't worried about the communicability of the disease. My date caught them instead, most likely off the sash.

That was my last Battalion Ball and my penultimate stage with the Band. I graduated from high school in June 1945, in that uneasy period between VE and VJ Day, just before they dropped the first bomb, and at the annual Cadet Inspection of that year I was awarded the Most Efficient Band N.C.O. Medal, which I wore on my chest for the first time on our VE Day parade, a riotous occasion.

The end of the war punctuated my love affair with the Band because I had to go to work. I meant to go to college of course, and eventually did so two years later; but I was short of money and there could be no question of my father's sending me as he was then at the absolute nadir of his financial career. Like a good many of those who achieved a Sergeancy, I decided to stay on, partly in the desperate ambition of earning an even higher grade, Quartermaster-Sergeant perhaps or even, if anything untoward should happen to Perce McIlwraith, Bugle-Major. It was an unrealistic and adolescent ambition because nothing was going to happen to Perce; several years elapsed before his company transferred him out of town, and by then the Band had so evolved that my love affair with it was long long gone.

I tried to keep up to practices even though I had a full-time job in the Civil Service; but there was a lot of reorganization going on at Oakdale and little by little I fell out of touch. For the first time, in the winter of 1945–46, Mr. Thompson introduced a wholly new kind of march, a complicated species developed during the second war, featuring rudimentary harmonics. The bugle section was split into four, two sections of open bugles, and two of crook. Each section had—and this was genuinely revolutionary and a great credit to Mr. Thompson—an independent musical line to play which required much greater prowess on the bugle than we had been accustomed to display. We regularly had to produce the sixth note on the instrument, and sometimes even the seventh, a thing extremely difficult to do. And we had to learn not to listen to what the other sections were playing and stick to our own line.

Our first march of this type was called "Field of Glory." It took us all winter to master it—it was like a symphony to us—and we meant to create a sensation with it, but there were two defects in the production. Everybody else in town, even Boy Scout bands, had the same number. And no matter what band played it, no matter how carefully rehearsed, it sounded crazily incoherent as though we had our signals crossed and were playing two quite different marches at the same time. For some reason, the harmonics simply wouldn't blend into a meaningful whole.

In vain did Mr. Thompson introduce variations on the idea; in vain did we practise and practise. It was a question of a search for a new musical form that didn't exist. I didn't understand then, but I do now, that Mr. Thompson was in the position of Haydn in 1792, confronted with the Opus 1 of the young Beethoven, those revolutionary trios. He knew blindly and obscurely that there were new forms to be created and explored, that the old forms had been worked up to their zenith by himself and Mozart (I mean Haydn, not Mr. Thompson) but he had grown too old to discover the new forms. Mr. Thompson might, with the aging Haydn, have written *hin ist alle meine kraft* at the last page of his latest efforts.

I left the Band in the spring of 1947, having decided that it was time to put away childish things, and having saved a certain amount of money, I started to college that fall. From first to last my love affair with the Band had lasted thirteen years, and I guess that was time enough.

I moved away from the immediate neighbourhood of Oakdale, and became involved with the usual collegiate misadventures. I took a flat on Sussex Avenue near the corner of Huron, so as to be near the centres of under-graduate activity. I began to drink beer and get around to the pubs with the boys, and I thought my twenty-first birthday the happiest day of my life. I acquired a card-sized birth certificate and started to tell the waiters in beverage rooms not to bug me about my age. I looked sixteen then but in the interval I've aged. Nobody asks me to prove my age nowadays, and I wish to God they would, such is the perversity of man.

Sometimes on a fine night in the spring or fall, I'd be sitting by the kitchen window in our flat on Sussex, drinking an ale with my roommates, and way, way off across town, softly at first as they marched down from the upper campus, and then with perfect clarity, I would hear the Band practising, and if I had had enough to drink, and sometimes even if I hadn't, I'd feel a wave of longing and nostalgia. I would want to sober up, hustle uptown on the Avenue Road bus, and take my old place in the last rank of the bugles. But I couldn't have done it; my lip had gone soft and I wouldn't be able to hit the sixth note.

I couldn't escape the Band though. Now and then I'd see them on the street during a parade, or in a newsreel of a Royal visit, or at a football game. Around the University there were always people from Oakdale with a similar sentimental attachment. Through one of them who'd been in a later class than mine I heard about the later stages of the Band's history, sometime around the summer of 1951. There had been a lot of palace rivalry within the group, between the Brothers and Mr. Thompson. The out of town engagements with the large fees had stopped coming, the Band wasn't the draw or the novelty that it had been fifteen years before. Perhaps attachment to the Crown and the British connection had generally been enfeebled, I don't know, but there was feeling among the Brothers that the Band ought to break new ground, that it should somehow look different.

Then around 1953 I heard that Mr. Thompson was out. I wish I could narrate that final interview. But maybe there wasn't any such scene, maybe he quit. But I don't see how he could have quit, it wasn't in him to do it. He couldn't have done it.

They replaced him by Warren Haggerty, an Oakdale grad, a former Sergeant-Drummer and ex-Air Force officer, a real punk. He lasted two years. After that they appointed a boy younger than I, who'd been in first year high school when I was doing Senior Matric, and was therefore five years my junior. I couldn't see then, and I don't now, how little Norm Hutchings could have the effrontery to stand up there in Mr. Thompson's place, but he was too young to have appreciated "Tommy" Thompson, he was a creature of the Haggerty regime and can't have known what he was doing.

They did a lot of things to the Band, to revive it as a Toronto institution. They discarded the bugles and drums that Senator Mulhearne had donated, and, my God, they'd only seen ten years' service, they might as well have been brand-new. Nowadays they have a slew of bastard trumpets; "valve bugles" they're called, soprano, tenor and baritone, and they try to play things like "The Tennessee Waltz" and "Tzena, Tzena, Tzena," and even "Rock Around the Clock" and they violate the integrity of the organization, the way Andre Previn plays jazz piano. I hope that Mr. Thompson can't hear the practices but I'm afraid that he can.

Last summer I met a group of Oakdale bandsmen on a Toronto streetcar; they were wearing what they call their summer uniform, a shoddy sweatshirt, a $2.98 item, and sleazy cotton trousers of a vile light blue, the colour of faded bluejeans. They don't wear gold capes any more, winter or summer, and they have some sort of plumed shako, and they look like ushers in a second-run movie palace. Nothing endures.

So I imagine Mr. Thompson, as old as the century, which would put him in his early sixties, sitting in the summer twilight on the veranda of his house, which must be paid for by now. He'll be getting on to retirement age, if he hasn't already reached it. But perhaps he left Canada Packers when he left the Band; I don't know and I haven't any decent way of finding out. It would have been hard for him to carry on at the office, don't you see, because in a way he loved that goddam Band.

I think of him sitting upright in a porch chair somewhere on Belsize Drive or one of the little residential streets in through there, between Yonge and Mount Pleasant, impassive in the changing light, hearing the dreadful new sound rolling across the city, miles and miles, to remind him, sitting innocently there, of past glories, things that are utterly vanished, that will never come back again, his face firm, his chest out even though he's seated, his face sunburnt an even red, eyes unblinking in the growing darkness, listening to the young in action.

And as the summer darkness comes on, the children riding their bicycles noiselessly along the quiet street, going home, shadows in the dark, I almost feel myself sitting on the veranda steps beside him, and I want to tell him what we thought of him, Perce McIlwraith, Johnny Delancey, Morgan Phelan, Ted McGarry, all of us who loved him in return. It's almost time to go inside now, but in the darkness, oh, in this last time, I can almost reach out and take him by the hand.

Acknowledgments

This book could not have been completed without the good humour, hard work and intelligent editing of John Sweet and the contributions of the following writers:

Margaret Atwood, extract from *Cat's Eye*. Used by permission of McClelland & Stewart, Inc., Toronto, The Canadian Publishers.

Roch Carrier, "The Hockey Sweater" from *The Hockey Sweater and Other Stories*, translated by Sheila Fischman, copyright © House of Anansi Press Limited, 1979. Reprinted with the permission of Stoddart Publishing Co. Limited, Don Mills, Ontario.

Wayson Choy, extract from *The Jade Peony* (Douglas & McIntyre, 1995), copyright © 1995 by Wayson Choy.

Robertson Davies, extract from *What's Bred in the Bone,* copyright © Robertson Davies, 1985. Reprinted by permission of Macmillan Canada.

Marian Engel, "The Smell of Sulphur" from *The Tattooed Woman* by Marian Engel. Copyright © The Estate of Marian Engel, 1985. Reprinted by permission of Penguin Books Canada Limited.

Timothy Findley, "War" from *Dinner Along the Amazon* by Timothy Findley. Copyright © Pebble Productions, Inc., 1984. Reprinted by permission of Penguin Books Canada Limited.

Barbara Gowdy, "Body and Soul" from *We So Seldom Look on Love,* published by Somerville House Books. Copyright © 1992 Barbara Gowdy. Reprinted by permission of the author.

Hugh Hood, "Silver Bugles, Cymbals, Golden Silks" from *Flying a Red Kite,* copyright © Hugh Hood, 1996.

Isabel Huggan, "Jack of Hearts" is reprinted from *The Elizabeth Stories* by permission of Oberon Press.

A.M. Klein, "Kapusitchka" from *A.M. Klein: Short Stories,* edited by M.W. Steinberg (University of Toronto Press, 1983), copyright © University of Toronto Press, 1983. Reprinted by permission of University of Toronto Press Incorporated.

Margaret Laurence, extract from "Jericho's Brick Battlements" from *A Bird in the House* by Margaret Laurence. Used by permission of McClelland & Stewart, Inc., Toronto, The Canadian Publishers.

Alistair MacLeod, "To Everything There Is a Season" from *As Birds Bring Forth the Sun* by Alistair MacLeod. Used by permission of McClelland & Stewart, Inc., Toronto, The Canadian Publishers.

Joyce Marshall, "The Heights" from *Any Time at All and Other Stories* by Joyce Marshall. Used by permission of McClelland & Stewart, Inc., Toronto, The Canadian Publishers.

Anne Michaels, extract from *Fugitive Pieces.* Used by permission of McClelland & Stewart, Inc., Toronto, The Canadian Publishers.

W.O. Mitchell, extract from *Who Has Seen the Wind,* copyright © W.O. Mitchell, 1947. Reprinted by permission of Macmillan Canada.

L.M. Montgomery, extract from "A Tempest in the School Teapot." "L.M. Montgomery" is a trademark of Heirs of L.M. Montgomery Inc. "Anne of Green Gables" is a trademark and a Canadian official mark of the Anne of Green Gables Licensing Authority Inc.

Alice Munro, "Red Dress–1946" from *Dance of the Happy Shades and Other Stories* by Alice Munro (The Ryerson Press, 1968), copyright © Alice Munro, 1968. Reprinted by permission of McGraw-Hill Ryerson Limited.

Jacques Poulin, extract from *The Jimmy Trilogy*, translated by Sheila Fischman (Anansi, 1979), copyright © House of Anansi Press Limited 1979. *Jimmy* was first published in French by Les Éditions du Jour (1969) and reissued in 1978 by Les Éditions Leméac. Reprinted with the permission of Stoddart Publishing Co. Limited, Don Mills, Ontario.

Nino Ricci, extract from *In a Glass House*. Used by permission of McClelland & Stewart, Inc., Toronto, The Canadian Publishers.

Sinclair Ross, "Cornet at Night" from *The Lamp at Noon and Other Stories* by Sinclair Ross. Used by permission of McClelland & Stewart, Inc., Toronto, The Canadian Publishers.

Diane Schoemperlen, "Hockey Night in Canada" from *Hockey Night in Canada and Other Stories* reprinted by permission of Quarry Press Inc.

Guy Vanderhaeghe, "Drummer" from *Man Descending* by Guy Vanderhaeghe, copyright © 1982 by Guy Vanderhaeghe. Reprinted by permission of Macmillan Canada.